The Collected Thraxas

Thraxas Books Five and Six

Thraxas and the Sorcerers

Thraxas and the Dance of Death

Martin Scott

Thraxas and the Sorcerers
Copyright © Martin Millar 2001

Thraxas and the Dance of Death
Copyright © Martin Millar 2002

This edition published 2017 by Martin Millar

The moral right of the author has been asserted. All rights reserved. No part of this book may be reproduced or transmitted in any form or by any means without written permission from the copyright holder.

All characters in the publication are fictitious, and any resemblance to real persons, living or dead, is purely coincidental.

ISBN 978-1548353131

Thraxas and the Sorcerers

With the city still gripped by a fierce winter, the only thing to do is drink beer in front of a roaring fire. To Thraxas's annoyance, the city authorities won't let him rest. Every sorcerer in the west is heading for Turai, to elect a new leader. The Turanian government is desperate for their own candidate to win. This will require cheating, bribery and corruption on a massive scale. Naturally, they turn to Thraxas and Makri. As they do their best to support Lisutaris - herself a notably intoxicated sorcerer - the sorcerers' assemblage turns into the most riotously debauched affair ever seen in Turai.

Thraxas and the Dance of Death

"Why has no attempt been made to arrest Thraxas? Our inquiries indicate that Thraxas, a so called 'investigator,' has been at the scene of many unexplained deaths. Several landlords report that Thraxas, a huge man of bestial appetites, visited their taverns only minutes before these savage murders were committed…Thraxas has dabbled in the sorcerous arts, and may be in possession of several devastating Orcish spells. Why is this man still at liberty? And why was he ever granted the office of Tribune? Even in a city as corrupt as Turai, surely a man of such reputation should not be able to bribe his way into a lucrative government position…"

For more about Thraxas visit
www.thraxas.com
www.martinmillar.com

Cover Model: Madeline Rae Mason

Introduction to Thraxas Book Five

The world of Thraxas is often teetering on the brink of intoxication. In Thraxas and the Sorcerers, it falls over the edge. When the sorcerers meet in Turai to elect a new leader, the event sets new standards in debauchery. Naturally, Thraxas is at the centre of this. He may have failed at sorcery but he's not going to cede his position as the nation's greatest drinker without a struggle.

I'm rather jealous of my own fictional character. I wish I had Thraxas's capacity. I rather like the image of the hard-drinking author, banging his fist on the bar and demanding another drink. Sadly, I have a very low tolerance for alcohol, and drink mostly tea. To be fair to myself, I do make a good pot of tea.

Thraxas and the Sorcerers also features Lisutaris, Mistress of the Sky. She's been involved in the Thraxas series from the beginning, and she has a larger role in this novel. I'm fond of Lisutaris and her powerful sorcery, and she continues to feature strongly in the books that follow.

Martin Millar

Thraxas and the Sorcerers

Chapter One

Turai is in the grip of one of the fiercest winters in memory. Ice lies in thick sheets over the frozen streets. Snow falls incessantly from the grey sky. The north wind whips it through the alleyways, where it comes to rest in huge banks deep enough to bury a man. The citizens groan in frozen misery and the church sends up prayers for relief. The poor huddle miserably in their slums while the wealthy hide behind the walls of their mansions. In the taverns, great log fires struggle to keep the cruel weather at bay. Deep inside the imperial palace, the King's sorcerers expend their powers in keeping the Royal Family warm. Winter in Turai is hell.

Three hours before dawn, the snow is falling heavily and the wind is howling. No creature dares show its face. The beggars, whores, dogs, dwa addicts, thieves and drunks that normally infest the streets have vanished. Even the lunatics have better sense than to invite death in the appalling cold. No one is outside. No one would be so foolish. Except for me. I'm Thraxas the Investigator. In the course of my work, I often do foolish things.

I'm down at the docks, looking for a man the Transport Guild suspects of stealing shipments of dragon scales. Dragon scales are valuable items. The Guild has hired me because it believes that one of its officials has been stealing from their harbour-front warehouses. The idea is that I catch him in the act. It never seemed like that great an idea to me, but I needed the money.

I'm hiding behind a low wall in the freezing darkness. I can feel the frost collecting on my face. I'm tired, hungry and I need a beer. My legs have gone numb. I'm as cold as the ice queen's grave and that's a lot colder than I want to be. There's no sign of the suspect, who goes by the name of Rezox. No sign of anyone. Why would there be? Only a crazy person would be out on a night like this. I've been shivering for two hours and if he doesn't show up in the next few minutes I'm giving up and going home. Dragon scales may be valuable but they're not worth freezing to death for. The only thing that's keeping me alive is the spell that warms my cloak, but the warming spell is wearing thin.

I think I hear something. I'm no more than ten yards from the warehouse though it's difficult to make out anything through the driving snow. The warehouse door opens. A large man wrapped in furs emerges, carrying a box. That's good enough for me. I've no intention of hanging round any longer than I have to, so I struggle to my feet and clamber over the low wall. Unsheathing my sword, I walk up behind him. The howling wind prevents Rezox from hearing my approach, and when I bark out his name he spins round in alarm.

'Rezox. I'm arresting you for stealing dragon scales. Let's go.'

Rezox stares at me while the snow settles on the furs that shroud his face and body. 'Thraxas the Investigator,' he mutters finally, low down so it's difficult to catch.

'Let's go,' I repeat.

'And why would I go with you?'

'Because I'm freezing to death out here and if you don't start walking I'm going to slug you and carry you off. Easy or difficult, I don't mind, just so long as it's quick.'

Despite the interruption to his criminal activities, Rezox doesn't seem perturbed. He lays down the box carefully then stares at me again. 'So what do you want?'

'A warm bed. Let's go.'

'You want money?'

He's trying to bribe me. Of course. The cold has made me slow-witted. I shake my head. I don't want money.

'Gold?'

I shake my head again.

'Women?'

I stare at him blankly. I just want to get home. Wrapped in his furs, Rezox doesn't look cold, but he's puzzled. 'Are you saying you can't be bribed?'

'Just get in the cart, Rezox. I'm cold and I want to go home.'

The wind intensifies and Rezox has to raise his voice to make himself heard. 'Everyone in Turai can be bribed. I've paid off Senators. I'm damned if I'm going to be arrested by a cheap private investigator from Twelve Seas. What is it you want?'

I don't seem to want anything. Rezox claps his hands. The snow muffles the sound, but it's enough to bring two men out from the warehouse, each one carrying a sword and neither looking like he'll mind using it. 'Let's be reasonable, Thraxas. Just take a little money and walk away. Hell, it's not like the Transport Guild can't spare a few dragon scales.'

I raise my sword a couple of inches. Rezox has one final attempt at talking me out of making the arrest.

'You'll die for nothing, Thraxas. Take the money. No one will ever know. What are the Guild paying you? Thirty gurans? I'll give you a hundred.'

I remain silent. The two thugs advance. Normally on a case I'd be carrying some spell for dealing with emergencies, but right now I'm using all of my very limited supply of sorcery just to keep warm. The snow flies into my eyes, making me blink.

As the man on my left lunges in, I step nimbly to one side, bring my blade down on his wrist then kick his legs so he crashes to the ground. The second man leaps at me. I parry his blow, twisting my own blade in such a manner that his flies from his hand, spinning through the air to land in the snowdrift behind us. I punch him in the face. He loses his footing and lands with a dull thud.

I stare at Rezox. 'Were these the best you could find?'

Rezox screams at the men to get up and attack me again. I look down at them.

'Better get going. You just used up the last of my patience. Attack me again and I'll kill you.'

They're petty thugs. Not good for much, but smart enough to know when they're about to die. They scramble to their feet and without so much as glancing at Rezox stumble off into the darkness. I place the point of my sword at Rezox's throat.

'Let's go.' I lead him off to the next warehouse, where I've left a small wagon and a horse. The horse is none too pleased about being left in the cold space, and snorts angrily as we arrive.

'I'll split the dragon scales with you,' says Rezox as I load him into the cart. I don't reply. We set off. Technically it's illegal to ride horses or wagons in the city at night, but on a night like this there won't be any civil guards around, and I've no intention of struggling on foot to the Transport Guild's headquarters.

'You're a fool,' he sneers. 'You're too stupid to know what you're doing. What does the Guild mean to you? They're just as corrupt as everyone else.'

'Maybe. But they hired me to arrest a thief. And you're the thief. So here we are.'

Rezox can't understand why I care. Neither can I.

'I'll hire a lawyer and beat the charge in court.'

I shrug. He probably will. Turai is corrupt. There are plenty of clever lawyers ready to defend men like Rezox. The warming spell has worn off and my cloak offers me no protection from the elements. I'm numb with cold. Rezox still looks comfortable in his luxurious fur. He should have tried to bribe me with that.

Chapter Two

Next morning I sleep late. I'd sleep later if Makri didn't barge into my room complaining about the weather.

'Is this stupid winter ever going to end?' Makri is young and she hasn't been in the city that long. She isn't used to our climate yet. The seasons in Turai may be grim, but they're very regular.

'Sure it'll end. In two or three weeks. And how many times have I told you not to barge into my room in the morning?'

Makri shrugs. 'I don't know. Forty, fifty, something like that. Will it get hot in two weeks?'

'No. After winter we get the cold rainy season. It's also terrible.'

'I hate this place,' declares Makri, with feeling. 'The summer's too hot, the autumn's too wet and the winter's too cold. Who'd build a city here? It just goes to show that Humans are foolish.'

Makri is actually half Human herself, along with one quarter Orc and one quarter Elf. Which race she chooses to criticise depends on the circumstances. By now I've dragged myself out of bed and opened my first beer of the day. My rooms are freezing. I throw some wood on the fire, which is still smouldering from the night before.

'At least the Elves have the good sense to live in the Southern Isles where it's hot. I still don't see why we had to come back so quickly.'

Six weeks ago we were far south on Avula, one of the largest Elvish islands. After some initial unpleasantness - the Elves panicking about Makri's Orcish blood, me being slung into prison, the usual sort of thing - life smoothed itself out and we were settling down for a pleasant vacation, more or less welcomed by all. Unfortunately, Deputy Consul Cicerius and Prince Dees-Akan wouldn't let us stay, claiming that they were needed back in Turai for important business. All Turanians were obliged to board ship and set off homewards in some of the worst weather I've ever experienced, and I've sailed through a lot of bad weather. Makri, a very poor sailor, set some kind of record for sea sickness. She swore on more than one occasion she was going to kill Cicerius for making her endure such a journey. When we put in at Turai and found ourselves in the middle of such a fierce winter, I was tempted to agree with her.

I tell Makri to stop prowling around. 'If you have to infest my rooms at this time in the morning, at least sit down.'

'I can't sit down. I've got too much energy. I want to go to college. Why do they shut it in winter?'

'Because most students wouldn't want to fight their way through snowdrifts to get there. Neither would the professors.'

The twenty-one-year-old ex-gladiator is a very keen student and finds this interruption to her studies extremely frustrating. Yesterday she struggled all the way up town to the Imperial Library, only to find that it too was closed.

'I was furious. Don't librarians have a duty to the public?'

'It'll be open again soon, when the sorcerers arrive in town.'

'I can't wait. I can't stand doing nothing. Are you tracking anyone violent just now? Do you need me to kill them?'

'I'm afraid not.'

Makri continues to pace up and down. She's been in an odd mood since we got back from Avula and I'm not sure why. I wouldn't care, if it wasn't for the fact that she keeps waking me up in the mornings, and I'm finding it wearing. Twenty years ago I could march all night and fight all day. These days I need my sleep. She asks me how I got on last night, and I tell her that everything went fine.

'Just hung around outside the warehouse till Rezox showed up. Nothing to it really, he had two thugs along but they weren't what you'd call fighters. I chased them off, Rezox tried to bribe me, I refused and now he's in the custody of the civil guards, charged with stealing dragon scales.'

'Who wants dragon scales?'

'Elegant women.'

'What for?'

'Jewellery.'

'Aren't dragon scales too big for jewellery?'

'The jewellers cut them to size then sell them to rich women who want to sparkle. Costs a lot for a pair of dragon-scale earrings.'

'Did the Transport Guild pay you well?'

'Standard thirty gurans a day. I thought I wouldn't have to work all winter with the money we won on Avula.'

Whilst there, Makri trained a young Elf to fight. She did this so effectively that the young Elf won the junior tournament. As this Elf was previously the weakest, most pathetic Elf on the island, I was able to pick up a bundle by shrewdly backing her at long odds. It was a gambling triumph, one which was rather marred by a run of bad luck at the card table on the journey home.

'It was foolish to lose your money.'

'What else was I meant to do on the ship? At least I enjoyed my share. What did you do with yours?'

Makri doesn't answer. In all probability she gave it to the Association of Gentlewomen. More fool her. There are some rich women in the Association, but Makri says she has to do her bit. She gets back to complaining about the weather. 'I hate the cold. I have to wear too many clothes. It doesn't feel right. Why won't they open the library? How am I meant to practise with my axe when it's too cold to go outside? You know Gurd warned me for taking some thazis from behind the bar? As if he can't spare it. I hate working here. I hate Turai. I hate Twelve Seas worse. Why is it so cold? At least in the gladiator slave pits no one froze to death. What's the point of living in a place like this? Nothing ever happens. I loathe it. I need a new nose stud, I'm bored with this one. You know that young guy that comes in the tavern, he works at the tannery? He had the nerve to ask me out, and only last month I heard him saying how anyone with Orcish blood should be run out the city. I was going to punch him but Gurd complains if I hit the customers. It gets me down. Don't you ever tidy your room?'

'Makri, would you get the hell out of here? It's bad enough you wake me up without standing around complaining about everything and generally being as miserable as a Niojan whore. Take this thazis stick. Maybe smoking it will improve your mood. Now leave me alone. You know I like to enjoy my first beer of the day in peace.'

'Are you still annoyed about the Sorcerers Assemblage?'

'Of course I'm still annoyed. All the world's top sorcerers are arriving in Turai, and there's nothing I like better than being reminded that I'm a washout when it comes to sorcery.'

I studied magic when I was young but I never completed my apprenticeship. I only ever learned the basics and I was never good enough to join the Sorcerers Guild. Since then I've struggled my way round the world as a soldier, a mercenary and finally an investigator. Which has been tough, and since I passed forty, somewhat tougher. There are a lot cushier ways of growing old than pursuing criminals round Twelve Seas, the rough part of a rough city.

'You wouldn't have been happy as a sorcerer,' says Makri. 'I can't see you sitting round the Palace casting horoscopes.'

I shrug. It doesn't sound too bad. It's comfortable at the Palace. I know, I used to be a Senior investigator for Palace Security. They got rid of me some time ago. I drank too much. Now I drink more, but I'm my own man. Makri and I both live in rooms above the Avenging Axe, one of Twelve Seas' more convivial taverns. Makri earns her living working as a barmaid, which she doesn't particularly enjoy, but it pays for her studies and the occasional new weapon. She glances out of the window.

'Still snowing. Well, I'm not hanging round in here. I'm going to see Samanatius.'

'Samanatius? The quack philosopher?'

'He's not a quack. Samanatius is sharp as an Elf's ear and the most brilliant thinker in the west.'

I snort in derision. 'All he does is sit around talking about the mysteries of the universe.'

'He does not. He talks about ethics, morals, all sorts of things.'

'Great. See if he can teach you anything useful. Like how to earn money, for instance.'

'Samanatius isn't interested in money,' says Makri, defensively.

'Everyone is interested in money.'

'Well, he isn't. He doesn't even charge for his classes.'

'So the man is an idiot,' I say. 'How good can a philosopher be if he doesn't charge anything? If he had any talent he'd be raking it in. Anyone who does anything for free in this city has to have something wrong with them.'

Makri shakes her head. 'Sometimes your stupidity baffles me, Thraxas.'

'Thanks for waking me up to tell me that.'

Makri asks if she can borrow the magic warm cloak.

'Okay. I'm not planning on going anywhere.' I hand it over. 'Don't give it to that cheap philosopher.'

'Samanatius is indifferent to the climactic conditions.'

'He would be.'

Makri wraps herself in the cloak. 'This feels better. I hate this city. Who would live here?'

She departs, still cursing the weather. I shake my head. Her moods are definitely getting worse. I finish my first beer and move on swiftly to a second. The Sorcerers Assemblage is depressing me. It's many years since it's been held in Turai and it's quite a big deal for the city, with so many powerful sorcerers from all over the West heading our way. They're due to elect a new head of the Guild, and that's always a major event. Despite the predilection of sorcerers for sitting around palaces having an easy time of it, they are of great importance to every state because without them we'd be doomed in the event of war with the Orcs. The Orcs outnumber us, and last time they marched over from the east it was only the power of our Human sorcerers which held them off long enough for the Elves to come to our rescue.

Downstairs in the tavern, Tanrose is making food, ready for the lunchtime drinkers. Despite the fierceness of the winter, trade here is not too bad. Even the biting cold can't keep the population of Twelve Seas away from Gurd's ale. Gurd, a northern Barbarian, knows how to serve his ale. Tanrose greets me jovially. We get on well, partly because of my frank admiration for her excellent cooking. Even in the depths of winter, when fresh meat is impossible to come by, Tanrose manages to make salted venison into an admirable pie. I take a large portion and sit at the bar with another tankard.

'Have you seen Makri today?' asks Tanrose.

'She woke me up. Felt the need to complain about a few things.'

'Have you noticed that she's been in an odd mood since coming back from Avula?'

'Yes. But Makri's often in funny moods, I try to ignore them.'

To my surprise this brings a hostile response from the cook. 'What do you mean, *you try to ignore them?* That's not very nice.'

'Nice? What do you expect? I'm an investigator. I track down criminals. I like Makri well enough, but I'm not the sort of man to help her with her problems.'

Tanrose looks annoyed. 'Don't you realise how much Makri relies on you?'

'No.'

'Well you should.'

Not liking the way this conversation is going, I try concentrating on my venison pie. Tanrose won't let it drop.

'Makri grew up in a gladiator slave pit. Since she arrived in Turai she's had a hard time. You're probably her best friend. You should listen to her more.'

I choke back my angry response. As always, Tanrose, as the maker of the best venison pies in the city, has me at a disadvantage. I can't afford to offend her. 'Come on, Tanrose. You know I'm a wash-out when it comes to personal problems. Why do you think my wife left me? Makri's twenty-two years younger than me. I don't know what the hell her worries are.'

'Yes you do. She tells you. You just refuse to listen. Do you know she had her first romantic experiences on Avula?'

I down my beer and ask for another. This is really too much for me at this time of day.

'Yes, I had some idea… '

'So now she's confused.'

'Can't you sort her out?'

Tanrose smiles, fairly grimly. 'Not as well as you, Thraxas. She trusts you. God knows why. Probably because you're good with a sword. It always impresses her.'

I'm starting to feel trapped. There's nothing I want to discuss less than Makri's first romantic involvements. Tanrose dangles another slice of venison pie in front of me.

'Well, all right, dammit. I'll listen if she brings up the subject. But only under extreme protest. I haven't had a romance for fifteen years. Longer maybe. I've forgotten what it's like. When it comes to love I'm about as much use as a one-legged gladiator. I don't want to hear about her encounters with a young Elf.'

'I think it left her rather depressed.'

'She's always depressed.'

'No she isn't.'

'Well, there's always something wrong. She's a quarter Orc and a quarter Elf. That's bound to lead to problems. What makes you think I can help?'

'Have another slice of pie,' says Tanrose.

I take the venison pie and another beer back upstairs to my rooms. My fire has gone out. I try lighting it with a simple spell. It doesn't work. It's a poor start to the day. I curse. Life in Turai is bad enough without having to act as nursemaid to Makri.

Chapter Three

Despite the ice, snow and general misery, many Turanians are still working hard. The Transport Guild rides wagons over almost impassable roads, distributing food and supplies around the city. The blacksmiths in their forges hammer out iron wheel-rims to keep the wagons going. Whores wrap up as warmly as they can and walk the streets gamely. The Civil Guard still patrol, or at least the lower ranks do, though their officers remain comfortable in their stations. The Messengers Guild count it as a point of honour to always make it to their destination. The young messenger who climbs the stairs to my outside door looks as though he's had a difficult journey. His cloak is caked with snow and his face is blue with the cold. I rip open the scroll and read the message. It's from Cicerius, Turai's Deputy Consul. That's a bad start. Cicerius wants me to visit him immediately. That's worse.

I can't work up any enthusiasm for visiting Cicerius. I've had a lot of dealings with the Deputy Consul recently. On the whole these have worked out well enough, but he's never an easy man to work for. He's Turai's most honest politician - possibly Turai's only honest politician - and the city's most brilliant lawyer, but he's also cold, austere and unsympathetic to any private investigator who feels the need to interrupt his work to take in the occasional beer. On more than one occasion Cicerius, on finding me drinking while in pursuit of a criminal, has delivered the sort of stinging reprimand that makes him such a feared opponent in the law courts or the Senate. I can only take so much of this. Furthermore, while he is a fair man, he's never found it necessary to bump up my fee, even when I've done him sterling service. He comes from the traditional line of aristocrats who think that the lower classes should be satisfied with a reasonable rate of pay for a fair day's work. In view of the dangers I've faced on his behalf, I'd be inclined to interpret *reasonable* a good deal more generously.

I can't ignore the summons. I'm desperate to make it out of Twelve Seas and back into the wealthier parts of town. I'm never going to do that unless I make some inroads into Turai's aristocracy. Since I was thrown out of my job at the Palace I've hardly had a client who wasn't a lowlife. It's never going to earn me enough to pay the rent in Thamlin, home of the upper classes. And home of a few rather select investigators, I reflect, as I make ready to leave. You wouldn't catch anyone from the Venarius Investigation Agency freezing to death on the docks in mid-winter.

I remember Makri has borrowed my magic warm cloak. 'Damn the woman!' I roar. I can't believe I have to venture out in these freezing temperatures without the warm cloak. How could I be so foolish? Now Makri gets to stay nice and comfy while listening to that fraud of a philosopher Samanatius. Meanwhile Thraxas, on his way to do a proper man's job, has to freeze to death. Damn it.

I rummage around in the chest in the corner of my bedroom and drag out a couple of old cloaks and tunics. I try putting on an extra layer of clothes but it's difficult, because my waistline has expanded dramatically in the past few years and nothing seems to fit. Finally I just have to wrap an ancient cloak over my normal attire, cram on a fur hat I once took from a deceased Orc and venture out. The wind goes straight through me. By the time I'm halfway along Quintessence Street I'm as cold as the ice queen's grave, and getting colder.

The city's Prefects have been doing their best to keep the main roads passable. If I can make it to Moon and Stars Boulevard I should be able to catch a landus up town, but getting there through the side roads is almost impossible. The streets are already treacherous with ice, and fresh snow is falling all the time. I haven't been out in weather like this since my regiment fought in the far north, and that was a long time ago, when I was a lot lighter and nimbler of foot. By the time I make it to the Boulevard I'm wet, shivering and cursing Makri for tricking me into giving her the warm cloak.

I have a stroke of good fortune when a one-horse cab drops a merchant off right in front of me. I climb in and tell the driver to take me to the Thamlin. The landus crawls up the Boulevard, through Pashish and over the river. Here the streets are a little clearer, but the gardens are snow-bound and the fountains are frozen over. The summons was to Cicerius's home rather than the

Imperial Palace, and the driver, on hearing the address, gives me his opinions on Cicerius, which aren't very high.

'Okay, the guy is famous for his honesty,' says the driver. 'But so what? He commissions a new statue of himself every year. That's vanity on a big scale. Anyway, he's a Traditional and they're as corrupt as they come. I tell you, the way the rich are bleeding this city I'll be pleased if Lodius and the Populares party throw them all out. How's a landus driver meant to make a living the way they keep piling on the taxes? You know how much horse feed has gone up in the last year?'

The King and his administration are not universally popular. Plenty of people would like to see some changes. I sympathise, more or less, but I prefer to stay out of politics.

The landus deposits me outside Cicerius's large town house. There's a Securitus Guildsman huddled over a small fire in a hut at the gate who checks my invitation before ushering me in. I hurry up the path past the frozen bushes and beat on the door, meanwhile thinking that this job had better be worth the journey. A servant answers the door. I show her my invitation. She looks at me like I'm probably a man who forges invitations, then withdraws to consult with someone inside. I'm left freezing on the step. I struggle to keep my temper under control. It takes a long time for the door to open again. This time the servant motions me inside.

'What took you so long? A man could die out there. You want to have your nice garden cluttered up with dead investigators?'

I'm ushered into a guest room. I remove my outer cloak and start to thaw myself out in front of the fire. Whilst I'm in the process of this, a young girl, nine or ten, arrives and stares at me. The daughter of one of the servants, I presume, from her rather unkempt appearance.

'You're fat,' she says.

'And you're ugly,' I reply, seeing no reason to be insulted by the children of the domestic help. The kid immediately bursts into tears and retreats from the room, which cheers me a little. She should have known better than to cross swords with Thraxas. Thirty seconds later Cicerius appears. Clutching the hem of his toga is the same young girl, sobbing hysterically and denouncing me as the man who insulted her.

'What have you been saying to my daughter?' demands Cicerius, fixing me with his piercing eyes.

'Your daughter? I didn't know you had a daughter.'

'Do you normally insult the children you encounter in your clients' houses?'

'Hey, she started it,' I protest.

Cicerius does his best to calm his daughter before sending her off to find her mother. The little brat is still in tears and Cicerius is pained. This has got our interview off to a bad start. With Cicerius, that usually seems to happen.

'Have you been drinking?'

'I've always been drinking. But don't let it stop you from offering me some wine. You know the landus drivers in Turai are turning against the Traditionals?'

'For what reason?'

'Too many taxes.'

Cicerius dismisses this with the slightest movement of his head. He's not about to discuss government policy with me. On the wall of the guest room is a large painting of Cicerius addressing the Senate, and there's a bust of him in a niche in the corner. The landus driver was right about his vanity.

'I need your help,' he says. 'Though, as always when we meet, I wonder why.'

'Presumably you've got a job which is unsuitable for the better class of investigator.'

'Not exactly. I hired the better class of investigator but he fell sick.'

'Okay, so I'm second choice.'

'Third.'

'You're really selling me the job, Deputy Consul. Maybe you'd better just describe it.'

'I want you to act as an observer at the Sorcerers Assemblage.'

'Sorry. Can't do it. Thanks for the offer, I'll see myself out.'

'What?' Cicerius is startled by my abrupt refusal. 'Why can't you do it?'

'Personal reasons,' I reply, and head for the door. I'm not about to tell the Deputy Consul that attending the Sorcerers Assemblage would make me feel small, powerless, insignificant and a general failure in life.

Cicerius plants himself in front of me. 'Personal reasons? That is not an acceptable reason for refusing. I'm not offering you this job for fun. I'm offering you it because it's a service that Turai needs from you. When the city needs you, personal reasons have no significance. Now kindly sit down and listen.'

The Deputy Consul could easily make my life in Turai very awkward. He wouldn't have to pull too many strings to have my licence revoked. So I sit down and listen, and drink his wine, but I don't make any pretence I'm enjoying it.

'You are aware that the sorcerers are to elect a new Head of their Guild?'

I am. It's an important matter for Turai, as well as every other Human nation. The Sorcerers Guild in each land has its own organisation and its own officials, but unlike many of the other Guilds, the sorcerers have an international dimension. While a member of the Turanian Bakers Guild would probably not be too interested in the Simnian Bakers Guild, every magic user in the west looks up to the leader of the Sorcerers Guild. The post carries a lot of weight and brings a great deal of prestige.

'Our King and Consul are most keen that a Turanian is elected.'

I'm not surprised. Turai has been slipping in political importance for a long time now. We used to be a big voice in the League of City States, but that organisation has now almost fallen apart, riven by internal rivalries, leaving the small state of Turai dangerously exposed. We're in the front line against the Orcs to the east. To make things worse, Nioj, our northern neighbour and historical enemy, has spent the last decade making threatening noises. King Lamachus would like nothing better than to swallow us up, and if he decides to do it there doesn't seem much prospect of anyone else coming to our aid. Turai is still a good friend of the Elves, but the Elves are a long way away. It would make a lot of sense to cement the Sorcerers Guild to our city state.

I can see problems ahead. 'Who have we got for the post? There are a lot of powerful sorcerers in other countries. The way Turanian sorcerers have been dying in the past few years, I don't see who we could nominate.'

Cicerius nods, and sips some wine from a silver goblet. 'We had hopes for Tas of the Eastern Lightning. Very powerful.'

'But not very loyal. It's probably just as well he got killed, he'd have sold us out in the end. I guess Mirius Eagle Rider would have been the next best choice till he handed in his toga. But who else is there? Kemlath Orc Slayer got himself exiled, Old Hasius the Brilliant is too old, and Harmon Half Elf doesn't qualify for head of the Human sorcerers Guild.'

'We considered Melus the Fair,' says Cicerius. 'She is strong. But she's already employed as stadium sorcerer and the people like her. Removing her from that post would be very unpopular. However, we do have another excellent sorcerer. Lisutaris, Mistress of the Sky.'

I raise my eyebrows. 'You're not serious.'

'Why not? Lisutaris is very, very powerful. It was she who overcame the eight-mile terror which almost destroyed the city last year. She has a good reputation at home and abroad because she fought valiantly in the last Orc War. Even now people still talk about the way she brought down a flight of war dragons.'

'I was there. I remember the incident. And very impressive it was. But that was more than fifteen years ago. Before Lisutaris developed into the city's most enthusiastic thazis user.'

Cicerius pretends not to understand me. 'Does she use thazis?'

'Does she? Come on, Cicerius. Lisutaris, Mistress of the Sky, might be a heavy-duty sorcerer, but she lives for the weed.'

Cicerius is untroubled. 'In these decadent times, Thraxas, we cannot set our standards as high as we once might have. You know as well as I do that a great deal of degeneracy has taken root in the Sorcerers Guild as well as elsewhere. Dwa abuse is common, and the drinking habits of many of our sorcerers leave a great deal to be desired. For some reason sorcerers seem very prone to this. Compared to dwa and alcohol, thazis is a mild substance. I do not approve of it, but I don't see it as a serious impediment. You, for instance, use thazis quite openly, despite it still being illegal.'

I doubt that Cicerius fully appreciates the nature of Lisutaris's habit. Many people use the occasional stick to calm them down. On a busy night, the Avenging Axe is thick with thazis smoke. But Lisutaris's liking for thazis is on a different level. She actually invented a new kind of water pipe to enable her to ingest more. She spends half her life in a world of dreams. Last time I was at her villa I found her comatose on the floor after successfully developing a spell for making the plants grow faster. Still, none of this is really my concern. Lisutaris is not a bad sort as sorcerers go, and I'd be happy enough to see her as Head of the Guild.

'So why do you need me?'

'Because we have good reason to fear that the election will not be as fair as we would wish,' replies Cicerius. 'Your job would be to ensure that it is.'

Cicerius's daughter appears behind him. She makes a face at me. I let it pass. Cicerius carries on. 'There are other candidates for the post. Other nations are equally keen to succeed. We believe that some of these lands may not be averse to using underhand tactics.'

'Unlike Turai?'

'Unlike Turai.'

'So you're not wanting me to do anything illegal?'

'If you are caught doing anything illegal, the government will disown you.'

'That's not quite the same thing.'

Cicerius shrugs.

'Am I being hired to make sure the election is fair, or to make sure Lisutaris is elected?'

'We are confident that if the election is fair, then Lisutaris will be elected,' replies the Deputy Consul.

'In other words, I'm to stop at nothing to get her the post?'

Cicerius's lips twitch, which is as close as he generally comes to smiling. 'It's very important to Turai that Lisutaris secures the position. However, I repeat, if you are implicated in anything illegal, the government will disown you.'

'I don't really understand why I'm the man for the job. Wouldn't it be better to send someone from Palace Security?'

'I have selected you.'

It's possible the Deputy Consul is having problems with Palace Security. It's headed by Rittius, a bitter rival of his. Cicerius doesn't elaborate, but he points out that I am well qualified for the mission. 'You have good investigating skills. You have some knowledge of sorcery, albeit slight. And your uncouth manners will not offend the sorcerers as much as they might offend others.'

'I guess not. Sorcerers can be pretty uncouth themselves when they get some wine inside them.'

The Deputy Consul acknowledges that this is true. 'Turai will not, of course, be relying solely on you. We will have many representatives catering to the needs of the visiting sorcerers. Every effort will be made to make them look favourably on Turai.'

I finish off my wine. 'The fact remains that I don't want to go to the Sorcerers Assemblage. And I don't need the work. I won a lot of money on our trip to Avula.'

'You lost it all before you returned to Turai and are now sorely in need.'

'How do you know that?'

'I have my own sources of information. You will go to the Assemblage.'

Every time I end up working for the Deputy Consul, it's something I'd rather not be doing. It never seems to bother him.

'You know the sorcerers don't allow civilians at the Assemblage? It's Guild members and their staff only, and they're strict about it. So unless you can get me a position as Lisutaris's secretary, they're not going to let me in.'

'I doubt that you would be an acceptable secretary for Lisutaris,' replies Cicerius. 'But I have already dealt with the problem. The Sorcerers Guild does allow several observers from the government of the host city to attend, as a matter of courtesy. I will be there for much of the time.'

'You're the Deputy Consul. If I walk into the Assemblage claiming to be a government official they'll be down on me like a bad spell.'

Cicerius makes an impatient gesture. 'As I said, I have dealt with the problem. You will be there as a representative of the citizens of Turai. I am nominating you as a Tribune of the People.'

'A what?'

'A Tribune of the People. Are you not familiar with this post? It used to be a famous position in Turai. There were six Tribunes of the People, and they played an important role in the governance of the city. They were, as the name implies, responsible for representing the interests of the general population in city affairs. Three were elected by the population and three were nominated by the King and his administration.'

'When was this?'

'The institution fell into disuse about one hundred and fifty years ago. But it is still within my power to nominate Tribunes. I have already appointed Sulinius and Visus, both Senators' sons, to assist at the Assemblage. You will be the third.'

I drink more wine. It's a fine vintage. Though not given to excessive drinking, Cicerius keeps his cellars well stocked. An aristocrat has to, or he'd lose status.

'Why was the post of Tribune abandoned?'

'They fell out of favour with the King when they became too keen on supporting radical policies. After some civil unrest it was felt they were no longer necessary, which was wise. It is far better to leave administration to the King and his officials. But none of this need concern you. You are not expected to do anything as Tribune. It is merely a convenient way of gaining access to the Assemblage.'

I'm dubious. 'Are you sure I don't have to do anything? If there are any official duties involved, I'm not interested.'

Cicerius assures me there are no duties involved. 'Look on it as a temporary honorary post.'

'Is there a salary?'

'No. But we will be paying you for your time. Now listen carefully. We're facing formidable opposition. The Simnians have nominated one of their own sorcerers, and the Simnians are enemies of Turai. It is vital that their candidate is not elected. Unfortunately, Lasat, Axe of Gold, acting head of the Sorcerers

Guild, is believed to favour them, which makes our task more difficult. Turai will have to make a great effort to ensure that Lisutaris gathers sufficient votes to at least make it into the final stages of the process. Are you familiar with Tilupasis, widow of Senator Gerinius?'

'I've heard of her. Runs some sort of intellectual salon.'

'She is commonly described as Turai's most influential woman.'

'Didn't she publicly criticise you a while back? Something to do with wasting money on a statue?'

Cicerius brushes this away. 'We have had our disagreements. Tilupasis has an unfortunate habit of speaking out of turn. Nonetheless, she is a woman of considerable influence. She's proved herself to be a highly efficient organiser, and the King himself was pleased at the reception she gave for our Elvish visitors last year. Consul Kalius feels that she can play an important role in the vote-winning process.'

Cicerius, practised speaker that he is, doesn't give away too much in the way of unguarded emotions, but I get the feeling he's not entirely convinced about this. Women are discouraged from participating in politics in Turai, and an aristocratic Traditional like the Deputy Consul never feels wholly comfortable with any sign of female influence in the city. However, Cicerius can't disregard the views of the Consul, his superior.

'Kalius trusts Tilupasis—' continues Cicerius.

I bet he does. They're strongly rumoured to be having an affair.

'—and indeed, there is every reason to believe she will perform her duties of hospitality well. I've already instructed Visus and Sulinius to listen to her views respectfully, and I now tell you the same. With Tilupasis to organise our hospitality, Visus and Sulinius to cater to the sorcerers' needs, and you to ensure there is nothing untoward going on, I'm confident Turai can succeed.'

Cicerius carries on in this manner for some time. My spirits sink. Arrogant sorcerers, wealthy young senators' sons and Turai's most influential matron. What a collection. I'll be the only ignobly born person in the whole place and probably as welcome as an Orc at an Elvish wedding. *Thraxas, Tribune of the People.* That's going to cause a few laughs when word gets around Twelve Seas.

Chapter Four

The journey home is grim. I never figured I'd come so close to death just riding in a landus along Quintessence Street. Not for the first time I bitterly regret not saving enough of my winnings from Avula to buy some furs. I burst into the Avenging Axe and beg Tanrose to provide me with some hot food, before positioning myself as close to the fire as I can get without actually stepping over the grate. Makri is wiping tables and collecting tankards.

'Have a good time with the philosopher?' I say, cuttingly. 'Nice and warm in my cloak?'

'Yes thank you,' responds Makri. 'The magic cloak is a great creation.'

'Well, it's the last time you get your hands on it. I nearly died out there. Damn that Cicerius, he's not human. You know he wants me to go to the Sorcerers Assemblage?'

I'm feeling angry about all things sorcerous. It's ridiculous to hold their Assemblage in the depths of winter. 'They're only doing it to show off. No one else can move because of the snow, but the sorcerers will all come rolling into the city boasting about how easy it was for them to manipulate the weather, and what pleasant journeys they had. Braggarts, all of them. This job is a waste of time. Who cares who gets the post as Head of the Guild?'

'Samanatius says it's a very important position,' says Makri.

'He would. Shouldn't you be bringing me a beer instead of talking about philosophy all the time?'

'There's nothing wrong with philosophy.'

'It's a waste of time.'

'It's enriching,' says Makri.

I find this very annoying. 'If you were enriched you wouldn't have to wear that chainmail bikini to earn tips.'

'Samanatius says that women who are obliged to exhibit themselves to make a living are not degraded by the experience,' says Makri stiffly. 'The audience are.'

'Samanatius is an idiot. Bring me a beer.'

'Get your own beer,' says Makri, which is hardly the way for any barmaid to talk to a customer. She should learn some manners.

I get my own beer and return to the fire to think gloomy thoughts. I know most of the sorcerers in Turai, and plenty others from around the world. It's no secret that I failed my apprenticeship all those years ago, but I don't like my nose being rubbed in it. I still advertise myself as a sorcerous investigator to bring in business, though the spells I can work are pathetic, child's play compared to their powers.

'If any sorcerer laughs at me, I'm going to punch him right in the face.' I finger my necklace. It's a spell protection charm, and a good one. I might need it if things get rough.

Gurd had the excellent sense to provide the tavern with a plentiful supply of logs for the winter, and the Avenging Axe is warm enough to comfort the coldest guest. It's warm enough to allow Makri to wear the tiny chainmail bikini. I shouldn't have mocked her for it. It's not like she's crazy about it herself. She relies on it to earn tips, a stratagem which has proved successful over the past year, which is not really surprising, given Makri's figure. Mercenaries who've been all round the world and seen everything there is to see can still be struck dumb when she appears. Tanrose says that Makri's beauty will one day get her married to a Senator or a prince, but given that Makri has Orcish blood, pointed ears and plenty of attitude, I reckon she's more likely to end up dead in a gutter, probably not long after me. I never figure she's that beautiful anyway, but I gave up thinking about women a long time ago, so I'm a poor judge.

I finish my beer. Makri ignores my request for another. I swear at her. She swears back at me. Other drinkers laugh. Her moods are really getting me down. I retreat upstairs. My magic warm cloak is on the bed. I'll have to charge it up again before I go out tonight. I've a small piece of business to attend to - checking up on a woman for a jealous husband - but after that my diary is empty. Cicerius was right, I do need the work.

Makri strides into my room. 'Thraxas, can I–'

'Will you stop marching into my room uninvited?'

A tear trickles from Makri's eye. I've never seen Makri cry before, at least not in misery. A few tears of joy after massacring some opponents, maybe. She hurries from the room. It's strange behaviour.

Outside it's snowing again. I wish I didn't have to go out. I've been watching the activities of the wife of a wealthy merchant for two weeks now. He's suspicious of her and is paying me for reports of her movements. Normally I'd be glad of the work - no danger and not too strenuous - but it's been tough in the cold weather. So far I haven't found the wife doing anything particularly odd. The only visitors that ever call are representatives from high-class clothing concerns, make-up artists, hairdressers and the like. There's one beautician who looks in every day, but this is standard behaviour for any rich Turanian woman. The merchant has no objections to his wife beautifying herself, and he's starting to think he may have misjudged her.

I wrap myself in the warm cloak, fit on my sword and depart before Makri can bother me again with her moody behaviour. As expected, the assignment turns out to be a waste of time. If the merchant's wife has thoughts of being unfaithful, she's probably waiting till the summer months, when her husband is away trading in foreign lands, which would be the smart thing to do.

I'm relieved when midnight rolls around. It's another foul night and my magic warm cloak is starting to lose potency. I hurry off through the snow to the house of Astrath Triple Moon. Astrath is an old friend. He's a powerful sorcerer and might have expected to be a candidate for Head of the Guild himself had it not been for some irregularities in the chariot races when he was employed as resident sorcerer at the Stadium Superbius. The Stadium pays a sorcerer to ensure that no magic is used to interfere with the races. When a rumour spread that Astrath Triple Moon had been taking bribes to look the other way while a certain powerful Senator hired a sorcerer to help his chariots romp home easy winners, there was a lot of bad feeling in the city. Astrath faced prosecution. Fortunately for him, I managed to gather - and when I say gather, I mean fake - enough evidence in his favour to make prosecution impossible. Astrath was allowed to resign quietly provided he never showed his face in the stadium again. Thanks to me, he also escaped expulsion from the Sorcerers Guild, so he's entitled to attend the Assemblage, although whether he's planning to, I don't know. It might be a touchy subject. Astrath isn't welcome in polite circles these days and I'm not certain how he stands with the other sorcerers.

Astrath's house is reasonably comfortable, but not really the sort of place a powerful sorcerer would expect to live. In Thamlin, Harmon Half Elf has a villa with grounds so large he holds a horse race every year for apprentices, but here in Pashish you'd be hard pushed to fit a horse into Astrath's back yard. He greets me warmly, as always. It's a relief for him to see a friendly face from the old days.

'Thraxas, I've been expecting you. Some wine?'

'Beer would be better. And let me get myself in front of your fire, my warm cloak is starting to cool off.'

Astrath makes a living casting horoscopes, selling healing potions and such like, but there's not much money around in Pashish. There's not much money anywhere south of the river in Turai, unless you count the Brotherhood, who control the criminal activity. They always do well, but you couldn't say anyone else was prospering. Astrath only has one servant and she's finished for the day, so he leads me inside himself, and takes my cloak.

'I'll charge it up for you before you leave. What are you doing out on the streets in this weather?'

I tell him about my fruitless tailing of the merchant's wife. 'The woman is completely blameless as far as I can see. Obsessed with beauty treatments, but having met the husband I can understand why she'd want a hobby.'

We sit and chat about this and that. I let Astrath get some wine inside him before raising the subject of the Assemblage.

'Are you planning on attending?'

The sorcerer strokes his beard. Most male sorcerers in Turai are bearded, and they wear rainbow cloaks, the mark of their guild.

'I'm not certain. I'm still a member, but–'

He shrugs. I tell him he should go. 'Be a shame to miss seeing your old friends.'

'There's a lot of old friends not keen to see me these days.'

'People in the Palace maybe. But your fellow sorcerers? Do they care about a little trouble with the law? It's not like you broke the Guild's rules. Hell, if the Assemblage banned every sorcerer who'd had a run-in with their city authorities, the place would be empty. I'm forever getting Gorsius Starfinder out of trouble.'

Astrath smiles. Gorsius Starfinder, who holds a respectable post at the Palace these days, does have an unfortunate tendency to get drunk in brothels and cause a scene.

'Maybe you're right. It's a long time since they've held the Assemblage in Turai, be a shame to miss it.'

Astrath knows that the Turanians are nominating Lisutaris for Head of the Guild. He doesn't give much for her chances. 'I still hear all the gossip. Sunstorm Ramius from Simnia is the favourite. He's sharp as an Elf's ear and he has a lot of friends. And if he doesn't win it, there's a few others not far behind. Rokim the Bright from Samsarina, for instance. The Samsarinans control a lot of votes. Or Darius Cloud Walker. He impressed a lot of people when he brought down that stray dragon right in the middle of the Abelasian sorcerers' drinking contest. A man like that carries a lot of weight with sorcerers.'

'True. But Lisutaris is powerful too.'

'Maybe. But everyone in the Guild knows she's not always in a fit state to take care of business. Or even put on her own shoes.'

He looks at me knowingly. 'Are the authorities sending you to fix the election?'

'Absolutely not. Just to see it's fair.'

'The sorcerers have plenty of ways of their own to make things fair. Lasat, Axe of Gold, and Charius the Wise are running things till the new chief is elected, and no one's going to slip anything by that pair.'

'Then I'll have an easy time of it.'

Astrath lets it go. He probably suspects there's more to my mission than I'm admitting, but he doesn't press the point.

'So you're reckoning on Sunstorm Ramius, Rokim the Bright and Darius Cloud Walker as the main candidates? Abelasi is small and far away, so Darius wouldn't affect Turai much one way or another. Rokim the Bright wouldn't be too bad, but Samsarina is a long way off. No chance of help arriving quickly if Turai is in trouble. The worst choice would be Sunstorm Ramius. It's a long time since Turai has been friends with Simnia.'

Astrath brings me more beer. After discussing the convention for a while, we get to reminiscing about old times. Eventually I doze off on the couch. Astrath shakes me awake and points me towards the guest room. I sleep well under the sorcerer's roof and leave next day without waking him. My cloak has been fully recharged and keeps me warm as I tread carefully over the icy streets back to Twelve Seas. There are few people around, though I notice several dwa dealers scurrying along about their business. Nothing interferes with the dwa trade. I'm planning to stop at Minarixa's bakery to buy some pastries for breakfast, but I'm surprised to find a small crowd outside her shop, standing and staring in spite of the cold. A few Civil Guards are holding back the onlookers. This is worrying. I depend on Minarixa's bakery almost as much as Tanrose's pies. If they've been robbed and the ovens aren't fired up yet it's really going to spoil my day. I arrive just as Captain Rallee, wrapped in a black government cloak, emerges from the premises. He's scowling.

'Trouble?'

'Trouble. Minarixa's dead.'

I gasp. Not my favourite baker. The crowd moan as the body is brought out wrapped in a shroud. The baker was one of Twelve Seas' most popular characters.

'What happened?'

'Overdose,' says the Captain.

I stare at him like he's crazy. 'An overdose? Minarixa?'

He nods.

'It can't be. Not Minarixa. She didn't take dwa.'

'She certainly took enough last night,' says Captain Rallee.

It's some time since I've seen him looking so depressed. The Civil Guards loved that baker's shop. I stare dumbly as Minarixa's body is loaded onto a wagon and driven away through the falling snow, then I walk home, cursing. Word has already reached the Avenging Axe. Gurd, Tanrose and Makri are as miserable as three

Niojan whores. No one can believe that our cherished baker has gone and died of an overdose.

'Such a respectable woman,' says Gurd, shaking his head. Gurd, sturdy barbarian that he is, finds it impossible to understand why the city has been gripped by the plague of dwa.

'Why did she do it? Surely she was a happy woman?'

'She kept that bakery going through the worst times,' says Tanrose, sadly. 'Orc wars, riots, even the famine. She kept it going when the True Church tried to have it made illegal for women to own businesses. I can't believe she's finally gone like this.'

The event casts further gloom over Twelve Seas. Citizens, struggling with the weather, beset by poverty and surrounded by corruption, curse the powdered plant that has brought so much misery in the past few years. Makri is madder than a mad dragon at Minarixa's death. Minarixa was the local organiser for the Association of Gentlewomen. The Association dedicates itself to raising the status of women in Turai, and Makri supports it to the extent of helping to collect money, a thankless task in Twelve Seas. She spends a long time expressing her outrage that such a fine woman as Minarixa should succumb to a drug overdose.

'Are you going to investigate?'

I shrug. 'What's to investigate? She took too much dwa. So did about twenty other people in Twelve Seas this month. You've seen the bodies.'

Makri remains furious. When Captain Rallee calls in late in the evening for a beer to unwind after a hard day, she demands to know what he's going to do about the death.

'Nothing,' replies the Captain, gloomily.

'Shouldn't you be arresting whoever sold her the dwa?'

'How? You think we could find a witness? Or make anything stick in court? No chance. All the dwa trade is controlled by the Brotherhood and no one's going to give evidence against them. Anyway, you arrest one dwa dealer and another appears on the street before the day is out.'

'I've never seen you arresting even one,' says Makri.

Captain Rallee shifts uncomfortably. Makri's right, but it's not the Captain's fault. He's as honest as they come but his superiors aren't. 'I'm as angry as you about Minarixa. But no one is going to pay for her death. That's just the way it is.'

'If I meet her dealer I'm going to gut him,' says Makri.

'Fine with me,' says Captain Rallee. 'I'll be happy to look the other way.'

'I hate this place,' says Makri, and goes upstairs to read some mathematics treatise and curse the weather, the Brotherhood and everything else in Turai. Makri escaped from the Orcish gladiator slave pits a couple of years ago, an event involving such incredible carnage that tales of it have resonated throughout the Orcish lands, according to reliable reports. She made her way over to Turai on hearing tales of its fine cultural tradition, but while she admits that Turai does contain a great amount of art and learning, she refuses to admit that our level of civilisation is much better than the Orcs. Sometimes I'm inclined to agree with her, though in the Orc-hating city of Turai, it's not an opinion I'd voice in public.

Dwa is now plaguing all the Human lands. A few months ago on Avula I discovered it was starting to make inroads into Elvish society. It's said the Orcs encourage the trade, to weaken us. If that's true, it's a good plan. It's working. Captain Rallee buys me a beer, not a common event, though the Captain and I go back a long way. We don't get on as well as we used to but we've still got some kind of connection. We drink to the baker.

'Congratulations on finding the dragon-scale thief,' says Rallee.

He must be emotional. The last time the Captain complimented me on anything, I'd just killed an Orc and tossed him from the city walls, which was sixteen years ago at least.

'What's this I hear about you being some sort of government official?'

I explain to him that Cicerius is making me a Tribune of the People.

'What the hell is that?'

'Some old post that used to exist a hundred and fifty years ago.'

'I've never heard of it. Does it involve staying sober?'

'Not as far as I know. I'm not planning on staying that sober at the Assemblage.'

The Captain grins. The fire illuminates his long yellow hair, picking out his handsome features. 'Better take care you don't offend someone.'

'I'd be more likely to offend the sorcerers if I was sober.'

'True enough. When I heard our government were putting up Lisutaris for Head of the Guild, I thought they were crazy. Everyone knows she's not exactly sober. But who knows? It might be in her favour. Sorcerers, they never could control themselves.'

'You remember the time we were camped up north and Harmon Half Elf was meant to be keeping watch?' asks Gurd, bringing up an old war memory.

'Sure,' replies the Captain. 'He got so drunk he thought our pack mule was a troll and blasted it with a fire spell.'

'He burned all our supplies so we ended up eating the mule!'

We all laugh, and call for more beer, and we spend the night telling war stories and drinking.

'It was different in those days,' says Gurd, some time after midnight. 'The Orcs were always attacking us. We had to fight to stay alive. But there wasn't any dwa. I liked it better then.'

Chapter Five

The Assemblage is due to start in three days' time. Already sorcerers are arriving in the city, though there's little sign of them in Twelve Seas. They're either staying as guests of Turanian sorcerers in Truth is Beauty Lane or else living in villas in Thamlin rented by their guild. Some of the more adventurous may be visiting the Kushni quarter in the centre of town, where there's a lot of diversion in the way of whores, gambling, drinking and dwa, but none ventures as far south as Twelve Seas. This doesn't mean we're not interested in them. The local citizens read news of each new arrival in the *Renowned and Truthful Chronicle of All the World's Events*, the cheap and poorly produced news sheet that brings the population of Turai its regular dose of gossip and scandal. Faced as we are with so many enemies, it's comforting for Turanians to have powerful sorcerers within our walls. When it's learned that I'm to attend the Assemblage, people are impressed, although fairly amused at the thought of me being some sort of government official.

'Of course,' as Chiaraxi, the local healer, points out, 'it's not as if our officials are all sober, responsible citizens. From what I've seen of these degenerates in the Senate, Thraxas would fit right in.'

'Only if they could make a special outsize toga,' replies Rox, who should stick to selling fish.

Bolstered by such support, I'm wrapping up all other business. The Transport Guild has paid me for the apprehension of Rezox and I've been to visit the suspicious merchant with regard to his wife. He's a timber dealer by the name of Rixad. While I can't say he's the friendliest client I've ever had, he does take my opinions seriously and he doesn't quibble over payment. Rixad is around fifty, overweight and not the handsomest man in the city. I can see he might be suspicious of his glamorous young wife, but if he wants to use his wealth to scoop up a beauty in need of money, it's almost bound to happen. His wife might have thought it a wise move to swap the uncertain life of an actress for the luxury of an important merchant's household, but she's probably bored by now.

'I checked out her visitors but there's nothing suspicious. Standard crowd - dressers, beauticians - cater for all the richest women in the city. I expect it's costing you a bundle, but apart from that you've nothing to worry about.'

Rixad nods. 'The last bill from Copro was for more than a shipload of timber. I don't mind. It keeps her happy.'

Copro is quite a well-known figure. One of our finest beauticians. Since arriving in Turai he's attained such a reputation that the female aristocracy fight for his services. Princess Du Akan swears by him, I believe. He's been a frequent visitor to Rixad's wife, but as Copro is rumoured to have a close relationship with his young male assistant, he's not a man you have to worry about your wife misbehaving with.

I make my way home, reasonably satisfied. I'm still in a bad mood about having to attend the Assemblage, but at least it will be warm. The temperature has dropped even further and the streets are quieter than I've ever seen them. Only the most vital services are still operating, and many of the population are obliged to chip blocks of ice from frozen aqueducts and thaw them out for drinking water. I arrive at the Avenging Axe just as Makri is climbing the outside stairs to my office.

'I just had an argument with the dealer who sold dwa to Minarixa,' she says. 'Do you think there might be any trouble?'

'How bad was the argument?'

'He's dead.'

I mutter the minor incantation to open my door and hurry inside. 'Of course there will be trouble. Did anyone see you?'

Makri doesn't think so. 'The alley was dark and it was snowing.'

'Did you have to kill him?'

Makri shrugs. 'I wasn't planning to. I was just going to beat him. He pulled a knife so I ran him through.'

I swear it was only last week that Makri was telling me in glowing terms about some lecture she'd attended concerning the importance of moral behaviour at all times.

'You think this was moral?'

'He deserved it.'

'I'm sure Samanatius would be highly impressed. If the Brotherhood find out they'll be down on us like a bad spell. I don't fancy trying to escape the city when the gates are frozen shut. Do you always have to do things which lead to trouble?'

Makri opens her mouth to reply but instead she starts to cry. I stare at her in complete astonishment. She's never reacted like this before. When I shout at her, she normally just shouts back louder, and maybe reaches for her axe. Faced with a tearful Makri, I have no idea what to do. She slumps down heavily on the couch and continues to cry. I wonder if I could escape downstairs for a beer.

'Um...well, it might not turn out so bad...dwa dealers get killed all the time. Maybe the Brotherhood won't care too much.'

Tears trickle down Makri's face. I'm trapped.

'What's going on? Is it something, eh... personal?'

Makri seems reluctant to talk.

'Okay, maybe you could tell me later, I've got some important—'

'Are you trying to get rid of me?' she demands.

'What do you mean? I was trying to be sympathetic. If you're just going to sit there all day being as miserable as a Niojan whore, what do you expect me to do? I'm a busy man.'

'Well, that's fine, I wouldn't want to bother you,' says Makri angrily. 'I won't bother saving you next time you get in trouble.'

'Makri, the last thing in the world I want to do is discuss your private life, but Tanrose says I have to, so spill it.'

'You expect me to tell you about my private life? No chance.'

'That's fine with me, I don't want to hear it anyway.'

'All right, I'll tell you,' says Makri. She sniffs, and drinks some of my klee. 'I slept with an Elf on Avula. I've been miserable ever since.'

I silently curse Tanrose. She should be dealing with this sort of thing. 'Right…well…you know…I'm sure it will work out fine.'

Makri dabs her eyes and looks at me. 'Is that it? Is that the best you can do?'

I spread my arms wide and contrive to look hopeless. 'I might be number one chariot when it comes to investigating, and sharp as an Elf's ear at the race track, but I never claimed to be any good on emotional problems. I assume this is an emotional problem?'

'What did you think it was?'

'With you it's hard to tell. If it turns out you stabbed the Elf I wouldn't be surprised.'

Makri starts crying again. I wish the Brotherhood would attack. A good sword fight would take her mind off it. Makri never had a lover before, and now appears to be suffering some sort of crisis.

'Wasn't that what you wanted? I mean, an Elf, leafy glades and such like? Better than some lowlife in Twelve Seas anyway. The first time I was with a woman I was fourteen, drunk, and her pimp came in halfway through to check I had enough money.'

'Why hasn't See-ath been in touch?' wails Makri. 'He's ignoring me. Wasn't it important?'

'He's thousands of miles away on an Elvish island. How's he going to get in touch?'

'He could send a message.'

'How?'

'He could've used a sorcerer.'

'Makri, sorcerers can sometimes communicate over long distances but it's not easy. Only a powerful sorcerer could contact Turai from Avula, and he'd need plenty of help from the right conjunctions of the moons, not to mention calm weather and some good fortune. It's a difficult business. I really don't think your young Elf could persuade the local sorcerer to send a message to his girlfriend, no matter how much he wanted to.'

'Fine,' says Makri, angrily. 'Be on his side then.' She stands up and storms out the room.

I take a hefty slug of klee. I'm unnerved. I resolve to have a strong word with Tanrose. I shouldn't be dealing with this, I'm far too busy investigating. I take another drink and realise I'm feeling angry about the whole thing, though I'm not sure why.

There's a knock on my outside door. I answer it warily, fearing that the Brotherhood may be here to ask questions about their sudden loss of a dwa dealer. It turns out to be Lisutaris, Mistress of the Sky. I'm moderately pleased to see her and welcome her in. It's probably a good idea to talk to her before the Assemblage, though I'm surprised she's travelled to Twelve Seas. If I was a powerful sorcerer living in the pleasant environs of Truth is Beauty Lane, nothing would get me south of the river.

Lisutaris has high cheekbones, a lot of fair hair and carries herself elegantly. She's only a few years younger than me but you wouldn't know it. The years have not taken such a toll on her. Of course, I've hard a hard life. She's attractive, and rather glamorous when she takes the notion, though when she arrives she's wrapped in a sensible amount of fur, and her rainbow cloak is a practical winter model rather than the fancy thing she sometimes wears.

My rooms are extremely untidy. Lisutaris isn't overly concerned about the niceties, however, and sweeps some junk off a chair before sitting down and enquiring if I can provide her with some wine to keep her circulation moving while she prepares thazis for consumption.

'I've no wine. Beer?'

Lisutaris nods, and concentrates on her thazis. Most people smoke thazis in small sticks but Lisutaris, when separated from her water pipe, constructs far larger versions, and she proceeds to do this while I bring her ale. In no time the room reeks of thazis and Lisutaris is looking more comfortable.

'It's cold as the ice queen's grave out there,' she mutters. 'I've got a warming spell on my cloak, my hat, my boots and my carriage, and I'm still shivering.'

I ask her what brings her to Twelve Seas.

'I hear you're going to the Assemblage as Cicerius's representative. Did he ask you to fix the election for me?'

'Not exactly. Just to make sure it wasn't fixed against you. Do you care?'

Lisutaris shrugs. 'Not particularly. It will be bad for Turai if the Simnian gets the post, but what the hell, the Orcs will destroy the city soon enough, either that or Nioj will.'

'The King thinks that having you as head of the Sorcerers Guild will give us protection.'

'It might. Who knows?' Lisutaris inhales more thazis smoke. 'What I mainly want to happen at the Assemblage,' she continues, 'is for me not to get killed.'

'You think that's likely?'

'I received an anonymous message saying an Assassin was on his way.'

Lisutaris is short on details. She's brought the message with her and hands it over. A small piece of paper with neat handwriting.

You may be in danger from an Assassin at the Assemblage. Covinius is coming.

There's nothing else. Nothing else to see, that is, though a piece of paper can often yield a lot to sorcerous investigation. I tell Lisutaris I'll get to work on it.

'Did you inform the Civil Guard?'

'Yes. But the Guards won't be allowed into the Assemblage. That's why I want to hire you.'

I tell Lisutaris that strictly she doesn't have to. Cicerius has already hired me to work on her behalf. Lisutaris insists she'd be happier if she hired me directly, and there's some sense in this, so I accept a retainer fee from her.

'It's very hard to get any information about the Assassins. But I'll do my best. Most probably it's just some crank.'

'Who is Covinius?' asks Lisutaris.

'A member of the Simnian Assassins Guild. He has an evil reputation. People say he's never failed on a mission.'

'That doesn't make me feel any better,' says Lisutaris, frowning. 'I don't want this job enough to get killed for it.'

Lisutaris is strong enough to carry a powerful protection spell at all times. This will turn a blade, but there's no saying how many ways a murderous expert like Covinius could find to get around it. I repeat that there's probably nothing in it, but in truth I'm worried.

A freezing draught from under the door is ·badly affecting my feet. I kick an old cushion over to cover the gap. Lisutaris smiles. She isn't the snobbish type. Back in the war she slept in a tent by the walls like everyone else. I realise I rather like her. I'll be sorry if she ends up with an assassin's dart in her heart.

'I need someone to watch my back,' says the Sorcerer.

'Didn't you just hire me for that?'

'Yes. But you're going to be busy with other things at the Assemblage. I want to recruit Makri as a bodyguard.'

This doesn't seem like a bad idea. If you want a bodyguard, Makri is a good choice, providing you don't mind her killing a few extra people every now and then. With the Guild College being closed for the winter, she's got time on her hands.

'I think she'll be pleased to do it. Cheer her up, probably.'

'Has Makri been unhappy?'

In other circumstances it would be strange that the well-bred Mistress of the Sky would even know Makri, but they've met through the Association of Gentlewomen. So I believe anyway, though the Association keeps its business secret.

'Fairly unhappy. Personal problems. I sorted most of it out.'

Lisutaris's attention is starting to wander. When I ask her about the Assemblage it takes a few moments for her to reply.

'How exactly is the new head of the Guild chosen? Is it a straight election or is there some sort of test?'

'Both. The sorcerers vote on the candidates and the top two go on to a final elimination.'

'Which involves?'

'A test inside the magic space.'

'What test?'

The Mistress of the Sky doesn't know. Charius the Wise will set the test, and he's keeping the details close to his chest.

'With any luck we'll be looking for thazis plants,' says Lisutaris, who's fairly single-minded about her pleasures these days. I show her along the corridor to Makri's room and leave her at the door before heading downstairs for a beer. I get myself round a Happy Guildsman jumbo tankard of ale and inform Gurd that his barmaid will be missing for a few days, as she's about to perform the duties of bodyguard for Turai's leading sorcerer. Gurd looks relieved. He's also been suffering at the hands of Makri's moods. Since Tanrose told him it was due to some emotional difficulties, he's been terrified that Makri might broach the subject with him. Gurd has enough emotional problems of his own. He's attracted to Tanrose and never quite knows what to do about it.

'It will take her mind off things,' says Gurd. 'Why did she want to get involved with an Elf anyway?'

'I don't know. Probably thinks they're handsome.'

'Why would she care about that? A good fighter and a good provider, that's what a man should be.'

Sensing that Gurd is now worrying that Tanrose might not think he's handsome enough, I change the subject. 'I'm about to look after an election. Not a job I ever thought I'd end up doing.'

'You think it will be fair?'

'I'll make sure it is. Turai is depending on me, and I'm depending on the hefty fee from Cicerius.'

'But what about all the magic they'll be using?' asks Gurd. As a northern barbarian, he's never been too comfortable with magic.

'It won't matter. If there's anything irregular going on I'll pick it up. Easy as bribing a Senator for a man of my experience.'

The tavern fills up as the evening draws on. The fierce winter is not harming Gurd's business too much. People would rather be drinking in the warmth of the Avenging Axe than huddling miserably at home. I load up with several bowls of stew, then depart upstairs with beer. I look in on Makri to see if she's taken the job as bodyguard. Lisutaris is still here. She's lying unconscious on the floor surrounded by the remains of numerous enormous thazis sticks. Makri is comatose beside her. The room is so thick with smoke I can barely see the far wall. I shake my head.

'You'll be a fine new head of the Sorcerers Guild,' I mutter, and leave them to it. If Cicerius could see her now, I figure he'd be regretting his choice.

Chapter Six

I take the paper to Astrath Triple Moon and ask him to work on it for me. He asks if I can give him any more information about it. A good sorcerer can often glean information from an object but only if he has something to go on, something to anchor the enquiry. Left to his own devices, Astrath might scan the city for days and not link the paper to anything. 'It might not even have originated in Turai.'

'It did. I checked the watermark. The paper was made and sold right here in the city. And it's a woman's handwriting.'

'How do you know?' asks Astrath.

'I know. I'm an investigator. The message was handed in at the Messengers Guild post in the middle of Royal Boulevard, which doesn't narrow it down much. That's a busy station, and the man on duty doesn't remember who brought it in. But I have a hunch. Not that many people in Turai would have heard of Covinius. A few people at Palace Security maybe, but they don't employ women. But there is one woman who'd know all about him. And she's based in Kushni, not far from that messenger post. Hanama.'

'Hanama?'

'One of our own assassins. She might send a warning to Lisutaris.'

'Wouldn't that be against the assassins' rules?'

'Hanama seems to be playing by her own set these days.'

Astrath Triple Moon agrees to check it out, and I carry on with my preparations for the Assemblage. Cicerius is providing me with expenses money so I'll be okay for beer. Makri complains about the weather and is even more irritating than usual.

'Maybe she should sail back to Elf-land,' suggests Gurd, after clearing up the tavern following a fight between Makri and three dock workers she claimed had insulted her. 'A barmaid has to expect a few insults, it's part of the job.'

Two days later I'm standing outside a large hall at the edge of Thamlin, just outside the grounds of the Imperial Palace. The grounds are frozen white. The trees are frosted, the ponds and fountains iced over. Snow is falling heavily and the assembled soldiery and civil guards stand miserably in shivering ranks. They're gathered here because the King himself has been making a speech to the sorcerers, welcoming them to the Assemblage and wishing them a pleasant time in the city state of Turai.

I'm stuck outside because I wasn't invited to this part of the ceremony, which demonstrates that Tribune of the People is not that great a thing to be. While I'm waiting to be let in, I reflect sadly that a few years ago, when I was senior investigator at Palace Security, I'd see the King regularly. I doubt he'd recognise me these days. If he did he wouldn't acknowledge me. A man who's been bounced out of his job for drunkenness at the Palace no longer has enough status to be noticed by the King. I wonder if Rittius will show up at the Assemblage. He's the current head of Palace Security and a bitter enemy of mine. I've done him plenty of bad turns and he's paid them all back. Last year he took me to court and damn near bankrupted me. I shiver. Maybe I can persuade one of the sorcerers here to show me a more effective spell for warming my cloak.

It's a relief when the King and his retinue emerge from the building and ride off through the blizzard. I trudge forward to the huge portico that leads into the Royal Hall. This is one of the largest buildings in Turai, almost as big as the Senate. It dates from a few hundred years ago but, as with Turai's other public buildings, it's kept in excellent repair by the King. He likes his public works to look impressive, and he's not short of money since the trade route from the south opened up a few years back, and the gold mines in the north ran into some very productive veins of ore.

'Sorcerers and their staff only,' says a young woman at the door. Her blue cloak signifies that she's an apprentice.

I bring out my letter bearing Cicerius's seal and flash it in her direction. 'Official Turanian government representative.'

She studies the paper. 'Tribune of the People? What's that?'

'A very important position,' I reply, and march past. After standing outside in the cold for what seems like hours I'm not about to explain my business to the hired help. Once inside, my first task is to find beer. After making some enquiries I find that refreshments are served in the Room of Saints at the back of the hall. It's already crowded and no one is looking at the statues, frescoes and mosaics of our great religious figures. Drinking is already underway. The sorcerers, no doubt bored by the King's speech, are keen to get on with the business of enjoying themselves. Normally in a crowded inn I'd use my body weight to force my way through, but here I'm rather more circumspect. It's absolutely forbidden for a sorcerer to blast anyone with a spell at the Assemblage - it would lead to immediate expulsion - but I don't want to offend anyone unnecessarily. Not yet anyway. I'll get round to it soon enough.

I grab a beer and a small bottle of klee and head back to the main hall, where I look around to see if there are any faces I recognise. I'm due to meet Cicerius but I want to get my bearings first and see if I can learn anything useful. The main room of the Royal Hall is vast. Frescoes decorate the walls and ceilings, and a huge and intricate mosaic depicting the triumphs of Saint Quatinius covers the floor. In every corner there are statues of past heroes of Turai. The stained-glass windows are noted for their beauty and contain some of the finest surviving work of Usax, Turai's greatest artist. Fine though the stained glass is, it doesn't let in a great amount of the dim winter light, and torches are lit at regular intervals along the walls.

The great room is full of sorcerers of every description. Each is wearing his or her best cloak, which makes for an impressive collection of rainbows. In the middle of the floor a group of Turanians are holding court, welcoming friends and allies. Old Hasius the Brilliant, Chief Investigating Sorcerer at the Abode of Justice, stands beside Harmon Half Elf and Melus the Fair. Next to them Gorsius Starfinder is guzzling wine, and Tirini Snake Smiter

- our most glamorous sorcerer, and the only one to wear a rainbow cloak made of transparent muslin - is showing off her smile to some younger admirers. All Turai's most powerful sorcerers, standing in a group like they haven't a care in the world. I immediately feel irritated. Close to them are some of our younger adepts: Lanius Suncatcher, the new Chief Sorcerer at Palace Security, along with Capali Comet Rider and Orius Fire Tamer. They irritate me as well. Lisutaris, Mistress of the Sky, doesn't seem to be here yet. Still wrapped around her water pipe, no doubt. As Turanian candidate for Head of the Guild, the woman is going to be a disaster. There again, I can't see many of these people staying sober for the whole week.

Despite the gathering of so many magic workers under one roof, there's no real sorcery going on. Though sorcerers are not as a rule modest, it would be regarded as bad taste to show off one's powers in such company. Here and there someone might use his illuminated staff to check under his seat for his tankard, or place a large object discreetly inside a magic pocket, but there are no demonstrations of great power. Today is for meeting old friends, relaxing, and hearing news from round the world. Demonstrations of power can wait, and so can the election, which won't happen for a few days yet.

I'm still waiting for Astrath's report on the piece of paper. He's decided to attend the Assemblage so I'm hoping to learn something from him later. I wonder if the message was genuine. I hope not. Covinius means trouble. Even for an assassin he seems to be almost intangible. No one has ever seen him, and that bothers me. In what guise is he planning to appear? Though the sorcerers are strict about who they admit to the Assemblage, an experienced assassin like Covinius would have no trouble in assuming a convincing identity. The worrying thought strikes me that he might actually be a sorcerer. I've never heard of a sorcerous assassin, but there's always a first time. It's hard enough gaining any information about the Assassins Guild here in Turai. As for their equivalent in Simnia, who knows?

Cicerius appears at my side, resplendent in the green-edged toga which denotes his rank. 'Where is Lisutaris?' he enquires.

'Not here yet.'

'Not here yet?' The Deputy Consul is incredulous. 'How can she be late at a time like this?'

Cicerius can't quite understand that not everyone is desperate to do their duty for Turai all the time. He scans the room, tutting in frustration. 'Come with me,' he instructs. 'While we await the arrival of our candidate, I shall introduce you to your fellow Tribunes, and Tilupasis.'

Cicerius ushers me into a small side room, one of the many which adjoin the hall. There we find Tilupasis, Visus and Sulinius. Cicerius introduces us formally. Tilupasis is thirty-five, with nothing flashy in her appearance. She's wealthy, fashionable enough, but not much given to frivolity. A politician's wife and, since the death of her husband, something of a politician herself. I know our Senators take her seriously. She has the ear of the Consul, and friends at the Palace, and the ability to do people favours. Visus and Sulinius are both around twenty, young men just embarking on their careers. Sulinius is the son of Praetor Capatius, the richest man in Turai, and Visus is also of aristocratic parentage. They both look fresh-faced and handsome in their white togas, and eager to perform their tasks well. Becoming a Tribune of the People in order to attend the Sorcerers Assemblage is an unconventional start to a political career, but if they do well, Cicerius will look favourably on them.

Tilupasis informs the Deputy Consul that the Assemblage has begun satisfactorily. The sorcerers are settling in well. More importantly, Tilupasis has already made a count of probable votes, and thinks Lisutaris is in with a chance.

'Sunstorm Ramius is the favourite to win, but there are a lot of sorcerers here who haven't decided who to vote for. I'm certain we can get Lisutaris elected provided she puts up a good showing.'

Cicerius is pleased. He entreats his two young Tribunes to work hard for Turai. He tells me to let him know the moment I suspect any hint of treachery by any other delegation. 'Above all, be sure to act in a manner which brings only credit to Turai. It's vital that we show our visitors that Turanians are people of high moral standards. Do nothing which could be interpreted otherwise.'

Cicerius departs. Tilupasis turns to us. 'Disregard everything the Deputy Consul just said,' she tells us briskly. 'Turai needs to win this election and I'm here to make sure we do. If we can gather enough votes fairly, all well and good. If not, we'll buy them. I have an endless supply of gold, silver, wine, whores, pretty boys, dwa and thazis to keep the sorcerers happy. Personal favours, political favours, anything. Whatever they need, we provide. Understand?'

The two young Tribunes gape. This is not what they were expecting. I'm unsurprised. It's exactly what I was expecting. You don't win a post like Head of the Sorcerers Guild by fair play and good behaviour. Cicerius knows it too, though he's not intending to dirty his hands with the details. That's Tilupasis's job, and from her introduction I'd say she was going to be good at it. She starts handing out detailed instructions to Visus and Sulinius as to which sorcerers they are to approach. I'm becoming increasingly uncomfortable. I never like being told what to do, and I fear I'm about to be ordered about in a manner quite unsuitable for a private investigator. My mood, already poor, worsens.

'Thraxas. I'm not depending on you to charm anyone, or manoeuvre for votes. We'll take care of that. I need you to look after Lisutaris and inform me immediately if you get wind of anything going on which may damage her chances.'

'Fine. I'll start in the Room of Saints. I could do with another beer.'

I'm hoping this might annoy her.

'A good choice,' says Tilupasis, unperturbed. 'Let me escort you there.' She leads me out into the main hall. I'm wearing my best cloak but I'm still shabby beside her. Tilupasis is conservatively but fashionably dressed in a white robe with just enough jewellery to let people know she's got wealth on her side. The hall is now crowded and we pause to allow two blonde-haired female sorcerers to pass.

'From the far north,' says Tilupasis. 'I already have their votes.'

'Did it cost much?'

'Some gold, a dragon-scale necklace or two. They were quite reasonable.'

Her eyes come to rest on one of the more exotic figures in the hall, a tall young woman in a cloak which is mainly gold, with the rainbow pattern visible only at the collar. The woman is dark-skinned and has hair so long as to make me suspect it's been sorcerously enhanced, stretching down almost to her knees. In amongst the dark mass of hair are several golden streaks and some beads which brilliantly reflect the torchlight. I've never seen so much hair on one person. It's an impressive sight. Beneath her spectacular golden cloak she's wearing a somewhat more functional tunic and leggings, marking her out as a visitor from outside the city. Very few Turanian women ever wear male attire, apart from Makri, and some of the lower-class market workers.

'Princess Direeva?'

'Yes. One of the most powerful sorcerers in the Wastelands.'

'Not an associate of Horm the Dead, I hope?'

Horm the Dead, a renegade half-Orc sorcerer, almost destroyed Turai last year.

Tilupasis shakes her head. 'Her lands are far south of his. I don't think they're friends.'

Turanians tend to be suspicious of anyone who lives in the Wastelands, the long stretch of ungoverned territory that separates us from the Orcs in the east.

'Better to have her as a friend than an enemy, I suppose,' I mutter.

'More than that. Princess Direeva is of huge importance in this election. She influences a great many votes.'

'She does?'

'Of course. Her father's kingdom, the Southern Hills, is rich in sorcery. It has to be, being so close to the Orcs. Without magical protection they'd have been overrun long ago. There are ten sorcerers here directly under her sway. But that's not all. The Wastelands are full of tiny regions that look to them for leadership. When you count up all the sorcerers from these regions, it comes to something like thirty votes. That could be enough to sway the election. I believe she favours Darius, the Abelasian, so winning over Princess Direeva is one of the most important tasks I have.'

The Princess stands rather aloof from the crowd. She's attended by two apprentices in blue cloaks but makes no attempt to mingle with the other sorcerers. Tilupasis excuses herself, and heads over to begin her offensive on Direeva. I'm surprised that the young woman has thirty votes under her control. Already I'm feeling slightly baffled by the complexity of the election.

I've spotted Sunstorm Ramius on the far side of the room and I'm keen to gain an impression of the Simnian. He's a man of medium height and build, around fifty-five but showing no effects of age. His beard is short and well-trimmed and he stands erect with something of the manner of a soldier. Ramius won himself a fine reputation during the last Orc Wars and he looks like a man who wouldn't flinch in the face of danger. Around him are a large collection of friends and admirers, and from the way they hang on to his words I can tell that he carries a lot of weight round here.

Charismatic and powerful, I reflect. Bad news for Lisutaris. But good to know. Apart from my official business here, there's the ever-important matter of gambling on the result. If I can't succeed in getting Lisutaris elected I'm at least planning to back the winner. Honest Mox has been taking bets on the outcome of this election, but I've been holding off till I get a chance to study the form in person. My first impression is that Sunstorm Ramius is probably worth his place as favourite.

I hang around on the fringes of the group who surround Ramius. They're talking of the election and I listen keenly because there are other candidates to consider. Lisutaris, Rokim, Darius and Ramius may be the early favourites, but that's not to say there won't be a strong showing from anyone else. Surprise candidates have been known to win the post before, creeping through the pack when the Assemblage has been unable to make up its mind. Or else bribing their way to power, though the sorcerers will never admit that this has happened.

I'm heading back to the bar for a fresh tankard of ale when a slight stir in the hall heralds the arrival of Lisutaris, Mistress of the Sky. She enters quite grandly, as befits her rank, with a young female apprentice beside her and Makri bringing up the rear. Lisutaris is extravagantly coiffured and wears her finest rainbow cloak over a white robe which trails elegantly behind her as she walks. She has silver Elvish bangles, a silver tiara, a necklace of three rows of emeralds and a pair of gold shoes that must have cost the equivalent of a shipload of grain.

Behind her Makri is wearing her full light body armour, something I've rarely seen. Usually when she gets into a fight in Twelve Seas there's no time to be donning armour. She brought it with her from the Orc lands and it's made of black leather partly covered with chainmail, which will turn most blades. Makri carries her helmet under her arm, and while she isn't openly wearing a blade - this is not allowed at the Assemblage - I've no doubt that she has a knife concealed somewhere, and Lisutaris will be carrying her swords in a magic pocket. Anyone with an experienced eye can see that the wearer of such a suit is a person who knows how to fight; a worthwhile bodyguard. It makes for an impressive entrance. Lisutaris looks like a sorcerer who means business.

I make my way over to greet them. Lisutaris is already surrounded by sorcerers and, not for the first time, Makri also finds herself the object of some interest. Makri's reddish skin tone gives away her Orcish blood - any sorcerer would sense it anyway - and I can see that people are already wondering who this exotic creature is that walks behind Lisutaris wearing Orcish armour with the gait of a warrior.

'Nice entrance.'

'You think so?' says Makri. 'I was worried about the armour. But Lisutaris wanted her bodyguard to look businesslike.'

'Probably a wise move. Why are you late? The water pipe?'

'Only partly,' says Makri. 'Lisutaris was having her hair done by Copro.'

'I guess that explains it. How did you like our finest beautician?'

'He's okay,' says Makri, noncommittally. 'He offered to show me his new range of make-up from Samsarina. I told him I didn't need it.'

After her tough upbringing in the gladiator pits Makri still professes contempt for the softness of our Turanian aristocracy, though in recent months she's moderated her hostility towards make-up, particularly in the field of colouring her nails.

'Does Lisutaris have your swords?'

Makri shakes her head. 'I've got them. She lent me a magic purse.' She pats her hip. 'I've got two swords, three knives and an axe in here.'

A magic purse is a container of the magic space. You can put anything inside and it loses all mass and volume. It's a small manifestation of the magic space in which some of the sorcerous tests will later be carried out. It's illegal to walk around Turai with a magic purse, but the Consul has suspended this law for the duration of the Assemblage.

Two young sorcerers - Samsarinan, from their clothes - are attempting to edge their way past me to greet Lisutaris. Or possibly to introduce themselves to Makri. I leave them to it. Maybe if Makri gets involved with someone else she'll stop being miserable about the Elf. I'm picking up a beer when a heavy hand pounds me on the back.

'Thraxas? Is that you?'

I turn round to find a large sorcerer with a red face and a bushy grey beard smiling at me. I don't recognise him.

'It's me. Irith!'

'Irith Victorious?'

'The same! You've put on weight!'

'So have you.'

I slap him on the back enthusiastically. I haven't seen Irith Victorious for more than twenty years. When I was a mercenary down in Juval, Irith was a hired sorcerer in the same army. It was the first time I met Gurd. The war was messy and confused, and the only relief was the klee, provisions and occasional good times supplied by Irith Victorious. He was a slim youth in those days, but from the size of his waistline I'd say he'd carried on with the good times.

'What are you doing now?'

'I made good. King's Chief Sorcerer in Juval. You wouldn't have thought that was going to happen when we were wandering around in that jungle! What are you doing here?'

Irith knows I never made it as a sorcerer. When he learns I'm working for the Deputy Consul he roars with laughter. I find myself roaring with laughter too. I always liked Irith.

'There's six sorcerers from Juval here and we're looking for a good time. Come and meet them!'

I go to meet them. They turn out to be six of the largest, most jovial sorcerers ever made, each with a loud voice, a large belly and a mission in life to get as much ale inside him as possible, all the while shouting for more beer, more stories about the old days and more serving girls to sit on their knee.

'The election?' yells one of them, who's drinking a huge flagon of ale while another hovers at his side. 'Who cares? Hey, can anyone else do this?'

He mutters a word and the floating tankard rises and starts emptying beer into his mouth. I'm impressed. It's one of the finest spells I've ever seen. His companions bellow with laughter and start trying to emulate the feat. Soon beer is flowing in all directions. Waitresses are scurrying this way and that with fresh supplies, and Irith Victorious is claiming in the loudest of voices that he doesn't care what anyone says, he was the real champion at the last Juvalian sorcerers' drinking contest and anyone who says otherwise is an Orc-lover.

'The Juvalian drinking contest is as nothing compared to the feats of Thraxas of Turai!' I bawl, and start on a fresh tankard.

'Turai?' screams Irith. 'No one can drink in this city. Too cold! I've been as cold as a frozen pixie since I got here. Southern heat, that's what makes a drinker!'

'Southern heat? I've seen a two-fingered troll drink more than a Juvalian sorcerer. Haven't you finished that tankard yet?'

I call for more beer. 'And charge it to Cicerius!'

We toast the Deputy Consul, and then the Deputy Consul in Juval, or some such official. I don't quite catch the title.

'Anyone betting on the election?' I enquire, some time later.

Irith is a gambler but he's not as enthusiastic about betting on the contest as I thought he might be, even though he knows there's a woman working in the kitchens whose actual purpose is to act as a runner, taking bets to a bookmaker. He doesn't fancy the odds.

'Sunstorm Ramius is the strong favourite and they're only offering one to two. Hardly seems worth it. I can never get excited about an odds-on bet.'

I nod. Risking twenty gurans to win only ten isn't that attractive a prospect to a fun-loving sorcerer like Irith. Myself, I might go for it at the chariot races if I was certain I was backing the winner. Here at the Assemblage, I'm not so sure. Having seen Tilupasis swinging into action, it doesn't seem impossible that Lisutaris might win. I heard Tilupasis telling young Visus in strong terms that she didn't care how old the Chief sorcerer from Misan was, it was his duty to show her round the city and make sure she was having a good time. As the elderly sorcerer departed on Visus's arm she looked pretty happy, so that's probably a few more votes for Turai. Furthermore, I'm on Lisutaris's side and I have a lot of confidence in my abilities.

'Number one chariot,' I tell Irith.

'What at?'

'Investigating. Drinking. Fighting. Getting votes. Lots of things. Sharp as an Elf's ear. Where's the beer?'

Providing Lisutaris, Mistress of the Sky, can avoid appearing in public looking like she's just unwillingly detached herself from her water pipe and is having trouble putting one foot in front of the other, I reckon she's in with a chance. Most people like her, she's maintained her good reputation from the wars, and she can muster a lot of charm when she has to. A few beers later it's as clear as day that I should be placing a hefty bet on the Mistress of the Sky, so I head for the kitchens to do just that, picking up a plate of venison and a huge peach pie on the way. I get back to drinking with the Juvalians, and entertain one and all with a fine story of my exploits in the war between Juval, Abelasi and Pargada, twenty-four years ago.

'It was the first time I met Gurd, and we gave the Pargadans hell, I can tell you.'

Some hours later a tired-looking attendant suggests to us that as the Royal Hall has now completely emptied of sorcerers, it may be time for us to go home. I clamber to my feet, bid farewell to Irith and his companions, step lightly over the one or two Juvalian sorcerers now lying prostrate on the floor, and stumble out the building. I'd say the Assemblage has gone well so far. Far more enjoyable than I anticipated. I wonder what happened to Lisutaris and Makri. I shrug. Powerful sorcerer and ferocious warrior. They can look after themselves. At the door I run into Tilupasis. She looks as fresh and elegant as she did at the start of the day.

'Get many votes?' I ask.

'I believe so.'

'I may have secured the support of the Juvalians.'

'You mean you out-drank them?'

'I did. It was a close-run thing, but I was drinking for Turai.'

Tilupasis laughs, quite elegantly. 'Good.'

'Good?' I was hoping she'd be annoyed. It still bothers me that I'm obliged to be here working for the government.

'I have Visus and Sulinius to charm those who need to be charmed. But for those who need to be drunk into submission, I have you. I told Cicerius you'd be a good man to have on our side.'

Tilupasis departs. Going to snuggle up with the Consul maybe. I have a peculiar feeling I've been outsmarted somehow. To hell with them. Outside, the only landus I can find doesn't want to take me south of the river. I'm obliged to raise my fist and inform the driver that his landus is going south, with or without him. We set off through the snow. The streets are quiet. I'm cold. It wasn't such a bad day.

Chapter Seven

Astrath Triple Moon sends me a message apologising for his non-appearance at the Assemblage, claiming illness. The message ends with the brief sentence, *Paper came from Hanama.*

I mull this over with my morning beer. Astrath has good powers of sorcerous investigation and his results can generally be trusted. My hunch was correct. It was Hanama who warned Lisutaris about Covinius. This means I'll have to talk to her. Talking to Assassins is never something I enjoy doing. I finish my beer, warm up my cloak and set off through the snow for the Assemblage. Once there I nose around for a while, check that Makri is looking after Lisutaris, then get round to drinking with Irith and his companions. In the rooms and corridors of the Royal Hall, the electioneering is gathering pace. So far I've had little involvement in the machinations of Tilupasis, although she does ask me to escort young Sulinius to a secluded location behind the hall.

'He's carrying a lot of gold and I don't want him to get robbed.'

The gold buys the votes of four sorcerers from Carsan. Tilupasis is well satisfied. 'Let the Simnians try to match that.'

'Are they busy with bribery as well?'

'Of course. So are the Abelasians. But they lack the advantage of being at home. I have access to the King's vaults. We can outspend them.'

The only other task I'm given is to call in at a local Civil Guard station to bail out two Samsarinans who found themselves in some trouble after an argument at the card table in a tavern. Tilupasis refunds their losses, promises to show them a more hospitable venue for gambling the next night, and charms them sufficiently to make some inroads on the Samsarinan delegation. Samsarina have their own candidate, Rokim the Bright, but Tilupasis hopes to persuade them to switch their eighteen votes to Lisutaris if things seem hopeless for their candidate.

'Eighteen second-choice votes,' she says. 'At present they're attached to the Simnian, but I'm hoping we can sway them.'

Tilupasis is proving to be a highly efficient, and has boundless energy. Her main worry is Princess Direeva. In a tight contest the thirty sorcerers under her influence are looking more important than ever, but they're intending to vote for Darius Cloud Walker, the Abelasian. Direeva has known Darius for a long time, and trusts him.

'I can't seem to get to Direeva. Her representative rebuffed a very generous offer. She doesn't appear to want for anything. She wasn't interested in gold and she didn't seem to take to either Visus or Sulinius.'

At least Lisutaris is holding up, just about. Accompanied by Makri, she greets her fellow sorcerers, quite charmingly from what

I can tell, disappearing only occasionally to indulge her need for thazis. So far she hasn't disgraced Turai by falling over in public. I've informed Tilupasis and Cicerius about the possible involvement of a Simnian Assassin. Cicerius is sceptical.

'Palace Security would have notified me if Covinius had entered Turai,' says the Deputy Consul. 'I can't believe that Lisutaris is in danger of being assassinated. The election is keenly contested but there has never been an assassination. Who is meant to have hired him?'

'I don't know yet. I'll check it out as soon as I can.'

Tilupasis promises to discreetly inform the other Turanian sorcerers of the warning so they can watch out for Lisutaris, just in case the threat turns out to be real. Which, along with Makri, gives her quite a lot of protection. I've sent a message to Hanama requesting a meeting but have had no reply as yet. I excuse myself from Tilupasis as it seems like a long time since I had a beer. Close to the Room of Saints, I bump into Makri.

'Any trouble?'

Makri shakes her head. 'No trouble.'

At this moment Princess Direeva appears at our side. Ignoring me, she introduces herself to Makri.

'I am Princess Direeva,' she says. 'And you are?'

'Makri.'

The Princess nods. 'I thought so. Champion gladiator of all the Orc lands, I believe?' Princess Direeva is apparently impressed. 'I understand you were undefeated for five years?'

'Six,' says Makri.

'Really? And you once fought a dragon in the arena?'

'I did.'

Direeva seems intrigued. Her extraordinary hair sways gently as she talks, making the gold streaks and glittering beads sparkle in the light. There may be a touch of Orcish blood about the Princess herself. Though only Human sorcerers can stand for the post of Guild leader, there are various sorcerers in attendance with Elvish blood in their veins, so I suppose a little Orc isn't such a surprise. The sorcerers are not as formal as many of the city's guilds. Makri would be bounced right out of a meeting of the goldsmiths, but goldsmiths are always very concerned about etiquette.

I've heard Makri bragging about her accomplishments in the arena enough times already, and Princess Direeva shows no interest in talking to me, so I slip off. In the Room of Saints Tilupasis is encouraging some Pargadans to drink more wine. She asks me what Princess Direeva wanted with Makri.

'Just a friendly chat, as far as I could tell.'

'Really?' Tilupasis's eyes light up. 'Excellent. We may have found something the Princess is interested in.'

I spend the rest of the day drinking with Irith Victorious. He asks me how I'm coping with my official duties.

'It's all right. Better than rowing a slave galley. It wasn't like I had anything else planned for the winter.'

One of Irith's companions teaches me an improved warming spell for my cloak. Now I'm warm and I have plenty of free beer. I'm starting to enjoy this assignment. The light fades early and I arrive home in darkness. I take care climbing the stairs to my office. I may be full of beer but Thraxas, number one chariot among Turai's investigators, has never been known to fall off his own staircase. I'm nearly as happy as a drunken mercenary. These sorcerers from Juval know how to enjoy themselves. Maybe I should move down there. Be better than this lousy city.

'Better than this lousy city!' I yell into the darkness. There's no one around and I take the opportunity to bellow the last verse of an old army drinking song, before entering my office in a cheerful manner and finding Makri, Lisutaris and Princess Direeva all unconscious on the floor. Darius Cloud Walker is lying dead beside them with Makri's knife in his back. I blink. It isn't a sight I was expecting. The sheer awfulness of the situation almost paralyses me. The room stinks of dwa and thazis. I'm full of beer. I can't cope with a dead sorcerer. I'm still trying to take it in when there's a knock on the door and a voice I recognise shouts my name.

'Thraxas. We want to talk to you.'

It's Karlox, an enforcer for the Brotherhood. I mutter a foul curse at Makri for landing me in this situation. From the look of her face I'd say she's been indulging in more dwa than she can handle. If the overdose doesn't kill her I swear I'll do it myself.

My first thought is to kill Karlox, get on a horse, ride out of town and keep going. The situation is so grim as to defy description. When Cicerius hired me to help Lisutaris, he wasn't expecting me to lure her rivals to my office and have them murdered, which is what this is going to look like. I'm heading for the scaffold in the company of Makri, and that's going to make a fine story for the Renowned and Truthful Chronicle.

'Open up, Thraxas,' shouts Karlox. 'I know you're in there.'

Karlox may be dumb as an Orc but he's a loyal member of the Brotherhood, not the sort of man to give in easily. I've a shrewd idea he's here investigating the recent death of their dwa dealer, and that's a big enough problem in itself. Makri killed him and at this moment she's unconscious and there's an important sorcerer dead on the floor. It would be easy to panic. Fortunately I'm not a man to panic. I weigh up the situation. I doubt that Karlox is here alone. He knows he couldn't get the better of me without help. If he's here with a gang, they'll be able to break down the door, minor locking spell or not. The one thing I can't afford to happen is for any witnesses to see Darius lying alongside Makri. Particularly as it's Makri's knife that's sticking in his back.

If I move the body I'll be in endless difficulties later. If I don't move it I'll be in endless difficulties right now. Karlox beats on the door and I can hear him giving orders to start breaking it down. I hoist the unfortunate Darius over my shoulder and stagger to the inner door. Darius doesn't weigh that much. The shock of these events has sobered me up just enough not to fall and break my neck as I make my way down the stairs and through to the back of the tavern. To my surprise, Gurd and Tanrose are still about, making preparations for tomorrow's food.

'What—?'

'Can't stop. Go upstairs and look after Makri till I get back. The Brotherhood are about to break the door down.'

Gurd picks up his axe and they depart swiftly. I carry on through to the yard. Ideally I'd like to dump the body as far away as possible, but I can't risk being seen from the front of the tavern, so

I can think of nothing better to do than heave the body over the wall into the next yard. It's a high wall and I'm panting with the exertion. The snow billows around me, muffling any sound.

I pray that no one has seen my actions. Not that it will matter in a day or two, when the sorcerer's companions start working their spells, looking for Darius. I've just committed a serious crime and I've no idea how I'm going to escape the consequences. Without pausing to catch my breath I hurry back upstairs to find Gurd and Tanrose confronting Karlox and six others. They've forced the door, breaking the lock. Gurd is outraged at the damage to his property, but the Brotherhood men are more interested in the sight of Makri, Lisutaris and Princess Direeva lying on the floor. My room is still thick with thazis smoke and reeks of burnt dwa.

'Been having a party?' rasps Karlox.

I unsheathe my sword and stand beside Gurd. With his axe in his hand the old Barbarian is still a formidable sight.

'Time to leave,' I say.

'Where did you get the dwa?' says Karlox, which is quite a shrewd question for such a stupid guy. I'm not planning on answering, though it's a question I'll be putting to Makri. I tell Karlox brusquely that he's got about ten seconds to leave my office or suffer the consequences. He eyes my blade, and Gurd's axe.

'Why so upset, fat man? We're just asking a few polite questions about the death of one of our men. You got something to hide? Or are you just wanting time alone with the doped girls?'

His men guffaw.

'You've given me plenty to report,' says Karlox. With that he turns and strides out of the room, followed by his men. I immediately shut the door and place my locking spell on it, for all the good that will do.

'What's going on?' asks Gurd, but I'm already bending down over Makri. I'm mad as hell at the woman but I don't want her to expire from dwa. She's inexperienced in its use. Or I thought she was. Lesada leaves, from the Elvish Isles, serve me mainly as hangover cures but I've seen an Elvish healer use them to bring a person out of a dwa trance. I crush a couple in some water and pour some down Makri's throat. She coughs, sits up and looks around her curiously.

'What's happening?' she says.

'A good question.'

She looks round the room. I ask her if she notices anything missing.

'Like what?'

'Like a sorcerer maybe?'

'Right. Darius. Where is he?'

'He's lying in a snowdrift in the next yard. Did you kill him?'

Makri looks puzzled. 'Of course not. Why would I?'

'Who knows? When I got here Darius was dead and your knife was still sticking in his back. I had to hide the body. If we don't move fast we're all heading for a swift execution. So help me wake up these two and tell me what's been going on.'

Gurd and Tanrose want to stay and help but I banish them from the room. The less they're involved the better. I set about trying to revive Princess Direeva, while Makri gets to work on Lisutaris.

'What were you thinking of, taking dwa? You know what happened to Minarixa.'

Makri shrugs. 'I was depressed.'

I don't have time to be outraged. Makri tells me that after the Assemblage ended Lisutaris said she didn't want to go back to Thamlin. 'She said she'd show Princess Direeva the bad part of town. Direeva seemed keen to accompany us.'

'Why did you bring Darius?'

'He just sort of tagged along. I think he liked Direeva.'

Lisutaris and Direeva come slowly back to consciousness, aided by Lesada leaves and deat, a foul herbal drink traditionally taken to sober up. They're both confused and don't yet realise the urgency of the situation.

'I need to sleep,' says Lisutaris.

'You need to sleep? You'll be going for a very long sleep if we don't do something about this. As soon as Darius is missed, his sorcerer buddies will start scanning the city for him. They'll locate his body soon enough. Then they'll start looking back in time to find out what happened. That might take days or weeks but they'll succeed in the end. And thanks to you invading my office I'm now involved in this disaster.'

'Yes, fine, it's an aggravating situation,' says Lisutaris, coldly. 'But you ranting isn't going to help. What are we going to do?'

'Firstly you could tell me who killed Darius Cloud Walker.'

Everyone looks blank. All three claim that he was still alive last time they could remember.

'So someone just waited till you'd conveniently all drugged yourselves into a stupor then snuck into my office and used Makri's knife to kill him? The Civil Guards are going to love that story.'

'Did you examine the body?' asks Lisutaris.

'Of course not. The Brotherhood were breaking the door down.'

We fall silent. The notion of a mysterious stranger isn't impressing anyone here. It's not going to impress the Sorcerers Guild or the Turanian authorities.

'Why did you leave the Assemblage without telling me?'

'You were having such a good time with the Juvalian sorcerers, that's why,' says Makri.

'Indeed,' says Princess Direeva. 'Such a good time that I do not see how you can criticise others for their pleasures.'

'My pleasures didn't involve a dead sorcerer who was second favourite for Head of the Guild. Congratulations, Lisutaris, you just lost a rival. Which makes you a pretty good suspect. Anyway, we've sat here talking long enough, it's time to do something.'

'Why must you do anything?' enquires Direeva. As she sits on the couch her hair trails on the floor. It must be inconvenient on occasion.

'To save my own skin.'

I'm mostly concerned about Makri but I'm not about to say that. And lingering at the back of my mind in an annoying manner is the thought that if I'm to help Lisutaris win the election, which I was hired to do, I can't let her be involved in any of this. Keeping her out of it is not going to be easy, but I never give up on a client.

'Lisutaris, can you put some sort of sorcerous shield over the night's events? Cover everything so it can't be looked at?'

The Mistress of the Sky considers this. I know she's aching for some thazis. If she lights another stick I'll be tempted to slug her.

'Probably, for a while. I've hidden events before. But if the whole Sorcerers Guild starts looking I'm not going to be able to shut them out for long. Even on his own, Old Hasius the Brilliant would get through eventually.'

'I too have hidden events,' says Princess Direeva. 'I will add my powers to yours.'

'That will buy us some time. Meanwhile I'll try and find out who killed Darius. That doesn't get us off the hook, seeing as we're concealing a crime, but it will help. If I can find the killer we might be able to divert attention from any of you being involved.'

'How do you know we weren't?' asks Direeva.

The young Princess doesn't seem to be treating this as seriously as she should. Perhaps she believes that if she finds herself in trouble she can claim diplomatic immunity and ride back to the Wastelands. Maybe she's right, but that's not going to help anyone else.

'I don't. You're all suspects. I'm just hoping I can find a better one.' I rise to my feet. 'Get busy on the spell. I'm going to move the body further away. The Civil Guard aren't fools. If they find Darius lying dead right next to the Avenging Axe they'll know I had something to do with it and that will lead back to you. And whatever you do, don't get stoned again, it will lead to disaster.' I pause at the door and turn to Makri. 'Where did you get the dwa?'

'I stole it from the dealer.'

'Very moral behaviour. At least he was selling it at a fair price.'

Outside it's bitterly cold. I haven't had time to recharge my warm cloak. Snow is falling in thick sheets and there's not a soul in sight. It takes me a while to get a horse saddled up and fitted on to a wagon, and longer to retrieve the now frozen body of Darius. I sling it in the cart, cover it with a blanket and set off. My mood is grim. It wasn't helped by the difficulty I had removing Makri's knife from the corpse.

The Sorcerers Guild is not going to give up easily on this one. It might take them one day or three months but I have no doubt that some time in the future they will be staring at a magical picture of me riding in a cart with Darius's body. That's going to be hard to explain, and it's not going to do much for Lisutaris's chances in the election. Almost worse is the realisation that I'm going to have to report all this to Cicerius. He's my client. I've withheld information from Cicerius before but there is no way I can keep this from him. For all I know the death of the Abelasian sorcerer might lead Turai into war. I can't let that happen without warning the Deputy Consul. I dread to think what the man is going to say, and try as I might, I can't think of a means of explaining the situation that doesn't put me in a bad light. Thinking it over while I'm looking for a suitable snowdrift in which to dump Darius, I don't come up with anything I like.

Chapter Eight

I'm used to being abused by officials. Often on a case I end up being told by a Prefect or Captain of the Guard how much better Turai would be without me. I've been lectured by the best of them, but nothing compares to the lecture Cicerius gives me when I wake him up at three in the morning to inform him that Lisutaris, Mistress of the Sky, has just got herself mixed up with the mysterious death of Darius Cloud Walker.

This man is noted for the power of his rhetoric. In the courts he regularly tears his opponents to shreds. Some of his speeches have become so famous that copies of them are used in schools to teach students how to construct an argument. Cicerius's argument on this occasion demonstrates mainly that as a protector of Turanian interests I am as much use as a one-legged gladiator, if that.

'I hired you to help Turai, not plunge us into war with the Abelasian confederacy! Never in my most fevered imaginings could I have dreamed of the chaos that would result from involving you in this affair!'

'Steady on, Cicerius,' I protest. 'I'm not to blame. It wasn't me that got stoned in Twelve Seas with Darius. It was Lisutaris.'

'You were meant to be looking after her. And what were you doing? Drinking and trading jokes with these degenerate sorcerers from Juval! Did I not specifically warn you not to do that?'

'Very probably. I wasn't expecting things to go wrong so quickly.'

Even as I speak I know this sounds feeble.

'You yourself warned of some involvement by an assassin. Did you expect him to wait until you were ready?'

Once again I am subjected to Cicerius's invective. I have to raise my voice to stop him. 'Okay, it's bad. I thought that having Makri as a bodyguard would keep Lisutaris out of trouble. That turned out to be a mistake.'

At the mention of Makri's name Cicerius fulminates some more about the foolishness of placing trust in a woman with Orcish blood. I find myself defending her, which I don't feel much like doing. 'If an attempt is made on Lisutaris's life, you'll still be pleased she's got Makri to protect her. And it's all very well coming down on me like a bad spell for messing things up, but if it wasn't for me we'd be in a lot worse position. If I hadn't got rid of the body the Brotherhood would have found Darius lying there with Lisutaris and Direeva, and what would have happened then? You'd be paying blackmail money to the Brotherhood till the King's vaults were empty. At least I've bought us some time.'

Cicerius is aware that the respite is temporary. He knows as well as I do that when the sorcerers start looking they'll eventually find out the truth.

'You have bought us time? For what?'

'For me to find the killer.'

'And if that turns out to be Lisutaris? Or your companion?'

'It won't.'

'How can you be sure?'

'I'm not sure. But I've talked to them both and my intuition tells me they're innocent. As for Princess Direeva, I'm not so certain.'

'If an unknown assailant did enter your office and kill Darius, have you not made everything worse by moving the body and hiding the crime?'

'There was no time to work things out when the Brotherhood were beating on the door. As far as I knew, either Direeva, Makri or Lisutaris had stabbed Darius, and I couldn't let that be discovered. Anyway, no matter who did kill him, would you really have wanted that scene to be made public? It would have ended Lisutaris's chances of election.'

Cicerius shakes his head. 'Had she been taking dwa?'

'I don't think so. Direeva had.'

'This curse is going to destroy us.'

Cicerius's son was involved in a dwa scandal last year, and when we were on Avula, the Deputy Consul was badly shaken to discover that the drug had now taken root on the Elvish Isles.

'If things carry on like this the Orcs will sweep us away. What do you propose doing to rescue Turai from this calamity?'

'Lisutaris and Direeva are making a hiding spell.'

'Can we trust Direeva?'

'I don't know. Ask Tilupasis, she's been working on her. We have to take the risk, it'll cover our tracks for a while. The spell would be a lot stronger if they got help from Old Hasius.'

'You mean involve the Chief sorcerer at the Abode of Justice in covering up a murder?'

Cicerius is a stickler for the law. He's been known to go against his own party to uphold the constitution. And yet such is the seriousness of the matter for Turai that he doesn't immediately dismiss my suggestion. 'To save the city I might be prepared to sanction such an illegal action. But I doubt if it could be kept secret. Hasius's apprentice is a supporter of Senator Lodius. If Lodius learns of this we're finished.'

Senator Lodius leads the opposition party, the Populares. They're fierce opponents of Cicerius and would leap at the opportunity to catch him out in such an illicit plan.

'All right, Hasius is out. And Gorsius is too unreliable. But Melus the Fair is a friend of Lisutaris. She might be able to help, and you could trust her. She wouldn't sell out Lisutaris because they're companions in the Association of Gentlewomen.'

'Kindly do not bring that organisation into the picture,' says Cicerius acidly. 'They are nothing but trouble.'

'As you wish. But Lisutaris could do with her help. Anyway, with the hiding spell working I've got some time to investigate.'

'How long?'

'I don't know. It depends on the alignments of the moons at the time of the murder. If they're unfavourable it might take the Sorcerers Guild a week or so to break through. Lisutaris is going back to her villa to check her books. Which is where I'm heading right now. She's going to try and look at the events herself before she starts hiding them. If she can get a good picture of the murder we'll be a step ahead of everyone else and I might be able to clear things up before everything goes to hell.'

Cicerius is far from soothed. With the situation being as it is in Turai, it's hard to know who he can trust. He'd like to get the Civil Guard to discreetly investigate but many of the guards are in the pay of either the Brotherhood or their rivals the Society of Friends, and those that aren't might be supporters of the Populares.

'I'd say it's safest to tell no one.'

'And trust you to fix everything?'

'No. Trust me to find out the truth, then get Tilupasis to fix everything. She's an efficient woman. You think I could have some more wine before I set off? It's cold out there.'

'Get drunk on your own time,' says Cicerius, with feeling.

I set off, leaving a highly agitated Deputy Consul behind me. I'm none too calm myself. Cicerius might have been right about calling the guards straight away. But my intuition told me to move the body and I've lived on my intuition for a long time now. I ride towards Truth is Beauty Lane, home of the sorcerers. The wind pierces my cloak like a series of sharp knives. I can't ever remember being so cold. I'd never have taken the damned case if I'd known it was going to involve so much outdoor activity.

Lights are burning in Lisutaris's villa, and despite the lateness of the hour a servant takes my horse for stabling while another leads me inside. The house reeks of thazis. I find the Mistress of the Sky sitting at her water pipe in the company of Makri and Princess Direeva. The walls are hung with Elvish tapestries of green and gold. Numerous well-tended plants surround the large windows that look out over the gardens. It's a beautiful room, decorated by one of the fashionable designers now found necessary by Turai's upper classes. Warm too, though there is no fire. Such is the ingenuity of Turai's architects that large villas now have systems for leading hot air through pipes under the floors to warm the houses. Unlike the frozen masses in Twelve Seas, the wealthy of Turai never have to shiver. No torches burn on the walls. The bright illumination in the room is provided entirely by Lisutaris's illuminated staff, which rests in a corner, bathing the room in light.

Makri has removed her armour to display the man's tunic she generally wears. Princess Direeva's tunic and leggings are somewhat similar and it makes for an odd contrast with Lisutaris's flowing robes.

'How was the Deputy Consul?' asks the sorcerer.

'He regrets nominating you for the post. And Makri, I wouldn't count on his help for getting into the university.'

Makri's face falls. She has a serious ambition to enter the Imperial University, and without powerful assistance that will never happen. Seeing her disappointed face, I'm oddly pleased. Revenge for all the trouble she's been causing me recently. Lisutaris motions towards the water pipe, inviting me to try it.

'Do you ever do anything else?' I say, angrily.

'As you wish,' says Lisutaris.

'I wasn't refusing. I just wondered if you ever did anything else.'

I take a long pull at the pipe. The thazis is so strong that I'm obliged to sit down. I do feel calmer.

'You're just in time,' announces the Sorcerer. 'We have the hiding spell ready. Before using it I shall look for the killer.'

Beside her is a golden saucer full of kuriya. In this dark liquid, an experienced practitioner can sometimes read the secrets of the past. It's a difficult art. I've occasionally gleaned secrets from the kuriya but my success rate is low. However, my powers are as nothing compared to Lisutaris's. Before using kuriya I'd have to spend a long time getting myself in to the correct state of mind. Lisutaris is far beyond this. With no preparation, not even a deep breath, she waves her hand over the saucer. The room immediately goes cooler and the black liquid starts to glow. We crane our necks to see the picture that begins to form.

It's a picture of my office. Very clear. You can see yesterday's dirty plates lying on the table. As the picture spreads to fill the saucer I observe Makri and Direeva lying unconscious on the floor. Darius Cloud Walker is nearby, also comatose. Lisutaris doesn't seem to be around. The door opens and she enters. She treads softly through the room and bends down over Makri. She reaches down and comes up with a knife. And then she pounces on Darius and sticks the knife in his back. Next, she disappears from the room, leaving the sorcerer bleeding to death. The picture fades. I look around at my companions. All three of them are struck dumb.

'Well, that seems unequivocal,' I say. 'No room for argument there. So what are we going to do now? And why the hell did you have to stab him with Makri's knife? If you hated the man that much, couldn't you just have blasted him with a spell?'

The Mistress of the Sky is still unable to speak. She stares at the now dark liquid, unblinking, horrified.

'Snap out of it,' I tell her. 'And get busy with the hiding spell. You'd better make it good, because if anyone ever needed a hiding spell, it's you.'

Chapter Nine

I awake feeling unusually comfortable, and very warm. I realise I'm not at home. I'm in a guest room at Lisutaris's villa. Lisutaris the killer. I'd never have picked her for a murderer. My clothes are draped over a bronze statue by the window. I get out of bed and get dressed. Outside the room a servant asks me if I'd like breakfast.

'I'll take a beer and whatever else you have. Is Lisutaris up yet?'

She isn't. Downstairs I pick up my beer, and some roasted fowl from a selection of silver platters in the dining room, and finish them off quickly. I'm not planning on hanging around. Unfortunately, before I can make my exit Lisutaris appears, a thazis stick in her hand. She doesn't look like she's slept well.

'I didn't kill him,' she says.

She said that last night as well. I don't reply.

'Don't you believe me?'

'No.'

'Someone faked that magical picture.'

I continue not to believe her. It looked pretty damn convincing to me and it would stand up in court.

'I'm telling you, someone faked it.'

'No one could fake that.'

'I thought you always supported your clients.'

'I do. That's why I haven't turned you over to the Guard.'

'But you don't believe I'm innocent?'

'No.'

Makri enters the breakfast chamber. 'What's going on?'

'Thraxas believes I killed Darius Cloud Walker. He's unhappy to be stuck with a murderer for a client.'

'Lisutaris isn't a murderer,' says Makri. 'You have to help.'

'I don't have to do anything.'

We stare at each other in silence. The Mistress of the Sky inhales from her thazis stick. 'Those pictures were good,' she says. 'Even with all my power I couldn't prove they were faked. They'll fool other sorcerers.'

'There's no reason to think they were faked,' I point out. 'And even if they were, what happened to the real past? A sorcerer can hide the past but no one can erase it. You looked in the kuriya ten times or more and you couldn't find the real events. Or what you say are the real events. So we're talking two major discrepancies here, neither of which can be done by sorcery. One, erasing reality, and two, faking a new reality. Temporarily hiding the past is one thing, but erasing and faking can't be done. You know that better than me. Why don't you tell me what really happened?'

'You've known me for a long time,' says Lisutaris. 'We were standing on the same piece of city wall when it collapsed under dragon attack.'

'Kemlath Orc Slayer was standing there as well. And last year I got him exiled from the city.'

'But he was guilty!' explodes Makri. 'Lisutaris didn't kill Darius. Why would she? You have to help. No one else knows how to investigate things like you.'

I take another beer. I really don't like this.

'How good is the hiding spell?' I ask, after a while.

'Good. Better with Direeva's power added to my own.'

'You don't sound certain that will last.'

Lisutaris isn't certain. Princess Direeva departed the villa last night after seeing the pictures of Lisutaris knifing Darius. Darius represents the nation of Abelasi, and they're friends of Direeva's.

'If Direeva thinks you killed him she's not going to keep helping.'

I can see Tilupasis will be hard pressed to get Direeva's votes for Turai, but that might be the least of our problems now. I ask Lisutaris about the alignment of the moons, important in sorcerous enquiries concerning the past.

'Not so good. The sorcerers will have the alignments in their favour in two or three days.'

Lisutaris sits down heavily as if crushed by the weight of her troubles. I finish my beer. Somewhere south of here, Darius Cloud Walker is lying in a snowdrift. He deserved better.

'I suggest you recruit Melus to boost the hiding spell. Say nothing to anyone. And pack a bag.'

'Why?'

'Because the most likely outcome is that we're all fleeing the city, one step ahead of the Civil Guard.'

I grab another beer and walk out of the villa. There's no way this one is turning out well. Last night there was another heavy fall of snow. The land around the city will be impassable. Unless you're a sorcerer, of course. I'll probably end up climbing the scaffold myself while Lisutaris makes her escape. I just can't see any good outcome. It's going to need something superhuman to prevent it. I'm a forty-three-year-old investigator, badly overweight, and I drink too much. No one would accuse me of being superhuman.

Back at the Avenging Axe, Gurd looks at me questioningly. 'Who did it?' he asks.

'Lisutaris, looks like.'

'What are you going to do?'

'Get her off the hook. Or try to.'

Gurd raises his eyebrows. He knows that protecting a murderer is not a job I'd volunteer for.

'Can you do it?'

'I'm number one chariot in this business.'

'But can you do it?'

I shake my head. 'No one could do it.'

Upstairs in my office I sit and stare out at the snow. After a while I get out my klee and sip the fierce spirit till I feel better. I set up my niarit board and play through a game or two. The room feels cold so I stoke up the fire. It doesn't make me warm so I lie on the couch and drag a blanket over me. I really should be doing something. I drink some more klee and fall asleep.

I'm woken by Makri. She says she's come to apologise.

'What for?'

'For taking dwa and getting unconscious when I should have been watching Lisutaris. I'm sorry.'

I haul myself upright. 'Sorry? No need to apologise to me. You can do what you like.'

'Okay, I said I was sorry.'

'Stop apologising. I don't care what you do.'

'Stop giving me a hard time,' protests Makri.

'I'm not giving you a hard time.'

'Yes you are. You're deliberately making me feel bad by saying I don't need to apologise.'

'You don't.'

'Stop doing that,' says Makri, and looks cross.

'Makri, you can fill yourself full of as much dwa as you like. I don't care.'

'Well, that's fine. I don't care if you care or not.'

'I don't.'

'You shouldn't.'

'I won't.'

'Then we're fine,' says Makri.

'Completely fine.'

Makri storms out of the room. I pick up my klee and wonder what I'm meant to do at the Assemblage today. Look for clues? Protect Lisutaris? Kill her other main rivals?

Makri storms back into the room. 'What's the idea of going on and on about me taking dwa, when you drink so much?'

'I wasn't going on and on.'

'You're being intolerable. I'm going to tell Tanrose.'

'You're what?'

'I'm going to tell Tanrose.'

'You? The number one gladiator and genius philosophy student? You're going to run away and tell tales?'

'Okay!' screams Makri. 'I was feeling bad about See-ath! I just wanted to not feel bad for a little while! Stop tormenting me!'

Makri grabs the bottle of klee and takes a slug. I pick up my cloak. There's no time to charge it up, which means I'm in for a cold journey to the Royal Hall.

'Do you want me to put some stuff in this magic pocket?' asks Makri. 'Lisutaris let me keep it for the week. I've got two swords, three knives and my axe in here. You have to be prepared when you're a bodyguard.'

'And you're a great bodyguard.'

'Stop insulting me,' says Makri. 'I said I was sorry.'

We have to trudge for a long way through the frozen streets before we find a landus. It takes us ages to travel up Moon and Stars Boulevard. There is little traffic on the streets but the road is partially blocked near the harbour by a collapsed aqueduct, and the landus has to pick its way carefully through a mess of fallen masonry and huge blocks of ice. Workmen, moving slowly in the freezing cold, are trying to clear the way.

'Samanatius teaches here,' says Makri, and looks concerned.

I have no mental energy to waste on Samanatius. 'Are you sure you can't remember anything else about last night?'

Makri shrugs. She's keeping her head warm with the floppy green hat she brought back from Avula. It's ridiculous. 'I told you everything. Lisutaris wanted to show Princess Direeva some interesting bits of the city. So we came to Twelve Seas. Darius was friends with Direeva so he tagged along. I took them to the Avenging Axe. We went in your office because my room is small and cold, and after a while we got to drinking klee–'

'You were drinking klee? Whose klee?'

'Yours, of course. I thought you wouldn't mind; after all, you're meant to be helping Lisutaris.'

'And you all passed out and next thing you know Darius is dead?'

'That's right.'

'And you didn't see anyone else the whole time? Didn't sense anyone following you in Twelve Seas?'

'No.'

Snow falls from the bleak sky. Without a warming spell my cloak is useless. I shiver. 'What about Direeva? How was she with Darius?'

'Friendly. Maybe not as friendly as he wanted to be.'

'You think she might have resented his attentions?'

'Maybe. But not enough to kill him. He wasn't trying to force himself on her.'

'You fell asleep before Direeva. You don't know what happened after that.'

Makri admits this is true, but she doesn't believe that anything bad enough could have occurred to make Direeva kill the sorcerer. I doubt this myself, though I'm still suspicious of the Princess.

'I notice Direeva seemed to take to you.'

Makri looks embarrassed. She changes the subject. 'You know those pictures of Lisutaris killing Darius were faked.'

'I don't know that at all. Faking a scene like that and sending it into the past would be a fantastically difficult thing to do. It's the sort of thing you read in stories about sorcerers, but I'm not certain there's any sorcerer in the world who could really do it. So where does that leave us? The same pictures will appear when anyone else looks. If it really didn't happen, the sorcerer who forged it has strength I've never encountered before, or access to some spells no one else knows.'

Despite the evidence Makri is still convinced that Lisutaris didn't kill Darius.

'Why?'

'Intuition.'

I don't dismiss Makri's intuition but I trust my own better. And it's not sending me anything very positive right now. Maybe it's the cold. 'What a mess,' I mutter.

All the while I'm wondering about Covinius, the assassin. Could he have anything to do with this? I need to talk to Hanama, and quickly. We arrive at the Royal Hall. Lisutaris hasn't yet turned up.

'She'll be having her hair done by Copro,' Makri tells me. 'She's hired him for every morning of the Assemblage. Wants to make a good impression.'

'She's going to make a hell of an impression soon.'

All around the sorcerers are arriving, greeting each other. Many of them are notably less ebullient than yesterday. The mood will pick up when their hangovers fade. I look around for Irith Victorious. I'm planning on discreetly pumping him for information on Darius Cloud Walker. Juval borders Abelasi and the sorcerers should know each other well. Maybe someone else wanted Darius out of the way. Before I leave Makri I bring up the subject of the Turanian Assassins Guild. In particular, Hanama, number three in the hierarchy.

'You're friendly with Hanama.'

'No I'm not.'

'Well, you're as friendly as a person can be with an assassin. I need to talk to her but she's not answering my messages. Before I'm reduced to storming their headquarters, how about you have a word with her?'

'I'm not friendly with her,' protests Makri.

'You meet at gatherings of the Association of Gentlewomen.'

'She doesn't go to meetings,' says Makri.

She's lying. I guess it's meant to be a secret.

Tilupasis takes the bad news much better than Cicerius. For her it's just another problem to be solved, like buying votes. 'You must keep it quiet and find out the truth,' she instructs, like it's the easiest thing in the world. 'Once you find out the truth, Consul Kalius and Praetor Samilius will arrest the murderer without involving Lisutaris. It need not spoil her chances of winning.'

'It will spoil them plenty if she really did it.'

'Nothing will spoil Lisutaris's chances of election while I'm running her campaign,' says Tilupasis firmly. 'If she's guilty of murder then you'll have to find some way of disguising the fact.'

'And how am I meant to do that?'

'You're a sorcerous investigator. It's what you do.'

'What I do is catch petty thugs, slug them and send them to jail. Large-scale conspiracy isn't my forte. If the Sorcerers Guild catches me trying to hoodwink them they'll be down on me like a bad spell.'

'I have great confidence in you,' says Tilupasis. 'Keep me informed of developments and let me know if you need money. I'll instruct my operatives to learn what they can to assist you. Now, how is your companion Makri getting along with Princess Direeva? I'm very optimistic about this.'

'I doubt Makri will enjoy being used as bait for Direeva's votes.'

What Makri might enjoy doesn't concern Tilupasis. She departs to carry on the campaign and I depart for a beer. Irith Victorious is sitting at a table, looking a little the worse for wear.

'How are you today, Irith?'

'Not quite as happy as an Elf in a tree,' he replies. 'Won't feel like myself till I get a few drinks in. Care to join me?'

'Of course.'

Today there are some organised events at the Assemblage. Meetings for learning new spells, swapping lore from around the west, that sort of thing. Irith tells me he isn't quite up to learning anything new right now, though he is in the market for a magic pocket which can store beer without it going stale.

I'm looking for information on Darius. As a means of raising the subject I tell Irith I placed a bet on Lisutaris.

'Rash behaviour, Thraxas. Sunstorm Ramius is the man, I'm sure. Though I'd rather see Darius or Lisutaris in the post. Even Rokim, though I'm not keen on Samsarinans as a rule. Ramius is too much of an old soldier for me, he'll have the Guild declaring war on the Orcs at the first excuse. Me, I like my life more peaceful. You think Lisutaris is keen on going to war?'

'Only if the thazis plants are threatened.'

'I might vote for her. I admire a woman with a respectable hobby.'

Other Juvalian sorcerers drift in, each in a similar state to Irith. I pick up some useful information. Mainly of the negative sort, however. Darius has no obvious enemies. Gets on with most people, apart from his apprentices. As sorcerers are always firing their apprentices, that's not much to go on, but I file it away to check out later. I nose around for more, but as it's not yet known that Darius Cloud Walker has handed in his toga, I can't press too much for fear of giving myself away.

Sunstorm Ramius strides through the room, greeting us as he passes. 'Just off to teach some Samsarinans how to purify poisoned water with a simple spell. Care to come along?'

The Juvalians decline. They're not quite in the mood for instruction today. Ramius smiles indulgently. I get the impression he doesn't entirely approve of the manners of the Juvalians, but as a man who's looking for votes he can't go around being rude to the electorate.

'What sort of candidate is he?' says Irith. 'Didn't even offer to buy us a drink. Anyone seen Darius? He ought to be good for a beer or two. Thraxas, is Lisutaris handing out any free thazis?'

I grin at the large sorcerer. 'I take it you're not planning on much studying at the Assemblage?'

His companions guffaw at the notion.

'I haven't learned a new spell in fifteen years,' replies Irith. 'I've got plenty already. Who needs more? Are you going to talk all morning or are you going to finish that beer?'

A few hours later, slightly the worse for wear, I wander off in search of Lisutaris, finding her in a corner of the main hall, sitting beside Makri. Makri is again wearing her full armour but the effect is spoiled by her floppy green hat, which is the sort of thing sported only by small Elvish children.

Makri tells me she bought a new stud for her nose. 'It's magic. Look, if you touch it, it goes gold. Touch it again it goes silver. Then it goes gold... '

'Then it goes silver. That's great. Any information?'

I'm looking at Lisutaris. She's looking at the ceiling. Or possibly the sky. I frown. 'I take it your recent troubles haven't led you to lay off the thazis?'

Lisutaris slumps forward onto the table.

'She's under a lot of stress,' says Makri.

I glance around. Approaching us is a delegation of sorcerers from Mattesh.

'For God's sake, Makri, can't you keep her under control? If these sorcerers see her like this they're never going to vote for her. Get her out of here.'

Makri stands up. She sways, clutches at her head, and sits down again. 'Sorry,' she says.

I glare at her. 'As a bodyguard you're about as much use as a eunuch in a brothel.'

'Wouldn't a eunuch be some use in a brothel?' says Makri.

'What?'

'He could guard the woman. Or maybe just help out around the place.'

I glare at her. 'That's not the point of the saying.'

'Well it's a stupid saying. It hasn't been thought through properly.'

'Could we discuss this some other time?'

'Not my fault if Turanian similes are rubbish,' says Makri.

The sorcerers draw near. I hoist Lisutaris to her feet and start walking her rapidly in the other direction.

'Tell me about your new spell for protecting a whole city!' I boom, trying to give a good impression while I drag the number one Turanian sorcerer to the safety of a side room. Makri struggles along behind us. I dump the Mistress of the Sky on a couch. Makri slumps beside her. I take out my flask of klee and pour a healthy dose down my throat.

'Have you been encouraging Lisutaris to drink?' comes an angry voice behind me.

It's Cicerius. He saw us heading this way and followed us in. I protest my innocence. Cicerius looks at us like we've just crawled out from under a rock. He demands to know why I've been spending the day drinking when I should be trying to get Lisutaris out of the mess she's in. I feel confused, angry, full of beer and bereft of a good reply. I slump down beside Makri.

'I've got a new nose stud,' says Makri. 'You touch it, it goes gold. Then it goes silver.'

'A fine trio you make,' rages the Deputy Consul. 'None of you can even stand. God knows what I was thinking when I entrusted the welfare of our great city into your hands.'

Cicerius's assistant Hansius rushes through the door. 'Deputy Consul!' he gasps. 'Word from Twelve Seas. The Civil Guards have just found the body of Darius Cloud Walker! He's been murdered!'

Outside, the Assemblage is already in uproar as the news spreads.

'Need more thazis,' mumbles Lisutaris, then closes her eyes. I notice that her hair is very finely arranged. And her make-up is perfect. The early morning beauty sessions are really paying off.

Chapter Ten

I pour some kuriya into a saucer. No one speaks. Makri looks uncomfortable. Cicerius is agitated. Tilupasis remains calm. We're gathered in Cicerius's private room at the Royal Hall and I'm preparing to show them what happened at the Avenging Axe.

'What you are about to see is hidden from all other eyes by the spell cast by Lisutaris, Mistress of the Sky, and Princess Direeva. I've only got access because Lisutaris has given me a key.'

I take out a scrap of parchment and intone a brief incantation, Lisutaris's key. Cicerius and Tilupasis draw closer to the saucer. The air cools. A picture starts to form. My untidy office. I really should clean it up some time. Makri, Direeva and Darius are unconscious on the floor. Lisutaris enters, stabs Darius, then departs. The picture fades. Seeing it again, I don't like it any better.

Cicerius controls his agitation. Though sometimes excitable, he's not a man to panic in a crisis. 'How many people have seen that?'

'Just us. It's well hidden from everyone else. The sorcerers will get through eventually but it will take a while.'

'It looked very real to me,' continues Cicerius. 'Are you convinced by Lisutaris's protestations of innocence?'

I shrug. 'I've taken her on as a client.'

'You do not sound convinced.'

Makri breaks into the conversation. 'She's innocent! I was there, I know she didn't stab Darius.'

'You were unconscious.'

'I was the last to fall asleep. Lisutaris didn't do it.'

Tilupasis wonders about the magic required to falsify the past. 'My knowledge of sorcery is limited. Is it possible that the pictures are, as Lisutaris claims, fakes?'

'Maybe.'

'Please be more specific,' says Cicerius.

'There are three different things involved here. Hiding, erasing, and making. Hiding means concealing the past. Plenty of sorcerers can do that, at least for a while. The other two are not so easy. Lisutaris and Direeva searched for the real events before they made their hiding spell, but they couldn't find them. They couldn't find anything else apart from the pictures of Lisutaris killing Darius. So if there were other real events, someone has erased them. But no one has ever perfected such an erasement spell. Every sorcerer at the Assemblage would tell you the same. The obvious conclusion is that there was no erasing, which would mean the events as depicted are true, Lisutaris is the killer.

'The same goes for a making spell, something to create the illusion of events happening, a good enough illusion to fool a sorcerer who checks back in time. Again, no such spell has ever been perfected. It's a difficult thing even to imagine, painting a convincing picture of real events and placing it in the past. What we saw there was my office, complete with junk. Could someone fake that in every detail? I doubt it. Again, the obvious conclusion is that we're looking at the real events.'

'Whether Lisutaris murdered Darius or not, we can't let it be known,' says Tilupasis.

I point out that not everyone feels so comfortable about covering up a murder. Tilupasis gives the slightest of shrugs. She's quite comfortable with it. We look towards Cicerius.

'If the Sorcerers Guild will eventually discover the truth, it might be better for Turai to come straight out and admit that this has happened,' he says. 'Lisutaris would be sent into permanent exile at the very least. She might even hang for it. Turai would lose influence, but at least we wouldn't be found guilty of complicity in the murder of the chief sorcerer of another country. If we try and cover this up and it goes wrong, the Abelasian Confederacy and the other states in the south will turn against Turai. We already have numerous enemies.'

We fall silent while Cicerius weighs up his options. It's his decision and for once I don't feel like barging in with my own opinions.

'If Lisutaris is innocent, as she claims, what chance do you have of uncovering the real murderer?'

'A reasonable chance. Maybe less than reasonable. I've no leads and I'll be up against sorcery no one has encountered before. Which is not to say I won't find anything. Criminals generally leave some traces behind, even sorcerous criminals. The problem is time. We don't know how long it will take for the Guild to break through the hiding spell.'

Cicerius drums his fingers lightly on the table. Finally he makes a decision. 'Carry on with your investigation. We shall continue with our efforts to have Lisutaris elected as Head of the Guild.'

Hansius appears at the door, Cicerius is needed for a conference with Lasat, Axe of Gold. He departs swiftly.

'Now that Darius is no longer in the running, I should be able to win over some of these southern votes,' says Tilupasis. 'Keep watching Lisutaris. And Makri, be nice to Princess Direeva. This is now more important than ever. With Darius out of the running we have an excellent chance of winning her over.'

'Not if she decides to believe that Lisutaris killed Darius.'

'You must persuade her otherwise,' instructs Tilupasis. She hurries off.

'What exactly do I have to do to get Princess Direeva's votes?' asks Makri.

'I don't know. I was never any good at politics.'

I stare at the now blank pool of kuriya. After the spell, the temperature in the room has again risen. The authorities have made it warm for the sorcerers. Anything to keep them happy.

'It's unfortunate the body was discovered so quickly.'

'You should've dumped it in a deeper snowdrift,' says Makri. 'Do you have any suspects?'

'Lisutaris, mainly. Maybe Sunstorm Ramius. He had something to gain from Darius's death. Got rid of a rival.' I'm not fooling myself. Darius wasn't really a rival to Ramius. There was no sign of him picking up enough support to overhaul the Simnian. Nonetheless, I'm suspicious of Ramius. He's arrogant, powerful and successful, and that's three things I dislike in a sorcerer.

'It's time to go to work. Have you shaken off the thazis?'

'Yes.'

'Does the Imperial Library have much about sorcery?'

'The largest collection in the west,' says Makri. 'How can you possibly not know that?'

'I've been cultivating ignorance for a long time. Take Lisutaris home then meet me there as soon as you can. I need to do some research into spell-casting and I'm terrible at using a catalogue.'

There's great agitation in the main hall as the sorcerers congregate to discuss the murder. They come pouring from all corners of the building, workshops abandoned. Even the Juvalians emerge from the Room of Saints, drinks in hand. Illuminated staffs are fired up all over the hall, as if to cast light on the affair. Sunstorm Ramius is deep in discussion with other important sorcerers. It won't be long before they start looking for the killer. Again I get the urge to ride out of town. If they conjure up a picture of me dumping the body, the whole Guild will be down on me like a bad spell. If the sorcerers don't just blast me on the spot, the Civil Guards will prosecute. Either way, my prospects are poor. Astrath Triple Moon is standing alone on the fringes of the crowd.

'Any news on the knife?'

The sorcerer is worried. 'No. It's been wiped. Is it the knife which...'

His voice tails off. I tell him I'd rather not give him any more details. Astrath accepts this. He'd rather not know. He promises to keep on working but he's deeply troubled to find himself involved in such an affair.

'I owe you a lot, Thraxas, but if the Guild really gets on my back it's going to be difficult to lie to them.'

I take the opportunity to ask Astrath if he knows of any spell, or any sorcerer, who could create a sequence of fake events lasting almost a full minute, and send it back into the past. He doesn't.

'I don't think it could be done. Not by us, or the Elves, or the Orcs. Every detail of a long scene? There would just be too many things to control. And what about the real events? It's one thing to hide them for a while, but unless you completely erased them somehow they'd keep bursting through any illusion.'

The news spreads that Darius was found in a snowdrift, stabbed to death. Those sorcerers who are familiar with Turai explain to those who are not that Twelve Seas is the bad part of the city near the harbour, where crime is rampant. There's a lot of nodding of heads. The immediate impression is that the Abelasian must have gone there seeking either dwa or a prostitute, neither of which would be particularly strange for a sorcerer on holiday.

Princess Direeva and her apprentice remain aloof from the masses. There's no telling how the Princess will react if she finds herself being questioned by the Guards. Will she maintain silence, to help Makri and Lisutaris? Or tell what she knows, claim diplomatic immunity and depart swiftly? Already with Direeva and Astrath it seems like there are too many people who might be indiscreet. Even if Lisutaris's spell miraculously hides the events of the murder for weeks from sorcerers, I can't see the Civil Guard being baffled for long. They know how to follow a trail. I can't imagine the addled Mistress of the Sky standing up to prolonged questioning. I curse the day I ever became involved with the woman. It would have been better all round if the dragons she brought down had fallen on top of her.

It's time to visit Hanama. There's a Messengers Guild post in the entrance hall, placed there for the convenience of the sorcerers. The young messenger who takes my scroll looks surprised when he sees that it's addressed to the headquarters of the Assassins Guild, but he hurries off, keen to do his duty. These young messengers are always keen. I've no idea why. I hurry from the Assemblage and pick up a landus outside. Shortly afterwards I'm sitting in a tavern on the outskirts of the notorious Kushni quarter. Kushni is a hive of drinking dens, gambling dens, dwa houses, whorehouses and anything else disreputable you might wish for. In the summer it's a seething, sweltering mass of decadent humanity. Even in the depths of winter, trade goes on at an unhealthy pace. The Assassins have their headquarters nearby. I've informed Hanama that if she ignores this message I'm going to march in and call out for her in a loud voice. I figure that ought to bring her out. No assassin likes hearing their name shouted out loud; they're a private sort of people.

A young prostitute with red ribbons in her hair sidles up to the table. I ignore her. Her young male companion then approaches. He's also got red ribbons in his hair. I don't think the Whores Guild admits men. I could be wrong. I ignore him as well. A dwa dealer offers me some Choirs of Angels, cheap. I tell him to get lost. The dealer's friend gets insistent. I take a dagger from my pocket and lay it on the table. They sneer at me and mouth a few insults but they leave me alone. There are plenty of willing customers to cater for. No need to argue with a big angry man with a knife.

Hanama arrives in the dark garb of a common market worker. Each time I've encountered her I've been surprised by how young she looks. From her many reported exploits she can't be much under thirty, but she's a small, slender woman, dark-haired but very pale-skinned. With the aid of a little disguise she could pass as a child. The thought of Hanama dressing up as a child before disposing of another victim makes me shudder. I loathe the Assassins. Hanama is as cold as an Orc's heart. The fact that I fought beside her last year doesn't make me like her any better.

Hanama refuses my offer of beer.

'Staying sober? Got an assassination coming up?'

Not the best introduction perhaps, but it's hard to find the right tone when you're talking to a woman who has famously killed all sorts of important people. It's said she once killed an Elf Lord, an Orc Lord and a Senator all in one day. Hanama stares at me, pale and expressionless. She's not pleased at my method of bringing her to a meeting. I wonder whether I could knock her out with a sleep spell before she got her knife in my throat. I'm not carrying any spells. I'd better not offend her too much.

'I'm looking for some information about Covinius.'

'An assassin from Simnia, as is public knowledge, I believe.'

'But public knowledge doesn't go any further. Like whether it's a man or a woman. Or what Covinius looks like. Or whether he actually comes from Simnia.'

'I know no more about him.'

'What brings him to Turai?'

'I did not know that he was in Turai.'

'Then why did you send a message to Lisutaris warning her?'

This has to take Hanama by surprise but you couldn't tell from her expression. She denies it coolly. I tell her to stop wasting time.

'I know you sent the message. You might be number one chariot at murder but when it comes to covering your tracks you're a washout. I worked out it was you in a couple of minutes, and I've got sorcerous proof to back me up.'

The tiniest hint of colour touches Hanama's cheeks for a second or two. I think I might actually have embarrassed her.

'Don't feel bad. Investigating's my business. No one else knows you've been sending messages.'

If Hanama's Guild knew, she'd be in trouble. The Assassins generally strive to avoid becoming embroiled in the world of politics. Neither would Hanama's companions be pleased to know of her involvement in the Association of Gentlewomen.

'I'm presuming you warned Lisutaris because of that Association?'

Hanama remains silent. I point out that as I'm responsible for Lisutaris's well-being, along with Makri, it would make a lot more sense to tell me what she knows. Hanama considers it while I calculate the chances of leaving the tavern alive if I'm forced to blackmail her.

'You know Lisutaris is quite likely to end up dead at the hands of Covinius?'

This seems to sway her. 'An informant who works for my organisation was fatally wounded last week. Before dying he informed us that Covinius was heading to Turai. He had encountered him in the course of his work. The nature of this informant's mission is secret, and unconnected with either Lisutaris or the Sorcerers Assemblage, so I am unable to tell you any more.

But it did occur to me that if Simnia were bringing an assassin with them, Lisutaris would be the likely target. She is Ramius's main rival.'

I'm dissatisfied with this. Other than confirming that Covinius is in town, Hanama hasn't really told me anything.

'There's nothing more to tell. I do not discuss our private affairs with anyone. Sending the message was the most I could do.'

Hanama stands up and leaves swiftly. I toss some money on the table for my beer and depart, angry. Talking to assassins always bothers me. It's not far to the Imperial Library. This is a magnificent piece of architecture but it's a place I rarely visit. All those scrolls make me feel inadequate. And I don't like the way the assistants walk around so quietly in their togas. They make a man feel like he doesn't belong. There's a whole room devoted to sorcerous learning but that's as far as I get. When I start trying to work out the catalogue I develop a serious mental block and am obliged to wait till Makri shows up, which takes a while. When she finally waltzes in I'm annoyed to see the staff greet her in a friendly manner. She grew up in an Orcish slave pit. I'm a native-born citizen of Turai. They ought to show me more respect.

'What do you expect?' whispers Makri. 'You once spilled beer over a manuscript.'

'Not much beer. You think they'd have forgotten by now. How's Lisutaris?'

'Glued to the water pipe. She's taking it all badly. You know, I'm starting to think she might not be such a great candidate for head of the Sorcerers Guild. I like her but I can't see her spending much time looking after Guild affairs.'

'You just realised that?'

'Well, you're the one who betted on her,' Makri points out.

'That was before I realised that helping her would mean covering up a murder. I'm going to have to work hard to pick up my winnings.'

'Is that why you took her as a client?'

'It tipped the balance. Did you leave her safe?'

Makri thinks so. Lisutaris's house is full of servants and attendants and Makri left instructions that they should be wary of strangers.

'Not that that's going to help much if the great assassin Covinius decides to pay a visit. I've seen Hanama. She didn't tell me much. But Covinius is definitely in town.'

'Did he kill Darius Cloud Walker?'

'Who knows? I'll have to try and find out more.' A passing library assistant frowns at me. I lower my voice. 'I need to find out what kind of spell could possibly make it appear as if Lisutaris killed Darius. I've been racking my brains but I can't think of anything. Neither can Astrath.'

Makri seems distracted. I study my companion suspiciously.

'Did you take a turn on the water pipe?'

'No. Stop treating me like I'm Turai's biggest drug abuser. There were special circumstances. I was depressed. Did you know that Jir-ar-Eth the Avulan sorcerer is here?'

'What about it?'

'You told me no one could travel from the Elvish Isles to Turai in winter.'

'Jir-ar-Eth set off early, shortly after we left.'

'Then why didn't See-ath send me a message with him?'

'Possibly Lord Kalith's sorcerer felt he had more important things to do than carry love letters. Do you have to go on about See-ath all the time?'

'It's important,' says Makri.

I shake my head helplessly. 'Try and concentrate, we've got work to do.' I describe to Makri what I'm after and we get busy at the catalogue, looking for a spell. Two spells probably, one to hide the real events and one to create the false ones. It's sounding more and more unlikely. The pictures of Lisutaris killing Darius were very clear. I can't think why Lisutaris would have done that, but just because I can't think of a motive doesn't mean it didn't happen. I've come across stranger things. Perhaps the thazis is driving her mad. At such extreme levels, who knows what it might do?

'Did Lisutaris share your dwa?'

'Stop going on about dwa,' hisses Makri. 'I said I was sorry.'

We struggle through tome after tome, scroll after scroll. Faced with this task I quickly tire. I hate this catalogue. I'd rather be on a stake-out in a freezing alleyway.

'Can't they organise it in a way a man can understand?'

'It's perfectly logical.'

'What do these numbers mean? I can't make any sense of it.'

'It's the classification system,' explains Makri. 'It tells you where to find things.'

'Why isn't it clearer?'

'It's very clear. You just don't understand it.'

I struggle on, working my way through books listing spells for every conceivable occasion. If I wanted to learn how to attack a Troll, I'd be fine. If I needed to know how to tell what the weather is like two hundred miles away, I could locate the right incantation. I even come across a spell for testing the strength of beer, and that's something I'd be interested in. But for what I'm looking for, there's nothing. 'This is hopeless. I've said all along it couldn't be done. All right, I might be the worst magic user in Turai. I can't do much more than heat up a cloak or send an opponent to sleep. But I understand the principles of sorcery, and its limitations. I think we're going to have to face it. Lisutaris is guilty.'

'You don't really believe that,' protests Makri. 'You just can't stand being in the library any longer. You can't abandon a client simply because you don't understand the classification system.'

'Don't bet on it. Anyway, I can't concentrate any more. If I don't eat soon I'm going to expire. I suggest we go to the hostelry across the road, and try again later.'

Makri isn't hungry. 'I don't like giving up on research. I want to go all through the catalogue.'

I admire her persistence, but I can't carry on myself. 'Meet me in the tavern when you've run out of energy. Maybe once my belly's full I'll come up with an idea.'

The Imperial Library stands in a magnificent square, flanked by an enormous church and the Honourable Merchants Association's building. All these workers need refreshment and there are several small taverns tucked away round the corner. I choose The Scholar, which, despite its name, seems a welcoming enough establishment.

The short walk from the library to the tavern is an ordeal. The wind slices through me and snow whips into my face. By the time I arrive my cloak is encrusted with tiny particles of ice and I hang it close to the fire to dry. At this time in the afternoon the tavern is empty, save for two young men, probably students, who sit at a table with two small jars of ale, studying a scroll. I order the special haunch of salted beef, then take my beer and sit in a prime spot in front of the fire to thaw out.

Another few winters like this will finish me off. Fleeing south towards the sun might not be such a bad idea. I'm in a tough spot. Already the most powerful sorcerers will be turning their attention to the matter of Darius. They'll find their way blocked by Lisutaris's spell, but for how long? What if Lisutaris was too addled to cast it properly? The Civil Guard might be looking for me at this very moment. For the first time in my career I start to think I may be in over my head. I can't fight the Sorcerers Guild. It's foolish to try. I pick at my salt beef without much enthusiasm, finishing it only with the aid of an extra portion of sauce and another beer. The door slams, an icy gust rushes into the tavern and Makri staggers in.

'Move over from that fire, Thraxas, I'm as cold as the ice queen's grave.'

Before she has time to even sit down, the landlord appears and brusquely informs her that women are not permitted in this establishment. Makri gapes.

'Are you serious?'

He's completely serious. It's their regular policy. In truth, it's not that unusual in some of the more respectable sections of the city.

Makri has not been herself recently. With the emotional upset over See-ath and the overindulgence in substances - for which I blame Lisutaris - she's not really been exhibiting the hard edge I've come to expect. In some ways that's not such a bad thing. Makri continually getting into fights can be wearing. On the other hand, Makri being emotional is pretty wearing as well. As the landlord asks her to leave she snaps right back into character and places her face as close to his as she can get, which is close enough, though he's a large man and quite a lot taller than her.

'I just struggled through the snow to get here. I'm not planning on leaving right now.'

The landlord makes the unforgivable mistake of laying his hand on her shoulder to lead her out. Makri immediately lands him such a fearsome kick in the groin that the students at the far end of the tavern shrink back in terror. The landlord collapses to the floor. Makri grabs a table and hurls it on top of him. She glares down at his prostrate body.

'I will be taking this matter up with the Association of Gentlewomen,' she says.

Outside the snow is falling faster and heavier.

'Can you believe that?' yells Makri, over the howling wind.

We struggle down the street till we reach another tavern, The Diligent Apprentice. Makri marches in. I follow with my hand on the hilt of my sword, ready for trouble. A friendly-looking landlady greets us as we enter. Makri seems almost disappointed.

'Are you going to complain about me hitting the landlord?' she demands, as we sit down with two beers and two glasses of klee.

'No. I didn't like the tavern much anyway.' A year ago I'd have objected to Makri's behaviour. Now, I'm more sympathetic. Or maybe I'm just used to it.

'Did they really not serve women? Or just women with Orcish blood?'

'I don't know. Probably both. It wasn't much of a place. Their haunch of beef was adequate at best. I think I'll pick up another meal while I'm here.'

Makri grins. 'I always get depressed when life is too peaceful. All those years being a gladiator, I suppose. I need to fight every now and then, and it's been a long time since I was in a fight.'

I point out to her that only a few days ago she killed a dwa dealer.

'I forgot about that. It wasn't really what you'd call a fight.'

'After that you got in a brawl with those three dock workers.'

'What are you doing, keeping records?'

'How are you ever going to manage if you get to the Imperial University? They frown on violence.'

'I can probably wean myself off it.'

Makri drinks heartily of her ale.

'Don't get too cheerful, Makri, we're still in a hell of a situation. The Sorcerers Guild could be looking at pictures of our involvement in a murder right now.'

Makri slaps the table. 'I almost forgot. I found a spell!' She brings out a sheet of paper and reads from it. 'A spell for wiping out events in the past. With this incantation an experienced practitioner can erase all traces of events, so that they can never be seen, even by sorcerous enquiry.''

Makri looks up from her notes. 'You wouldn't believe the obscure place I found this. I swear no one else could have located it. It wasn't in the main sorcery collection, it was hidden away in-'

'Yes, Makri, I already know you're number one chariot in the library. Let me see the spell.'

I study Makri's copy. It's very interesting, a spell the like of which I've never encountered. It claims that if worked properly it can erase almost a full hour.

'I'm certain no one in Turai has ever worked this. Where did it originate?'

'Developed in the Southern Hills, according to the catalogue.'

I raise my eyebrows. Princess Direeva lives in the Southern Hills. 'We might be on to something. But this doesn't account for everything. It might work for erasing events but it's not a spell for creating new ones.'

'I'm sure it's relevant,' says Makri. 'You know how when things happen during an investigation and it seems like a coincidence, you generally get suspicious? Well, take a look at the ingredients for the spell.' She hands over another sheet of paper. The spell requires a healthy dose of dragon scales.

'And only recently you were hunting for a dragon-scale thief.'

It is a coincidence. And Makri's correct. In my line of work, coincidences always make me suspicious.

Chapter Eleven

The landus driver doesn't want to take us to Twelve Seas. These uptown drivers hate to go south of the river.

'I'm a Tribune of the People.'

'Never heard of you.'

It takes a lot of argument to persuade him. I'm deep in thought as we travel down Moon and Stars Boulevard. I want to follow up the dragon scales, which means I have to talk to Rezox. As I just put him in prison he isn't going to be keen to talk to me. Not in a friendly manner anyhow. Some abuse, possibly. I tell the landus to stop, and then hurry into a small way-station which acts as a forwarding post for the Messengers Guild where I quickly scribble a message to the Deputy Consul.

We travel on. The driver complains about the cold. Makri complains about the cold. She ought to put on a little weight.

'If you weren't so scrawny you wouldn't feel it so much.'

'Princess Direeva said I had a perfect figure.'

'I bet she did. Keep working your charms, you'll get her votes.'

'I don't want to charm anyone into voting,' says Makri. 'The whole thing is corrupt and I don't approve.' She shivers. 'Are you claiming you don't feel the cold?'

I scoff at the suggestion. 'You call this cold? It doesn't compare to the conditions I experienced up in Nioj. I've camped out for a month in weather worse than this.'

'You're a liar,' says Makri, still quite cheerful after her fight.

There is great confusion at the corner of Quintessence Street where the aqueduct has collapsed. Workmen are still struggling to clear the area but there seems to be some other activity going on. A gaggle of citizens are arguing furiously. Civil Guards are arriving on the scene. I urge the driver to edge his way past but Makri calls for him to halt.

'What's happening here? These men are standing in front of Samanatius's academy.'

Samanatius's so-called academy is a miserable hall surrounded by equally miserable slums. Makri insists she's going to take a look.

'Fine, you can walk the rest of the way.'

Makri departs and the landus driver manoeuvres his way into Quintessence Street and along to the Avenging Axe. Inside the tavern I fill up with food and beer and enquire of Gurd if anyone has been here asking questions. No one has, which means that Lisutaris's hiding spell is working for now. I'd like to spend a few hours in front of the fire but I can't stay for long, though I refuse to leave the tavern till I've recharged my magic warm cloak.

In my office I find Casax, along with Orius Fire Tamer. Casax is head of the local chapter of the Brotherhood. A very important man in Twelve Seas. All crime is controlled by the Brotherhood. Since Casax took over, crime has been doing very well. Orius Fire Tamer is a young and recently qualified sorcerer who seems to have hooked up with the Brotherhood.

'Don't you know how to knock and wait politely?' I demand.

'Never learned that,' answers Casax.

He's wrapped in an enormous fur. He doesn't look cold. I notice he's grown his hair a little longer, and tied it at the back. Casax has a fair complexion, but he's weatherbeaten, a man who started out at the docks a long time ago and worked his way up. A calm, strong, intelligent man, and very dangerous.

'Having a good time at the Assemblage?'

'The time of my life.'

'Orius tells me you've been enjoying yourself,' says Casax.

I'm uncomfortable. A Brotherhood boss doesn't pay social visits for no reason.

'You've been enjoying yourself a lot recently. Rolling around with Lisutaris and Princess Direeva, from what I hear.'

'You've been hearing things that are none of your business.'

Casax raises his eyebrows a fraction. Last year I found myself more or less on the same side as Casax in a case involving the chariot races. A fortunate occurrence, and since then the Brotherhood have left me alone. It doesn't mean much. The Brotherhood are never well-disposed towards investigators.

He leans forward. 'You know anything about the death of a dwa dealer?'

'Which one? They die a lot.'

'Orius here thought he might be picking up a little Orcish aura round the death scene.'

I glance at the sorcerer, then back to Casax. 'So?'

'Your young companion is part Orc. And handy with a sword.'

'Plenty of people are handy with a sword in Twelve Seas. And she's not the only person in town with Orc blood.'

Casax glances round the room. 'Is this it?'

'What do you mean?'

'I mean is this all you have? Two tiny rooms full of junk? Furniture fit for a slum?'

'It suits me fine.'

'You don't have something salted away? Gold in the bank?'

I look at him blankly.

'Why do you do it?' he asks.

'Do what?'

'Investigate.'

'I got thrown out of my last job for being a useless drunk.'

'You could still do better for yourself. Rezox would have paid you to let him go. So would plenty of others. You could live a lot better.'

The Brotherhood boss rises to his feet.

'If you came here to give your pet sorcerer a chance to see what he could learn, you're going to be disappointed,' I tell him.

Orius Fire Tamer sneers at me. 'You think you have any power to affect me?'

'I think I could toss a knife in your throat before you got a spell ready, kid.'

Casax almost grins. 'He might, Orius. He's a tough guy, Thraxas. Not so tough that he'd bother me, but tough enough, when he's sober.' He turns to me. 'If your Orc friend killed my dealer I'll be down on her like a bad spell. Not that I miss the dealer. But I've got a position to maintain. You understand.'

They depart. I open my klee. The bottle is almost finished. I make a mental note to buy more. Makri appears.

'Was it about the dwa dealer?'

'So they said. But I think Casax was more interested in what Lisutaris and Direeva were doing here. He won't learn anything from Orius. That runt isn't going to get through a hiding spell cast by Lisutaris. What's the kid think he's doing, linking up with the Brotherhood? When I was his age–'

'Thraxas,' says Makri, loudly. 'Be quiet. I have something important to tell you.'

'If this is about See-ath, I don't–'

'It's not about See-ath. It's about Samanatius. They're trying to evict him.'

'What?'

'The landlord wants to demolish the block. He's using the collapse of the aqueduct as an excuse. He's been trying to get rid of Samanatius and the other tenants for months now, he wants to make money on the land.'

I'm staring at Makri in bewilderment. I can't think why she's telling me this. It almost sounds like she expects me to do something about it.

'You have to do something about it.'

I finish off my klee. 'Me? What? Why?'

'The owner got the go-ahead from Prefect Drinius, but it's illegal to demolish the block without permission from the Consul's office.'

I shrug. 'Happens all the time. If the local Prefect says its okay, the owner's not going to wait for the Consul to screw things up. Just mean another bribe to pay.'

'They can't evict Samanatius! He's a great man. You have to stop it.'

'Makri, what gives you this bizarre idea that I could do anything? I'm an investigator, not a planning inspector.'

'You're a Tribune of the People. You can halt any building work by referring it to the Senate for adjudication.'

My head swims. 'What?'

'It's part of the power invested in the Tribunes. They could do lots of things to protect the poor. Stopping landlords from demolishing buildings was one of them.'

'You're crazy.'

'I'm not. I looked it up in the library.'

'That was a hundred and fifty years ago.'

'Their powers were never rescinded.'

'But I'm not a real Tribune. It's only a device to get me into the Assemblage.'

'It doesn't matter,' declares Makri firmly. 'Cicerius made you a Tribune and it's legal. You now have the full power of the Tribunate behind you and you have to do something.'

I grab for the klee. It's empty. There must be a beer round here somewhere. 'Makri, this is insane. I'm sorry your buddy's getting evicted but I can't stop it. What is Cicerius going to say if I suddenly start using my supposed power to order the local Prefect around? The Senate would go crazy. So would the Palace, probably. I'd have the whole government on my back. Who is the landlord anyway?'

'Praetor Capatius.'

'Capatius? The richest man in Turai? Controls about forty seats in the Senate? Sure, Makri, I'll take him on any time. I'll just tell him to please stop behaving badly. Be reasonable.'

'You can do it,' insists Makri. 'It's part of your power.'

'I don't have any power,' I roar, frustrated by her insistence. 'And have you forgotten what else is going on right now? I'm in the middle of a case that's probably going to end with me rowing a slave galley and Lisutaris dangling on a rope. I've got sorcerers, the Deputy Consul, and an election to worry about, not to mention Covinius, deadly assassin. And you expect me to march up to Prefect Drinius and say, 'Excuse me, you have to stop this eviction because I'm a Tribune of the People'?'

'Yes.'

'Forget it.'

'Samanatius will not be evicted.'

'I can't prevent it.'

'I'll kill anyone who tries,' threatens Makri.

'Good luck. Now excuse me, I've got an investigation to be getting on with.'

I grab my warm cloak and depart swiftly. Stop the eviction indeed. Use my powers as Tribune of the People. That would certainly give the local population something to laugh about.

They'd still be laughing when Praetor Capatius hired twenty armed men to chase me out of Twelve Seas.

It takes a long time to find a landus. I'm cold. I wish I had more beer inside me. I wish I wasn't always having to visit the Deputy Consul. For a man who paid good money to hire me, he shows a great lack of enthusiasm to see me when I finally roll up at his house.

'What do you want?'

'Beer. But it's usually in short supply round here, so I'll take whatever you've got.'

'Have you disturbed me merely to request alcohol? I have an important appointment with Tilupasis.'

'She's an efficient woman, Tilupasis. Sharp as an Elf's ear. You ought to make her a Senator. I need to talk to Rezox. I threw him in the slammer a week or so back and I need quick access. It's to help Lisutaris.'

For all that he's a crusty specimen and was a poor soldier, Cicerius can move quickly when he needs to. He's known for his quick wits in the Senate. As soon as I hold up the possibility of helping Lisutaris, he moves into action, dashing off an official letter and granting permission for me to visit Rezox in prison. When I mention that Rezox may not be forthcoming with the important information, he replies brusquely that he can deal with that if necessary. 'His crime was to steal dragon scales from a warehouse? Tell me on the way why this is important. If he seems disinclined to co-operate, I can offer him his freedom.'

I wasn't planning on taking Cicerius along with me but he insists. Inside he's no calmer than me. We're just waiting for the scandal to blow up in our faces. The Deputy Consul lives in fear of anything damaging the interests of his beloved Turai. Furthermore, the repercussions of Lisutaris's arrest would hand a huge slice of harmful ammunition to Senator Lodius, head of the Populares. The opposition party would use Lisutaris's downfall to smear Cicerius, and by association Consul Kalius, and even the King.

We hurry to the prison in Cicerius's official carriage. He still maintains that things would never have gone so badly wrong if I had looked after Lisutaris properly.

'It could be worse. Certain members of the population of Twelve Seas are suggesting I use my Tribune's powers to stop Praetor Capatius carrying out an eviction.'

Cicerius is incredulous. 'What? You will do no such thing.'

'Don't worry, I wasn't planning to. Although they have a point. It's hardly fair of the Praetor to use the cover of a fierce winter to evict the poor. You'd think the man had enough money already without tearing down his slums.'

I know this will annoy Cicerius. Capatius is a strong supporter of the Traditionals and a large contributor to their funds.

'Presumably Capatius is set on improving the people's housing conditions,' says the Deputy Consul.

I laugh, which annoys him. 'Capatius is set on improving his bank balance. Which is odd really, seeing as he owns his own bank. Doesn't it bother the Traditionals that some of your supporters spend their whole life bleeding the poor?'

'I do not intend to discuss Turanian politics with an investigator,' says Cicerius.

He doesn't mind discussing politics when it suits him. We've arrived at the prison. We hurry inside. A Captain of the Guards salutes the Deputy Consul and leads us to Rezox. Cicerius's assistant Hansius, arriving before us, has arranged for the interview in a private room. He's an efficient young man, Hansius. He'll go far. In detention, Rezox looks about as miserable as a Niojan whore, and the sight of me arriving doesn't cheer him up. Cicerius begins to speak. Not having time for long speeches, I interrupt.

'Rezox. I need to know who you were passing the dragon scales on to. Tell us and Cicerius will get you out of jail.'

'Is that true?'

'Sure it's true. Cicerius has the green-edged toga. He can authorise it. So long as you tell me now.'

Rezox weighs things up. If he's worried about the morality of selling out his partner, it doesn't delay him for more than five seconds. 'Coralex,' he says.

'Coralex?' Cicerius is surprised. 'I know of him. He's a respectable importer of wine.'

Coralex is the biggest disposer of stolen property in Turai. I thought everyone knew that. 'Cicerius, you're much too trusting. Okay, I'm off to see Coralex.'

Before departing, I inform Cicerius that the threat from Covinius is now very real. 'I don't know if he had anything to do with Darius's murder but I'm sure he's in Turai. There's a strong chance his target is Lisutaris.'

'Why do you say that?'

'He's a Simnian Assassin, isn't he? Sunstorm Ramius might be favourite to win the election but that doesn't mean the Simnians won't try to get rid of the opposition.'

'I regard that as unlikely,' replies Cicerius. 'Simnia has never attempted assassination in the sorcerers' contest.'

'There's a first time for everything.'

'Might his purpose in Turai be unconnected with the Assemblage?'

'It might but we ought to assume the worst. Can you provide any more of a bodyguard for Lisutaris?'

The Deputy Consul nods. 'Is Coralex really a disposer of stolen goods?' he asks.

'One of the biggest.'

Cicerius shakes his head sadly. 'I have purchased wine from his warehouse. Some citizens have lost all sense of morality.'

I depart swiftly on the trail of the dragon scales. My sense of morality went into decline a long time ago. It kept getting in the way of my work.

Chapter Twelve

Honest Mox's bookmaking establishment is closed for the first time in living memory. The gambling fraternity of Twelve Seas are stunned. I'm standing outside in the snow with about twenty others, looking forlornly at the locked front door

'What happened?'

'His son just died. From dwa.'

The frustrated gamblers shake their heads. It's almost too bad to contemplate. We never thought we'd see the day when Mox had to close. There's a general feeling that if we can make our way here through the bad weather, Mox ought to at least be able to keep his shop open. People start drifting away, heading north towards the next bookmaker. It's a frustrating occurrence. I was planning to lay off a little money on Ramius. As Lisutaris is likely to be thrown out of the competition I really wanted to cover my losses with another bet. I've no time to visit another bookmaker. I need to see Coralex in a hurry. I curse. This job just gets worse and worse.

The wind howls down from the north. By the time I reach Coralex's house in Golden Crescent, home of the richest merchants, I'm about as angry as a Troll with a toothache. The servant who answers the door tries to keep me out and I just walk over him. They don't build many domestic servants that can stand up to me. Another functionary attempts to hold me back and I bat him out of the way. Coralex appears at the top of the stairs. I've encountered him before in the course of my work, though I've never invaded his home before. I march up the stairs and grab him by the collar.

'Coralex. I'm in a hurry. You got some dragon scales recently from a crooked merchant named Rezox. I want to know who you sold them to.'

'Throw this man out of the house,' yells Coralex.

An employee hurries into view, a more formidable specimen than the domestic servants. He's tall and he carries a sword. I slam Coralex into him then grab him and tumble him downstairs. I turn back to Coralex. 'As I was saying. What happened to the dragon scales? Stop stammering, I don't have time. I'm here with the backing of Deputy Consul Cicerius, and if I have to toss you downstairs, the Deputy will move Heaven, Earth and the three moons to see I don't get prosecuted. He's already very upset by what he just learned about you.'

The merchant hesitates. I touch my dagger. 'Spill it.'

Coralex spills it. At his age, he isn't going to get off lightly from a trip down the stairs. A man of his wealth naturally has a very long staircase.

I leave the house with a lot of information, and curses raining down on me from Coralex, his wife, and a very pretty daughter who probably doesn't know that her father deals in stolen goods. Outside the snow catches me in the face. I shake it off. Now that I've really offended someone, I feel like I'm working well. I have a list of the people who've recently bought dragon scales, and there's a good chance that the mysterious spell-worker will be among them. Back in Twelve Seas I buy a bundle of logs from a street vendor, stoke up the fire, open a beer and prepare to study the list. I'm interrupted by a knock at the door. I wrench it open and am surprised to find Senator Lodius, leader of Turai's opposition party, and sworn enemy of Cicerius. I've never spoken to Lodius though he did once vehemently denounce me to the Senate. The Chronicle ran a full report, listing many of my previous misdemeanours.

'Are you busy?' he enquires, politely.

The Senator is a man of medium height, about fifty or so but well preserved. He has something of an aristocratic air, though he styles himself leader of the democratic Populares party. He's not particularly imposing in appearance but he's handsome enough for a political leader, with blue eyes, short grey hair neatly styled and a well-cut toga just visible under a thick woollen cloak. He's a powerful orator, and he has a lot of support in this city.

'I'm busy. But come in anyway.'

I don't know why he's here. Lodius is far too important to be visiting me. I've never liked the man - he always gives me the impression of a politician who'd hitch his wagon to any cause which might bring him to power - but if he's here to offer me some lucrative work I might be prepared to change my opinion. The Senator is accompanied by two assistants, or bodyguards more likely. Turanian politics can be violent. I kick some junk under the table, draw out a chair and motion the Senator to take a seat. He accepts my offer of beer. He takes the bottle, doesn't mind that I don't have any goblets to hand, and gets right down to business.

'I understand you are busy, at the Sorcerers Assemblage?'

At the mention of the Assemblage I'm immediately on my guard.

'I wish you success,' he says. 'It will be a fine thing for the city if our candidate is elected.'

I'm expecting Lodius to start in with some criticism of Cicerius and the Traditionals, but that doesn't seem to be what he's here for.

'I'm hoping, however, that you will have time to perform another function. Have you heard of the impending demolition of the buildings around the collapsed aqueduct?'

'Yes.'

'Are you aware that the proposal to clear the area will make four hundred Turanians homeless?'

I wasn't, though the way landlords crowd people into the slums, it's not really a surprise.

'Praetor Capatius wants to develop the land for profit,' continues Lodius. 'As the richest man in the city, the Praetor has no regard for the rights of the ordinary citizen.'

By this time I'm eyeing the Senator warily. I don't like where this is going.

'Are you aware of your powers as Tribune of the People?'

'I've a rough idea.'

The Senator nods. Then he asks me what I'm planning to do.

'I wasn't planning to do anything.'

'Surely you do not wish to see these people made homeless, particularly in the middle of such a fierce winter?'

'I'd sooner they were warm and cosy. But I'm not really a Tribune. I was only given the post so I could get into the Assemblage.'

'Nonetheless, you have the power. Are you afraid that Cicerius would disapprove of you acting against his friend Capatius?'

'Not particularly. I just don't see myself as a politician. And I'm busy.'

'Too busy to help your fellow citizens?'

If there's one thing you can be sure of it's that Lodius doesn't care about his fellow citizens either, but he's backing me into an awkward corner.

'Yes. I'm too busy. I'm already helping Turai by assisting Lisutaris. I can't help everyone. You're head of a political party, why don't you stop the evictions?'

'I don't have the power. By some quirk of history, only the Tribunes could do that. A Tribune can insist that every legal step is followed to the letter in the matter of city development. Naturally, that was not what Cicerius had in mind when he appointed you, but the fact remains that you can prevent the eviction by referring the matter to the Senate. Once that has been done, I will take over.'

'Would this have anything to do with you needing four hundred votes in a vital ward that has an election next year?'

'I am concerned only with the plight of the poor.'

We stare at each other for a while. I'm wondering what pressure Lodius can bring to bear. While I don't relish having him as a political enemy, Cicerius and the Traditionals still have more power. The Consul, Turai's highest official, is always a Traditional, and they're the party of the King. The last thing I want to do is end up an enemy of the King. The whole thing is extremely aggravating for a man who tries to stay out of politics. I inform the Senator that, sad as I am to see hardship among my fellow citizens, I'm not about to enter the political arena by vetoing Praetor Capatius. Senator Lodius sips his beer, and turns to speak to one of his assistants.

'Ivitius. Tell me again what you saw when you were visiting your cousin in Quintessence Street.'

'Thraxas dumping a body over a wall,' says Ivitius.

'And what night was that?'

'The same night Darius Cloud Walker was killed.'

Lodius turns back to me. 'A very troubling affair. I understand the Sorcerers Guild is currently extending its full powers to find out what happened to Darius. From what I hear, someone has cast a mystical shield over the events. The sorcerers are baffled, at least for the moment. Of course, they're lacking specific information. All they know is that the body was found in a snowdrift in Twelve Seas. If they had more facts - for instance, the exact location of the killing, and the identity of those around the victim at the time - I have no doubt they could quickly learn the truth.'

I can't think of anything to say. I'm all out of words.

'My carriage is outside,' says the Senator. 'I'll take you to the site of the eviction. Nothing formal in the way of documentation is required. It is merely necessary for you to speak to the person in charge, one Vadinex, an employee of Capatius's. Tell him you're referring the matter to the Senate. Work will then cease, pending investigation.'

I still can't think of anything to say. I get my cloak. We ride in silence along Quintessence Street. The snow and ice are thick on the ground, but Lodius has a sturdy carriage pulled by two equally sturdy horses and we reach the site of the eviction a lot quicker than I'd like. The snow is falling on a dismal scene of workmen, city officials, lawyers, civil guards and poor tenants, all arguing bitterly. Violence is in the air as the Civil Guards hold back the crowd. Some of the slum dwellers scream from upstairs windows, aiming their anger at Vadinex, the man in charge.

I knew Vadinex in my army days. He stands about six and a half feet tall and he's built like a bull. Once at a siege he won a commendation for being the first man over the wall. Praetor Capatius uses him for difficult assignments. Evicting a few poor tenants is all in a day's work for him. I really don't want to be doing this. I notice Captain Rallee among the guards, and make my way towards him. Before I get there, a figure bursts through the crowd brandishing an axe. It's Makri, clad in a thick cloak and her floppy hat, and bristling with weapons.

'You're not going to evict Samanatius,' she yells.

An elderly figure in a plain cloak, presumably the philosopher himself, steps forward through the blizzard to lay his hand on her shoulder, indicating, I think, that he doesn't wish to see violence done. Vadinex confronts Makri. She raises her axe. I step forward.

'Stop!' I yell.

I have a loud voice when necessary, and a lot of bulk. It's hard to miss me, even in a snowstorm.

'I'm halting this work. As Tribune of the People, I am referring the matter to the Senate.'

There is general astonishment. Captain Rallee actually laughs. Vadinex doesn't seem so amused. 'What the hell are you talking about, Thraxas? Get out of my way.'

Various others now step forward in support of my statement. Several cold-looking lawyers, accompanied by armed men, courtesy of Lodius, announce that the eviction cannot go ahead.

'The Tribune has spoken.'

Everyone looks at me. I feel foolish. Senator Lodius has now stepped into the fray. As people recognise him they realise this is not a joke. Captain Rallee addresses Vadinex. 'The lawyers say it's legal. It has to go to the Senate. You can't carry out the eviction.'

Vadinex starts to protest but Captain Rallee cuts him short. 'It's the law. And if you keep me standing here in this snowstorm any longer, I'm liable to throw you in prison for assaulting a Civil Guard. Eviction over. Everybody go home.'

Vadinex eyes me with loathing. 'The Praetor will be down on you like a bad spell for this,' he growls.

Makri hurries over. 'Stay away or I'll kill you,' she spits at him.

Vadinex always had a short temper. Were the area not so thick with Civil Guards, he'd quite likely attack her. I'd like to see Makri killing Vadinex. The way the huge man looks at her before he departs, she may yet get the chance. He moves off, taking his companions with him.

'Thraxas, you were wonderful!' enthuses Makri. 'I knew you'd come through in the end. Come and meet Samanatius!'

I shake the elderly philosopher's hand. He thanks me warmly, but when he looks into my eyes I know he knows I'm not here of my own free will. All around, tenants of the slums are congratulating me for rescuing them from Vadinex.

'Good work,' booms Senator Lodius, and gets round to letting everyone know that he is the man responsible for their salvation. The congratulations fail to give me a warm glow. Makri might be as happy as an Elf in a tree that Samanatius has a reprieve, but I've got other things to worry about.

'Where's Lisutaris? You're meant to be protecting her.'

Makri tells me she's asleep in her room at the Avenging Axe. Direeva is with her.

I frown. 'I'm starting to get suspicious of Direeva. I don't like the way she keeps sticking to Lisutaris.'

'Tilupasis likes it. Tilupasis seems to have a lot of influence, even with the Consul.'

'She ought to. They're having an affair. Well, according to scurrilous rumour anyway, and I generally trust that. Do a good job for Tilupasis and she might help with the university.'

'I already thought of that.'

I ask Makri if Tilupasis is a supporter of the Association of Gentlewomen. Makri doesn't think she is, which strikes her as odd.

'Maybe she thinks she's doing fine already,' I suggest.

Makri isn't enjoying her employment as bodyguard. 'I expected I might have to kill the occasional attacker and maybe fight off a few assassins. I never thought it would involve being nursemaid to a woman who can't stand upright after lunchtime. What were you thinking of, nominating her for Head of the Sorcerers Guild?'

'I didn't nominate her. Cicerius did. Is she still going at the water pipe?'

'Like a hungry dragon chewing on a carcass. How does she ever remember any spells? You can't remember them even when you're sober.'

'She studied more than me.'

'It was terrible at the Assemblage. I had to keep dragging her away from visiting sorcerers so they wouldn't see how doped she was. Isn't she meant to be impressing people?'

Despite her recent lapses, Makri does have something of a puritanical streak, which now appears to be resurfacing. She thinks that people should get on with their work, and Lisutaris is certainly failing to do this. I agree that Lisutaris can't be impressing the sorcerers with her performance.

'The delegation from Turai are doing their best. The other two Tribunes have been spreading so much hospitality around that some of our guests are now so sated with sex, alcohol and dwa that they'd vote for anyone they were told to.'

'Does Lisutaris have enough votes to win?' asks Makri.

'Probably not enough to defeat Ramius. But remember, our candidate only has to make it into the top two.'

'Those two go into some sort of final contest,' Makri points out. 'How is Lisutaris going to manage that?'

'Who knows? It wouldn't surprise me if Tilupasis was working on some way of cheating right now.'

At the Avenging Axe, Makri goes to check on Lisutaris. I've barely time to load up with stew, venison and yams before I'm back at work, studying the list of recipients of dragon scales. It's an interesting collection, containing the names of quite a few aristocratic Turanians. These rich ladies like to make their hair sparkle with dragon scales, but it seems as if they prefer to buy them at a discount, even if it's illegal. Coralex and Rezox were doing a good trade. Clients include Praetor Capatius, Prefect Galwinius, several other Senators and various high-up city officials. Rich merchants too, including Rixad, who I was working for recently. I'm not surprised. He was keen to keep his wife happy, and nothing says I love you better than a sprinkling of well-cut dragon scales.

Few people on the list have any knowledge of sorcery. I can't see Capatius or Galwinius cooking up a magical brew. The name of Tirini Snake Smiter catches my eye. She might buy dragon scales for making spells. She is a sorcerer. But she's also a woman who loves to display herself to her best advantage, and I'm inclined to believe she wanted to make her hair sparkle rather than work some malevolent spell. Tirini would be an unlikely murderer. She never dabbles in politics, or crime, to my knowledge, being more concerned with party-going, scandalous romances and generally enjoying herself. The only other name of note is Princess Direeva. She recently bought dragon scales from Coralex. I muse on this. In my eyes Direeva is already a suspect for the murder of Darius. No known motive but plenty of opportunity. And now it turns out that she's been clandestinely buying the main ingredient for a hitherto unknown spell of erasement. Unfortunately Direeva also wears beads made from dragon scales in her hair. I think I noticed some dragon scale earrings too. If I confront her she'll simply say she needed new jewellery.

I need a drink. As a private citizen, my recent obligation to act in an official capacity has unnerved me. I'm grateful it's midwinter. People have enough problems without paying too much attention to the startling sight of Thraxas suddenly appearing as a minor politician. With any luck it will soon be forgotten about. It had better be, I'm not planning on defending anyone else's rights.

Chapter Thirteen

Next morning at Lisutaris's villa I find Makri sitting in front of a well-laden breakfast table.

'Lisutaris still unconscious?'

'No, wide awake.'

I'm surprised. 'What happened? The water pipe break from overuse?'

'Lisutaris never starts on the water pipe till Copro's done her hair. She needs to be fully alert for the morning beauty treatments. Copro wouldn't like it if she wasn't paying attention. He's quite temperamental.'

Discussing Copro, I feel quite temperamental myself. 'I need to see her.'

'Copro doesn't like to be interrupted when he's working.'

'Goddammit, are you serious? I'm trying to get her off a murder rap and she's too busy getting her hair done?'

'You can't expect an important sorcerer like Lisutaris to turn up at the Assemblage with her hair in poor condition,' says Makri. 'It's hardly going to impress people.'

'They're voting for top sorcerer, not fashion woman of the year.'

'No one's going to vote for her if they think she's not making an effort,' asserts Makri.

'How come you're a fan of Copro all of a sudden? I thought you didn't like him.' I stare at Makri suspiciously. 'There's something different about you.'

'No there isn't.'

'Yes there is. Your hair is different.'

'Just a little rearrangement,' says Makri, defensively. 'Copro said it would show off my cheekbones better.'

'Your cheekbones? What's got into you? When you arrived in Turai you couldn't stop talking about how ridiculous the rich women were.'

'I'm just fitting in,' says Makri, calmly. 'As Lisutaris's bodyguard I can't be arguing with her hairdresser. It would create all sorts of difficulties.' She studies her fingernails. 'Do you think I should get my nails done? I'm not really happy with this colour.'

'What's wrong with it?'

'It clashes with the chainmail.'

Makri holds her fingers over a piece of chainmail, and peers in the mirror. 'You remember how I wondered about being blonde after we saw all those blonde Elvish women? What do you think?'

'I think you should stop talking nonsense. Yesterday you were going to chop up Vadinex with your axe, and today you're wittering on about your hair.'

'I don't see the two things as mutually exclusive.'

'Life was easier when you were an ignorant barbarian.'

'I was never an ignorant barbarian.'

'You didn't used to ramble on about hair and make-up. When you arrived in Turai all you wanted to do was attend the university.'

'I still do.'

'What happened to Makri the demented swordswoman?'

'Make your mind up, Thraxas. Only last week you were lecturing me about killing the dwa dealer. You want me to kill someone? Fine. Just point me in the right direction.'

'I don't want you to kill anyone.'

'Don't worry about me,' says Makri, warming to the topic. 'I'll kill anyone that needs killing. Orcs, Humans, Elves, Trolls, dragons, mythical beasts–'

'Will you shut up about killing things?'

'So now I'm not meant to talk about killing people or hairstyles? Is there any subject you'd be happy with?'

'Solving a murder would be a good choice. How long is Lisutaris going to be?'

'I think she's scheduled for a manicure as well. Copro brought his best assistant, and a nail specialist.'

Makri is showing little interest in the food in front of her, so I pile up a plate for a good second breakfast, meanwhile silently cursing Copro and his ilk. When I was young the city wasn't full of beauticians. Old Consul Juvenius would have thrown Copro off the walls, and a good thing too.

'So what do you think?' says Makri.

'About what?'

'Dying my hair blonde.'

'I think you'll look like a prostitute. Stop asking me about it.'

'Do you have to be so unpleasant? Looking after Lisutaris is stressful. I need some relaxation.'

Unable to take any more of this, I carry my plate over to the window and stare out at the ice-covered garden. There's some commotion in the long hallway and a messenger rushes in calling for Makri. He hands her a slip of paper. Makri breaks the seal and looks concerned.

'Bad news at the Assemblage.'

'The sorcerers have got through–?'

'No. Sunstorm Ramius has dispatched Troverus to take Princess Direeva to dinner. Tilupasis is very concerned.'

Makri rises to her feet. 'I have to intercept them.'

'Who is Troverus?' I ask, feeling confused.

'Handsomest young man in Simnia, according to all reports. Tilupasis has been worried about him. That Ramius, he's cunning.'

Makri starts making ready to leave. She has a determined look in her eyes. 'I won't allow it. No handsomest young man in Simnia is going to charm Direeva into voting for Sunstorm Ramius.'

She hurries to don her armour, and throws her weapons into the small purse which contains the magic pocket. All the while she's muttering about the perfidy of the Simnians. 'It's underhand tactics. I'll show them.'

'I thought you weren't keen on this vote-winning business. You said it was corrupt.'

'It is. But I refuse to be defeated. Look after Lisutaris till she gets to the Assemblage. And whatever you do, don't insult Copro. He's extremely temperamental.'

Makri takes a final, dissatisfied look at her nails, then hurries out. I sit down to finish off the food on the table, and ring for beer. The young servant who arrives has a noticeable rural accent. No doubt a sturdy and sensible woman from the outlying farmlands.

'What do you think of Copro?' I ask.

'He's a great man. They should make him a Senator.'

I study her face. 'Was there much beauty treatment back on the farm?'

She shakes her head. 'That's why I moved to the city.'

The city is doomed. Eventually Lisutaris emerges, accompanied by Copro and his two helpers.

'Thraxas.' Lisutaris greets me graciously. She's wide awake and alert, the first time I've seen her like this since the Assemblage began. Copro is still fussing round her with a comb. He's thin, dark, a little younger than I imagined. And not quite as lisping, though I wouldn't want him on my side in a sword fight. I doubt he'd handle a blade as well as his comb. I note with displeasure that beneath his long hair, jewelled earrings glisten on his earlobes. A number of guilds in Turai use plain gold earrings as a mark of rank, but few men would wear jewels in their ears, apart from the foppish sons of wealthy Senators.

Copro motions extravagantly towards Lisutaris. 'Do you like it?'

'It's wonderful. Lisutaris, we have to get to the Assemblage. Cicerius is starting to complain about your late appearances. And Tilupasis is giving me a hard time.'

Lisutaris tells me she'll be ready in an instant, and departs upstairs.

'I love your friend Makri,' says Copro. 'Such a savage beauty.'

I grunt, and sit down.

'She really should let me do more with her hair.'

Makri has a vast unruly mane, remarkable in its own way. I can't see her taking to any of the controlled styles favoured by Turai's aristocrats. To my disappointment, Copro agrees with me.

'Of course, Makri would not suit such a stylised coiffure. Her magnificent features would only be diminished. But a little styling to bring out her radiance, her force of character. A style the Abelasians call Summer Lightning. It would be breathtaking. I already did much the same for Princess Direeva.'

'You attend Direeva?'

'Princess Direeva insists on the best. I have often been called to the Southern Hills.'

Not really wanting to engage in conversation with Copro, I busy myself with my beer, but Copro apparently finds me more interesting than I find him, because he sits down facing me at the table. 'You have such a fascinating job. Is it dangerous, tracking down all those criminals?'

'Yes.'

'Is it exciting?'

'No. But I need the money.'

Copro studies me. I'm just waiting for him to make some crack about my appearance. I've got long hair tied back in a ponytail, and if he suggests styling it I'm going to sling him out the front door. He asks me some more questions about my work and I grunt some replies. All the time I'm wishing that I wasn't here in Lisutaris's villa, and remembering that when I did live in the better part of town, I never felt all that comfortable about it. Finally Copro gives up on me and converses with Lisutaris's apprentice about new styles just in from Abelasi. Summer fashions apparently, although I can't see why they want to talk about summer fashions when we're still in the middle of winter.

Copro arrived in Turai with nothing, and now he's rich. For all the hand-waving and vacuous conversation, I'd be willing to bet he's a shrewd enough operator underneath, and smart enough never to be singed by a dragon. Tiring of the conversation, I go in search of the Lisutaris. Servants look on with disapproval as I approach her private chambers, but I ignore them and find her in her room, sucking on her water pipe.

'Time to go,' I say, and drag her to her feet.

She looks at me with surprise. 'I can't believe you just laid your hand on me.'

'It was either that or kill the beautician.'

'The last time anyone laid a hand on me I punished them with a heart attack spell.'

'I'd be surprised if you could remember a spell for a runny nose. Don't you ever get sick of thazis dreams? Get your warm cloak on, we're due at the Assemblage. You've got an election to win. Cicerius is paying me to make it happen. So let's go,'

Lisutaris looks with longing at the water pipe.

'Touch that pipe again and I'm going to slug you.' I say.

'I'd kill you if you did.'

'And then who'd get you off the murder rap? Face it, Lisutaris, you need me. So let's go.'

Lisutaris looks at me with dislike. 'I didn't realise how unpleasant you were.'

'Then you're the only person in Turai who didn't. I'm famous for being unpleasant. Now get ready before I pick you up and throw you in the carriage.'

Lisutaris bundles about a hundred sticks of thazis into a magic pocket and starts smoking them on the way to the Assemblage. We're hardly out of Truth is Beauty Lane when her head starts lolling about. I grab the thazis from her hand and toss it out the carriage window.

'What's the matter with you? You used to be a great sorcerer and now you're about as much use as a one-legged gladiator.'

She shakes her head. 'I'm worried I might have killed Darius.'

'You seemed sure you didn't.'

'I'm not so sure now,' she says, and takes another thazis stick from her magic pocket. Lisutaris, Mistress of the Sky, is starting to fall apart. By the time we get to the Assemblage she's unsteady on her feet. Tilupasis intercepts her at the door and leads her off to some private room. Makri and Princess Direeva are looking on.

'She wasn't like this ten years ago,' says Direeva. Her hair sways gently. The dragon scales, finely cut by a jeweller, sparkle brilliantly in the torchlight.

'Just our bad luck that Sunstorm Ramius is a clean-living sort of sorcerer.'

Direeva enquires if I've made any progress on the case. I'm noncommittal. 'I'll get there in the end. Depends how much time I have. How is the hiding spell?'

'Strong enough for now,' replies the Princess.

Last night Melus the Fair visited Lisutaris's villa to add her power to the incantation, strengthening the spell. I hope we can trust Melus. She's sharp as an Elf's ear and has close ties to Lisutaris, but it's one more person who might give us away. The weight of events is getting to me. Makri wonders what would happen if Lisutaris managed to win the election and was then found to be implicated in the murder.

'Hard to say. As far as I understand the sorcerers' rules, the Head of the Guild can't be expelled. Lasat, Axe of Gold, is the temporary leader, but once he confirms the new sorcerer in their post they can't be removed. Given that important upper-class citizens in Turai are usually allowed the opportunity to slip off into exile before being convicted of a serious crime, Lisutaris might still end up as Head of the Guild, exiled in another city.'

'Could she ever return to Turai?'

'Maybe, when the heat died down. I think Cicerius is hoping for something like that, if I can't clear her name. Won't help you or me, though.'

I'm firmly of the Turanian lower classes. Even my name marks me out as such. If I'm implicated in a murder, no one will look the other way while I flee into exile. Makri has intercepted Princess Direeva before her appointment with Troverus. She's doing her best to keep her entertained with tales of her exploits in the gladiatorial arena. Direeva seems interested.

'I too have often had to fight. When my grandfather died my uncle attempted to seize the kingdom from my father. It took two years of warfare till my father was secure. My uncle hired an army of Orcish mercenaries, and it was only with help from the Abelasians that we overcame them. Darius Cloud Walker was our ally. We will miss him.'

A cunning look comes into Makri's eyes. 'Yes, it's a terrible loss. But now you have thirty votes to spare, I expect you'll be transferring them to Lisutaris.'

'Is that why you have been hospitable?' says Direeva, stiffly.

'Of course not,' replies Makri, a little flustered. 'I'm naturally hospitable to any woman who can lead an army. But now your friend has been brutally murdered, you have to vote for someone. I mean, it's a shame your old ally ended up in a snowdrift but you can't dwell on the past. Voting for Lisutaris seems like the natural thing to do, given that Darius was unfortunately killed in Thraxas's office...with my knife...' Makri's voice tails off. She holds up her hand. 'Do you like this nail varnish? I'm not sure about it.'

Direeva laughs, quite heartily for a Princess. 'If you get exiled from Turai you can stay with me in the Southern Hills,' she says. 'I may vote for Lisutaris. I can see why Turai is desperate for her to win. I didn't realise your strength was so diminished. You're extremely vulnerable to attack from the Orcs.'

'They haven't recovered from the beating we gave them last time,' I say.

Princess Direeva isn't so sure. 'It's difficult to predict when a new leader may arise to unite the Orcish nations and lead them against the West.'

I've been through one Orc war and I don't expect to live out my days without seeing another so I'm interested in Direeva's opinions.

'You weren't expecting it last time,' she continues. 'King Bhergaz of Aztol was of no special importance, till the neighbouring country asked him to intervene in their succession dispute. He put his own cousin in charge, took control of the eastern trade route, started dealing in gold and slaves and became rich. Soon he was calling himself Bhergaz the Fierce and raising an army to conquer the region. Once he got Rezaz the Butcher on his side he became effective leader of all the Orc lands. You remember what happened after that.'

I certainly do. Without the timely intervention of the Elvish armies, Turai would now be a province of Aztol.

'It's true that Aztol hasn't recovered from defeat,' continues the Princess. 'But Gzak is growing stronger. It's a rich land and a lot of Orcs still look up to Gzak for its victories last century.'

'So you think Gzak will invade?' asks Makri. She doesn't sound too distressed by the prospect. Here in Turai she can never find enough Orcs to kill.

'It's possible. But hard to predict. It takes something special to unite the Orcs. Who knows if one of the current warring Princes might be destined for greatness? Have you heard of young Prince Amrag of Kose who just overthrew the King? He was abandoned as a bastard child, so the story goes, but his brilliant guerrilla warfare proved too much for the army to contend with. He has a reputation as a very charismatic Orc.'

I nod. I've heard of Prince Amrag. Charismatic, savage and successful, so they say. 'Isn't there some weird story that he's not entirely Orc?'

'Mixed blood, according to some,' answers Direeva. 'A little Human perhaps. Some of the wilder stories even say he has Elvish blood, though I find that impossible to believe. But even the fact that such stories gather around Amrag shows he's an Orc to set their imaginations rolling.'

I get a brief vision of the horrors of the last war. I banish it with an effort. There's no time to dwell on that, or on what may be to come. 'I have to do something about the current crisis. I'm no closer to finding the murderer. And now we know Covinius is here, Lisutaris is in danger.'

'I'll see if Hanama can learn any more,' says Makri, unexpectedly.

'What changed your mind?'

'You helped Samanatius.'

Poor Makri. If she wasn't so naive she'd know I'd never have gone near the eviction without being blackmailed into it. Makri turns back to Direeva but the Princess has now switched her attention to a young man wearing a well-cut rainbow cloak whose bright golden hair tumbles over his shoulders in a raffish manner. Troverus, we presume.

'Where'd he come from?' demands Makri, not pleased at being outflanked by the young Simnian sorcerer. 'You think he's handsome?'

I shrug.

'I don't think he's that handsome,' says Makri. 'Look at all that girly blond hair.'

'You like girly blond hair.'

'Yes, it's really attractive, now you mention it,' says Makri. 'Excuse me, I have to get between them.'

Makri plants herself firmly between Direeva and Troverus and eyes the Simnian like a hostile attacking force. 'I understand that venereal disease is rampant in Simnia,' she says. 'How do you cope with that?'

I leave her to the struggle. Things may be bad but at least Tilupasis doesn't have me trying to charm anyone. The Assemblage continues to be the one bright spot in a frozen city. If the murder of Darius has cast a shadow over proceedings, you wouldn't guess it from the behaviour of Irith Victorious and his jolly Juvalian companions. Behind the scenes the senior sorcerers may be working assiduously, but in the main hall, behaviour has become riotous. Cicerius is shaken.

'I was not quite prepared for this,' he admits. Nearby, some dark-skinned southern sorcerers are engaged in a contest to see who can levitate the largest barrel of beer. 'At least we have their votes,' says Cicerius, moving swiftly to avoid a floating river of ale. 'We sent a wagonload of beer to their lodgings.'

With Darius out of the way, it seems certain that Ramius will win the vote. Lisutaris is still favourite to gain second place, ahead of Rokim, but there's been an unexpectedly good showing by a sorcerer named Almalas.

'A Niojan, of all things,' says Cicerius, animatedly.

Nioj, our large northern neighbour, is one of the biggest threats to Turai's security. If they gain control of the Sorcerers Guild we might as well surrender to King Lamachus.

'How can a Niojan be making gains?' I ask. 'No one likes Niojans. They're religious fundamentalists. Their church isn't even that keen on sorcery. They don't drink, don't have fun, don't do anything except pray.'

'Sober habits are not universally despised,' retorts Cicerius.

'We're talking sorcerers here. Whoever heard of a sorcerer voting for a man who doesn't drink?'

Cicerius admits it's strange.

'Has he been spreading his Niojan gold around?'

'Probably. But remember, many northern states look to Nioj for protection from the Orcs. Almalas's sober habits may not be so unwelcome to those who worry about imminent attack. Also, he's a war hero, at least as much as Lisutaris or Ramius.'

'I remember Almalas. I guess he was good enough in the war. His sorcery wasn't on a par with Lisutaris's, though.'

'He is at least able to walk around unaided, which helps,' says Cicerius, in a withering tone. 'What about the hiding spell?'

'Still in place. It's been boosted by Direeva and Melus the Fair.'

'Have you eliminated Princess Direeva from suspicion?'

'No. I haven't eliminated her. I still don't like the way she's sticking close to Lisutaris. I have some other leads, though. There's an apprentice used to work for Darius who got the boot after being accused of embezzling funds, and left threatening to kill Darius. The apprentice was last heard of in Mattesh, still practising sorcery and threatening revenge. And I've got a lead on the erasure spell.'

The air starts turning orange as the southern sorcerers begin to show off their illuminated staffs. Three days into the convention, inhibitions are fading and there's more magic in evidence. The Royal Hall is not a place to visit if you don't like surprises.

'I can hardly bear to go into the main room,' confesses Cicerius. 'Every time I do I seem to get covered in beer or wine.'

Cicerius's assistant Hansius approaches briskly. He leans over to whisper in the Deputy Consul's ear, though as the nearby sorcerers have now started up a raucous drinking song, it's difficult to hear anything. Cicerius listens briefly before dismissing Hansius.

'Bad news. Sunstorm Ramius and Old Hasius the Brilliant have let it be known they are close to uncovering the hidden events. Ramius is keen to do this. It will enhance his reputation.'

'Couldn't you do something to get Hasius off the case? He's sharp as an Elf's ear when it comes to looking back in time. Isn't there some other matter at the Abode of Justice which requires his urgent attention?'

'Unfortunately not,' replies Cicerius. 'The King has granted permission for Hasius to remain here and help. He naturally wishes to give all possible aid to the Sorcerers Assemblage.'

'I take it the King doesn't actually know our own candidate is prime suspect?'

Cicerius shakes his head, and looks grim. 'You must at least hold them off till after the election,' he tells me. 'We depend on it. Now, about this matter of Praetor Capatius and the eviction.'

I'm expecting Cicerius to chew me out over this one, but the Deputy Consul for once seems to perceive that I was in an impossible position.

'It was clever of Senator Lodius to spot that you could aid him in this matter. It did not occur to me when I nominated you as Tribune of the People that this might happen. I regret that it's granted the Populares party a small victory. However, in the scheme of things it doesn't matter too much. Whatever happens, do not be drawn into further such actions.'

'I'll try my best.'

Tilupasis joins us, neatly sidestepping a levitated goblet. In the midst of the uproar she remains unruffled and elegant. She gives a brief report to the Deputy Consul. Two days away from the vote, things are looking reasonably good, but she's worried about the growing support for Almalas.

'Sareepa Lightning-Strikes-the-Mountain seems quite taken with him. God knows why.'

Cicerius is perturbed. Sareepa Lightning-Strikes-the-Mountain is head of the Sorcerers Guild in Mattesh, our southern neighbour.

'They have a lot of influence. Sareepa probably controls twelve votes. We can't let them go to Nioj.'

'Didn't we already pay Sareepa?'

'She gave the gold back,' explains Tilupasis. 'After listening to Almalas talking about a sorcerer's duty, she says she regrets even considering taking an immoral bribe.' Tilupasis spreads her arms in despair. 'What am I meant to do with a senior sorcerer who suddenly gets religion?'

'Increase the bribe?'

'It won't work.'

'Send a young Tribune to her private chambers.'

'I already tried. She sent him away. And she instructed her delegation that thazis and dwa would no longer be tolerated. The woman's gone mad with moral behaviour. Damn that priest sorcerer Almalas.'

Tilupasis turns to me. 'Thraxas, didn't you know Sareepa Lightning-Strikes-the-Mountain when you were an apprentice?'

'Sure. She used to distil klee in a cauldron and invite young mercenaries to sample it, as I recall. The woman was never more than one step away from being slung out of the apprentices' college. Weird that she should suddenly become respectable.'

'You have to change her back.'

'Pardon?'

'Get her drinking again. Once she has some klee inside her she'll forget this Niojan ethical nonsense and take our bribe.'

I point out that I'm already busy doing various other vital tasks, and besides, I'm not what you'd call a skilful diplomat.

'How important are Sareepa's votes?' Cicerius asks Tilupasis.

'Absolutely vital.'

Cicerius draws himself up to his full height, adjusts his toga, and turns to me. 'I'm ordering you to get her intoxicated,' he says. 'Don't argue. You're clearly the man for the job.'

Chapter Fourteen

Irith Victorious is lying belly-up on the floor of the drinking area. His companions are laid out beside him on a bed of tangled rainbow cloaks. Tilupasis ordered the closure of a busy local tavern in order to divert its entire supply of ale to the Juvalian sorcerers. When that proved insufficient she ordered the next tavern to close, bringing in its beer and klee as reinforcements. Finally overwhelmed by the flood of free alcohol, the Juvalians are now rarely conscious, and spend their days in a stupor, awakening only to drink. They've promised to cast their votes for Lisutaris.

Not far away, the five members of the Misan delegation are sleeping off the effects of high-quality dwa, courtesy of Tilupasis. She had the drug brought in from the confiscated supplies stored at the Abode of Justice. Officially these mounds of dwa should have been destroyed, but Tilupasis seems to have the authority to do just about anything. Four sorcerers from the far western state of Kamara who once strode confidently into the Royal Hall are now unfit to leave their private quarters after a forty-eight-hour orgy of unprecedented degeneracy. Some of the Kamaran tastes were, strictly speaking, illegal in Turai, but not beyond the organisational powers of Tilupasis and the city's efficient brothel keepers. The Kamarans have promised that when they recover, they'll be sure to vote for Lisutaris.

What Sunstorm Ramius makes of all this I don't know. I'm certain his Simnian delegation has also been indulging in bribery but I can't imagine it's on anything like the vast scale of corruption wrought by Tilupasis on behalf of our city. Thanks to us, the Sorcerers Assemblage has descended into an unparalleled orgy of illicit gold, extravagant drunkenness, wanton sex and extreme drug abuse. It makes a man proud to be Turanian.

'You Turanians are a filthy, degenerate nation,' says Sareepa Lightning-Strikes-the-Mountain.

I've sought her out to say a friendly hello. It's not going well.

'I cannot believe the way the sorcerers are behaving. I blame Turai, the entire city is corrupt.'

'It's really not so bad...'

'It is vile,' insists Sareepa. 'Thank God for Almalas. He's a beacon of light in this foul den of corruption.'

Is this really the same Sareepa Lightning-Strikes-the-Mountain I used to know? When we were sixteen, she'd already worked her way through the male population of the district and was looking to neighbouring towns for new lovers.

'Why are prayer calls ignored?' she demands.

'A little laxity is common at these events.'

'A little laxity? Not for the Niojans. They pray six times a day. Would that others would follow their example. Thraxas, you must escape from this iniquity. I will introduce you to Almalas.'

'Could we perhaps discuss this over a bottle of wine?' I venture, remembering my mission.

Sareepa looks as if she's about to explode. 'Wine? Do you realise–'

At this moment some sorcerers stumble between us in drunken pursuit of a levitated beer barrel. 'A flagon of klee to the man who brings it down,' shouts one of their number, and starts firing bolts of light from his staff. Sareepa is rendered temporarily speechless. Realising that alcohol is not the best subject to be discussing, I turn the conversation to Darius's apprentice. 'He left Abelasi with a powerful dislike of Darius. Settled in Mattesh, I believe?'

Sareepa knows the apprentice in question. 'Quite a powerful sorcerer these days. He's here with us.'

'With you? How?'

It turns out that said apprentice finished his studies, took up Matteshan citizenship, and is now a fully fledged sorcerer in attendance with the rest of the delegation.

'He still hated Darius,' agrees Sareepa. 'But don't go suspecting him of murder. My delegation is firmly under my control.'

I ask for an introduction anyway, which Sareepa agrees to make, providing I'm sober. The woman really hates alcohol. It's a sad state of affairs.

'Have you ever come across a spell for making a new version of reality and sending it back in time?' I ask.

'There's no such spell,' replies Sareepa. 'No one could do that.'

Moments later I'm apprehended by a furious Makri. 'You know what happened? I was just telling Direeva how I once killed three Trolls in the arena when that creepy Troverus smiled in this really annoying manner and said he'd come to the Assemblage to forget about unpleasant things like fighting and then whisked Direeva off for dinner!'

'Couldn't you have stopped them?'

'I was too taken aback by anyone wanting to forget about fighting,' complains Makri. 'By the time I recovered, they were gone. Damn that Troverus. I don't trust him at all. Right this moment he's charming Direeva over a bottle of wine, and who knows what'll happen after that? He's not that handsome anyway. See-ath was a lot better-looking and he never said he was bored with my fighting stories. I hate these smooth-talking Simnians. What am I meant to do now?'

'I've no idea. Ask Tilupasis, she's the expert.'

'Come and help me. You could detain Troverus with some tedious war story while I charm Direeva.'

'Can't do it. I need to go out and investigate.'

As I leave the hall I pass a tall man with a long beard who's wearing the most sober rainbow cloak ever woven. It's hard to imagine a rainbow cloak could be so dull. He's talking in a deep voice to a large crowd of younger sorcerers who appear to be hanging on his every word, which is some achievement, with the uproar on all sides. Almalas, I presume. Niojan sorcerers rarely take on fancy names. I listen to him for a while, but as he seems to be talking about honour, duty and such like, I quickly lose interest.

The rest of the afternoon is spent travelling round the frozen city, checking out people who bought dragon scales from Coralex. It gets me nowhere. I'm not even sure what I'm looking for. Someone who's been buying scales but doesn't look like they'd wear them in their hair. Someone who looks like they could work an erasure spell never before used in Turai. No one I visit fits the bill. Just a lot of aristocratic women with plenty of jewellery. Or merchants' wives on the way up, also with plenty of jewellery. Even a Captain of the Guards, who's buying jewels for a girl he'll never be rich enough to marry.

The last name on my list is Rixad, the merchant whose wife I was recently tailing. He isn't pleased to see me. People who once hired me often aren't, even when I've done a good job for them. The results are the same as everywhere else. Rixad bought the scales for his wife. His wife likes plenty of decoration. Rixad makes it clear he's not keen for me to hang around. Now he trusts his wife again he doesn't want her finding out he was checking up on her. He'll always be checking up on her. He should have married someone less demanding. She should have carried on as an actress till someone better came along.

Outside, the snow is still falling. As I walk through the northern outskirts of Pashish I notice two legs protruding stiffly from a snowdrift. A beggar, frozen to death. It's not even a bad part of town. Thinking of the wealth that's pouring into the Assemblage, I get annoyed. A little of that money could have housed a beggar for the winter instead of disappearing down the throat of some corpulent freeloader. Like Irith. Like me. I stop feeling annoyed and start feeling depressed. I want to go home but I have to go back to the Assemblage to check up on Lisutaris and report to Cicerius. I shiver. I've learned two new spells for warming my cloak but it never seems to keep out the cold.

I make my report to Cicerius, including my failure with Sareepa Lightning-Strikes-the-Mountain.

'You must try again,' he says.

'All right, I'll try again. Where's Lisutaris?'

'Unconscious. Sulinius and Visus took her to my private room.'

'Is she losing votes, being so intoxicated?'

Cicerius no longer knows. With half the Assemblage now permanently under the influence of dwa or thazis, it might even be in her favour.

'And we've spread plenty of gold around,' I point out.

The Deputy Consul nods. He doesn't look that happy about it.

'You wish we had a nice clean candidate like Almalas?'

'Yes. But we don't.'

'Don't worry, Cicerius. If Lisutaris is elected, you'll get plenty of credit.'

Cicerius would enjoy getting the credit. He's not enjoying the process. At this moment Makri and Lisutaris wander past. Makri has discarded her body armour and is wearing only her chainmail bikini. It has to be the smallest bikini ever seen in Turai. It's not even on properly. Lisutaris is fully dressed but completely drenched, possibly from an unsuccessful experiment with beer levitation. Both have huge thazis sticks hanging from their lips, creating a mushroom-shaped cloud of smoke above their heads.

Cicerius looks at them with horror. 'Were Visus and Sulinius not–'

'I broke out,' says Lisutaris, her speech slurred. 'Had to console Makri.'

'Failed with Direeva,' says Makri. 'Sorry about that. Simnian outmanoeuvred me. Tell Tilupasis she should have him killed.'

'Thraxas has to charm Sareepa,' says Lisutaris.

'Tough assignment,' says Makri. She laughs. Her thazis stick falls from her lips and is extinguished by the beer that drips from Lisutaris's cloak. Lisutaris mutters a word and the thazis flies from the floor into Makri's hand, and relights itself. At least the Mistress of the Sky hasn't completely forgotten how to work magic. It's fortunate that entry into the Assemblage is so closely regulated. Were the ordinary citizens of Turai to see their leaders freely distributing illegal substances, there would be consternation. Or jealousy, maybe.

'You're looking as miserable as a Niojan whore,' says Lisutaris. 'Have some thazis.'

'Take them home,' says Cicerius, sounding as close to desperate as I've ever heard him.

Lisutaris and Makri want to go to Twelve Seas rather than Thamlin. I don't argue. It's as well for me to stay close to Lisutaris. Makri isn't in a state to do much in the way of guarding her. I sneak them out a side door and into an official carriage. On the journey back to Twelve Seas, Makri wakes up.

'Did you bring my armour?'

'Yes.'

'Keep it safe,' says Makri, and goes back to sleep. I've wrapped my cloak around her to stop her freezing. The carriage takes a long, long time to make the journey. The streets are next to impassable and the driver has to coax the horses through the falling snow. I'm cold as the ice queen's grave. I've been cold for weeks. I'm sick of it. Getting my companions up the stairs to my office is difficult. Before we're more than halfway up, a large band of men emerge from the snowstorm.

'Thraxas!' they call.

I take out my sword. I don't recognise them. Not the standard Brotherhood thugs of Twelve Seas. There must be twenty of them, all armed.

'What?'

'We're here on business.'

'Whose business?'

'Praetor Capatius's business.'

Their leader steps forward. 'The Praetor outranks you, Tribune. It wasn't very bright to go against him.'

'It wasn't very bright of the Praetor to send you after me. I'm working for the Deputy Consul and he outranks Capatius.'

'Really?' says the leader. 'How about that?'

Hearing the voices, Makri once more wakens. She sees the situation and quickly pulls a sword out of her magic pocket. As she raises it, it slips from her hand and clatters down the stairs. Makri has never dropped her sword before.

'Damn,' she says, and pulls out another blade. She loses her footing on the icy stairs and tumbles down in a heap. The men laugh at the sight. Makri attempts to rise, but can't make it to her feet. Capatius's men advance.

'Don't you believe in the legal process?' I say, descending the stairs to stand over Makri's prone figure. Were I on my own I'd already be inside the tavern with a locking spell on the door, but I can't leave my companions out here. Even without the threat of Capatius's men, they'd freeze to death soon enough. The situation is hopeless. Faced with overwhelming odds, I've sometimes managed to overcome my opponents with a simple sleep spell. Due to the freezing weather, I'm not carrying any spells. Just a sword. Good as I am with a sword, I'm not going to be able to beat twenty men. I'm going to die as a result of my unwilling opposition to the eviction. I knew I should have stayed out of politics.

The first man is no more than three feet away when a voice sounds behind me.

'I'm cold.' It's Lisutaris. She's cold. 'What's happening?'

'We're being attacked.'

I raise my sword to parry the first blow. Suddenly the twenty men are tossed backwards like feathers in a storm. Seconds after preparing to meet my death I'm looking at a bundle of unconscious thugs. I glance round. Lisutaris, still unable to make it on to her feet, has raised herself to her knees with the aid of the railings.

'Good spell,' I call.

'You're welcome,' replies Lisutaris. 'I can't get up. Help me inside.'

I toss Makri over my shoulder and march upstairs.

'At least you can still do sorcery,' I say as I take Lisutaris inside.

'Of course I can still do sorcery. I'm number one chariot. Put some logs on the fire. It's freezing in here.' I throw some logs on the fire. Lisutaris waves her hand and they burst into a roaring blaze. I wish I could do that. I should have studied more.

Chapter Fifteen

Next morning I'm sitting over a beer and a plate of stew at the bar with Gurd and Tanrose. Tanrose makes excellent stew, flavouring it with herbs she grows in the back yard. Gurd and I have cooked a lot of stew on our campaigns round the world but we never had any particular talent for it. For all that I detest Twelve Seas, it's a comfort to be able to eat good meals made by Tanrose. The Avenging Axe is not yet open and would be quiet were it not for the furious sounds of combat emanating from the back yard.

'Makri is madder than a mad dragon,' says Gurd.

Fortunately Makri is not angry with me. Not even with the filthy city of Turai. She's angry with herself. She is appalled to have fallen over in front of an opponent. Early in the morning Tanrose was surprised to discover a bleary-eyed but fully armed Makri preparing to do battle with the wooden targets in the yard. Since then she's been practising her weaponry, oblivious to the biting cold. The noise of battle halts as Makri rushes in to pick up one of the long knives she keeps secreted behind the bar.

'You haven't eaten,' says Tanrose. 'Have some stew.'

'No time,' says Makri. 'I fell over. I'm a disgrace.'

Makri hurries out, clutching her knife. I carry on with my stew, and take another ale.

'She pushes herself too hard,' says Gurd. 'Even the best warrior can't fight all the time. Look at Thraxas. He was a fine companion in war and he spent half his time too drunk to walk.'

There's some truth in this. But I was a better horseman in those days.

'Makri is getting stranger,' I muse.

'Stranger?'

'In the past week she's been miserable about See-ath the Avulan Elf. Then she was the determined bodyguard. Right after that she was getting stoned with Lisutaris and right after that she was back to being organised, rescuing Samanatius. Then she was being intellectual at the library and right afterwards getting stoned again. Now she's back to being mad axewoman. I don't understand it. She should just pick a personality and stick with it. It's not normal, changing all the time.'

'Perhaps it's the mixed blood,' suggests Gurd.

I'm inclined to agree.

'I expect it will drive her mad in the end.'

'Pointed ears.'

'Always leads to trouble.'

'Nonsense,' scoffs Tanrose. 'She's just young and enthusiastic.'

'Enthusiastic? About everything?'

'Of course. Makri is full of passion. Don't you remember what that was like?'

'No, I don't remember. Another beer if you please, Gurd.'

I wonder if I was ever passionate about my wife. My memory seems hazy on the subject. Lisutaris appears in the bar. She spent the night on Makri's floor and her fine robe is crumpled. Her make-up is smeared and her hair is badly in need of attention.

'I'd better get back to Thamlin and clean up before the Assemblage. Big banquet today. And then the vote.'

Lisutaris shows no enthusiasm for the banquet or the election. She sits with us at the bar, but refuses the breakfast offered by Tanrose. Though Tanrose is becoming used to the odd collection of characters who pass through the Avenging Axe these days, she's still surprised at the sight of Turai's leading sorcerer, as purebred an aristocrat as Turai can offer, slumped unhappily at the bar, looking like a tavern dancer after a rough night.

'How is the Assemblage?' asks Tanrose, politely.

'Awful,' replies Lisutaris. 'They're trying to kill me.'

I'm perturbed. The Mistress of the Sky's nerves don't seem to be what they once were. An excess of thazis can lead to feelings of persecution, I believe.

'We're not certain anyone is trying to kill you,' I say, in an attempt to be reassuring.

'We are. Yesterday a Simnian sorcerer whispered something in my ear. I did her a favour a long time ago and she came to repay it. She told me that Sunstorm Ramius definitely did hire an Assassin before he left Simnia.'

'Can you trust that information?'

'Yes.'

So now we have it confirmed. Ramius has engaged the services of Covinius to kill Lisutaris.

'We'll protect you. No client of mine is falling to an Assassin.'

Lisutaris turns her head to stare at me. 'Any idea what Covinius looks like yet?'

'No,' I admit.

She shakes her head sadly. Lisutaris is suffering. She was fine in battle but the thought of an Assassin on her tail, and the pressure of the Sorcerers Guild trying to break the hiding spell, is really getting to her. It's getting to me too. I call Makri in from the back yard. She's caked with sweat and the falling snow has dampened her hair so the points of her ears show through.

'Time to be a bodyguard. Ramius did hire an assassin.'

'Good,' says Makri. 'I'll kill him.'

She's back in fighting mode. I hope it lasts.

All over Turai there's great interest in the outcome of today's election, though few people in the city are aware of what has really gone on at the Assemblage. Even the Renowned and Truthful Chronicle, normally privy to most of the city's dirty secrets, has remained strangely silent about the scandalous happenings, which is odd. The Chronicle loves scandal, and they're sharp as an Elf's ear at dredging it up. Even the Royal Family has trouble keeping its affairs out of the news-sheet. Possibly Tilupasis is responsible. It wouldn't surprise me if she's blackmailing the editor.

I'm fretting about my appearance at the Royal Hall. For one thing I'm not going to be admitted to the feast, which is galling for a man who likes his food. For another there's the risk of Old Hasius and his friends suddenly breaking through the hiding spell. I haven't made any progress on finding the real murderer of Darius, unless the real murderer is Lisutaris, in which case I don't want to make any progress. Then there's the matter of Sareepa Lightning-Strikes-the-Mountain. I'm meant to be winning her over. A hopeless endeavour. That woman is never going to vote for Lisutaris. Not after yesterday's display of inebriation. Damn Sareepa. If there's one thing I can't stand it's a person who gives up drinking. It shows a great weakness of character.

Makri's having problems of her own in the vote-winning department. As she leaves with Lisutaris she's muttering that a certain blond-haired Simnian is going to find himself on the wrong end of a sharp sword if he keeps on being charming to Princess Direeva. 'How about if I just kill him? We could pretend he was the Assassin. Could you fake some evidence?'

They depart to visit Copro, who's going to have his work cut out getting Lisutaris into shape for today's appearance. I don't like the beautician any better than I did before. He might be number one chariot at styling hair, but what sort of achievement is that for a man? The amusing thought strikes me that if Copro were not the useless specimen of humanity he is, his work would make him an excellent assassin. Gets into all the best houses, and no one would ever suspect.

Only sorcerers are allowed at the banquet, no exceptions allowed, so for a large part of the day I'm exiled to the Room of Saints. My two fellow Tribunes are with me, along with those others granted access to the Assemblage who aren't sorcerers - personal staff, a few government representatives and such like. Hansius and Tilupasis drift around, carrying on with the hospitality to anyone that needs it. Sulinius and Visus look tired. When Cicerius handed them over to Tilupasis they were expecting to be involved in some light diplomacy: showing our visitors round the city, making introductions, that sort of thing. They were surprised to find themselves plunged into an endless round of bribery and corruption. To be fair to them, the young aristocrats have adapted well. It'll be good preparation for their careers in the Senate. Both are worrying about the upcoming election.

'Tilupasis still isn't certain Lisutaris is going to make it. Rokim the Bright is still in the picture and Almalas has been taking votes from everyone.'

'Your companion Makri seems to be losing ground with Direeva.'

There's a certain tone in Sulinius's voice as he mentions Makri. When he becomes a Senator and gets his own villa, he's never going to let a woman with Orcish blood through the front door. Visus asks me about Sareepa and I admit I've made no progress.

'It's difficult. Sareepa's gone religious thanks to Almalas. Tilupasis should've given me more notice.'

'I managed to win over the Pargadan delegation in a single hour,' says Sulinius, grandly.

'That's because the Pargadans are notorious dwa addicts and you brought them a wagonload. Anyone could have done that.'

'Perhaps if you did not concern yourself with meddling in city politics…'

Sulinius is aware of my interfering with the Praetor's business. Not having any intention of apologising, I tell him sharply that if his father insists on throwing poor people out into the snow, he has to expect some opposition. 'And tell him if he tries sending any more men after me, then Lisutaris, Mistress of the Sky, will smite him with a plague spell.'

'Lisutaris would not come to your aid.'

'Oh no? I was fighting beside Lisutaris before you were born. She already blasted your father's thugs once. She'll help me again.'

I wonder if she really would. Having the Mistress of the Sky as head of the Sorcerers Guild would be no bad thing if she felt obligated to me for a few favours. Good reason to clear her name. Maybe I shouldn't have been rude to her. At least I wasn't violent. The great door opens and a flood of sorcerers, led by Irith Victorious, announce the end of the banquet. I hear him complaining about them only serving wine with the meal as he hastens towards the bar, showing surprising speed for a man of his size. 'Beer, and make it quick,' he yells at a waitress.

There are only a few hours left till the election. I take the opportunity to talk with the Matteshan sorcerer who once served as apprentice to Darius.

'I didn't kill him, if that's what this is about,' he states flatly. 'I was with the other Matteshan sorcerers when he was killed.'

That's not a great alibi. They'd lie for him if necessary.

'Darius got through a lot of apprentices. None of them liked him much better than I did. I'm not the only sorcerer who started off in Abelasi then went elsewhere after being sacked by Cloud Walker. My predecessor, Rosin-kar, swore he'd kill him one day. The one before him left in disgrace. I think he's with the Pargadans now.'

Tilupasis approaches me as I head back for the Room of Saints. 'How are things progressing with Sareepa?'

'Badly.'

'You must try again.'

'I'm busy looking for ex-apprentices of Darius. They seem to have spread round the world.'

'Work on Sareepa.'

'Doesn't anyone want me to solve this murder?'

'Of course,' says Tilupasis. 'But the hiding spell will work for a little longer. It is more important that Lisutaris performs well in the election.'

Makri rushes up and confronts Tilupasis. 'Can't you do something about this Troverus? He's sticking about as close as a poultice to Direeva. I can't get near the woman.'

'Keep trying,' instructs Tilupasis.

'Is that the best advice you have? It's not working. When you told me to charm Princess Direeva - and don't think I didn't notice there was something dubious in that whole concept - you didn't say I'd have a rival who wins prizes for being handsome.'

Faced with defeat, Makri clenches her fists in frustration. 'You can't trust a man as good-looking as that. He probably likes boys, right? Send him some boys to distract him.'

'He doesn't like boys. I made enquiries.'

'He doesn't? Well, send him some gold.'

Tilupasis shakes her head. 'Troverus is already wealthy. He doesn't want money.'

Makri explodes with anger. 'How come I'm the only one that's up against someone incorruptible? It's hardly fair. What am I meant to do?'

'You could sleep with him,' I suggest.

'I don't want to sleep with him. He's creepy. I'm here as a bodyguard, not a comfort woman.'

'I really must go,' says Tilupasis. 'The Pargadans need more dwa. I trust the two of you to work things out.'

'Is that what Tilupasis wants me to do?' says Makri. 'She can forget it. I'm not going to sleep with just any sorcerer that fancies a good time.'

'God help anyone who thinks he'd have a good time with you.'

'I didn't notice See-ath complaining,' retorts Makri. 'Anyway, your idea is stupid. Direeva isn't going to thank me for stealing her suitor, is she?'

A tall man in a toga greets Makri politely as he passes.

'Who's that?'

'A mathematician from Simnia. He's here with the delegation. He's the only civilised person I've met in this place. Yesterday he told about his work on prime number theory. Do you know–'

'Fascinating, Makri. Nothing interests me more than mathematics. I have work to do. Sareepa has twelve votes.'

'Direeva has thirty,' counters Makri, and we go our separate ways.

The election is drawing near. Time for one last attempt on Sareepa. She's sitting at one of the top tables in the main hall, placed there by Tilupasis to flatter her. Sareepa herself appears calm, but her fellow Matteshan sorcerers are unhappy. No doubt they've been forbidden by Sareepa to overindulge. I've never seen a group of sorcerers more in need of a drink. Most of the people in the hall are carrying on with their previous intemperate behaviour. Goblets, tankards and bottles glint in the light from the flaming torches on the walls, and it's obvious the Matteshans are aching to join in the fun. Tough break, arriving at the biggest binge in the sorcerers' calendar only to find that your leader has developed a puritanical streak.

I'm about to make one last desperate effort to end Sareepa's sober behaviour. Not just for the good of Turai. Sareepa Lightning-Strikes-the-Mountain has fallen under the thrall of Nioj. The woman needs help. I'm carrying a bottle of the finest klee Turai can offer. Distilled in the mountains, this liquid could burn a dragon's throat. They don't make liquor like this in Mattesh. Before Sareepa realises what's happening, I'm standing beside her at the table, pouring it into the empty glasses of her delegation.

'What do you think you're doing?' demands Sareepa Lightning-Strikes-the-Mountain.

'Part of my Tribunate duties. A toast to the King of Mattesh.'

At these words Sareepa's companions' eyes light up. No Matteshan can refuse a toast to the King. It would be disloyal. They raise their glasses and look towards their leader expectantly. Very reluctantly, Sareepa raises her goblet, all the while staring at me in a manner which would cause grave concern were I not wearing such a fine spell protection necklace. We drink. There is a moment's stunned silence as the fiery liquid hits their throats. Sareepa coughs. I fill up her goblet again in a manoeuvre so swift that only an expert at the bottle like myself could pull it off.

'A toast to the Queen!'

'The Queen!' yell the delegation, filling up their own glasses.

'A toast? To who?' enquires Sulinius, appearing at that moment, as I've asked him to.

'The Queen.'

Sulinius grabs a goblet. 'The Queen!!'

He drinks. Everybody drinks. You can't not drink when a foreigner is toasting your Queen.

'And the King!' says Sulinius, and drinks again.

I'm already filling glasses. 'To Mattesh!' I cry.

No Matteshan can refuse a toast to their country. It would be disloyal. We drink. I break open another bottle.

'Let me see that,' says Sareepa.

I hand it over.

'Interesting... from the mountains?'

'Yes. Finest quality.'

The sorcerers wait expectantly.

'A toast to the King,' says Sareepa, and starts pouring herself another large one.

An hour or so later, Sareepa Lightning-Strikes-the-Mountain is challenging the Simnians at the next table to a drinking contest. 'You Simnian dogs couldn't drink if you fell in a barrel of ale!'

Before leaving the Matteshan sorcerers I ask them if any of them have heard of a spell for making a new version of reality and sending it back into the past. None of them have.

'There's no such spell.'

I'm getting sick of hearing that.

Tilupasis and Cicerius are waiting for me in the Room of Saints.

'What happened with Sareepa?'

'I got her drunk. Better have the apothecary standing by. Klee laced with dwa has been known to cause fatalities.'

'And her votes?'

'Heading for Turai. By the third bottle she was cursing all Niojans.'

Tilupasis roundly congratulates me. 'It was a fine plan.'

'Sharp as an Elf's ear,' I mumble, and look round for a chair. Even by my standards, I've drunk a lot of klee. Makri is sitting at a table nearby, with Direeva and Troverus. Makri looks aggressive, Troverus looks unruffled and Direeva looks interested.

'I can out-drink any Simnian sorcerer,' declares Makri, and downs the goblet of klee in front of her. Troverus does the same. Makri refills the goblets. They drink again.

'No one likes a Simnian,' says Makri. 'Direeva is never going to be impressed with a weakling like you.'

A few goblets later, Makri's face goes a horrible shade of green and she is obliged to hurry from the room. I find her in the corridor, throwing up into a pot plant.

'Goddammit,' she gasps, still retching.

'You were never going to win a klee-drinking contest,' I say, and hunt around in my bag for a Lesada leaf to make her feel better. Makri takes the leaf and washes it down with my beer.

'I couldn't think of anything else. Everything I do, Troverus does better. He knows more about art and culture than me. He's been everywhere and done everything. Everything he says is witty. Princess Direeva is eating out of his hand. She's bound to vote for Ramius.'

As the leaf takes effect her colour returns to normal. I advise her to give up.

'Give up?'

'Why not? You don't really care who Direeva votes for.'

'It's not in my nature to give up,' says Makri, then vomits noisily into the pot plant again.

'I didn't become champion gladiator by giving up.'

She's sick once more. I wince. It's a painful sight.

'Give me another leaf.'

Makri hauls herself to her feet. 'I have an idea,' she says, and stumbles off in the direction of the Room of Saints. I follow on, interested to see what Makri's new strategy might be. Possibly some learned disquisition of political theory, learned from Samanatius? Makri weaves her way across to Direeva, knocking over several sorcerers on the way. She stands in front of Troverus, lays her hand on his rainbow cloak and yanks him to his feet.

'I'm getting really sick of you,' she says, and then punches him in the face hard enough for him to tumble unconscious to the floor. Princess Direeva looks startled.

'Don't vote for the Simnians,' says Makri to Direeva. 'I don't like them. Turai is a disgusting city but Lisutaris is a good woman and she's given you a lot of thazis.'

'And if I need military help?' says Direeva.

'Call on me,' says Makri, and slumps down beside her. 'I'll sort them out. Number one chariot at fighting.'

Irith Victorious is occupying a large couch in the corner. I take him a beer and join him in a final drinking session before his fellow sorcerers drag him off to vote. The Room of Saints empties. Makri appears at my side. She's unsteady on her feet and her speech is slurred.

'That seemed to go well,' she tells me.

In the distance, Troverus's companions are carrying him off.

'Do you want this couch?' says Makri.

'You can have it.'

'I don't need it. I've been practising with weapons. Stayed sober all day, more or less.'

Makri plummets to the floor. Electioneering. It's tough. I help her on to the couch then sink into a nearby chair where I doze off quite comfortably.

I awaken to the news that Sunstorm Ramius has won the vote, with Lisutaris in second place. Both of them will now go forward to the final test. Turai has accomplished the first part of its mission. Cicerius makes a gracious speech to everyone in the Room of Saints, thanking them for their support, and indicating that though most of the credit belongs to him, others were involved in an important capacity. Some time later Tilupasis arrives at our side. 'Congratulations to you both,' she says.

Makri wakes and vomits over the edge of the couch. She's not the drinker I am. Tilupasis is unperturbed, and motions to an assistant to bring a cleaner.

'I'll call a landus to take you home. As long as we can keep Lisutaris's name clear for another day, we're in with a chance of having a Turanian head of the Sorcerers Guild. Is the concealment spell holding up?'

'Yes.'

'How long will it last?'

'I don't know.'

'Why not?'

'I'm too drunk to think.'

Tilupasis smiles. She smiles a lot. I doubt she ever means it but it still seems to hide her insincerity. I help Makri to her feet and we head for the door. The sorcerers will now carry on with their celebrations but I need a rest. As we pass through the main hall, Hansius hurries up to us.

'Trouble,' he says, and motions for us to follow. He leads us to a room at the far end of the hall I've not been in before, a room reserved for the senior sorcerers. Inside, Old Hasius the Brilliant, Sunstorm Ramius, Lasat, Axe of Gold, and Charius the Wise are deep in conference with Cicerius. They're talking in low voices but I catch enough to know that we're in trouble.

'Lisutaris, Mistress of the Sky, killed Darius Cloud Walker.'

Cicerius protests. 'This is impossible.'

'We have seen clear pictures,' insists Ramius. 'She must be apprehended immediately.'

Ramius becomes aware of our presence. He ignores me, but when he sees Makri he recognises her immediately.

'That woman was in the room with Darius when he died. As was Princess Direeva. What has been happening in this city? Deputy Consul, are you going to send for the Guards or must I rouse the Council of Sorcerers to apprehend Lisutaris?'

At this moment Tilupasis strides confidently into the room. 'I have sent for Consul Kalius. He will be here shortly. Until then, this news must not be allowed to spread.'

'And why not?' demands Lasat.

'It may prejudice Lisutaris's chances in the final test.'

'The final test? Lisutaris will not be entering any final test. As Presiding sorcerer I am disqualifying her immediately.'

If Tilupasis has a reply to this, she saves it for now, but she motions for Hansius to shut the door.

'Consul Kalius will take care of the matter.'

Lasat, Axe of Gold, reluctantly agrees to await the arrival of Turai's highest official, but I can't see it doing anything but buying us a few minutes' grace. Lasat is not the sort of person to be pushed around by city officials. He's the leader of the Samsarinan Sorcerers Guild, the senior sorcerer present at the Assemblage, and one of the most powerful people in the West. He's not about to take orders from Tilupasis or Cicerius. He'd bring down the city wall before buckling under to a mere government official.

Beside me Makri still looks unwell. I wonder if she might be sick again. On one memorable occasion she threw up over Prince Dees Akan's sandals. Taking aim at the Consul's feet would certainly lighten things up. Vomiting over Lasat, Axe of Gold, would be even more sensational.

The noise of celebrating sorcerers drifts into the room, but we wait, quiet and grim, for Kalius to arrive.

Chapter Sixteen

Consul Kalius is the city's highest official. Praetor Samilius is head of the Civil Guard. Old Hasius the Brilliant is Chief Investigating Sorcerer at the Abode of Justice. Rittius is in charge of Palace Security and Orius Fire Tamer is his Senior Investigating sorcerer. Along with Lasat, Axe of Gold, Charius the Wise and Sunstorm Ramius, it makes for an impressive gathering. I don't like the way they're all looking at me.

'I firmly believe Lisutaris to be innocent.'

'We would like to believe you,' says Kalius.

'But we don't,' adds Ramius.

'What grounds do you have for thinking her to be innocent?'

Consul Kalius looks at me hopefully. I've got most of Turai's officialdom on my side. A rare occurrence. Unfortunately, it comes at a time when I'm faced with an almost impossible task. Now that Old Hasius the Brilliant and Lasat, Axe of Gold, have pierced the hiding spell, the pictures are very clear, and they never change. Lisutaris stabs Darius, every time. Praetor Samilius has enquired repeatedly of the sorcerers if there could be trickery involved, but they're adamant there could not be.

'No one possesses such power.'

'I told you, I discovered a spell that could do it.'

'You discovered it?' Ramius is cynical. Sorcerers never like to admit there might be spells they don't know.

'A spell to project false events into the past? It can't be done.'

'Well, not exactly project spells into the past. But a spell for erasing past events.'

Once more, I've had to explain my theory of a spell of erasement and a spell of making. To the non-sorcerers present it's confusing, and to the sorcerers it's unbelievable.

'I have checked repeatedly,' insists Old Hasius. 'And I firmly believe these to be the real events. If not, I would have located the true reality.'

'Not if it was erased.'

'Even if such an erasement spell was used successfully, how was the new reality created?'

'I don't know. But anyone who's good enough to do the first part might pull off the second. We can't be sure that Lisutaris committed the murder.'

I look round at the doubtful faces. The Turanian officials are desperate for Lisutaris to be innocent. Even against their better judgment they'd be willing to believe me, but I'm not making any impression on Lasat or Ramius. Cicerius, the most patriotic of Turanians, has hardly said a word. He's sitting in the corner looking as miserable as a Niojan whore, though that's not an expression I'd use to him right now, as Nioj is a sore point.

Almalas came third in the ballot. If Lisutaris is disqualified, he'll go into the final contest in her place. Not only will Turai suffer the monumental disgrace of having our candidate arrested for murder, we'll face the prospect of a hostile Head of the sorcerers Guild. Niojan or Simnian, neither one is going to rush to the aid of Turai.

'I feel you're not telling us everything,' says Samilius. The Praetor was appointed Civil Guard Chief as a political reward and he's not an experienced investigator, but he's shrewd enough. He suspects I've been involved in this more than I'm saying. So far no one realises that the murder took place in my rooms at the Avenging Axe, and I'm not about to enlighten them.

'I know no more than you,' I say. 'But I've been keeping close to Lisutaris since the Assemblage began and I'm sure she didn't kill Darius. She had no reason to.'

'We've seen her do it! In the presence of Princess Direeva and the other woman.'

'Both women of Orcish blood,' notes Sunstorm Ramius. 'I insist you inform the King and arrest Lisutaris.'

He looks to Lasat, Axe of Gold. The Senior sorcerer nods his head in agreement.

'We must at least wait till we hear what Lisutaris has to say,' says Cicerius. 'My assistant is looking for her now.'

At this moment Lisutaris arrives, accompanied by Hansius. Despite the gravity of the situation, the Mistress of the Sky remains calm. This might be due to thazis, but perhaps not. Back in the war, she never panicked under pressure. Before she can be questioned, Consul Kalius orders that those not directly involved be removed from the room. This means me, Makri and Tilupasis.

'Take them to a secure place and do not let them speak to anyone.' We're led away by a sergeant of the guard, through the main hall and along a short corridor to another room. I don't know if this performance fools anyone else, but it's obvious to me that the procedure has been worked out by Tilupasis and Kalius to give us some freedom to act. So it proves. Once secure in a private room, Tilupasis starts issuing orders.

'Makri. Go back and wait for Lisutaris. If they take her anywhere, follow them and make sure she's safe.'

Now that there's action afoot, Makri has ceased to look ill. She departs briskly. Tilupasis dismisses the sergeant.

'Did you get it?' she asks me.

'A good sorcerer could eavesdrop on our conversation.'

'Not here. We had this room lined with Red Elvish Cloth precisely for an occasion like this.'

Red Elvish Cloth forms a barrier to magic. No sorcerer can pry through it. It's fabulously expensive, and lining the room with it must have cost a fortune. I hand over a document. Tilupasis glances at it and seems satisfied. The document contains confidential details of an agreement between Lasat, Axe of Gold, and a wealthy Juvalian merchant named Berisat. They've been defrauding the King of Samsarina for the past three years by providing the royal mint with slightly impure gold. It's Lasat's job to test the purity of the metal used for Samsarina's coinage, and he's been illicitly letting the substandard gold through, and taking a healthy share of the profits. Getting my hands on the details cost me a great deal of effort, and Tilupasis a great deal of money.

'Is everything here?'

'I believe so.'

I pumped Irith Victorious for information when he was drunk. The Juvalians knew all about their merchant's shady dealings, though they were keeping the information for their own use. I hired a thief, who stealthily robbed the Juvalian delegation while they slept in their stupor. A successful operation, though what Samanatius the philosopher would say about the ethics of arranging for my own friends to be robbed, I don't like to think. I know what Gurd would say. He'd be disgusted.

'This should be sufficient to make Lasat cooperate,' says Tilupasis.

'Risky, don't you think? Blackmailing such a senior sorcerer?'

'I'll worry about the risk.'

'You won't be around to worry if Lasat decides to kill you.'

'Unlikely,' replies Tilupasis. 'Far easier to go along with Turai's natural desire to suppress the affair until it's been fully investigated.'

'What if Lasat just tells you to go to hell?'

'Then he's going to need all his sorcerous power to keep him from the scaffold once the King of Samsarina learns he's been defrauding the royal mint for the past three years.'

'I never figured Lasat as an embezzler.'

'He has a very bad dwa habit.'

'Really?'

'He keeps it quiet. This information will buy us time. Lasat will order Sunstorm Ramius not to reveal any details of the murder. Lisutaris will go forward into the final test tomorrow.'

I'm not especially happy at any of this. Though I generally leave ethics and morals to Makri, I can't help noticing I'm participating in blackmail to avoid the arrest of a murderer. 'Even if you keep Lasat quiet, you won't silence Sunstorm Ramius for ever. If Lisutaris beats him in the final test he'll squeal out loud that she's a murderer, no matter what Lasat says. Unless you have some way of blackmailing him too?'

Tilupasis shakes her head. 'Unfortunately, Sunstorm Ramius is free of any dark secrets. Don't think I haven't looked. You're right, it only buys us a little time. If Ramius loses the test he'll tell what he knows and every sorcerer in the west will have access to the pictures. Which means you have one more day to sort it out. So far all you've come up with is the possibility of an erasement spell. Not enough. We need the whole story and we need it quickly.'

I don't like the fact that I'm being lectured. I get enough of that from Cicerius. 'If you don't like my investigating, why didn't you ask someone else?'

'We have. You're not the only man currently trying to clear up this mess. None of you have come up with anything. It's time to get results.'

Tilupasis smiles at me. She's really well bred.

'So what have you got worked out for the final test?' I ask, as she makes to leave.

'Pardon?'

'The final test. Don't tell me you're going to leave it as a fair contest between Lisutaris and Ramius?'

'Lisutaris would stand an excellent chance of winning such a contest.'

'Maybe. But she'd stand more chance if Turai was planning to cheat on her behalf.'

'The nature of the test is still secret. It will be set by Charius the Wise. So far he's proved to be annoyingly incorruptible. We're still working on it,' says Tilupasis before departing to blackmail the Senior sorcerer in the west. I hope he never learns that I was involved. Lasat could blast me away without blinking an eye.

I shake my head. I've sobered up. I don't like it. I don't like anything. It's pretty clear why I was recruited for this job. No one would expect me to refuse to do anything shady provided I was paid well enough. A real sorcerer with loyalty to the guild wouldn't have been any use. The man they required had to know something about magic but never have been good enough to be admitted to the Sorcerers Guild. He needed to be keen enough for money to not mind much what he did to earn it. He needed to be not above using people for his own ends. I sigh. I'm the ideal man for the job.

I walk all the way home through the terrible winter. Back at the Avenging Axe I sit morosely in my room in front of the fire, staring at the shapes in the flames. After a while I get out my niarit board and play through a game. I drink some beer and stare out of the window. The sky is dull and overcast, same as it has been for weeks. It's getting me down. There's a knock at the door. I wrench it open. If it's the Brotherhood or Praetor Capatius's men come looking for trouble, that's fine with me. It's Samanatius the philosopher. That's not so fine. He asks if he can come in.

Samanatius is around sixty, fairly well preserved. His white hair and beard are well trimmed. He's dressed in a cheap cloak and his tunic has seen better days. Neither are suitable for the fierce weather but he doesn't appear to be suffering. He politely refuses my offer of beer.

'Forgive my intrusion. I wanted to thank you for your help. Many people would have suffered had the eviction been allowed to happen.'

I'm not in any mood for taking credit. I tell Samanatius in the plainest terms that I only helped because Senator Lodius blackmailed me into it.

'I know this already,' says Samanatius. 'But we still owe you thanks. I have no doubt that if you wished, you could have found a way to avoid coming to our aid. I am now in your debt. Please do not hesitate to ask if I can ever do you a favour.'

The philosopher bows, and departs as abruptly as he arrived. I don't quite know what to make of it. Or what to make of the man. I'm not feeling any sudden urge to join his philosophy school but I didn't dislike him as much as I thought I would.

The stain of blood is still visible on my rug. Darius Cloud Walker was killed right here in my room. So far I've done nothing about it. I should have made more progress. I should have spent more time investigating and less time drinking. I have to find out the truth. It's what I was hired to do. I banish all distractions from my mind, then sit down and think, for a long time.

Chapter Seventeen

I wake up in my chair with a bottle in my lap and a pain in my neck. It's morning. The fire has gone out and my room is freezing. Princess Direeva is sitting on the couch, reading my book of spells.

'Very out of date,' she says. 'Sorcery has moved on since this was written.'

'I haven't.'

'You never qualified. Why not?'

'I was never good at studying. Why are you here?'

My doors are secured with a locking spell, but a sorcerer like Direeva can walk right through any of my minor incantations.

'Are you cold?' she asks, as she sees me shiver.

'Yes.'

Direeva waves her hand. My fire bursts into life.

'Very clever. You got a spell for tidying my room?'

'I have,' says Direeva. 'But you wouldn't like it.'

'I take it you didn't come to Twelve Seas just to demonstrate your power?'

'Lighting a fire requires very little power. I really wonder why you didn't pursue your apprenticeship.'

'Change the subject. First thing in the morning, I hate talking about me failing.'

'As you wish.'

The Princess has never shown any signs of liking me. Sitting in my office she still has something of a disdainful air, as if she'd rather be elsewhere. It's annoying. It's not like I asked her to visit. She's welcome to go and disdain somewhere else. I ask her if news of Lisutaris's detection as a murderer has reached the ears of the Assemblage. It hasn't. Apparently Tilupasis has succeeded in silencing Lasat, Axe of Gold. You have to admire that woman. It takes nerve to blackmail a sorcerer.

'As far as the Assemblage knows, Lisutaris is in the happy position of coming second in the election and is now about to face the final test. That's why I'm here. I'm concerned for her safety. Covinius may decide that the magic space is a very good place in which to kill her.'

I don't understand this. Lisutaris and Sunstorm Ramius will enter the magic space to carry out the final test, whatever that may be, but the magic space in question will not be open to the public.

'Charius the Wise will create the magic space when he sets the test. No one else will be there.'

'Is Covinius not the master assassin?' says Direeva. 'May he not have means of following them? A person can die in the magic space just as well as anywhere else. The unpredictability of the dimension could make even a strong sorcerer like Lisutaris vulnerable to attack.'

There's something in what the Princess says. Outside, Covinius couldn't fire a dart into Lisutaris. Her protection spells would deflect it. But in magic space, they might not. Nothing is ever certain there. It's not a good place to visit.

I pile a few more logs into the hearth. I'll miss it when these sorcerers are no longer around to light my fire.

'I intend to follow Lisutaris into the magic space,' says Direeva. 'That way I can watch over her.'

'Since when are you so concerned about Lisutaris? Only yesterday you weren't even sure who you were going to vote for.'

'Makri won me over with her strong arguments,' says Direeva, and almost smiles. I doubt this is the whole truth. Direeva's father, the elderly ruler of the Southern Hills, probably isn't going to last much longer. Quite possibly Turai has secretly offered the Princess aid if she decides to dispute the succession with her brother.

'I never really cared for the Simnian,' says Direeva. 'Lisutaris will be a better Head of the Guild.'

'Charius and Lasat won't allow anyone else into the magic space.'

'I believe I can secretly open a portal. Before Lisutaris starts the test I will use a spell to connect us.'

'How difficult is that? Could other sorcerers do it?'

'Possibly.'

I've wondered for a while why Sunstorm Ramius and his Simnian delegation haven't been doing more in the way of bribery. They've seemed content to let Turai do its worst. Almost as if they were confident of winning the final test no matter what. Direeva's notion makes me wonder if they might be planning to send some help of their own into the magic space.

'If you're going in I want to come with you.'

'You do? I was thinking more of Makri.'

'No doubt she'll insist on coming as well.'

The dragon scales in Direeva's hair glint in the firelight, casting small flashes of reflected colour on to the walls.

'Ever work a spell with those dragon scales?'

Direeva shakes her head. 'No. I just use them to decorate my hair. Where is Makri?'

'I don't know. Last time I saw her she was going to watch Lisutaris's back. If Lisutaris hasn't been denounced as a murderer she should be with her in her villa.'

'Then we should go there,' suggests Direeva. 'And make preparations.'

I stretch. My neck hurts. I shouldn't fall asleep in chairs. I wonder if Direeva could fix it with a spell. I'm not going to ask. I'm hungry. I'd go and buy pastries from Minarixa's bakery if Minarixa wasn't dead from dwa. I get my cloak. It's cold. I don't warm it up. I don't want to show my poor magical skills in front of a major sorcerer. I take a quick beer from downstairs and ask Tanrose to throw some salted venison in a bag for me. Direeva has a carriage outside, driven by two of her attendants, each bearing the insignia of the royal house of the Southern Hills. They're grim men, and remain silent on the journey. I poke around in my bag and take out a hunk of venison. Direeva looks startled.

'I did not invite you to eat in my carriage.'

'I didn't invite you to interrupt my breakfast.'

'I don't allow people to speak to me like that in the Southern Hills.'

'Since you got drunk and collapsed on my floor, I figure I don't have to worry about etiquette.'

I'm angry. Angry that I'm making no progress. And angry at Direeva for thinking she can waltz into my rooms without an invitation. Direeva is displeased at my lack of civility and we ride in silence to the villa. There we find various servants, but no sign of Lisutaris or Makri.

'Copro is attending to the Mistress of the Sky.'

We wait in silence. It's the day of the final test and I can already feel some tension. I don't trust the Simnians. And Covinius will finally show his face, I'm sure.

Cicerius is expecting me to come up with something to clear Lisutaris. I haven't. It's a long time since I failed so badly on an important case. Makri arrives downstairs after ten minutes or so. Although her nails are freshly painted, she's frowning. Makri knows that she's in for a hard time if it all goes wrong and she finds herself being interrogated by the Civil Guard. The guards are not going to go easy on an alien woman with Orcish blood who can't come up with a good explanation as to why her knife was sticking in the corpse.

'I'll kill them all and leave the city,' she mutters. 'I don't suppose you've achieved a fantastic breakthrough?'

'Not yet. But I have good news. We're sneaking into the magic space to help Lisutaris in the test.'

'Good,' says Makri. 'Will it clear her name?'

'No. I'm still working on that.'

Direeva expresses some doubts about my powers of investigation. 'A woman could die waiting for you to help. What have you done so far?'

'A lot of thinking.'

'And?'

'And now I need a beer. How long till Lisutaris is ready?'

Makri isn't sure. 'She had a new outfit planned for the final test but Copro was doubtful about the whole concept. They're still discussing shoes.'

'I liked the gold ones she wore yesterday,' says Direeva.

'Me too,' says Makri. 'but they clash with the new necklace.'

I take a goblet of wine and wonder about the final test. Last time the sorcerers elected a new leader, the two candidates had to sorcerously dam a magical river which doubled in volume every two minutes. The winner brought down a mountain to act as a barrier, but some say it was lucky that the mountain just happened to appear in the magic space at the right time.

'Lisutaris will need her wits about her. Is she staying off the water pipe?'

'No.'

'She should be.'

'Well, she isn't.'

'Couldn't you encourage her?'

'Why me?' says Makri, becoming belligerent.

'You're her bodyguard.'

'She's still alive, isn't she?'

'No thanks to you.'

'What do you mean by that?'

'I mean as a bodyguard you're as much use as a one legged gladiator. When the Brotherhood knocked on my door you were unconscious, and when Capatius's thugs attacked us you collapsed in a heap.'

Makri is irate. 'Stop bringing that up. Who saved you last year when we were attacked by Orcs? Who defeated Yulis-ar-Key? He was about to chop your head off till I tossed him off that balcony.'

'I'd have managed.'

'Only if Yulis had stopped for a beer.'

'Do you have to argue all the time?' says Direeva, angrily.

'Who asked you to get involved?' I retort, aggressively.

'Who is it that is going to take us into the magic space?'

'I'd have found a way in anyway.'

'The only thing you'd find would be Lisutaris's wine cellar.'

Our nerves are beginning to fray. Fortunately Lisutaris arrives downstairs in time to prevent us from becoming violent. When we arrive at the Assemblage the atmosphere is unusually tense. The sorcerers are quieter. Whether this is because they've heard some ugly rumours or just because on this day they are required to tone down the celebrating, I don't know, but even Irith Victorious looks subdued. Cicerius practically bites my head off when I'm forced to report no progress on the murder.

'You think this is easy?' I protest. 'I'm trying to unravel a sorcerous plot the like of which no one has ever encountered before. Someone very smart entered my office to kill Darius and no one even knows why. Don't forget everything else I've had on my plate, like helping Tilupasis bribe our way to victory. And guarding Lisutaris against Covinius, whoever the hell Covinius is. When you gave me the job you didn't mention the Simnians had hired an Assassin to kill our candidate.'

'I am still not certain that is the case,' says the Deputy Consul.

'I am. Lisutaris knows that Sunstorm Ramius hired an assassin, and that's good enough for me.'

Sulinius hurries into the private room, looking harassed.

'How dare you arrive late on such an important day,' declares the Deputy Consul.

'Visus is dead,' gasps Sulinius.

'Dead?'

'A dwa overdose. Last night.'

Sulinius seems on the verge of tears at the death of his young companion. Cicerius is speechless.

'I'll see that it's kept quiet,' says Tilupasis, and leaves the room in a hurry. Cicerius recovers swiftly and tells Sulinius to pull himself together. 'It is time for all Turanians to do their duty.'

All the Turanians who appear in the Deputy Consul's room are already stressed from doing their duty. Praetor Samilius is resentful that he wasn't informed of events earlier, but he sullenly admits that none of his investigators have found out anything about anything. Old Hasius the Brilliant, briefly visiting before going to help with the final test, informs us sharply that he still believes Lisutaris to be guilty.

'I don't know why Lasat is allowing her to continue,' he says. 'But I do know that it is pointless.'

'The King's administration does not believe it to be pointless,' says Cicerius.

'Then the administration is acting more foolishly than usual.'

The Deputy Consul glares at Hasius, but the sorcerer is far too old and venerable to be intimidated by anyone. When Consul Kalius arrives, Hasius reminds him that he'd said all along that Lisutaris was not a suitable candidate. From the look on Kalius's face, he probably agrees, but he's stuck with it now.

The test is due to start in one hour. Charius will call Lisutaris and Ramius and the three of them will step into the mouth of the magic space. Charius will then give them their task. I draw Cicerius aside for a private word and inform him that Direeva believes she can penetrate the magic space. Cicerius is pleased, though he expresses some concern.

'If Turai is found to have interfered with the test, Lisutaris will be disqualified.'

'Direeva thinks she can get us in unobserved.'

Tilupasis returns from hushing up the death of Tribune Visus. 'An unfortunate occurrence.'

'Very,' agrees Cicerius. 'Young men should stay clear of dwa.'

I find this hard to take. 'Stay clear? He was practically ordered to take it. You ought to give him a medal, he died in the line of duty.'

'So you will enter the magic space with Direeva and Makri?' says Tilupasis, briskly ignoring my barb.

'That's the plan. If Covinius the Assassin arrives Direeva will distract him. Meanwhile Makri protects Lisutaris and I do whatever I can to help. If Sunstorm Ramius looks like he's winning, he's going to find me in his face. Have you managed to find out anything about the test?'

Tilupasis shakes her head. Charius has continued to be incorruptible.

'It might not matter. Lisutaris could probably dam a magic river as well as Ramius, providing she isn't too intoxicated.'

'And is she?'

'She's coming round.'

In the main hall the sorcerers are gathered in their delegations. Sobriety prevails, as is traditional. Even the most hardened hedonists are strongly discouraged from enjoying themselves while the test is in progress. I notice Irith and his large companions sitting at a table at the far side of the room. I'd like to greet them but I hesitate. I was discreet when I pumped them for information, and even more discreet when I arranged for the theft of their papers, but sorcerers often have finely developed intuition. I'd be surprised if they didn't work out what I was about, eventually.

So far at the Assemblage there has been little ceremony since the King's welcoming speech. Today is rather different, and once again all non-sorcerers are banished from the main hall as the two candidates approach the tall robed figures of Lasat, Axe of Gold, and Charius the Wise. Charius has a small globe in his hand, the artefact which he'll use to create the magic space. The last thing I see is Lisutaris laying her hand on the globe while the entire Guild looks on in silence. In a way, it's a sacred moment. I hurry to Cicerius's private room to get on with the business of corrupting it. Princess Direeva and Makri are already there. Makri reports that Lisutaris's mind is clear. 'I managed to get her focused.'

Direeva waves her hand to silence us. 'We must enter now.'

'Shouldn't we give them a start?'

'Not if you want to find out what the test is. Now be silent.'

Direeva takes a small fragment of dragon scale from her hair and holds it in the palm of her hand. She stares at it for a few seconds then mutters a sentence in one of the arcane sorcerers' languages. The room goes cool. An aura of green light forms round the dragon scale, growing in size till it's the height of a man.

'Let us go,' says the Princess, and steps into the light.

Makri walks quickly in behind her. I hesitate for a second. The magic space isn't a place I really want to visit again. I turn to

Cicerius. 'I'm adding this to my bill,' I say, then tramp forward into a place where the sun is a vile shade of purple and we're surrounded on all sides by a tall hedge.

'Where's the talking pig?' asks Makri, looking around.

The last time we were in the magic space we met a pig which was, as I remember, a fairly intelligent creature.

'It won't be here. We're in a different part of magic space.' I'm suddenly doubtful. 'Or are we? Is all magic space the same place?'

'Sort of,' replies Direeva, unhelpfully. 'This is the Maze of Aero. Do not separate or you will become lost. Remain silent while I bring us close to the entry point of the others.'

Direeva leads us through the maze. It's hard to keep our bearings as we're surrounded on all sides by the huge hedge. Everywhere looks the same but Direeva seems to know where she's going. Finally, after some twisting and turning, she leads us to a clearing wherein there is a small pool. On the other side of the pool a green light is beginning to glow. Direeva motions for us to withdraw behind the foliage. So far this magic space seems to be behaving itself reasonably well. The sun is a horrible colour but the hedge isn't doing anything weird. Not turning into giant mushrooms, for instance. You can't trust this place, though. If we get out without encountering an erupting volcano I'll count myself lucky. From behind the hedge I hear voices, first that of Charius the Wise.

'You are now in the Maze of Aero. Here is your test.'

'What is this?' enquires Lisutaris.

'A sequence of numbers,' replies Charius. 'Your task is to find the next number in the sequence and bring it to me. The first person to do so will be the winner.'

'What sort of test is that?' demands Lisutaris, sounding displeased.

'It is the test I have set you.'

'I'm not a mathematician. I do not count this as a proper test.'

There is no sound of protest from Sunstorm Ramius. Maybe he's a mathematician. Or maybe he's about to cheat. Already I'm highly suspicious. I peer round the hedge. Charius is disappearing into the green light and Ramius is exiting through the opposite gap in the hedge. Lisutaris, Mistress of the Sky, is dragging a large water pipe out of her personal magic pocket.

'That's not going to help,' I say, stepping forward.

Lisutaris looks round. 'Nothing's going to help. Look at this.'

She hands over a sheet of parchment. On it are written the numbers 391, 551, 713.

'Anyone know what the next number might be?'

No one knows.

'It seems like an odd sort of test,' says Direeva.

'Don't you know, Makri? You study mathematics.'

'I'll try and work it out,' says Makri, but she looks puzzled.

'You do that,' says Lisutaris, and takes hold of the water pipe.

'For God's sake, you can't just give up,' I shout. 'Not after all the effort we went to, to get you here. Do something.'

'What? I'm no good at numbers.'

'Summon up a mathematical spirit or something.'

'There's no such thing.'

'There must be some magical way of finding the next number. Otherwise Charius wouldn't have set it as a test.'

Direeva wonders, like me, if this might have been arranged in some way for Ramius to win. Perhaps the Simnians didn't bother bribing the sorcerers because they'd already bribed Charius.

'If he walks back in here in thirty seconds with the right number, I'm going to be pretty suspicious.'

A unicorn walks by. We ignore it.

'Maybe they have mathematical spirits in Simnia.'

'Maybe,' says Lisutaris. 'But not in Turai. I'm stumped.'

She lights the water pipe. I can't believe she's giving up so easily. Direeva suddenly makes a warning sound. Close to us, a green light is starting to glow. We all hurry behind the hedge, and peer round the edge just in time to see a dark shape disappearing into the forest.

'Covinius!' whispers Princess Direeva. 'He's come, as I thought he would.'

'Are you sure that was Covinius? I couldn't see his face.'

'Who else would it be?' Direeva steps forward. 'I will take care of him. Lisutaris, you must do what you can with the test.'

With that Direeva strides off. I turn to Makri. 'Stay here with Lisutaris.'

'Where are you going?'

'I'm going to see what I can find.'

'You'll get lost.'

'No I won't. I know all about sorcerous mazes. Maybe if I can rustle up a talking pig he'll know the next number in the sequence.'

'The next number,' grumbles Lisutaris. 'The whole thing is ridiculous. Who knows anything about mathematics?'

'Simnian sorcerers, perhaps.'

Lisutaris sits down. 'It's not a fair test,' she mutters, sounding irritatingly like a schoolchild. 'I was expecting to be damming a river. Or building a mountain. I could have done that.'

'Fair or not, we have to find it quick, before Ramius. I'm damned if I've come this far just to let a Simnian win.'

Lisutaris doesn't seem to care. She's given up. Her hair is still beautifully styled. At a reception at the Palace, other women would be eyeing her with envy.

Chapter Eighteen

I set off through the Maze of Aero, leaving Makri to guard Lisutaris. I'm guessing that despite her firm intentions of remaining sober, Makri will soon join in on the water pipe. It's a deficiency in her character, brought about by having pointed ears. It will serve them right if Covinius kills Direeva and then chops their heads off. Some bodyguard. Ever since Makri started blubbering about that damned Elf See-ath she's been as much use as a one-legged gladiator. Was that really Covinius who appeared? Direeva seemed certain, but so what? I don't trust her. I don't trust anyone. Lisutaris is a disaster. Makri's unreliable. Cicerius is hopeless. Tilupasis is a joke. Praetor Samilius couldn't investigate the theft of a baby's rattle. Everyone in Turai is useless. If it wasn't for me the city would have fallen long ago. I get out my sword and march through the maze. I dislike mazes, magical or not. They're irritating and pointless. Trust Charius the Wise to send us here. I turn a corner and almost bump into a small figure I recognise. It's Hanama, garbed in black, with a knife in her hand.

'You're not supposed to be here,' I tell her.

'Neither are you,' she replies.

'I've got more right than you.'

'No you haven't.'

'I'm a Tribune of the People. You're just an assassin.'

'Since when could a Tribune of the People - an honorary title at best - interfere with the sacred final test of the Sorcerers Guild?'

'Since I decided it was my duty.'

'Your duty? Very amusing. Step aside, investigator.'

'What are you doing here?'

'Protecting Lisutaris. So I have no time to talk,' says Hanama, and walks past. I stare at her retreating figure.

'I've got more right to be here than you!' I roar. 'I'm a Tribune!'

Hanama is now out of sight. Damn these Assassins. Always turning up when you don't want them. I walk on. By Hanama's standards she was quite talkative. Maybe she's warming to me. Another unicorn appears. Or maybe it's the one I saw earlier. They all look much the same. It trots in my direction. Perhaps it can help. In the magic space, anything is possible. The sun's just gone green, and the daisies are up to my waist.

'Greetings, unicorn. Have you seen a Simnian sorcerer called Sunstorm Ramius?'

The unicorn regards me in silence.

'About so high,' I say, waving my hand. 'Probably scowling.'

Behind me there's a burst of raucous laughter. 'He's trying to question a unicorn!'

I spin round. Quite a large squirrel is laughing at me.

'Don't you know unicorns can't talk?'

'I figured it was worth a try. I don't suppose you've seen Ramius?'

'The Simnian sorcerer? Ex-soldier type? I've seen him.'

The squirrel looks at me keenly. 'Do you have any thazis?'

'Yes, as it happens.'

I take out a stick and hand it over.

'Take the next right then keep to the left,' says the squirrel, then bounds off, thazis clutched tightly in one claw.

I walk on. I've just bribed a large squirrel with thazis. It's fine, if you don't think about it too much. The breeze is picking up and the daisies are still growing. It's getting colder. I think I hear voices so I creep forward quietly. When the voices grow louder I halt. Sunstorm Ramius is round the next corner.

'You have the question?'

'I do.'

There's the sound of paper passing from one hand to another. I risk a glance. Ramius is conferring with a tall man in a toga who talks with a Simnian accent. It's the mathematician Makri encountered at the Assemblage. This is outrageous behaviour. The final test is meant to be sacred. Like I always say, you can't trust a Simnian. The scholar studies Ramius's paper. Quill in hand, he makes some calculations.

'Hurry,' hisses Ramius. 'Lisutaris is already working on the problem.'

The scholar looks at him coldly. 'I am the finest mathematician in the west. No one will find the answer faster than I.'

He carries on scribbling. I'm tempted to advance and confront them with their perfidy. Without doubt Charius the Wise has been bribed to set some numerical test, and the Simnians had their mathematician ready to lend assistance. If Ramius wins I'm denouncing him as the fraud I've always known him to be.

Finally the mathematician seems satisfied. 'The answer is—'

Ramius silences him. 'Don't say it. Lisutaris may be listening. You can't trust these Turanians. Write it down and show it to me quickly.'

The scholar does as he's told. Ramius glances briefly at the answer then instructs him to take the paper away with him. The sorcerer pulls a small globe from a pocket in his cloak, waves his hand over it, and the familiar green light grows till it's large enough for his companion to step into, back to the real world. As Ramius turns round I withdraw quickly out of sight. Next second he marches round the corner and bumps into me. I beat him on the head with the pommel of my sword and he collapses in a heap.

'I'm appalled,' I say, staring at his prone figure. 'You Simnians, you're all cheats. And you were no use in the war.'

I hurry off as fast as I can. The air goes suddenly icy, and snow starts to fall. Winter has arrived in the magic space. That's all I need. A fierce wind blows the snow into my eyes. I curse. Ramius won't be out for long. If only the mathematician had written down the answer, I'd have stolen it. Maybe back in Turai there's someone who could work it out. That means getting out of here quickly. I need to find Direeva. The icy wind hinders my progress. I'm not wearing my magic warm cloak. Soon I'm as cold as the ice queen's grave and cursing all places magical where you can't depend on the weather to be consistent for two minutes.

The hedges have been flickering, threatening to disappear but never quite going. I'm concentrating on following my path back to Lisutaris and it doesn't immediately register that the hedge on my left has shrunk to just two feet tall. As I glance round, I catch sight of a figure walking along the next path. The snow is flying in my eyes, visibility is poor and I can't be certain, but I'd swear that the person I see is Copro, beautician to the aristocracy. He's carrying a crossbow. Immediately I attempt to leap the hedge. Unfortunately it chooses that moment to grow back to normal size and I bounce off with a face full of prickly leaves.

'Copro?' I mutter. 'With a crossbow?'

By dint of some fine navigational skills I bring myself back to where Lisutaris, Mistress of the Sky, and Makri are sitting beside the water pipe. I tell them what just happened.

'They brought in the mathematician?' says Makri. 'That's really unfair.'

'Didn't I say you can't trust a Simnian?'

'Yes, hundreds of times.'

'What's this about Copro?' asks Lisutaris.

'He's walking around the maze with a crossbow.'

'You imagined it.'

'Why would I do that?'

'Because we're in the magic space, where nothing is certain, and also there's a heavy snowstorm affecting visibility.'

Lisutaris is annoying me so much these days. I can't believe I ever liked her.

'I tell you it was Copro. Where's Direeva? I need to get out of here to find someone back in Turai who can answer the question.'

'Like who?'

'I don't know. I'll go to the university and look for a professor.'

'That'll take too long,' says Makri. 'How about Samanatius?'

'Could he do it?'

'He's the finest philosopher in the west.'

'But can he do sums?'

Makri thinks so. 'I've been trying to work it out myself,' she adds. 'But I haven't got anywhere.'

'Where is Direeva? I have to get out.'

'Use salt,' says Makri, who remembers that on a previous occasion I brought us out of the magic space by sprinkling salt on the ground. I'm dubious about trying this again.

'It might collapse the whole magic space, and then what would happen to the test?'

'Wouldn't work anyway,' says Lisutaris, looking up from her pipe. 'Charius's magic space is different. Stronger.'

'Can you send me back to Twelve Seas?'

'Yes. But it'll create a large disruption in the magic field. Charius the Wise will know something has happened. If we want to be discreet, we need Direeva.'

The snow starts coming down more heavily. Lisutaris waves her hand and a fire appears beside her. Direeva walks into the clearing and collapses, blood spurting from a bad wound in her shoulder, caused by a crossbow bolt which is deeply embedded in the flesh.

'Who did it?'

Direeva didn't see her assailant's face.

'It was Copro!' I yell.

'Why did they hire this investigator?' gasps Princess Direeva. 'He gets more foolish every day.'

I ignore this. 'Can you get me back to Twelve Seas?' I ask Direeva, as Lisutaris tends to her wound. The Princess regards me with distaste but, ignoring her injury, concentrates briefly and opens a breach in the magic space.

'You've got five minutes till it closes,' she says, as I step through, emerging at the corner of Quintessence Street.

I step over the rubble into Samanatius's academy. Inside the dingy hall Samanatius is lecturing a group of students. I march through their midst and take a firm grip on the philosopher's arm, drawing him to one side. 'Samanatius, about that favour you owe me. I need to find the next number in this sequence and I need it right now. It's to help Lisutaris.'

Samanatius grasps my meaning immediately. He excuses himself from his students and examines the paper I've thrust under his nose. After thirty seconds or so he nods.

'A sequence of products of prime numbers, I believe.'

I'm expecting him to start scribbling some notes, but apparently Samanatius has the mental capacity to work it out in his head.

'One zero seven three,' he says.

'Are you sure?'

'Quite certain. The sequence is—'

'No time for that. Thanks for your help.'

I hurry out of the academy, impressed by Samanatius's mental powers. Maybe he deserves his reputation as philosophy's number one chariot. I'm glad I saved him from eviction. I wonder what he's like at working out odds on the races. The green portal of light is still visible in the street, now wavering slightly. I throw myself through it, arriving back in the magic space some way from the clearing. Copro the beautician is advancing towards me, crossbow in his hand.

'So it's you!' I roar. 'You're Covinius. I've suspected this all along. It's a fine disguise, assassin, but not fine enough to fool Thraxas the Investigator.'

The maze alters again and I find myself on my own, surrounded on every side by vegetation. I swing my sword desperately in an effort to cut my way through to Lisutaris before Covinius can reach her. The hedge in front of me bursts apart and Makri appears, axe in hand.

'What's going on? The hedge just started growing all over us.'

'Did you see Copro?'

'Are you still on about that?' says Makri.

'I tell you, he's the assassin.'

'Why would he be? He's a hair stylist.'

'I've had my eye on him for a long time. He didn't fool me with his deft make-up and effeminate ways. The man is a deadly killer. Where's Lisutaris?'

'I don't know.'

'Then keep chopping.'

'This is more like the magic space I remember,' says Makri, as penguins start to wander through the snow. 'Do you have the answer?'

'Yes.'

'So have I,' says Makri.

I pause for a moment. 'What?'

'I have the answer. I worked it out.'

Makri looks pleased with herself. I'm irritated. 'It took you long enough. Couldn't you have done that before I set off?'

We start chopping through the maze again, calling for Lisutaris.

'You might give me some credit,' says Makri.

'What for?'

'For solving the puzzle.'

'I solved it first.'

'You didn't solve it at all,' contests Makri. 'You just asked Samanatius.'

'I got the answer, didn't I?'

Makri rests her axe. 'You're really getting on my nerves these days, Thraxas. Everything is always about you: *I did this, I did that.* Do you have any idea how tedious it is having to listen to your stories all the time? If it's not that, it's some vapid criticism of me for getting on with my life. I tell you, it's about time–'

'Will you stop acting like a pointy-eared Orc freak and keep chopping?'

Makri glares at me. The hedge beside us splits apart in a sheet of yellow flame and we find ourselves confronted by an angry-looking Sunstorm Ramius.

'Thraxas hit you on the head,' says Makri. 'I had nothing to do with it.'

Ramius hurls a spell at me. My protection charm saves my life but I'm tossed to the ground and lie in a heap. Seeing that I'm still alive, Ramius draws a sword and charges forward. He's almost upon me when Makri leaps forward and pounds him on the head with the flat of her axe.

'Apologise for calling me a pointy-eared Orc freak,' demands Makri.

I struggle to my feet. 'Are you crazy? There's no time.'

Suddenly Hanama appears.

'Hanama,' says Makri. 'Do you think it's right that this fat drunk can just go around insulting me all the time?'

'What are you asking her for?' I scream. 'She's an assassin, she doesn't care.'

'I resent the way you always imply I have no feelings,' says Hanama.

'Oh for God's sake, who's responsible for this? Is the Association of Gentlewomen driving you all insane?'

'I'm not familiar with them,' says Hanama.

'Never been to a meeting,' claims Makri.

We start hewing our way through the still-growing vegetation.

'I need a new place to live,' says Makri to Hanama. 'It's hell in the Avenging Axe with Thraxas rolling around drunk all the time. It's putting me off my food.'

The hedge in front of us once more erupts in flame. I get ready to fight, but rather than Ramius it's Lisutaris who appears, with Princess Direeva leaning on her shoulder.

'I still don't believe that Copro is Covinius,' says the sorcerer.

'Copro?' exclaims Hanama. 'Copro the beautician is Covinius?'

'According to Thraxas,' says Makri. 'But you know how untrustworthy he is.'

Makri asks Direeva if it could have been Copro who shot her but as the Princess didn't see her assailant's face, she can't say for sure.

'The bolt caught me unawares. My protection charm deflected it enough to save my life.'

'If he's the assassin, why didn't he try and kill me when he was doing my hair?' asks Lisutaris.

'Maybe professional ethics forbade it. We should discuss this later. Right now we have to get out of here. Ramius is unconscious and I have the answer, so if we can get back to Charius, you win the test.'

Seeing the sense in this, Lisutaris starts burning away the huge hedge that surrounds us and we make progress back towards the clearing. The snow has now stopped but the ground is frozen, and we slip and slide as we go. High in the sky the sun has gone blue and shrunk to a fraction of its normal size, as if mocking us. By this time Direeva is looking less than healthy. Blood is still seeping from her shoulder. I ask her if she has enough power left to get us discreetly home without alerting Charius. She thinks so.

'Here's the clearing,' cries Makri.

'There's Ramius,' cries Lisutaris.

He's dead. The Simnian sorcerer is lying in the clearing with a great gash in his neck. I turn to Lisutaris and demand to know if she killed him. She denies it. I shake my head. Just like she didn't kill Darius. 'It would have made my job a lot simpler if you'd told me you were going to butcher all your opponents. I'd have planned accordingly.'

'I have not killed anyone,' insists the Mistress of the Sky. 'Although this is going to be hard to explain to the Sorcerers Guild. They get suspicious if someone dies in the final test.'

'Don't worry,' I say. 'If things look bad for you, I'll just tell them you were too stoned to walk, let alone kill Ramius.'

'Is that a criticism?'

'You're damned right it's a criticism. When this is over I never want to see you and your water pipe again. And that includes Makri, Hanama and Direeva.'

I'm still annoyed that no one believes me about Copro. To hell with them all.

'I don't understand this,' says Makri. 'I thought it was Ramius who hired the assassin?'

'It was,' asserts Lisutaris.

'So why did he kill Ramius?'

'We don't know an assassin killed Ramius,' I point out, and incline my head towards Lisutaris.

Direeva starts preparing our exit. Lisutaris glares at me. 'You have to tell me the answer to the final test now,' she says, stiffly.

'Of course. Yet another thing I've sorted out for you.'

'So what is it?'

I open my mouth, then close it again. I've forgotten. The excitement has driven the answer out of my head. I stare at Lisutaris helplessly.

Makri guffaws with laughter. 'He's forgotten it. *Ha ha ha!* The big investigator forgot the answer. Thraxas, you're as much use as a one-legged gladiator. The talking pig was smarter than you.'

Makri turns to Lisutaris. 'Fortunately I worked out the solution. In my head. Using my mathematical skills. I didn't have to cheat like Thraxas, going to see Samanatius. I worked it out myself. I'm far smarter than he is. I worked it out by–'

'Perhaps you could tell me now?' suggests Lisutaris. 'I think Princess Direeva is about to faint.'

'It's 1073.'

With the last of her strength Direeva creates a portal for us to leave the magic space while Lisutaris makes a door of her own to take her back to the Assemblage. We take a last look at the body of Sunstorm Ramius, then depart.

'I still don't believe Copro is Covinius,' says Hanama, as we materialise back in Cicerius's private room. Cicerius is startled to see us arriving looking like we've been in a battle.

'Princess Direeva needs a doctor, and quick. We found the answer. Lisutaris will win the final test.'

'Excellent,' says Cicerius, meanwhile sending Hansius off for medical aid.

'Ramius is dead. His throat was cut.'

'That is not good.'

No one else was meant to be in the magic space, which leaves Lisutaris, Mistress of the Sky, as the only suspect.

'Tell me the details,' says Tilupasis.

Chapter Nineteen

My second meeting with Turai's leading officials is even more uncomfortable than the first.

'In brief, the situation is as follows,' says Consul Kalius. 'Lisutaris, Mistress of the Sky, has won the final test and is now due to be confirmed as Head of the Sorcerers Guild. Unfortunately she remains the main suspect for the murder of Darius Cloud Walker. Additionally, Sunstorm Ramius, one of the best-known sorcerers in the west, was killed during the test. Although you report that various other people had infiltrated the magic space, as far as the Sorcerers Guild is concerned there were only two people there - Ramius and Lisutaris. Naturally Lisutaris is now suspected of this murder.'

Kalius is worried. As Consul, he has a gold rim running round his toga. It's the only gold-rimmed toga in the whole city-state and he doesn't want to lose it. 'So what are we going to do?'

'Deflect criticism from Lisutaris,' replies Tilupasis promptly. 'There's no certainty that Ramius was murdered. People can die of natural causes in the magic space.'

'His throat was slit,' points out Kalius. 'It doesn't look natural. No one is going to believe he was attacked by a rogue unicorn. Who did kill him?'

'We believe the Simnian Assassin Covinius may be involved,' answers Tilupasis. 'I've already put this out as a rumour.'

'Why would a Simnian Assassin kill the Simnian sorcerer?'

'Internal politics?' suggests Cicerius, hopefully. 'Whatever the reason, we must spread the story that Covinius killed Ramius.'

Everyone agrees it's very unfortunate that Covinius chose this moment to attack Sunstorm Ramius. Had he killed him earlier in the week at the Assemblage, it wouldn't have looked so bad for Turai. With plenty of foreign sorcerers around we could have blamed anyone. Personally, I don't know what to think. Since learning that Simnia had hired an assassin I've been working on the assumption that he was here to kill Lisutaris. Now that doesn't seem to fit the facts, with Ramius being the victim. Unless Lisutaris really did kill Ramius, and the assassin felt unable to attack her in the magic space because of the presence of Direeva and Makri. Is Copro Covinius? I'm no longer sure, though he can't have been up to any good wandering around in the magic space with a crossbow. It has to have been him who shot Direeva.

I'd like to ask Hanama what she got up to after we parted, but Hanama has disappeared. Disappearing is a speciality of hers.

'How long do we have to sort this out?' asks Praetor Samilius.

'Six hours,' replies Tilupasis. 'Lisutaris is due to be confirmed as Head of the Guild this evening, but before that happens, Charius the Wise will denounce her as the killer. Nothing I can do will prevent him from speaking out at the confirmation.'

'Could we... eh... get to Charius?' suggests Samilius.

'No. He has resisted all our efforts and is now safely in the company of Lasat, Axe of Gold, and all the most powerful sorcerers in the Guild.'

Kalius asks Samilius if the Civil Guard have come up with anything useful. They haven't. All eyes turn to me.

'I have some leads. I'll get onto it.'

Not wishing to expose myself to further ridicule, I'm not planning on denouncing Copro till I have some proof against him. Though Turai's politicians aren't about to include me in their discussions of state policy, I'm well aware there's more riding on this now than just Lisutaris's welfare. The city state of Turai is small. We have gold which other nations crave. If Simnia was looking for an excuse to make war on us, the murder of their Chief Sorcerer isn't a bad one. If the Abelasians decide to join them because of Darius, Turai isn't going to be the safest place for a man to live.

So far all my efforts have come to nothing. Maybe I should have been more determined in questioning the sorcerers. I might have been if I hadn't been forced to spend time pumping the Juvalians for dirt about Lasat. Old Hasius the Brilliant again scans the city, but with so little to go on, even the efforts of such a formidable sorcerer are futile. I ask him once more if he's had any further thoughts on the matter of a spell for remaking reality.

'There is no such spell,' he repeats.

I'm really sick of hearing that.

Lisutaris is resting at her villa, waiting either to be confirmed as Head of the Sorcerers Guild or arraigned as a murderer. With her is Princess Direeva, recovering from her wound. Makri is with them, or so I thought. I'm surprised when she arrives at the Assemblage just as I'm leaving. I stare at her suspiciously. Last time I called her a pointy-eared Orc freak she attacked me with her axe.

'I've come to help,' she says. 'Providing you give me a fulsome apology.'

'You think I need your help?'

'You always need my help.'

I apologise. It'll only make life hell at the Avenging Axe if I don't. 'Any insult was purely accidental. Your pointed ears are just one of your numerous excellent features. Many people speak highly of them. And well done for solving the test, that was intelligent. Now why are you really here?'

'Lisutaris wanted me to make sure you didn't kill Copro. She thinks my duties as bodyguard should extend to protecting her favourite hairdresser.'

Cicerius provides us with an official carriage and we set off to visit Copro at his home in Thamlin. I tell Makri that no matter what Lisutaris thinks, Copro is up to something.

'I saw him in the magic space.'

Makri knows me well enough to realise I don't suffer from hallucinations. 'It wouldn't really surprise me if there was more to him than he's saying. He was amazingly skilful with his scissors. And for a beautician, he did have a surprising grasp of world politics.'

Makri wonders why Covinius, whoever he actually is, suddenly ended up killing Sunstorm Ramius instead of Lisutaris.

'I'm wondering that myself. Damned unreasonable, seeing as we've spent the week protecting Lisutaris. If he'd just got in touch beforehand and said he was here to assassinate Ramius, it would have been simpler all round.'

'Is it a crime you have to solve?' asks Makri.

'Definitely not. The Simnians can look after their own sorcerers. All I have to do is show that Lisutaris didn't do it.'

Copro lives in an impressive villa. Not quite as large as those belonging to our wealthy Senators, but big enough. Few tradespeople of any sort live in Thamlin. The average working Turanian dwells in far more humble surroundings, and even those whose skill or good fortune have made them rich - some of our goldsmiths, for instance - wouldn't be welcome here. But Copro seems to have attracted a higher status to himself. The grounds at the front of his house, now covered in snow, are in summer a marvel of exuberant good taste, with plants, trees and bushes arranged in glorious harmony according to his own design. As with hair, make-up and dress, Copro's gardens have had an effect on the fashions of the city. I trample on a frozen bush so it breaks.

'You don't like the man, do you?' says Makri.

'I don't. Where was he when I was defending the city against the Orcs? Sitting comfortably in the Palace. Now he lives in a villa and I've got two rooms above the Avenging Axe.'

'You really should address your self-loathing some time,' says Makri, brightly. I scowl at her, and march up the long path. Copro isn't in. A servant tells me so at the door, and after I bundle her out the way and search the house, it seems to be true. Other servants run around threatening to call the Civil Guard. I grab one of them and demand to know where Copro is. He claims not to know. I slap him. He falls down but when I drag him up he still doesn't know.

'I don't have time for this. Tell me where he is or I'll throw you down the stairs.'

The servant starts wailing. I drag him to the top of the stairs, then halt, and let him go. 'I sense sorcery.'

Makri looks interested. 'What sort?'

'Not sure. But I can always sense it. Someone has worked a spell in this house, not long ago.'

We start hunting again, straining to find the source of the magic. Finally I stop in front of a bookcase. I drag it out of the way. Behind it the wall looks much as it should do. I put my shoulder to it and it creaks. I throw my full weight at it and the wall gives way. It's thin wood, a panel hiding a secret room. Inside are books, charts, phials, an astrolabe and various other things normally found only in the workroom of a sorcerer. At the back of the room is a particularly ugly statue of some sort of demon with four arms.

'How interesting.'

'So he's a sorcerer as well as an assassin?'

'Will you stop calling me an assassin?' says Copro, materialising in the centre of the room.

Makri takes her twin swords from her magic purse.

Copro laughs. 'Do you imagine those can hurt me?'

Makri, not one for banter while she fights, waits silently, swords at the ready. Copro ignores her and speaks to me, telling me of the great enjoyment he obtained from monitoring the incompetence of my investigation.

'Do people hire you for your amusement value, fat man?'

'All the time. I crack them up at the Palace.'

'Well, I am not an assassin. I find myself baffled that you could think me to be Covinius.'

'I don't think you're Covinius. I used to, but it just occurred to me that you're Rosin-kar, from Abelasi. Once the disgruntled apprentice of Darius Cloud Walker.'

Copro looks less pleased. 'And what do you base that on?'

'Summer Lightning. An Abelasian hair-styling term, I believe.'

'That's hardly proof,' retorts Copro.

'Maybe not. But it was enough to get my intuition working. And it will be enough to get the Sorcerers Guild to investigate your past and link you with Darius's murder.

'Darius's murder? Lisutaris has been shown to be guilty.'

'You faked the evidence,' I say.

Copro smiles. 'You don't know how I did that, do you? I've spied on you, Thraxas, as you've toiled round the city, asking questions. Every sorcerer you came to, you asked the same question. Is there a spell for remaking reality? Everyone said no. No one knows how to do it, except me. I am the greatest sorcerer in the west, and the world will soon know it.'

By this time I'm starting to worry. From the tone of Copro's voice and the glint in his eye, I'd say I was dealing with a fairly insane beautician. Probably he never really got over being booted out by Darius.

'So why did you kill Darius?'

'I owed it to him.'

'Maybe. But why bother to frame Lisutaris for the murder?'

'I was well paid by Sunstorm Ramius. The Simnians were just as keen as the Turanians to eliminate opposition.'

'But why get involved?' exclaims Makri. 'You're such a great beautician. Weren't you happy doing that?'

'Moderately happy,' replies Copro. 'But in truth, I was finding it wearing. And I loath Lisutaris. Eternally sucking on that water pipe. The woman is a disgrace to sorcerers everywhere. While she and her kind have stagnated in the west, I have travelled the world. I've learned sorcery unheard of in these lands. I'll show the Guild who it was they refused to allow to finish his apprenticeship.'

Copro is looking madder all the time. 'I offered my services to Simnia. When Ramius was elected Head of the Guild my reward was to be Chief Sorcerer of the conquered lands.'

'What conquered lands?'

'Turai and Abelasi.'

'Tough on you it's all gone wrong. Ramius is dead and Lisutaris won.'

Copro's eye starts to twitch. 'I intended to kill her in the magic space. I didn't understand why she hadn't been arraigned for the murder. Despite the excellent job I did in framing her, Turai had somehow managed to keep her name clear. I found that most annoying.' Copro shrugs. 'No matter. She'll be tried for the murder eventually. And no one apart from you will ever realise I am Rosin-kar. I see you're wearing spell protection charms. It might take a while for me to wear them down. Rather than waste time I will now introduce you to one of my favourite creations.'

Copro claps his hands. The statue behind him opens its eyes, and steps forward. It raises its four arms, each one carrying a sword. I raise my own weapons to defend myself. Makri does the same. The statue advances a few steps then topples over with a terrific crash and lies motionless on the ground.

Makri looks puzzled. 'Is that it?'

Copro looks furious.

'Don't feel bad,' I tell him. 'Animating a statue is a really difficult thing to do.'

Copro claps his hands again and huge chagra cats appear from nowhere, rending at us with their claws. Makri starts fighting but I remain calm. I know these are illusions. I walk straight through one of them and they all vanish. Serpents slither down the walls and slide towards us. I feel them twining round my legs as I walk forward. It takes all my concentration to keep going. Illusionary or not, I hate to be covered with snakes. Dragon fire erupts from the walls, covering me in golden light, and a nameless demon jabs at my eyes with a spear. I ignore it all and keep walking. Finally I back Copro up against the far wall. The illusions fade away.

'You have a stronger will than one would suspect,' says Copro.

'Cheap illusions never bother me.'

'The Sword of Aracasan is no illusion,' says Copro, suddenly pulling a short blade from beneath his tunic.

I'm rather worried by this turn of events. The Sword of Aracasan, a fabulous item long thought lost to the world, has the property of making its bearer invincible in combat. Armed with such a blade, a novice could hew his way through an army.

'That's not really the sword of–'

Copro swings it at me. The blade travels faster than the eye can see, and were I not already protecting myself with my sword it would have taken my head off. As it is, the flat of my own blade slams into my face and I fly back across the room and bang my head on the four-armed statue. I try to rise but my legs no longer seem to be functioning. Copro smiles. The sword flickers in the air, again faster than the eye can see.

'A remarkable weapon,' he says, advancing towards me. He isn't paying much attention to Makri. Possibly Copro doesn't feel threatened by any woman whose hair he's styled. Makri leaps at him and engages him in combat, but even her gladiatorial skills can't overcome the Sword of Aracasan. They fight furiously for a minute or so, but each time Makri attempts to land a blow the magical sword parries it, and she's hard pushed to avoid the answering strokes. Finally she leaps backwards and yells.

'Get him, Thraxas!'

Copro turns towards me. Makri stabs him in the back. He slumps to the floor with a surprised look in his eye.

I struggle to my feet. Makri is looking sadly at the body. 'You should've stuck to the beauty trade. You were good at it.' She sighs. 'Lisutaris isn't going to be pleased.'

She looks more cheerful. 'On the other hand, I suppose this ends the case? I mean, we've killed the bad guy. That usually does it.'

'We've killed one bad guy. Covinius is still around and we don't have any proof it was him who killed Ramius.'

I'm bleeding. I rip a length of cloth from a towel and wrap it round my head. The villa is in chaos, with servants running around and screaming.

'Furthermore, I don't have any proof that Copro killed Darius. He confessed to us, but who's going to believe it?'

'When Samilius and the sorcerers come down to investigate, won't they find things? You know, auras and such like?'

'Maybe. Old Hasius and Lasat might find enough here to link Copro to the Avenging Axe and the death of Darius. There's still the matter of this remaking spell, though. If I knew how that was done, life would be easy.'

'Let's take the sword,' suggests Makri.

I reach down, but before I can grasp the hilt it vanishes.

'I guess we weren't worthy.'

I tell the servants that the head of the Civil Guard will be here soon to take care of the crime scene and if they touch anything they'll all be in big trouble. Having no more time to waste, we depart into the cold and make our way back to the Assemblage.

'Do you have any thazis?' asks Makri.

'Do you need to calm down?'

'No, I just want some.'

We light some sticks as we ride back to the Royal Hall.

'Lisutaris has better thazis,' says Makri.

'Is she planning on cutting down when she's Chief Sorcerer?'

Makri doesn't think so. 'She did say she might be able to get some excellent plants imported from the south once she had better contacts in the guild.'

'You're far too keen on thazis these days, Makri. And dwa. You used to be a pain in the neck when you were studying and working all the time, but at least you got things done. What happened?'

'I got sad about See-ath,' she says.

'Any chance of cheering up?'

'I'm feeling a bit better after the fight.'

Chapter Twenty

Though the main room at the Royal Hall is crowded with sorcerers awaiting the confirmation, there is little sign of celebration. Fatigue has set in, and dismay at the death of Sunstorm Ramius has sobered them up. Losing one sorcerer was bad enough. The death of a second makes this the most unfortunate Assemblage since the infamous episode in Samsarina twenty years ago when three drunken apprentices burned down a tavern in a dispute over a game of cards, killing themselves in the process. Sorcerers huddle in their delegations, discussing the various rumours that circulate through the building. As Lisutaris is about to become the new Head of the Guild, few sorcerers want to come right out and accuse her of killing Sunstorm Ramius. That might be a bad career move. But there are plenty of whispered comments, and much talk about foul tactics by the Turanians.

My report to Cicerius and Direeva is brief and to the point. 'Copro the beautician turned out to be Rosin-kar, onetime apprentice to Darius Cloud Walker. He's dead in his villa. As for Ramius, I'm nowhere, and since his body was hauled out of the magic space the sorcerers are starting to talk. I still think that Covinius was the most probable killer, but I don't have any proof.'

'We have proof,' says Cicerius.

I'm surprised. 'What do you mean, you have proof?'

'A witness saw Covinius emerge from the magic space.'

'What witness?'

'A man called Direxan, who's here with the Matteshan delegation. Not a sorcerer, he's a Matteshan Tribune.'

I don't understand this at all. Cicerius explains that Direxan was minding his own business outside the Royal Hall when a green portal of light suddenly opened and the notorious Covinius appeared. He dropped a knife, and disappeared into the snow. The knife had a fragment of cloth on it, which has been matched with Ramius's cloak.

'Is this true?' I demand.

'Absolutely. Direxan has already made a sworn statement in front of Consul Kalius and Lasat, Axe of Gold. It will shortly be announced to the Assemblage that the notorious assassin Covinius was the killer of Sunstorm Ramius. Lisutaris is in the clear.'

'But how did this Direxan identify Covinius? No one knows what he looks like.'

'Direxan does. He was present three years ago when Covinius assassinated his superior, the Deputy Consul of Mattesh.'

'It's extremely fortunate that such a good witness was available,' adds Tilupasis.

'More than fortunate,' I say.

'Presumably it was an internal affair involving Simnian politics,' says Cicerius. 'It was my opinion all along, you will recall, that we did not have to worry about Covinius. Our concern is Lisutaris. Have we enough evidence to clear her name with regard to the murder of Darius in your office?'

'No.'

'Why did you kill Copro before gaining such evidence?'

'He attacked me with a magical sword.'

Cicerius and Tilupasis stare at me. I suppose it does sound like a poor excuse.

'You must find evidence. The confirmation is in one hour.'

Two apprentices enter, with Charius the Wise in their wake. He regards Cicerius and Tilupasis with anger and struggles to control his manners. 'Are you still planning to have Lisutaris put forward as Head of the Guild?'

'Certainly.' Cicerius adopts his friendliest tone. 'She won the test.'

Charius's long moustache sways slightly as he draws himself to his full height to stare down at the Deputy Consul. 'I am well aware of the tactics employed by Turai to gain this post. I have never witnessed such a shameless display of illegal behaviour. You have used every underhand means at your disposal to unfairly influence the outcome of the election.'

Cicerius and Tilupasis, being politicians, are taking this calmly enough, but I can't resist butting in. After all, it was me that had to struggle round the magic space in a snowstorm. 'Come on, Charius. Are you trying to say that other nations weren't doing exactly the same? And as for that final test, whose novel idea was it to set some mathematical problem? Lisutaris could have beaten Ramius in any test of sorcery. Smart idea, setting a problem she couldn't do, then sending in a Simnian mathematician.'

Charius refuses to answer me. He still has more to say about Turai's infamous behaviour. 'You went too far with murder, Deputy Consul. You may have cleared Lisutaris of the death of Ramius - though I am not the only one with doubts about the veracity of your witness - but she still stands accused of killing Darius Cloud Walker. I will not allow her to be confirmed. Unless she withdraws I will expose her to the Assemblage. The pictures of her stabbing Darius will be made available to all.'

'It's a fake reality,' I say.

'There is no spell for faking such a reality.' Charius sweeps out of the room, his dark rainbow cloak trailing behind him.

'If there was, you wouldn't tell me about it,' I mutter.

Kalius walks in, his scribe and assistant behind him. 'Is Lisutaris ready to leave?'

'She is preparing,' replies Cicerius. 'Though we are still hoping to avoid that eventuality.'

Once again I'm obliged to muscle into the conversation. 'Leave? Leave for where?'

'Lisutaris must go into exile immediately,' says the Consul. 'There is no other option. Once Charius denounces her to the Sorcerers Assemblage there's no telling what may happen.'

'At least this way she may yet become Head of the Guild,' adds Cicerius. 'If we can one day find evidence to clear her, she may be able to return.'

Poor woman. Loses her favourite hairdresser then gets sent into exile, all in the same day. I curse myself. I've failed my client.

'Can't you buy us any more time?' I ask.

They can't. Even Tilupasis has come to the end of her resources. Time has now run out. We've failed. Damn it.

In the Room of Saints, Makri is sitting on her own. She's heard the news. 'It's not fair. She didn't kill Darius. Copro did.'

'I know. But we can't prove it. He covered it up with some spell that no one else believes exists. I'm stumped.'

Makri wonders if Lisutaris gets to be head of the Guild.

'I think that's a moot point. She won't be confirmed in the post. But I don't think the sorcerers' rules allow them to elect anyone else till she's dead.'

'That might not be too long,' says Makri.

It's true. If Turai's enemies in the Sorcerers Guild decide that they want a clear run at electing a new leader, Lisutaris will be vulnerable to attack in exile. We fall silent. There's around thirty minutes to the confirmation, an event which is not now going to happen. sorcerers drift in and out. From their ugly mood I'd say that Charius was already showing the pictures of Lisutaris wielding the knife. I drink a beer, and another.

'I like Lisutaris,' says Makri, bleakly.

I drink more beer. It's been a strange couple of weeks. Started off looking for a dragon-scale thief and finished off in the Maze of Aero. In between there was a lot of drinking and two murdered sorcerers. Most of the time I've been cold as the ice queen's grave and at the end of it I've accomplished nothing. I should stick to simple cases, like tailing ex-actresses for their suspicious husbands. I wonder how that couple are getting on now. Strange that I first encountered Copro giving the wife beauty treatment when he called at her house.

'Very strange really,' I say out loud.

Makri looks up from her beer. 'What's strange?'

'Copro. Visiting that actress. The one I was watching. He was giving her beauty treatment.'

'So?'

'So Copro was booked up with Senators' wives, Princesses, Lisutaris and her like. Why did he visit a merchant's wife? They were rich, but his other clients were richer. You might have thought it beneath him to take on the wife of a merchant.'

Dragon scales went through that house. It was on the list. I presumed they were for purposes of decoration. Maybe there was more to it. I haul myself to my feet and shake my head to clear it.

'Makri. Go outside and find some fast horses. Steal them if necessary.' I hurry into the main hall and burst into Cicerius's private room. I need documents and I need them fast. Minutes later I'm running through the hall and out into the entrance, where Almalas is still lecturing apprentices on the correct way for a sorcerer to conduct himself. Makri has two horses ready. Their owners aren't happy about it but Makri holds them off with the point of her sword.

'Official business,' I cry. 'You will be fully compensated.' I leap into the saddle and we set off through the driving snow.

Chapter Twenty-One

I arrive back at the Assemblage with a very tired horse and an unwilling companion. There I find that Lisutaris is refusing to leave the city.

'Why should I go into exile? I didn't kill anyone.'

'Even if you didn't, Charius can prove that you did. The authorities will have no choice but to put you on trial if you stay.'

'What do you mean, authorities?' demands Lisutaris, facing right up to the Consul. 'You're the authorities. And I'm Head of the Sorcerers Guild. No one is running me out of Turai.'

I've arrived back at the Assemblage with Habali, wife of Rixad, the woman I spent so much uncomfortable time watching in the freezing cold. Though I have important news I'm having trouble getting a word in. Faced with an uncomfortable exile, Lisutaris is mad as a mad dragon.

'You expect me to just set off through the winter and find a new place to live?'

'We will provide you with funds,' says Cicerius.

'And work towards your eventual recall,' adds Kalius.

'It's for the good of the city,' says Tilupasis. 'And your own. No one benefits if the Sorcerers Guild produces their pictures and demands you stand trial.'

'I'm sick of those pictures,' says Lisutaris, her voice rising. 'How about if I just blast anyone that tries to show them again? If anyone tries to chase me out of Turai I'll be down on them like a bad spell and that's that.'

Hardly rational, but Lisutaris is angrier than I've ever seen her. She should smoke some thazis. Might calm her down.

'If I could make a suggestion,' I say, barging my way through the assorted assistants and guards who ring the room. Since I became a Tribune, it's proved a lot easier to get places. A few weeks ago I'd have been about as welcome as an Orc at an Elvish wedding at a meeting of the Consul, Deputy Consul and head of the Civil Guard. Now they're almost pleased to see me, even though I'm aware I smell of beer. I wouldn't normally notice, but it clashes with Lisutaris's perfume.

Beside me Habali is nervous. When I persuaded - or threatened - her to accompany me, she wasn't expecting to have to face a roomful of arguing politicians. Before I can speak further the room starts filling up with sorcerers.

'Didn't I say there were to be no interruptions?' snaps Cicerius.

'I insisted,' retorts Charius the Wise. Behind him is a large delegation. He's brought the Chief Sorcerer from each country. Even Princess Direeva is here, her shoulder heavily bandaged.

'It's time,' says Charius.

Cicerius looks helplessly at Kalius. Kalius looks helplessly at Tilupasis.

'We require a little longer,' says Tilupasis. It's a hopeless task. Charius isn't going to wait any longer. Beside Charius, Lasat, Axe of Gold, is looking on with grim satisfaction. He may have been blackmailed into silence but he's not going to be sorry to see the Turanian disgraced.

'It's time–' repeats Charius.

'–for some explanations,' I say.

'Explanations?'

'About the remaking of reality.'

A general groan issues from the sorcerers present, all of whom know of my fruitless search for such a spell. I must have approached every delegation, and everyone has told me to forget it.

'I take it you've all now seen the pictures of Lisutaris, Mistress of the Sky, killing Darius Cloud Walker. And you've probably all heard my theory that someone erased what really happened. And all of you have told me there's no way a sorcerer could make some phoney pictures to replace it-'

Charius the Wise interrupts me. 'Must we listen to this man? He is already known as one of the principal troublemakers at the Assemblage. I insist that Lisutaris is arrested immediately.'

Strong sounds of approval come from all round the room. I'm losing my audience. I hold up my hand. 'You can insist all you want, Charius the Wise. But in Turai, no citizen can be arrested on a capital charge without the approval of the Tribunes. And I, Tribune Thraxas, withhold my approval until you hear me out.'

This sounds impressive. It isn't true, but it silences the room. I thrust Habali forward. 'You've all seen Lisutaris stabbing Darius. You say no spell could create the illusion. And you're right. There is no remaking spell. The pictures as conjured by Old Hasius are entirely accurate. A woman did walk into my office and stab Darius. But it wasn't Lisutaris. It was Habali, dressed to resemble her. Meet Habali, actress.'

My revelation is met by silence and a lot of puzzled looks.

'An actress? Impossible!' says someone, eventually.

'Not impossible at all. The room was dark. The only light came from the fire. In a wig, make up, and wearing the proper clothes, Habali was good enough to fool anyone. It fooled all of you. And me, which is more impressive, because I make my living by not being fooled. For all the world it looked as though Lisutaris murdered Darius, but she didn't. She wasn't in the room at the time. Copro entered my office and killed him, then used his sorcery to erase all trace of events. Then he sent Habali in dressed as Lisutaris and she pretended to stab Darius with one of those fake knives they use in the theatre with a retracting blade. All the time he was already dead.'

I turn to Habali. 'Isn't it so?'

For a moment I think Habali is going to let me down. Not surprisingly, she's not keen on confessing to conniving in a murder in the presence of these people. However, she's already carrying a written pardon signed by Cicerius and a promise of enough gold to leave the city and set up in another state where she won't be bothered by her tiresome husband. All in all, it's not a bad deal from her point of view.

'It's true. I did it. Copro paid me. I impersonated Lisutaris to make the illusion. I also helped in the first part of the plan. He obtained the dragon scales he needed for the erasure from me.'

The controversy that follows is long and loud. Figuring I've done my part, I mostly stay out of it. Using the authority of the Tribunate, I send an assistant off to the Room of Saints to bring me beer while the sorcerers once more conjure up the pictures of the murder.

'Look,' says Habali. 'I'm wearing the same earrings I have on now.'

'But you look so much like Lisutaris.'

'That's because Copro styled my wig and did my make-up.'

'He was such a great beautician,' sighs Tirini Snake Smiter, making her only contribution to the debate. The arguments continue. I take a seat. Makri sits down beside me.

'That was a good piece of investigative work,' she says.

'Thank you.'

'It sounds like we're winning the argument. Of course, I deserve a lot of the credit.'

'You do?'

'Certainly. I provided the answer to the final test. Do you want to know how I did it?'

I pretend to be interested. Makri launches into an explanation. 'The sequence was 391, 551, 713. I wasted some time trying to see if the difference between each pair of numbers was significant, but it didn't seem to be. Then I thought about prime numbers.'

'What's a prime number?'

'It doesn't divide by anything except itself and one. Three is a prime number, for instance, or seven. So I broke each of the numbers into their factors. It took a while but eventually I found that 391 was 17 times 23. 551 was the product of 19 and 29. Of course by then it was becoming clear. The third number, 713, turned out to be 23 times 31, which I knew it would. So by then anyone could see that the answer to the test, the next number in the sequence, would be 1073, which is the product of 29 and 37. Do you want me to write out the sequence of prime numbers to make it clearer?'

'No, you've explained it all very clearly. It was brilliant of you to find the answer.' I haven't understood a word Makri has said. I congratulate her again on a fine piece of work anyway.

Makri sips her beer. 'Easy really, but I was under a lot of pressure. Time was limited, the magic space was misbehaving and there were assassins and unicorns wandering about. Tell Cicerius to remember that when I need his help getting in to the university.'

'You're still going?'

'Of course I'm still going. Why wouldn't I?'

'I thought you might be taking up a career as a useless drug user instead.'

'Stop bringing that up,' says Makri. 'I was sad about See-ath.'

I get a final boost for the magic warm cloak from Lisutaris and let Makri wear it on the way home. She does deserve some reward.

Chapter Twenty-Two

Three days later I'm sitting comfortably in front of the fire at the Avenging Axe. It's early evening and the tavern is not yet crowded. I'm moderately satisfied. Lisutaris, Mistress of the Sky, is now Head of the Sorcerers Guild and I have been well paid for my efforts on her behalf.

'Fine efforts, though I say it myself.'

'Many times,' says Makri.

Makri is taking a break before the evening rush. Since the end of the Assemblage she's been in a benevolent mood. She struggles to manage on the money she gets at the Avenging Axe, so payment for her duties as bodyguard will make her life easier for a while.

'I got paid for fighting. Like being a gladiator really. Except when I was a gladiator I didn't get my hair done. Well, I did, in fact, but that Orc woman wasn't really up to the job. A shame about Copro.'

'I understand our female aristocracy is devastated.'

'Tirini Snake Smiter has sent to Pargada for their best man.'

'Why would she do that?' I ask. 'Doesn't everyone say she's already the most beautiful sorcerer in the world?'

'So?'

'So why does she need an expert beautician?'

Makri looks at me. 'I doubt you'd understand even if I explained it to you.'

Makri has cleaned her armour and carefully stored it away. Back at work and needing to earn tips, she's reverted to the chainmail bikini. The firelight glints on her skin. Sailors and workmen are pleased enough at the sight to hand over a little extra.

My winnings on the election were very modest. I picked up a little on Lisutaris, but I was so busy I missed out on several other good gambling opportunities. 'I hate to miss out on a bet. I'd have got more down if Honest Mox's son hadn't gone and killed himself with dwa.'

Minarixa the baker. Mox's son. And young Tribune Visus. The city's going to hell.

'Don't involve me in any gambling,' states Makri. 'I'm saving my money. I have fees to pay when the Guild College opens. I need to get back to studying. I'm far behind with rhetoric. Four days on Lisutaris's water pipe and I forgot all the best-known speeches from last century.'

I refrain from commenting.

'I'm still puzzled by the witness,' says Makri. 'Direxan. The Matteshan who saw Covinius emerge from the magic space after killing Ramius. You said no one had ever seen Covinius. Did Direxan really recognise him?'

I sip my beer. Gurd really knows how to serve his beer. And Tanrose really knows how to cook a venison pie. They should get together. They'd be an ideal couple.

'It was all arranged, I imagine.'

'Who by?'

'Cicerius. Or Tilupasis and her boyfriend the Consul.'

'You're losing me here.'

'Covinius was hired to kill Sunstorm Ramius. Turai hired him. I wasn't meant to know. I wouldn't have if Hanama hadn't accidentally learned about it.'

'You mean this city actually hired an Assassin to kill Lisutaris's main opponent?'

'So I believe. No wonder Cicerius kept telling me to ignore Covinius. He knew all along he wasn't a danger to Lisutaris.'

Simnia hired Copro. Turai hired Covinius. It was hard to sort it out. I wasn't really meant to. Makri muses on this for a while.

'Doesn't Cicerius make a big thing about being the most honest politician in Turai?'

'He does. And he's right, mostly. He never takes bribes and he never allows the prosecution of opponents on trumped-up charges. When it comes to foreign policy I suppose he has to be pragmatic.'

I drink my beer, and try and calculate the cost of winning the position of Head of the Guild. Two murders, several accidental deaths, and gold and dwa beyond count.

'An expensive victory. But worth it to the government. Especially as the city's masses will end up paying for it in taxes.'

'Are you still in trouble with Praetor Capatius?'

'No, Cicerius is keeping him off my back provided I don't do any more Tribune-like actions. Which I won't. Anyone looking for help in an eviction can go elsewhere.'

Senator Lodius sent me a payment for my services. I still don't like Lodius. I kept the payment.

'Am I still in trouble with the Brotherhood?' asks Makri.

I shake my head. The Traditionals have influence with the Brotherhood and Cicerius has smoothed that one out for us as well.

'Great,' says Makri. 'Everything worked out well.'

Lisutaris has been confirmed as Head of the Guild. The foreign sorcerers are already leaving the city. In a week they'll all be gone, apart from those still receiving treatment by the city's doctors after the excesses of the Assemblage.

'How is Sareepa Lightning-Strikes-the-Mountain?' asks Makri.

'Still sick. One of the worst cases of alcoholic poisoning the apothecaries have ever had to deal with, apparently. She'll thank me in the end.'

As the tavern begins to fill, Makri returns to work. I spend the evening drinking beer, and playing a game of rak with Captain Rallee and a few others.

'Damned sorcerers,' says Rallee. 'You know they were all immune to prosecution for dwa? City's going to hell.' Captain Rallee is in a foul temper due to being out on patrol on one of the coldest nights of the year. I'm not planning on leaving the comfort of the tavern for the rest of the winter. Now I've been paid, I don't have to. Come the spring, business should pick up. I just did some sterling service for the city and I'm expecting the city to be grateful. Between them, Cicerius and Lisutaris should be able to put a few wealthy clients my way. It's deep into the night by the time I make it upstairs to my rooms. My office is surprisingly warm. A fine fire is lit and an illuminated staff casts a warm glow over the shabby furnishings. Lisutaris, Mistress of the Sky, Makri and Princess Direeva are all slumped on the floor. I sigh. Makri's good intentions haven't lasted for long.

Direeva opens her eyes.

'For a woman who doesn't like me, you spend a lot of time in my room.'

Direeva shrugs, drunkenly.

'What really happened in the magic space?' I ask her.

Direeva doesn't look quite so drunk any more.

'You don't get on well with your brother. He controls the army and you control the sorcerers. Pretty soon the Southern Hills is going to erupt in a civil war. Turai would much rather have an alliance with Lisutaris's friend Princess Direeva than your brother.'

'What are you talking about, investigator?'

'Was Covinius even in Turai? No one ever saw him, apart from you and a phoney witness Tilupasis bribed.'

'Of course Covinius was in Turai. He killed Ramius.'

I look at her. 'Maybe he did. But an intelligent man might think it was you.'

'No one would mistake you for an intelligent man.'

'If Turai paid you to kill Ramius, I wouldn't be surprised. And I won't be surprised if Turai comes to your aid when you're making yourself Queen.'

The Princess laughs. 'A foolish theory. Was not Hanama the Turanian Assassin also in the magic space?'

'She was. Protecting her friend Lisutaris, I imagine. She might have killed Ramius. But I think you're a more likely candidate.'

I don't really care one way or the other.

'You expend a lot of effort in your work,' says Direeva.

'Is that a compliment?'

'No. Your work is pointless.'

'It's better than rowing a slave galley.'

I haul Makri to her feet and drag her along the corridor. Restricted space or not, she can entertain her friends in her own room. Direeva assists Lisutaris. 'Poor Copro,' mutters Lisutaris, coming briefly back to consciousness.

'Don't worry. There will be another brilliant young beautician emerging next season. Now you're Head of the Guild, you'll be number one client.'

'Sharp as an Elf's ear,' says Lisutaris, but whether she means herself, Copro or me, I'm not sure.

Now my room is clear of intoxicated sorcerers and barmaids, I have a final beer before going to bed. I wonder how long my term of office as Tribune is supposed to last. However long it is, I'm withdrawing from politics. A man should never get involved with these people. It's far too dangerous.

The End

Introduction to Thraxas Book Six

When I began writing Thraxas, I planned for it to be rather darker. More noirish. Sort of Dashiell Hammett meets sword and Sorcery. Thraxas does share some elements often associated with detective fiction. He's a solo investigator who's tough, and ready to defend himself. He drinks a lot and he's poor. He exists in a corrupt urban environment where he comes up against organised crime. He distrusts the police and tends to be hostile towards authority. He's loyal to his clients, and prepared to go a long way to defend them. Despite this, Thraxas didn't turn out very noirish at all. Partly that's because Thraxas's huge appetites for food and drink can drag him out any prolonged burst of soul searching. A good bowl of stew and five or six beers will usually make him view the world in a more optimistic light.

And also, I think, because Thraxas and Makri turned out to be something of a comedy double-act. At times their relationship seems to consist mainly of bickering and mutual insults, but really, Thraxas is rescued from a potentially bleak world by the presence of the young female warrior. Makri is too spirited and intelligent to be intimidated by Thraxas's blustering. She gives as good as she gets, and consequently they become friends, quite quickly. Thraxas is still walking down unfriendly streets, but he's no longer on his own.

Makri is tough too; in Thraxas and the Dance of Death, she's again employed as Lisutaris's bodyguard. Protecting the Head of the Sorcerers Guild is an important task, and Makri's employment signifies that she's no longer quite the outcast she was at the beginning of the series.

Martin Millar

Thraxas and the Dance of Death

Chapter One

It's summer. It's hot. The city stinks. I've just been described as a liar in court and subjected to a stream of hostile invective that would have made a statue flinch. Funds are low, I'm short of work and badly in need of beer. Life, in general, is tough. It's no time for my idiot companion Makri to be complaining about an examination.

'So you have to take an examination. You wanted to go to Guild College. What did you expect?'

'It's not just a written examination. I have to stand up and talk to the whole class. It's making me feel bad.'

'You used to fight in the gladiator slave pits. I thought you'd be used to an audience.'

Makri shakes her head violently, causing her huge mane of black hair to swing around the small of her back. Underneath all her hair Makri has pointed ears. This often leads to problems.

'That was different. I was killing Orcs. It never felt stressful like talking to a group of students. They're all merchants' sons with money and servants. They're always laughing at me for being a barmaid. And how am I meant to prepare for anything when this stupid city is as hot as Orcish hell and stinks like a sewer?'

Summer in Turai is never pleasant, and this summer is promising to be as bad as last year, when dogs and men keeled over in the street, overcome by the heat, and the main aqueduct into Twelve Seas was dry for a record eighteen days in a row. Makri continues to complain about her upcoming examination but I'm too annoyed about my recent experience in court to pay attention. A few months ago I arrested a thief down by the docks, name of Baxin. He was stealing Elvish wine. I apprehended him and delivered him, complete with evidence, to the Transport Guild. Unfortunately, being caught committing a crime has never stopped a Turanian criminal from putting up a strong defence in court. The devious, toga-clad lawyer Baxin hired to defend him made a good job of convincing the jury that Baxin was nothing more than the victim of a bad case of mistaken identity. The real criminal was the notoriously unreliable investigator Thraxas, a man with a city-wide reputation as a person of bad character.

'Damn it, no one was saying I had a bad character last winter when I saved this city from disgrace. Not to mention helping Lisutaris get elected as Head of the Sorcerers Guild. Then it was "Thank you, Thraxas, you're a hero."'

'Well, no one actually said that,' points out Makri.

'They should have.'

'I seem to remember several sorcerers saying you should be thrown in prison. And the Deputy Consul was very angry about you turning up drunk. And then the Consul threatened–'

'Yes, fine, Makri. You don't need to remind me of every detail of this city's ingratitude. If there was any justice I'd be living in a villa in Thamlin instead of a tavern in the bad part of town.'

We walk on through the intolerable heat. Packs of dogs lie listlessly on the baked mud roads and beggars slump in despair at every corner. Welcome to Twelve Seas, home to those city dwellers whose lives have not been going too well. Sailors without a ship, labourers without work, mercenaries without a war, broken-down prostitutes, pimps, thugs, runaways and the rest of the city's underclass all struggling to survive, and no one struggling more than sorcerous investigator Thraxas - ex-Palace employee, ex-soldier, ex-mercenary, currently broke, ageing, overweight, without prospects and really, really in need of a beer.

'I'm sure that everyone at College doesn't have to give a talk to the class,' continues Makri, apparently unaware that I have no interest in her problems. 'Professor Toarius is making me do it because he hates me. He just can't stand that I'm a woman. And he can't stand that I've got Orcish blood. Ever since I enrolled he's had it in for me. 'Don't do this, don't do that.' Petty restrictions everywhere. "You can't wear your sword to rhetoric class." "Don't threaten your philosophy tutor with an axe." I tell you, Thraxas, life for me is tough.'

'Very tough, Makri. Now please shut up about your damned examination.'

It's a long way down Moon and Stars Boulevard from the centre of the city to Twelve Seas. By the time we reach the corner of Quintessence Street I'm dripping with sweat. I'd buy a watermelon from the market if I hadn't lost every guran I had on an unwise wager on a chariot which might possibly have won the race had it not been driven by an Orc-loving charioteer with two left hands and a poor sense of direction. Down each narrow alleyway youths are dealing dwa, the powerful drug that has the city in its grip. The Civil Guard, bribed or intimidated by the Brotherhood, look the other way. Their customers eye us as we pass, wondering if we might be potential targets for a swift street robbery, but at the sight of the swords at Makri's hips, and my considerable bulk, they look away. No need to tangle with us when there are plenty of easier targets to be found.

The sun beats down cruelly. The crowds around the market stalls kick up clouds of choking dust. By the time we reach the Avenging Axe I'm practically begging for ale. I march through the doors, force my way through the afternoon drinkers and reach for the bar like a drowning man clutching at a rope.

'Beer. Quickly.'

The tavern is owned by Gurd, barbarian from the north, a man I've fought beside all over the world. Recognising the poor state I'm in, he omits the small talk and fills me up a tankard. I down it in one and take another.

'Bad day in court?'

'Very bad. They let Baxin go. So now I'm missing out on the conviction bonus. You wouldn't believe what the lawyers said about me. I've had it with this stinking city. A man can't do an honest day's work without some corrupt official grinding him into the dust.'

My tankard is empty. 'What's the matter? Beer in short supply?'

Gurd hands over a third. He grins. Gurd's around fifty, and after a life of mercenary wars he's content to settle down peacefully in his tavern. Once a ferocious fighter, he's now a rather mellower person than me. Of course, Gurd had the good sense to save enough money to buy an inn. Everything I ever earned I gambled away, or drank. By my fourth or fifth beer I'm complaining loudly to all who care to listen that Turai is undoubtedly the worst city in the west. 'I've been in Orcish hovels that were more civilised than this place. The next time the city authorities need me to bail them out of a crisis they can forget it. Let them look somewhere else.'

The beer doesn't lighten my mood. Even a substantial helping of Tanrose's stew can't cheer me up. As the tavern starts to fill up with dock workers coming off their afternoon shift at the warehouses, I grab another beer and head upstairs. I used to be a Senior Investigator at the Palace with a nice villa in Thamlin. Now I live in two rooms above a tavern. It doesn't make me feel good about my life. Makri lives in another room along the corridor. I bump into her as she emerges. She's changed into her chainmail bikini in readiness for her shift as a waitress.

'Cheered up any?' she asks.

'No.'

'Strange. Eight or nine beers usually does it. What's eating you? You've been criticised in court before. Now I think about it, weren't you criticised in the Senate only last year?'

'Yes. I've been lambasted by the best of them. Do you realise that I'm in exactly the same position I was when you arrived in this city a couple of years ago?'

'Drunk?'

'I mean broke. Without a coin to my name. Dependent on Gurd for ale on credit, till some degenerate walks through my door asking me to investigate a case which will no doubt involve me risking my life for a lousy thirty gurans a day. It's not right. Look what I've done for this city. Fought in the wars, held back the Niojans and repelled the Orcish hordes. Did anyone pin a medal on me for that? Forget it. Who was it saved our necks when Horm the Dead tried to wipe out Turai with his Eight-Mile Terror Spell? Me. And only this winter I got a Turanian elected Head of the Sorcerers Guild practically single-handed.'

'I helped with that.'

'True. That doesn't alter the fact that I deserve more than being stuck in this foul tavern. I ought to be employed by the Palace.'

'You were employed by the Palace. They bounced you out for being drunk.'

'That only goes to prove my point. There's no gratitude. I tell you, if that useless Deputy Consul Cicerius comes down here again begging for help I'm sending him away with a dragon's tooth up his nose. To hell with them all.'

'It's not fair,' says Makri.

'You're damn right it's not fair.'

'I don't see why I have to take this examination. I'm so busy waiting tables I hardly have time to study.'

I glare at Makri with loathing. As far as I can see, if a person who's part Elf, part Orc and part Human decides to slaughter her captors, escape to civilisation, then sign up for college, she's only got herself to blame for her problems. She could have remained a gladiator. Makri was good at that. Undefeated champion. She's just about the most savage fighter ever seen in the west. Slaughtering people is her speciality. Guild College is a foolish enterprise requiring long hours of study in rhetoric, philosophy, mathematics and God knows what else. No wonder she's stressed. The woman - and I use the term loosely - is next door to insane at the best of times; a result, I imagine, of having mixed blood, pointy ears and a general tendency to believe that all of life's difficulties can be solved with violence.

Makri departs downstairs. I take my beer to my room, slam the door, and clear some junk off the couch. I've had enough of this. I need a plan. There must be a way for a talented man to get ahead in this city. I finish my beer. After a while I drag a bottle of klee out of a drawer and start in on it. The klee burns my throat as it goes down. Finest quality, distilled in the hills. The sun streams in, through the holes in the curtains. My room is hotter than Orcish hell. No one can think in heat like this. I'm just going to finish my days in Twelve Seas broke, angry and unlamented. I finish the klee, toss the bottle in the bin, and fall asleep.

Chapter Two

I'm dreaming about the time I won a beer-drinking contest down in Abelasi. Seven opponents, and every one of them unconscious on the floor while I was still demanding more ale, and quickly. One of my finest moments. I'm rudely awakened by someone shaking my arm. I leap to my feet and make a grab for my sword.

'It's me,' says Makri.

I'm angry at the invasion. 'How often do I have to tell you to stay out of my room!' I yell at her. 'I swear if you walk in here uninvited again I'll run you through.'

'You couldn't run me through if I had both arms tied behind my back, you fat ox,' retorts Makri, never one to smooth over a disagreement.

I notice that Makri is not alone.

'You remember Dandelion?' she says.

My heart sinks. It plummets. Even in a city full of strange characters, Dandelion stands out as a particularly odd young woman. She hired me on a case last year, and while I admit this worked out all right in the end, the whole affair didn't endear her to me. Dandelion is weird. Not least among the things I dislike about her is her habit of walking around with bare feet, something I'm utterly unable to account for. In a city full of refuse-strewn streets, it defies common sense. You're liable to step on a dead rat, or maybe worse. Besides this, she wears a long skirt covered with patterns from the zodiac, and spouts rubbish about communing with nature. She hired me on behalf of the talking dolphins in the bay, which was probably to be expected.

'What do you want?' I grunt. 'The talking dolphins having problems again?'

The dolphins don't actually speak Turanian. Just a lot of strange whistles. I saw Dandelion communicating with them but I'm half-convinced she was making it up as she went along. Dandelion tries to smile, but she seems nervous. With my sword in my hand I guess I don't put people at ease. I sheathe it, just in case the woman has anything useful to say. She did pay me with several valuable antique coins, and I'm not in a position to turn away paying clients no matter how peculiar they might be.

'Dandelion has a warning for you,' says Makri.

Makri's keeping a straight face but I sense she's secretly amused. Springing Dandelion on me when I'm sleeping off ten beers is probably her idea of an excellent joke.

'A warning? From the dolphins?'

Dandelion shakes her head. 'Not from the dolphins. Though they're still very grateful for your assistance. You should visit them some time.'

'Next time I need to commune with nature I'll get right down to the beach. What's the warning?'

'You're about to be involved in terrible bloodshed.'

Dandelion gazes at me. I gaze back at her. There's a brief silence, interrupted only by the cries of the hawkers outside. At the foot of the steps leading down from my outer door to the street there's an ongoing dispute over territory between a woman who sells fish and a man who's set up a stall for sharpening blades. They've been screaming at each other all week.

'Terrible bloodshed? Is that it?'

Dandelion nods. I hunt around for my klee. It's finished.

'I'm an investigator. I'm always surrounded by bloodshed. Comes with the territory. People round here don't like being investigated.'

'You don't understand,' says Dandelion. 'I don't mean a little violence. Or even a few deaths. I mean many, many deaths, more deaths than you can count. An orgy of blood-letting such as you've never encountered before.'

My head's starting to hurt. The sight of Dandelion with her bare feet and odd clothes is irritating beyond measure. I'd like to bounce her down the stairs.

'Who gave you this warning? The Brotherhood? The Society of Friends?'

'No one gave it me. I read it in the stars.'

Makri fails to suppress a giggle. I stare at both of them with loathing. 'You read it in the stars?'

'Yes,' says Dandelion, nodding eagerly. 'Last night on the beach. I hurried here as fast as I could to warn you. Because I owe you–'

'Will you get out of my office!' I roar. 'Makri, how dare you bring this woman in here to bother me like this. If she's still here in five seconds I swear I'll kill you both. Don't you know I'm a busy man? Now get the hell out of here!'

Makri shepherds Dandelion from the room. She pauses at the door. 'Maybe you ought to listen to her, Thraxas. After all, she came up with the goods during the dolphin case.'

I tell Makri brusquely I'll be grateful if she never wastes my time again, and add a few curses I usually save for the race track. Makri departs, slamming the door. I open it to curse her again, then sit down heavily. My mood just got worse. I need more sleep. There's a knock on the outside door. I ignore it. It comes again. I continue to ignore it. My outside door is secured by a minor locking spell which is sufficient for keeping out most people, and I'm not in the mood for company. I lie down on my couch just as the door flies open and Lisutaris, Mistress of the Sky, strides into the room. Lisutaris, number one sorcerer in Turai. Number one sorcerer in the west, in fact, since she was elected Head of the Sorcerers Guild. She glares down at me.

'Why didn't you answer the door?'

'I was counting on the locking spell to keep out unwanted intruders.'

Lisutaris smiles. A locking spell placed by the likes of me is never going to be a problem for such a powerful sorcerer.

'Are you planning on lying there all day?'

I struggle to rise. Lisutaris is an important woman, and wealthy. She deserves respect, though as I've frequently seen her in a state of collapse due to overindulgence in the narcotic thazis, I don't feel the need to be too formal.

'Do you always greet your clients this way?'

'Only when I'm trying to sleep off the effect of beer. Is this a social call? And incidentally, why are you in disguise?'

'It's a professional call. I'm here to hire you. I'm in disguise because I don't want anyone to recognise me.'

Turai's sorcerers wear a distinctive rainbow cloak, and as Lisutaris is an aristocratic woman, she'd normally have a fine gown under her cloak, along with jewellery, gold sandals and the like. Instead she's dressed in the plain garb of the lower classes, though any observer could tell that her extravagant hair wasn't coiffured at one of the cheap establishments you'd find in Twelve Seas. Even in a plain robe, Lisutaris, Mistress of the Sky, is a striking woman. She's only a little younger than me, but she's always been an careful with her looks.

'I see nothing's changed around here,' she says, sweeping some junk off a chair and sitting down lightly. 'Is it absolutely necessary for you to live in such squalor?'

'Private investigation never pays that well.'

'You were well remunerated for your work at the Sorcerers Assemblage, I believe.'

'Not as well as I should have been. And some recent investments turned out less well than I anticipated.'

'You mean you lost it all at the chariot races?'

'That's right.'

Lisutaris nods. 'I also lost money at the last meeting. Of course, I can afford it. Well, Thraxas, as you're in need of money, I expect you'll be glad to take on the case.'

'Tell me about it.'

There's a slight delay while Lisutaris lights a thazis stick. She offers me one, which I accept. Thazis is a mild narcotic for most people, but Lisutaris is a very heavy user. She invented a new kind of water pipe and developed a spell for making the plants grow faster. The citizens of Turai are proud that one of our own was recently elected as Head of the Sorcerers Guild, but they might be surprised if they knew the full extent of Lisutaris's habit. Generally she's too intoxicated to walk by the end of the day.

'Have you heard of the sorcerer's green jewel?'

I shake my head. 'I never made it past apprentice. My sorcerous knowledge has a lot of gaps.'

'Not many people have heard of it. Even I was unaware of its existence till I became privy to government secrets after my election as Head of the Guild. The green jewel is Turai's guarantee against unexpected invasion. In the hands of a powerful sorcerer, the jewel acts as an all-seeing eye. No matter how private the Orcs might try to keep their affairs, we will always be able to tell when they're massing armies against us. It's an important piece of rock.'

I'm surprised to learn of this artefact, and a little puzzled by Lisutaris's explanation. 'It sounds like a handy thing to have. But doesn't the Sorcerers Guild have plenty of spells for giving us advance warning?'

'In theory, we do. However the Orcish Sorcerers Guild has spent the last fifteen years in a concentrated attempt to negate every one of them. There used to be twenty or more far-seeing spells we could use. Government intelligence now indicates this is down to two or three. The Orcs have successfully developed counter-spells to the rest. The Orcish Sorcerers Guild is a far more cohesive unit than most things in the east. Even when their states have been riven by internal wars, they've kept working away on the problem. If they come up with counter-spells to our few remaining incantations for tracking their movements, the green jewel will be the only thing standing between the west and oblivion.'

This talk of Orcish wars, while uncomfortable, has got my attention. I fought in the last one. So did Lisutaris, Gurd, and practically every other able-bodied Turanian who was old enough to wield a blade or chant a spell. In the climax of a savage and destructive conflict we threw them back from the walls, but it was a close thing till the Elves arrived. Without their aid, Turai would now be an outpost of the Orcish empire, or a pile of ruins.

'So the Orcish sorcerers have been busy and we're now dependent on the green jewel.'

'That's right,' says Lisutaris. 'I hope I've impressed you with the great importance of this item?'

'You have. So what about it?'

'It was entrusted to me.'

'And?'

'I lost it.'

'You lost it? How?'

'I put it in my bag when I went to the chariot races. That was not as careless as it might sound. To use the jewel properly, it's necessary for a sorcerer to become familiar with it, and learn its properties in all circumstances. Unfortunately when I returned home it was no longer in my bag. It may have dropped out when I was giving my secretary money to place a bet, and been taken immediately by some alert thief.'

'What chariot were you betting on?'

'City Destroyer.'

'Bad choice. I lost a bundle on that.'

'The jewel was–'

'Didn't you think there was something fishy about the way it dropped out of the running on the last lap? I think the charioteer may have been bribed.'

'Of course I looked for it at the time but–'

'I'm not convinced that Melus the Fair was the right choice for Stadium sorcerer. I'm sure there's some corruption going on that she's not picking up on.'

Lisutaris informs me coldly that she didn't come here to discuss our mutual misfortunes at the races. 'I've just lost the most important weapon in the nation's armoury and I need it back quickly. If word of this gets out, the King will have me expelled from the city. So I'd appreciate it if you'd start investigating without further delay.'

'No need to get upset. I was just sharing in your misfortunes. City Destroyer should have won that race at a canter. It's getting so a man can't make an honest bet these days.'

I notice that Lisutaris has a threatening glint in her eye. I get down to business. 'You'll need to tell me some more details.'

'The green jewel is set in a pendant, Elvish silverwork, quite distinctive. However, I don't require you to do much investigating. Though I was unable to find the pendant immediately - I didn't want to draw attention to my loss by performing a spell at the Stadium Superbius under the nose of Consul Kalius - as soon as I returned home I put my powers to use. I have now located the jewel. It's being held in a tavern next to the harbour. The Spiked Mace. Are you familiar with it?'

'Yes. It's the sort of place you'd expect stolen jewels to end up.'

'So I imagined. You will understand, Thraxas, that absolute secrecy is necessary. I can't allow the King, the Consul or any of my fellow sorcerers to learn that I've lost the jewel. That being the case, I am unable to stride into the tavern myself and start blasting people with spells. Explanations would be called for which I would be unwilling to provide.'

I understand well enough. In a city which hates and fears the Orcs, anyone found to have carelessly lost our most powerful protection against them would soon find their life not worth living. It is a shocking piece of carelessness on Lisutaris's part, though in truth it's not surprising. Her thazis habit is very severe.

'Why don't you just send someone from your household?'

'I deem it too much of a risk. Even if they were not recognised, there's no telling who might learn of the affair. Turanian servants are not known for their discretion. My secretary is absolutely loyal, but she is a young woman of rather delicate constitution and not suitable for a task such as this.'

From Lisutaris's description of events, it seems quite possible that the thief won't realise what he's got. He may believe he's holding nothing more than a normal piece of dress jewellery and try to sell it as soon as possible for a modest profit.

Lisutaris shifts uncomfortably in the sticky heat of my office. During the winter the Mistress of the Sky, like every other sorcerer, had warming spells on her apparel to fight off the bitter cold, but cooling oneself by sorcery is more difficult. A worried expression flits across her face. 'Given that discretion is essential, you won't start throwing your legal powers around, will you?'

I frown. I've been busy trying to forget that I had any legal powers. After many years as a private citizen, I was unexpectedly elevated to the position of Tribune of the People some months ago by Cicerius, the Deputy Consul. The Tribunate, a sort of official citizens' representative, was an extinct post till Cicerius nominated me last winter. He did this purely so I would be granted access to the Sorcerers Assemblage. It was never his intention, or mine, that I'd actually do anything official, but I was blackmailed into using my Tribune's powers to halt an eviction, something which carried with it various political ramifications. Since I'm always keen to avoid getting involved in Turai's murky political world, I've been playing down the Tribune bit as much as possible ever since, and have flatly refused to use the authority of the position again. It would only land me in trouble with some powerful party or other.

'Don't worry. The post was purely honorary. Senator Lodius forced me into action once, but that's it.'

The position of Tribune lasts for a year and I'm hoping that the last few months of my term will pass unnoticed by all, leaving me once more a private citizen. A man who goes around using political power in Turai needs a lot more protection than I have.

Lisutaris lights another thazis stick.

'You didn't gamble the jewel away, did you?'

She has the good grace to smile. 'No. I'm still wealthy. However, if the loss is made public, you would not be the only person to make that remark. The Stadium Superbius was an unfortunate place to lose the pendant and there has been some jealousy in certain circles since I was elected Head of the Guild.'

Lisutaris takes out her purse and lays some money on the table. 'Thirty gurans. Your standard retainer, I believe. There's one more thing. I positively must have the jewel back quickly. In four days' time I'm holding a masked ball and the Crown Prince will be there, along with Kalius and Cicerius. It's likely they will wish to view the jewel. Consul Kalius was, I know, somewhat dubious about letting me take it from the Palace.'

Anyone who saw Lisutaris stumbling around the Sorcerers Assemblage in a thazis-induced stupor would have been dubious about letting her take anything valuable home with her.

'Couldn't you cancel the ball?'

Apparently not. Lisutaris's masked ball is set to be a highlight of the social season. I wonder what it's like to have a social season.

'Well, don't worry. I'll get it back for you.'

'When you do, be sure not to stare into it,' says Lisutaris. 'It's a powerful sorcerous object. Handling the pendant for a short space of time is safe, but it could be hazardous for an untrained person to gaze deeply into the green jewel. It may induce fainting, or worse.'

Lisutaris is now on her third thazis stick. She finishes it, drops the end in my bin, and lights another.

'How is Makri?' Lisutaris is acquainted with Makri; she hired her to be her bodyguard at the Sorcerers Assemblage.

'Same as usual. Busy and bad-tempered.'

'I have something for her.'

The sorcerer hands me an envelope. Makri's name is written on it in the fancy script of a professional scribe. I promise to pass it on. I'm curious, but I figure it's none of my business, so after Lisutaris leaves I dump it in Makri's room. Then I douse myself with water to get rid of the last effects of the alcohol and thazis, and strap on my sword. Finally I load one spell - the most I can comfortably manage - into my memory and head out into the streets. Outside, the knife sharpener and the fish vendor are still arguing. It's bound to end in violence.

Chapter Three

At the foot of the stairs, I run into Moxalan, younger son of Honest Mox the bookmaker. Only son I should say, as his older sibling succumbed to an overdose of dwa last winter, around the same time that Minarixa the baker also died of an overdose. I miss the baker terribly. Life isn't the same without her pastries. I don't miss Mox's son, but as I do a lot of trade with the bookmaker, it's as well to be civil to his family. Moxalan is around nineteen, open-faced and friendly, not yet having taken on the mean and cunning look of the hardened bookmaker. His tunic is plain but well cut, and his sandals are expensive enough to let anyone know that his father's business isn't doing badly. We exchange greetings and he tells me that he's here to ask Makri for help with theories of architecture, which makes no sense to me.

'Theories of architecture?'

'For the Guild College. We're in the same class. I missed a lecture so I want Makri's notes.'

I didn't know Honest Mox was sending his son to Guild College, though it's not really a surprise. A man who's raking in as much cash as Mox can afford the fees. Mox, as a bookmaker, has very low social status and it's not uncommon for men of low status, on becoming wealthy, to try and improve the family lot by educating their sons and getting them into the civil service, or something similar.

'Not entering the family business, then?'

He shakes his head. 'I help out a little, but my father wants me to better myself. Is Makri in the tavern?'

'Yes. She's working.'

Moxalan is confident that Makri will have a full set of notes from the course. 'She's the best student. Much better than me. Did you know she's top of every class?'

Makri probably mentioned it but I don't pay that much attention. I notice that Moxalan's face goes a little dopey as he mentions Makri's name. I recognise the symptom. Young men, on seeing Makri's impressive figure crammed into two barely adequate strips of chainmail, tend to forget that their mothers want them to marry a sensible girl from a good family, and their fathers warned them to stay away from women with Orcish blood. What these young men don't realise is that their mothers were right. Life with Makri would be hell, no matter how fabulous they think her figure is. She'll never shake off the effects of growing up as a gladiator. At the first sign of a domestic argument, Makri would very likely behead her husband and paint her face with his blood.

'I thought she'd be with you,' says Moxalan.

'Why?'

'Because of the warning.' Moxalan explains that he's heard about Dandelion warning me of a bloodbath. In Twelve Seas, rumours travel fast. I'm aggravated, and not just because I don't like my private business becoming the stuff of gossip. The implication seems to be that if I'm in danger I need Makri to protect me. As if I didn't get along fine for years before she arrived.

'Don't worry about me,' I grunt, and take my leave.

The Spiked Mace is an unpleasant little establishment close to the harbour, full of drunken sailors and unruly stevedores. Unlike many of the local taverns, it's not owned by the Brotherhood, the criminal gang that controls most crime south of the river. That's good news for me. If I tried to remove stolen loot from the

Brotherhood, they'd be down on me like a bad spell. Most likely I'll find the pendant in the hands of some petty thief who'll be keen to sell it as soon as possible to raise money for his next dose of dwa. If he's desperate enough and lets me have it cheap, I might even make a profit on the deal. Lisutaris isn't going to gripe over a few gurans, not with the wealth she has. As usual, contact with a member of the Turanian aristocracy has left me envious. I've always been poor. Some years ago I worked my way up to a nice job as Senior Investigator at the Palace, with a big office, and lackeys to do the work. Then I drank myself out of the job. My father always said I'd come to nothing. So far I've been unable to prove him wrong.

The sun beats down. The streets are as hot as Orcish hell. I6nside the Spiked Mace it's worse. The heat mingles with the smell of ale and burning dwa. Thazis smoke drifts over the tables. The wooden beams overhead are blackened with age. The prostitute who patrols the area with red ribbons in her hair strives vainly to interest the largely inebriated clientele. There's a woman on the floor who looks like she might be dead. I shake my head. This is about as low as life gets. No civilised person would visit this tavern.

'Thraxas! We were wondering where you'd got to.'

I do come here occasionally. The barman, and owner of the establishment, is Gavarax, one-time captain of his own fighting trireme, till he was kicked out of the navy for failing to hand over booty to the King. He's dark-skinned and has a scar stretching from chin to eyebrow, a result of a naval encounter he's not shy of bragging about when the old salts get to remembering the old days. Taking a beer simply to be polite, I ask him if there's been anyone in trying to sell a stolen jewel. Gavarax isn't the sort of man who'd give information to the Civil Guard, but he knows me well enough to pass on anything that won't get him into trouble, providing there's something in it for him. Gavarax waits till the customer at the bar - a docker, from his red bandanna, but not one who's planning on working soon - departs unsteadily with his drink, before leaning over to inform me quietly that actually, yes, there was a man of that sort. I slide a few gurans over the bar.

'He's upstairs now in the private room. With a couple of others. Never seen them before.'

I make to leave. Gavarax grabs my arm. 'If you're going to kill anyone, go easy on the furniture.'

Making my way through the smoky, noisy room to the stairs at the back, I'm thinking that this case is going to be even easier than I anticipated. I climb the stairs and wait outside the room, listening. Not a sound. I boot the door open and march in, sleep spell ready, in case anyone is planning on resisting. There are four men in the room, but they're not going to do much resisting. Three of them are dead and the other one looks like he'll be joining them soon. Each one stabbed. It makes for a very large puddle of blood. I bend over the only one who's still breathing, albeit shallowly. He tries to look at me, but his eyes won't focus. 'I was on a beautiful golden ship,' he whispers. Then he coughs up blood and dies.

As last words go, they were fairly strange. I look round the room. The window at the back is open and there's blood on the sill. There's an alleyway outside and it's not too far to the ground. No problem making a getaway, though I'm wondering quite what sort of person it was who got away. Obviously a person or persons capable of taking care of themselves. The dead men are all wearing swords. Petty thieves are rarely trained fighters, but it's never that easy to kill four armed opponents.

Moving quickly, I start searching the bodies. They're still warm. I've handled plenty of corpses in my time but I don't enjoy it. I recognise one of them. Axaten, a petty thief, often worked at the Stadium Superbius, picking up whatever he could from careless race-goers. I don't recognise the other three. None of them has the pendant. All I find are a few coins in their purses. No tattoos, nothing identifying them as belonging to any organisation. I search the room, again without results.

I look down into the alley. An easy enough drop for a lighter person maybe, but with my bulk I'm not keen to try it out. Besides, there's the matter of four corpses to consider. I'd like nothing better than to leave them here and sneak out, but there's no point. Gavarax isn't going to cover for me. As soon as the bodies are found, he'll squeal to the Civil Guard and I'll be a handy suspect for murder. I curse mightily and retrace my steps downstairs to the bar. Gavarax isn't pleased.

'Four of them? All dead? The guards are going to love this.' His eyes narrow. 'Did you kill them?'

'I'm not that quick with a sword these days.'

Gavarax glances at my belly. He can believe it. He sends a boy off with a message and I wait in the dingy tavern for the guards to arrive. I'm now in for what will undoubtedly be an uncomfortable interrogation. I'm going to have more than a few words to say to Lisutaris, Mistress of the Sky.

Chapter Four

Approximately nine hours after finding the bodies, I climb out of a horse-drawn landus, pay the driver, and head up the long, long pathway to Lisutaris's villa. I've had six hours of questioning from the Civil Guard and two hours' sleep, and I'm not in what you'd call a good mood. The sight of Lisutaris's beautifully tended flower beds, trees and bushes doesn't make things any better. People with this sort of money generally don't find themselves on the wrong end of six hours' hostile questioning by a series of guards, each one dumb as an Orc and none of them looking like they'd mind knocking me around the room if I didn't come up with some better answers. If Captain Rallee hadn't appeared they probably would have. The Guards don't actually think I killed the four men in the Spiked Mace. Not Captain Rallee anyway, he knows me better, though some of his superiors think I'm capable of anything. Prefect Drinius, Head of the Guard in Twelve Seas, would like nothing better than to send me off to a prison galley. Rallee's more sensible, but the problem is I can never bring myself to tell the Guards too much about any case I'm working on. No matter how many times the Captain demanded I tell him what I was doing in the Mace, I just wasn't going to say that I was there looking for a pendant for Lisutaris. If I started identifying my clients every time I ran into trouble, I'd soon run out of clients.

Eventually Captain Rallee let me go, with the warning that he'd be down on me like a bad spell if I found myself in the vicinity of any more corpses on his beat. After assuring him that I'd endeavour to stay well clear of anyone dead, I took a hurried breakfast at the Avenging Axe and headed off to see Lisutaris. By the time I reach the front door - a very fancy affair, with a portal, engravings and gold fittings - I'm madder than a mad dragon and looking forward to batting some minion out of the way. Unfortunately the door is answered by a servant I've met several times previously, and she ushers me straight in.

'I'll tell the Mistress you're here,' she says, politely, and vanishes before I can think of a reason to fire off an angry retort.

I'm in a room overlooking the grounds. Vast, extensive gardens. More trees, flowers, bushes and landscaped pathways than a man would know what to do with, plus private fish ponds and an orchard which Lisutaris treats with sorcery to produce fresh fruit out of season. Last month she hosted a garden party for the city's Elvish ambassadors. It was delightful. So I read anyway. There wasn't any danger of me being invited.

The Mistress of the Sky drifts into the room. She's smiling, slightly vacantly. Lisutaris always starts early with her water pipe.

'Thraxas. This is very quick work. Congratulations.'

'I don't have the pendant.'

'You don't?'

'No. But I have four dead bodies and an even closer acquaintance with the Civil Guard.' I fill her in on yesterday's events. She's displeased to learn of my failure.

'So you don't know who these men were?'

'I recognised one of them. Axaten. Petty thief, works the stadium, or used to before he got his throat cut. Might well be the person who stole the pendant. I didn't know the other three and I don't know who killed them. I was hoping you might tell me.'

Lisutaris looks blank. 'What do you mean?'

'I mean you sent me to retrieve a jewel from a thief and I ended up in a slaughterhouse. Any idea why that might be?'

'No.'

'Do the words "I was on a beautiful golden ship" mean anything to you?'

'No. Is it a quotation?'

'I don't know. I never studied the great poets. But they were said to me by a dying man. I've seen plenty of dying men but no one ever used that particular phrase before.'

I look meaningfully at Lisutaris. She doesn't like the meaning.

'Are you suggesting I may have withheld information?'

'Well, have you?'

Lisutaris rises from her chair. 'Thraxas. I appreciated your help during the election. But possibly our close contact at that time has left you with the erroneous impression that you're free to come into my house and call me a liar. You are not.'

The Mistress of the Sky looks threatening. I tell her to calm down. She claps her hands and a servant enters carrying her thazis pipe on a tray.

'That's calmer than I intended. Can't you lay off that stuff for a single day?'

Lisutaris doesn't deign to answer. She makes me wait while she goes through the ritual of filling her pipe and lighting it. As she inhales for the first time, she rubs one gold-sandalled foot over the other, signifying pleasure, maybe.

'Surely there are any number of reasons why those men might have been killed? In a place like that?'

'True. Arguments among thieves can quickly turn murderous in Twelve Seas. But I don't like it that they were killed while they just happened to be in possession of such a valuable item. You're saying no one knows what this jewel does, but the way it looks to me, someone does. Either the person who stole it, or whoever's got it now. That makes everything a lot more difficult.'

'No one else could know the true value of that pendant.' Lisutaris is adamant. 'Its use is known only to the King, his senior ministers and the Head of the Sorcerers Guild.'

'Turai is corrupt from top to bottom. There are a lot of people well-versed in digging out secrets, particularly when there's a profit involved. How about your own household?'

'No one here knew of the pendant's true purpose, apart from my secretary, who's entirely trustworthy.'

'I'd like to talk to her.'

Lisutaris shakes her head. 'You will not speak to my secretary. You may take it from me that she's not a suspect in this matter.'

Lisutaris draws deeply on the thazis pipe. It was bad enough losing the pendant to a petty thief. If it's ended up in the hands of some gang who'll sell it to the highest bidder she's in big trouble, especially if the highest bidder turns out to be one of the Orcish nations. She pulls a slender cord that hangs by the door, summoning a servant. 'I'll locate the jewel again and you must retrieve it immediately.'

'Are you sure you don't want to bring someone else in?' I ask. 'Palace Security, for instance? Maybe it's time to let the Consul know what's happened.'

'If Kalius finds out about this he'll be down on me like a bad spell. I'm not ready to be expelled from the city just yet.'

A servant arrives carrying a golden bowl of an inky-black liquid, kuriya. In this pool a good sorcerer can often see versions of events both past and present. I've used it myself, with difficulty. These days I find it very hard to reach the required levels of concentration. Such is Lisutaris's power that she requires no preparation. She simply flutters her hand over the liquid and a picture starts to form.

'Another tavern,' mutters the Sorceress. 'The Mermaid. Do you know it?'

'I do. It's bad news. The Mermaid is run by the Brotherhood.'

'So?'

'Getting a jewel back from that organisation is a lot harder than getting it back from a petty thief. Still, there's always the chance they don't know what they're handling. If it's just ended up there as a result of some argument among thieves, I still might be able to retrieve it. Might mean making a larger payment, but if I pretend it's a family heirloom the owner is desperate to get back, there's no reason for them not to believe me.'

Lisutaris summons another servant and instructs her to bring me a bag of fifty guran pieces. 'Get it back. No matter what it costs.'

Workers have arrived in the garden outside and are putting up a large marquee. 'Preparations for the masked ball?'

Lisutaris nods. 'I must have the pendant back before the ball. I'm certain the Consul will ask about it. Did Makri get her invitation?'

'What?'

'Her invitation,' repeats Lisutaris.

'You invited Makri?'

'Yes. After all, she did excellent service for me as my bodyguard at the Sorcerers Assemblage. I felt she deserved some further reward. I have promised to introduce her to the Professor of Mathematics at the Imperial University.'

'What for? Nothing is going to make the University take Makri as a student.'

'Perhaps not,' agrees Lisutaris. 'However, she'll enjoy the ball.'

I stare out at the huge marquee. The workers, efficient in a way you rarely see in Twelve Seas, have already got it into shape and are carrying in tables, chairs and candlesticks. The servant returns with my bag of coins. Another servant leads me out to the carriage Lisutaris is providing for my journey.

The situation with the pendant is now extremely serious. It's going to take some clever work to retrieve it. However, I'm not thinking about this. I'm thinking about the gross injustice of Makri, barbarian gladiator who hardly knows how to use a fork or spoon, being invited to Lisutaris's smart party. No sign of an invitation for me, of course. Don't worry about Thraxas. He'll slog his way round town, fighting criminals and facing danger for you. He'll sit around in a Guards' cell for six hours, protecting your good name. Doesn't mean you have to invite him to your party. I'm quite happy drinking in the Avenging Axe in Twelve Seas with the rest of the struggling masses. Damn Lisutaris. I never liked the woman.

South of the river, my driver starts getting nervous. His duties for Lisutaris don't normally take him to this sort of place. In the sweltering heat it seems to take forever to work our way through the heavy traffic, wagons on their way to the harbour. When he finally offloads me in Twelve Seas, he spurs his horses and departs as swiftly as he can, pleased to be on his way.

'Thanks for the lift,' I mutter, and head into the Avenging Axe. Urgent business or not, I can't visit the Mermaid before eating something. I could do with a beer as well. Lisutaris broke out the wine for me, but these fine Elvish vintages don't satisfy a man. Outside the tavern I again run into Moxalan. He's in conversation with old Parax, the shoemaker.

'Was there much of a bloodbath?' Parax asks me, which is quite an odd question.

I shrug.

'Many deaths?'

'That's private business. And what do you care?'

'We're concerned about you,' says Parax.

If old Parax is concerned about me, it's the first I've heard about it. I wonder why the bookmaker's son is still hanging around. He must have got his architecture notes by now. Possibly he's come back to see Makri again, poor fool that he is. Suddenly violent shouting erupts from inside the tavern. I hurry in to find the place in chaos. Makri, axe in hand, is attempting to leave while Gurd and Tanrose are trying to hold her back. Several tables are overturned and the lunchtime drinkers are cowering in the corners. From the look of things I'd say it's been quite a struggle. Makri is a demon in a sword fight, but Gurd's a very strong man and he's managed to drag Makri to a halt. Not wishing to actually kill her employer, she twists round to face him.

'Gurd, I'm warning you. Let go of me now.'

Despite her skinny frame and Gurd's immense strength, Makri is quite capable of beating him in combat if she gets angry enough to use her weapons. Gurd knows this. He doesn't let go. I hurry forward and force my way in between them.

'What the hell is going on?'

'She's going to kill everyone at Guild College,' explains Tanrose.

I blink. 'What?'

'You heard her,' snarls Makri, and wrenches herself free to head for the door. I hurl myself after her.

'Makri. It's only an examination. Don't take it so personally.'

'It's not the examination,' growls Makri, and disappears through the door.

I look to Gurd for an explanation.

'She's been expelled for theft,' he says.

I rush out into the street. In these circumstances Makri really will slaughter everyone. Damn the woman and her temper, I don't have time for this. I catch up with her on the corner, trampling over a beggar who picked this unfortunate moment to accost her.

'Makri, instead of marching up Quintessence Street waving your axe, how about telling me what's going on?'

Makri halts. There's a look of murderous rage in her eyes I haven't seen since the last time I insulted her pointed ears.

'Some money went missing from the students' common room. Professor Toarius says I took it. He's expelled me. Now get out of my way while I go and kill him.'

'He says you took it? Was there an investigation?'

'So he claims. Get out of my way.'

'Stop telling me to get out of the way. Don't you think it might be better for someone to sort this out rather than you just killing the Professor? They'll arrest you and hang you.'

'No they won't. I'll kill everyone who tries and then I'll leave the city.'

'Well, that would be an alternative plan.'

A dog starts sniffing round Makri's ankles. She kicks it. It goes away whimpering. The way Makri is brandishing her axe it's lucky to still have its head. Despite the fact that Makri is barbaric, annoying and unreasonable, not to mention part Orc, she's one of the very few friends I have in this city. And while I'm not going to come out and admit it in public, she's been a lot of help in some of my recent cases. I'd probably regret it if she was hanged.

'Tell me what happened.'

Makri screws up her face. Not hastening to kill someone who's accused her of theft is taking a lot of effort. 'I went into college this morning. For my class in rhetoric. I had to go to the common room to leave my bag because I had two knives with me and they don't let me take them into class.'

'Why did you have two knives with you?'

'Why not?'

'Foolish question. Go on.'

'There are some lockers. I have a key. I locked my knives away then I went to my class. We were learning how to make a speech in court. About halfway through the lesson a student came in and said the Professor wanted to see me. That was unusual. Normally he tries to avoid me. So I went along to his office and he said that another student had lost some money from the common room and I'd been seen taking it! And then he expelled me!'

Makri's voice has been rising throughout this and as she finishes she's almost overcome with emotion. People stare at us, though not as much as they would have a year or so ago. The sight of Makri walking along Quintessence Street heavily armed is something the locals have become used to. As a woman with Orcish blood she's not exactly popular, but people know better than to get in her way.

'Makri. Go home. I'll fix things. I know the professor has it in for you. No doubt after the money went missing he was keen to jump to conclusions.'

'How dare he accuse me of theft!'

It is unjust. Makri is relentlessly honest. Gets me down at times.

'Yes, how dare he. But do you really want to be chased out of the city? After all the work you've done here? What about your plan to go to the Imperial University?'

'You laugh at that plan. Everyone laughs at it.'

'Of course I laugh at it. It's impossible. But you've managed to do other impossible things since you arrived, so what the hell, maybe you'll manage this one too. So stop threatening to kill your professor, and go back to the Avenging Axe. I'll go to the College, find out what's going on, and sort it out.'

Makri stares at me for a long time. It's alien to her nature to let another person fix a problem for her.

'Can you fix it today?'

'I can try.'

'If you fix it today then it's okay. If not, I swear I'll kill Toarius tomorrow, and every other person at the college if I feel like it.'

Makri spins on her heel to march back into the tavern. Then, as if remembering something, she spins round again. 'What's happening on the case you're working on?'

'It's gone bad.'

'Anyone dead?'

'Yes.'

'How many?'

I stare at her. 'What do you mean, how many?'

'I just wondered.'

'Four, if you must know. Why is everyone suddenly interested in my business?'

Makri marches back into the tavern. Not having had the chance to fill up on beer, I follow her. I head for the bar with a determined expression on my face, warning everyone to stay out of my path. Unfortunately this has no effect on Dandelion, who appears from nowhere and practically throws herself in front of me.

'I have terrible news,' she wails.

'If it's something to do with the stars, I'm not interested.'

'You must listen!'

'Can it wait till I get a beer?'

Apparently not. There's no putting the woman off. Dandelion is jumping up and down in her frenzied eagerness to tell me something. 'They're betting on the result. Even though I told them it was wrong.'

She's lost me completely here. 'What are you talking about?'

'Everyone is laying bets on how many deaths there are going to be in the case you're working on! It's because I warned you there was going to be a bloodbath! A bookmaker has been here and they're taking bets!'

'Dandelion!' says Makri, loudly. 'Don't distract Thraxas with your fanciful stories. He's a busy man.'

'She gets these strange ideas,' says Gurd, and looks guilty.

I stare at the pair of them. 'Is this true?'

'First I've heard about it,' says Makri. 'Shouldn't you be on your way to the college to clear me of theft?'

'That can wait. I wondered why you were so keen to know the exact body count.'

Makri contrives to look innocent. 'I wouldn't place a bet on such a tragedy as four deaths,' she says, in a dignified manner.

'Four?' Parax has been listening in the background. 'Did you say four? Already?' He turns to Moxalan. 'I want to raise my bet.'

There are some mutters of interest from various onlookers who seem to be heavily involved already.

'We could be looking at double figures,' says one of them.

I'm furious. 'Is the whole tavern in on this? I can't believe you'd all stoop so low!' I cry, taking in Gurd, Makri and the assembled lowlifes in one sweeping stare.

'Couldn't you just have stayed quiet?' says Makri to Dandelion.

'Don't pick on Dandelion,' I roar. 'She's the only honest person in the place. Makri, I'm appalled at you.'

A vocal faction want to know if it's true that the Sorcerers Guild has declared war on the Brotherhood. 'If they start throwing spells around we could be talking about fifty deaths. Maybe more.'

'If Thraxas gets killed, do we keep on counting?' demands Parax.

'No. It's clearly stated in the rules that Thraxas's death ends the body count,' says Moxalan.

'What rules?' I demand

'The rules of the contest. Don't look at me like that, Thraxas. I'm a bookmaker's son. Just because I'm going to college doesn't mean I've left the business.'

I shake my head. Sweat is pouring down my tunic. I never expected to find any trace of ethics among the clientele of the Avenging Axe, but even I'm surprised at this. It's immoral. Taking bets on how many deaths there are going to be in my current case? What's that going to do for my reputation? I curse everyone roundly. So irate am I that I actually march out of the tavern without picking up a beer and I can't remember the last time I did that. I need to get to the Mermaid to recover the pendant as quickly as possible, so I set off at a brisk pace, promising myself I'll have more than a few harsh words for Makri and Gurd when I get back.

Youthful dwa dealers hover round the alleyway that leads to the Mermaid. Close by are customers in various states of consciousness. Even in the open air the heavy aroma of burning dwa is easily discernible. The situation with this narcotic is now completely out of hand. Ten years ago the local youths would have been stealing fruit from the market. Now they're knifing strangers in the back for a few gurans. The violence of the gangs that control the trade has increased in proportion to the profits involved. The huge increase in illegal profits has led to city-wide corruption on unheard-of levels. Turai is a mess. It's not just the Orcs we need protecting from.

Lisutaris hired me to retrieve her pendant. I've failed once and I don't intend to fail again. I march towards the Mermaid ready to look Casax, the Brotherhood boss, squarely in the eye and demand the return of the jewel. This doesn't work out so well. Before I reach the door it bursts open and Casax, Karlox and about twenty of their associates rush out of the building, pursued by smoke and flames. The Mermaid is about to burn to the ground. I shake my head. It's turning into another really bad day.

Chapter Five

With its hot, dry summers, Turai is prone to serious outbreaks of fire. Fortunately, the city's fire-fighting services are well advanced. The best in the civilised world, some say. Given that much of the land is covered with tall wooden buildings crammed close to their neighbours, nothing else would do. Since half the city burned down around seventy years ago, there's been a sustained effort to improve our fire-fighting capabilities. The Prefect who runs each district is obliged to provide and maintain a sufficient number of water-carrying wagons, complete with equipment and emergency personnel to man them. This served us well during the last war, when the Orcish armies besieging Turai hurled fireballs over the walls with their siege devices, but failed to destroy the city. Around that time an army engineer developed an efficient new type of water pump which, in the hands of operators strong enough to keep the pistons moving, is capable of throwing water almost fifty yards. Equipped with this device, our fire-fighters have in recent years performed heroic service and are one of the few groups of people universally admired in Turai.

A great cry goes up for the fire services. An alarm bell is sounded and people look to the end of the alleyway, anxiously expecting horse-drawn wagons to appear. Nothing happens. No wagons come. As Casax the Brotherhood boss sees his headquarters starting to disappear in flames, he becomes agitated. He screams for his men to bring water from neighbouring houses, waving his fists to encourage them. The way the flames are taking hold, I doubt that this is going to do much good. Normally I'd enjoy seeing the Mermaid burning to the ground. However, it strikes me that it's hardly helpful to my immediate purposes. I approach Casax. He doesn't acknowledge me, being too busy trying to save the tavern to pay any attention to an unwelcome investigator. I grab him by the arm.

'Aren't you forgetting something, Casax?'

I point to a young man in a fancy cloak who's slumped in the alleyway, suffering either from inhaling smoke or, more probably, from shock at finding himself dragged out of a burning building in the nick of time.

'Your pet sorcerer.'

'What?'

'Orius. Or, to give him his full name, Orius Fire Tamer. Which name leads me to suspect he ought to be able to do something.'

Casax wastes no time. In seconds he's dragging the unfortunate young man up on to his feet. 'Put out the fire!'

Orius looks like he'd rather be elsewhere, concentrating on his recovery, and struggles to stand erect. I can't say I'm sympathetic. I never thought it was a good idea for the young sorcerer to get involved with the Brotherhood. Life as a gang member has its rewards, but it can be tough at times. Just when it seems that the flames must engulf the tavern, Orius manages to gather his concentration. He chants a spell. The flames seem to weaken. He chants again, and they go out. The crowd cheer. Orius Fire Tamer collapses in a heap. To give him his due, it was a nice piece of sorcery in difficult circumstances.

Casax doesn't waste any time congratulating his sorcerer. He needs to see that his headquarters have survived intact, so he strides swiftly into the tavern, motioning his henchmen to follow. I walk in after them, uninvited. The building hasn't fared too badly. Orius halted the flames before they really took hold. Coughing from the effects of the smoke that still hangs in the air, I look around. I don't quite know what I'm looking for and I don't get much of a chance to search before Casax spots me and angrily demands to know what I'm doing here.

'Just visiting. And you owe me for reminding you about Orius Fire Tamer.'

'I'll send you a present,' rasps Casax. 'Now get out of here.'

'You want to tell me how the fire started?'

'I don't want to tell you anything. Maybe you should be telling me something.'

I shake my head. 'All I know is that Prefect Drinius has been pocketing the money he should've been spending on fire wagons.'

'So what are you doing here? I get suspicious when investigators turn up just when my building is burning down.'

Casax stares at me. I stare back at him. We've had a few run-ins in the past. Nothing too serious. Nothing to make us lifelong friends either. All around, Brotherhood men are dampening down the last few tongues of flame and carrying boxes here and there, presumably illicit goods, or maybe Casax's records. Casax is an organised man. All Brotherhood bosses are. Organised and violent.

'I'm looking for a stolen jewel. In the shape of a pendant.'

'So?'

'It was stolen from a sorcerer. The sorcerer traced it here.'

'Then the sorcerer was mistaken.'

'I doubt it. And the sorcerer would pay well to get it back. It's a family heirloom.'

Before Casax can reply, he's interrupted by Karlox, a tough enforcer. 'They're dead,' says Karlox.

'Who's dead?'

'The three strangers who wanted to see you. They're still upstairs. But dead.'

'Burned?' asks Casax.

'No. Stabbed.'

Casax's brow furrows. 'What do you mean, stabbed? No one gets stabbed in here unless I say so.'

'They weren't by any chance three men who came here to sell you some stolen jewellery, were they?' I ask.

Casax stares at me. 'Time to leave. investigator.'

Knowing I'm not going to learn anything more, I turn to go. Casax calls after me. When I turn to face him again, he's got a mocking smile on his face. 'That makes seven, I believe.'

'Seven? Seven what?'

'Seven bodies. You want to give me and Karlox here any inside information? We might place a little wager with young Moxalan.'

His henchman Karlox laughs like this is a great joke. I try to disguise my feelings, without success. Now word of the betting in the Avenging Axe has reached the Brotherhood. Soon it will be all over Twelve Seas. All over the city, maybe. I'm fast becoming a laughing stock. Damn that idiot Dandelion and her foolish warnings about a bloodbath.

I haven't recovered the pendant, though my intuition is telling me that whoever the three guys were, they had it with them. Someone killed them, and made off with it, probably using the fire as a distraction. It was a neat piece of work. It's not easy removing stolen goods from under the noses of the Brotherhood. It's a relief to get out of the smoky building. Not much relief, though, as the sun hits me full in the face. Despite the commotion caused by the fire, the dwa dealers are still doing a brisk trade in the alleyway.

Three more dead. Seven since I started looking. A bloodbath? Perhaps Dandelion was right. Maybe she can read the stars. Maybe she can really talk to the dolphins. I wonder how many bodies Makri is betting on. I'd expect her to go for a high total. She's used to a lot of carnage. As I'm so annoyed at Makri, I'm tempted to refuse to investigate the accusation of theft against her. Let her sort it out herself. I sigh. If I let her sort it out herself she'll end up on the gallows. Cursing the woman for her foolish academic pretensions, I set off along the dusty road to the College.

The Guild College is sited at the edge of Pashish, a slightly less unpleasant area than Twelve Seas. The streets are still narrow but they're cleaner, and the aqueducts are in good repair. The tenements are less tall and better spaced. Here and there a small park serves as recreation for the families of artisans and lesser merchants. It's the sons of these artisans and lesser merchants who attend the Guild College, some in preparation for careers in government, and a few of them in preparation for the Imperial University. Makri is, I believe, the only woman to attend the College, gaining entrance only after some anonymous but wealthy woman with a point to prove promoted her case. The College, discovering to their dismay that their written constitution did not actually forbid it, found themselves the unwilling instructors of a mixed-blood ex-gladiator. To hear Makri tell it, they've been trying to get rid of her ever since.

To me it seems like a lot of trouble for nothing. I can't see what good a sound grounding in the arts of philosophy, rhetoric and mathematics is ever going to do her, and as for her ambition to attend the Imperial University, it's never going to happen. For one thing, their constitution does expressly forbid the admittance of women, and for another, if Makri ever walked through their marble portals, the uproar created by Turai's aristocracy would send a shock wave through the Senate. No Senator would want his son in the same class as Makri, with her Orcish blood, barbaric manners and propensity for wielding an axe.

The Guild College is not a grand affair. No grounds, no quadrangles with statues. Not even a fountain. It's a dark, old stone building that used to serve as the headquarters of the Honourable Merchants Association, till the Association moved to a better part of town. Its dim corridors are full of young students carrying scrolls and trying to look studious. Several elderly men in togas, presumably professors, stand around looking severe. Though the wearing of a toga is standard among Turai's upper classes, you don't see many of them south of the river.

Professor Toarius has a very fine toga, as I discover when I enter his office. Gaining entry was easier than I expected, the receptionist outside not being used to repelling large investigators. The Professor is elderly, grey-haired, aquiline-nosed and stuffed full of dignity. He's a man of some reputation among Turai's academics. He's on the board at the Imperial University and it's counted as a great favour from the Consul to the humble Guild College that the Professor was appointed to this position. I understand from Makri that Toarius rules the establishment in a manner which allows no room for debate. When I stride into his office he looks up from a dusty old book and frowns.

'Who let you in?' he demands.

'No one.'

'If this is some matter regarding your son's education, you will have to make an appointment.'

'I don't have a son. At least not to my knowledge. Although I did travel the world as a mercenary in my younger days, so I admit it's not impossible.' The room is crammed full of books and scrolls. As always when faced with evidence of learning, I'm uncomfortable. 'I'm here about Makri.'

The Professor goes rigid in his chair. 'Get out of my office,' he demands.

'What evidence do you have against her?'

Professor Toarius rises swiftly and pulls on a bell rope behind him. The clerk hurries in from the office outside.

'Call our security guards,' instructs the Professor.

This is worse than I expected. I'm surprised that Toarius is so unwilling to discuss the matter, and even more surprised that this place actually has security guards.

'You can't just expel Makri like this, Professor.'

'I already have. It was a mistake to allow her to attend the College, and now that she's committed theft I have no option but to permanently exclude her.'

The door opens behind me and two brawny individuals in rough brown tunics hurry into the room. I ignore them.

'You don't get my meaning, Professor. You can't expel Makri because I won't allow it.'

'You won't allow it? And how will you prevent it?'

'By referring the matter to the Senate. Allow me to introduce myself. I'm Thraxas, Tribune of the People.'

'Tribune? That post has been extinct for over a century.'

'Till recently revived by Deputy Consul Cicerius. I have the power to prevent any act of exclusion against any citizen of Turai without the matter being debated in the Senate. So before I'm forced to make the matter public, why don't we discuss it?'

'Do you think that the Senate will have the slightest interest in the fate of an Orcish thief?'

Makri isn't actually Orcish. She has one quarter Orcish blood, along with one quarter Elvish. Having grown up in an Orcish slave pit, she hates them. Calling her an Orc is a deadly insult. I can see why she found life under the Professor tough.

'The Senate will have to show an interest. It's the law, and Cicerius is a stickler for the law.'

'I am a good deal better acquainted with Deputy Consul Cicerius than you.' The Professor puts down his book. His frown deepens. 'Are you the same Thraxas who was denounced last year in the Senate for your part in the scandal concerning the Elvish cloth which went missing?'

'Yes. But I was later exonerated.'

'No doubt,' says the Professor drily. 'Few guilty men are convicted in this city. And now you claim to be an employee of the government? I have heard nothing about it.'

'I've been keeping it quiet. Nonetheless, it's true. I'm a Tribune of the People and I'm not letting you expel Makri. What evidence do you have that she stole the money?'

Professor Toarius doesn't want to discuss it. He abruptly orders his men to throw me out. They hesitate.

'I think this man really is a Tribune. I saw him stop an eviction a few months back...Senator Lodius was with him.'

The guards stand awkwardly, not quite knowing what to do. They don't want to offend the Professor, but neither do they want to end up being hauled in front of a Senate committee for interfering with official business. Professor Toarius solves the impasse by marching out of the room, muttering about the degeneracy of a city which can allow a man like me to walk around unpunished.

'Is he always like this?' I ask the guards.

'Yes.'

'You appreciate I really am a Tribune of the People? You can't throw me out of this place while I'm conducting an investigation.'

The guards shrug. I don't get the impression they're that desperate to do the Professor's bidding. Probably he's not the sort of man to inspire loyalty among his staff.

'You know Makri?'

The larger of the two guards almost smiles. 'We know her.'

'Violent temper,' adds his companion.

'Once chased some poor young guy round the building after he made some comment she didn't like. What does she expect? She doesn't exactly cover herself up a lot.'

I ask them what they know about the expulsion. They don't know much. 'We weren't involved. All we heard was that some money went missing and she took it. The Professor told us to make sure she didn't get back in the building.'

'Did you look into it at all?'

'Why would we?' asks the larger guard. 'We're just here to keep the dwa dealers outside from bothering the students. If the Professor expels someone, it's nothing to do with us.'

'She probably stole the money,' adds the other guard. 'I didn't mind the woman, but she is part Orcish. She was bound to start stealing sooner or later.'

'Good body, though. She should stick to being a dancer.'

I ask if they know of anyone who might fill me in on a few more details. They suggest Rabaxos.

'It was his money that went missing. Probably find him in the library. He's a little guy in a shabby tunic. Always got his nose in a scroll. Father owns a fishing boat but I guess being a fisherman isn't good enough for his son. Why are you so bothered about the girl anyway?'

A good question. I leave them without answering. It's hot and stuffy inside the old building but I've got more on my mind than the uncomfortable weather. I swore I wouldn't use my Tribunate powers again for any reason. Thanks to Makri, I've been forced into it. I know what's going to happen now. People are going to appear at my door, asking for help. Once the downtrodden masses learn that I've invoked my powers, they'll all be looking for assistance. Every person in Twelve Seas with some gripe against authority will be demanding action. I'd better strengthen my door-locking spell. I've no intention of spending my life helping the downtrodden masses; I'm downtrodden enough myself.

That's not the worst of it. Deputy Consul Cicerius was furious when I used my powers during the winter, particularly as it was to aid Senator Lodius, head of the opposition party. If I get involved in anything else of a similar nature, Cicerius will be down on me like a bad spell. Once a man gets involved in politics in this city, there's no telling what might happen. Time was when the Tribunes of the People were forever entering into the political fray. Some of them ended up being assassinated for their troubles, or dragged up in court on trumped-up charges by their opponents. To be a politician in this city you need a lot of backing, and a lot of backing is something I don't have.

When I remember that not only has Makri forced me into using my legal powers, as well as placing bets on how many corpses I'm liable to run into in the next few days, she's also received an invitation to Lisutaris's smart party, I start to seethe. Damn the woman. How can I be expected to get along in this city when I have to act as nursemaid to a pointy-eared ex-gladiator who doesn't know how to behave in a civilised society? It wasn't too long ago that she was terrifying the honest citizens of Twelve Seas by talking publicly about her menstruation problems, and if it's not that, it's killing a dwa dealer and bringing the Brotherhood down on my neck. Then there was the time she actually threw up over Prince Dees-Akan's sandals. *Low-life scum,* he called us afterwards, if I remember correctly. By the time I reach the library - another room containing an indecent amount of books and scrolls - I'm in a thoroughly bad mood. I demand to see Rabaxos and, ignoring the multitude of requests for me to keep my voice down, I keep on demanding till eventually a student leads me behind a book stack to a small table where a puny-looking individual with his hair tied back with a cheap piece of ribbon has his nose firmly in a scroll, written in the common Elvish tongue. I speak Elvish myself, though I don't go around studying it in libraries.

'I'm here investigating the theft of your money.'

He shrinks back in his chair.

'And if you don't tell me exactly what happened, I'll make sure you end up on a prison ship. It'll be a long time before you get to study an Elvish scroll again.'

Chapter Six

On my way back to the Avenging Axe, I call in at the local Messengers Guild station, sending a note to Lisutaris letting her know what's happened. I suggest she try to locate the jewel again and also suggest she uses her considerable powers of sorcery to find out what the hell is going on. Seven dead bodies is a lot for one pendant that no one is supposed to know about.

The sun is directly overhead and the streets are intolerably hot and dusty. There's little activity save for a bunch of ragged children splashing around in an old fountain that feeds off the local aqueduct. A few more days like this and the water supply is likely to dry up, which will probably lead to a riot. The mood I'm in, I wouldn't mind doing some rioting. I have the grimmest foreboding about what's going to happen now I've used my Tribune's powers. I'll have to send a report to an official at the Senate, and once that's made public, there's no telling what the result will be.

It's clear there was no proper inquiry at the Guild College. According to the young student Rabaxos he'd left the money in his locker for only a few minutes while he went to hand in a paper to one of his tutors. When he returned, the door had been forced open and the money was gone. I checked the lockers. They're little more than wooden boxes with a clasp. Anyone could have forced it in a few seconds. No one saw the theft, but Makri was observed by several students entering and leaving the locker room around the time of the incident. Apart from that, there doesn't seem to be any evidence against her. That doesn't mean the staff at the college were outraged by her expulsion. They all have much the same opinion as Professor Toarius: it was only a matter of time before Makri's Orcish blood came to the fore and she started stealing. Normally I'd be tempted to agree. You can't trust an Orc for a second. Even a small amount of Orcish blood makes a person unreliable. Everyone in Turai knows that. Unfortunately, I also know that Makri didn't steal the money, which means I have to find out who did. It's going to be a lot of work over a measly five gurans, and a lot of work for which I'm not going to be paid. I shake my head. As a general rule, I never investigate for free. It creates the wrong impression.

As for Lisutaris's green jewel, that case went bad as soon as it started. If the pendant really is the last reliable way of warning Turai against imminent Orcish invasion, it might be time to consider leaving the city. No matter what Lisutaris believes, someone else obviously knew all about the pendant, probably before it was stolen. You don't get multiple deaths and a burning tavern over any old piece of jewellery.

The fountain's centrepiece is a small statue of St. Quatinius talking to a whale, modelled on one of the numerous exploits of our city's patron. According to the story, the whale was full of religious knowledge. Perhaps signifying this, water pours from the beast's mouth. I shove a few children out the way and take a drink. I eye St. Quatinius.

'You want to help me sort this out?' I ask. He doesn't reply. To the best of my knowledge St. Quatinius has never come to my aid, though as I'm a man who frequently misses prayers, I suppose I can't complain.

Back at the Avenging Axe, I grumble to Tanrose about the undignified outbreak of gambling on matters which are not suitable for gambling, namely Thraxas-related deaths. I'm expecting a sympathetic ear from our kindly cook. Unfortunately Tanrose is in a bad mood and brushes aside my complaints. It's rare for Tanrose to be in a bad mood. Apparently she's been arguing with Gurd over payments for food deliveries. Gurd is at the far end of the bar, looking the other way, but when I take a beer and a plate of stew over to the far corner of the room he abandons his post at the bar and joins me. He's not happy either.

'Never accuse a cook of paying too much for her eggs and flour,' I advise him. 'It'll always lead to trouble. Makes them think you don't value their cooking.'

'It was an argument about nothing,' protests Gurd. 'Tanrose just yelled at me for no reason. It must be the heat.'

There's an awkward moment of silence. We both know that the usual reason for the rare moments of friction between them is Gurd's inability to express his emotions. He was a fine man with a sword or an axe - no one better - but when it comes to telling his cook he's sweet on her he just can't do it.

'You're going to have to say something sometime,' I say, uncomfortable as always about this type of conversation. 'It's no good just hanging round looking as miserable as a Niojan whore all day, then complaining about her bookkeeping when you can't think of anything else to say.'

Gurd shakes his head. In the tremendous heat his long grey hair is matted round his shoulders. 'It's not so easy,' he mutters.

'Women, they're all crazy,' says Parax the shoemaker, a very unwelcome intruder into the conversation.

I tell him to go away. 'And don't start asking for the latest body count.'

'We already heard about the last three,' says Parax. 'Seven so far. Makes my bet on twenty look pretty good.'

'Bexanos the ropemaker put a lot of money on twenty to twenty-five,' muses Gurd. 'You think it might get that high?'

'Gurd, what's got into you? How could you place bets on how many deaths there are going to be?'

'Why not?' says Gurd. 'A bet is a bet.'

He has a point there.

'There's no pleasing women,' says Parax, returning to his original theme. 'My wife, no man could live with her.'

Parax's wife might be happier if he spent more time actually making shoes and less sitting around in taverns, but I remain silent, not wishing to be drawn into this discussion.

'But we men, what do we do?' continues Parax. 'Pander to them. Run around performing their every whim. It's foolish, but that's life.'

By this time Gurd is shifting round in his seat uncomfortably, having no wish to hear his problems aired in public by anyone, particularly a shoemaker notorious for his lack of tact.

'Take Thraxas,' says Parax.

I sit up sharply. 'What about Thraxas?' I say.

'Well, where have you just been?'

I narrow my eyes. 'Working.'

'Investigating at the Guild College from what I hear. Trying to sort things out for Makri again.'

'What do you mean, *again?*'

'Come on,' scoffs Parax. 'You're always running round for that woman. You've been doing it ever since she arrived in the city.'

I should come back with a crushing rejoinder but the brazen audacity of Parax's words has left me temporarily speechless.

'Don't worry,' chuckles the shoemaker. 'Plenty of men have fallen for girls half their age. And she's got a fine figure, even if she does have Orc blood. Good enough to keep you warm in winter, eh, Thraxas?'

Noticing that I am now about to draw my sword and stab Parax, Gurd lays his hand on my arm. I manage to stifle the urge. 'Parax, you're as dumb as an Orc. Go and bother someone else.'

Parax, like the insensitive troublemaker he is, won't let it go. 'So how often do you work for free?'

'Never.'

'And how much is Makri paying you to sort out her problems?'

My bad temper gets a lot worse. Makri appears through the front door, cursing the heat. Perspiration makes her short man's tunic stick to her body.

'Have you been to the college?' she asks immediately.

Parax guffaws.

'What's so funny?' says Makri.

'Thraxas,' replies Parax, but noticing that I'm again attempting to draw my sword, he backs off, and moves away from our table. Makri pays him no further attention. She's too eager to know what happened at the College.

'Professor Toarius wouldn't speak to me,' I tell her. 'He seems to hate you. In fact everyone there seems to hate you.'

Makri looks crestfallen.

'But Rabaxos doesn't really think you stole his money. He didn't accuse you of the theft. Professor Toarius just leapt to that conclusion without any evidence as far as I can see. It's odd the Professor is so vehement. He must know he doesn't have enough evidence to stand up to an investigation.'

'He dislikes me enough not to care,' says Makri.

'Well, don't despair. And don't attack him with your axe. I'll sort it out. You can still do your examination.'

'I can? How?'

'I used my Tribune's powers to stop the expulsion. That means it has to go before the Senate for discussion, which will take weeks. As of now, you're still a student and can take the exam on schedule, in three days' time.'

Makri thanks me, quite effusively, though she's another one who's uncomfortable about showing emotion in public unless driven to it by rage. At the next table, Parax is sniggering. I rise to my feet. 'I have investigating to do,' I say, and depart briskly towards the stairs. I've barely sat down at my desk to consider matters when a messenger appears at my door carrying a missive from Lisutaris.

Have extended my powers. Believe that jewel has now been transported to Blind Horse tavern in Kushni. Proceed there immediately.

I shake my head. The Blind Horse in the Kushni quarter. I wouldn't have thought it possible, but the taverns are getting worse. The Blind Horse is the sort of place a man is grateful to come out of alive. If the clientele don't get you, the klee will. With such a dubious venue as my next destination, I attempt to load a couple of spells into my memory. It takes a lot of effort. My sorcerous powers, always slight, are getting weaker every day. I still advertise myself as a Sorcerous Investigator to bring in the public, but really my powers are becoming negligible. Every time a sorcerer uses a spell he has to relearn it before using it again, and these days I'm finding it very hard work.

The door starts shaking from some violent knocking. I wrench it open. Casax, local Brotherhood boss, strides in without waiting for an invitation. He looks round with distaste at the mess, which, if I remember correctly, he did last time he was here.

'This place is getting worse.'

'At least it hasn't burned to the ground.'

Casax smiles. 'We saved most of the important things. Now, would you like to tell me why my headquarters was set on fire? It's the sort of thing I should know.'

'Yes, I can see it's bad for your image.'

'Very bad. So who did it?'

'How would I know?'

Casax's eyes glint. 'Investigator, I'm asking you in a friendly manner. I'm feeling friendly because you had the presence of mind to remind that useless sorcerer of mine that he could put out the fire. Otherwise I'd be here with a dozen men. If you want me to come back with a dozen men I will. But I'd rather you just told me what was going on. I hear you went to the Spiked Mace looking for jewellery. Next thing four guys were dead and the Guards are questioning you. Then you come to the Mermaid and what do you know, the Mermaid is burning down and inside are three dead men who just happened to be selling stolen jewellery. Which makes me think you're on the trail of some pretty important gems.'

Casax takes a seat. 'Is it anything to do with the Orc girl and the Guild College?'

It's unpleasant to learn that Casax knows so much about my movements, but not a surprise. Casax is sharp as an Elf's ear and he has a lot of men working for him. Few things happen in Twelve Seas without Casax learning of it.

'No. Nothing to do with Makri. She's in a dispute over five gurans. Not enough to interest you.'

'Probably not. Though five gurans is five gurans.'

The sounds of arguing drift in from the street below. The vendors are still arguing.

'One of my captains has a son at the college,' says Casax. 'Wants him to get some qualifications and go to the University. You think that's a good idea?'

I shrug. 'Maybe. Better than a life of crime.'

'That depends on the criminal. Anyway, suppose the kid goes to the University and ends up at the Palace, or the Abode of Justice, taking bribes from Senators? You think that's not a life of crime?'

'Maybe he'll end up a professor. I believe they're still fairly free from corruption.'

'No one is free from corruption in Turai. Still, you might be right. Education, it's a bit of a mystery to me. I started in the business when I was six, running bets for a bookmaker. So I never had much time for school. But if my captain wants to send his son to the college, I'm not against it.'

He pauses, temporarily distracted by the increasing vehemence of the argument outside.

'Incidentally, this son I mentioned thinks that the Orc girl didn't take the money.'

'She didn't.'

'You'll have a hard time proving it. Up there Professor Toarius is the only one with authority. The Consul appointed him as a favour to the struggling citizens. I doubt he's going to pay much attention to you.'

'He might.'

'You want that I should use a little influence? Old Toarius will back down quick enough if he finds his staff are about to withdraw their labour. Or maybe not turning up to work at all due to some mysterious warnings.'

The Brotherhood could certainly close the College if they wanted to. No porter or delivery man is going to go against an instruction from their guild not to work, and the Brotherhood has great influence in the guilds.

'I'll sort it out. Why would you want to help anyway?'

Casax shrugs. 'I don't mind doing you a favour. Providing you tell me about the jewel. Who are you trying to recover it for?'

'That would be none of your business.'

'Not something I ever like to hear,' counters Casax. 'Everything in Twelve Seas is my business.'

'You might have the local guilds in awe of you but you don't scare me.'

'If Lisutaris hired you to find a jewel it must be a valuable item. Sorcerous probably.'

He knows about Lisutaris. I try not to look surprised.

'I read the message on your desk,' says Casax. I look foolishly at my desk, where Lisutaris's message to me is lying in plain view. I can't believe I've been so careless. He rises to leave.

'You know, I feel sort of sorry for that Orc girl. Working here all day and all night to pay for her classes. Especially as she's so good with a sword. She ought to work for me. Let me know if you need some help at the college. Be a lot easier than using your Tribune's powers. That's going to get you into big trouble.'

Casax departs. I stare at the message on my desk. Thraxas, number one chariot when it comes to investigating, as I've been known to say. But not so good at keeping my business private. I curse. Now the Brotherhood know I'm looking for an important item for Lisutaris, Mistress of the Sky, Head of the sorcerers Guild, there's no telling what's going to happen. Makri appears in my room without knocking. She asks how things are with the Lisutaris inquiry, which I told her about yesterday. A few months ago I realised to my surprise that I now tell Makri most of my business. There's no reason not to, but it breaks a long-term habit of complete privacy.

'It's all getting worse. Whoever set this thing in motion hasn't been discreet about it. Either the original thief, or the person who gave him the information, seems to have let half the city know how important that pendant is. Now Casax is on the trail.'

'How did he find out?'

'The Brotherhood have spies everywhere.'

Makri wonders how many people could know of the jewel.

'Very few, according to Lisutaris. The King, the Consul, the Deputy Consul, maybe a couple of senior sorcerers. None of them liable to open their mouths, but who knows who else might've got hold of some information and passed it on? All of these people have staff, and staff can be bribed. Lisutaris's secretary knew about the jewel's powers. I'd like to question her but Lisutaris forbids it for some reason.'

'She's very protective towards her secretary,' says Makri.

'How do you know that?'

'She told me at the Sorcerers Assemblage. While we were sharing a thazis stick. Some sort of young relation, I remember. Niece or something.'

'You're getting very intimate with our Chief Sorcerer.'

'You know she invited me to her masked ball?' says Makri.

'Really?'

'What costume should I wear?'

'Why would I want to discuss costumes with you? I'm still angry that you've been placing bets on my work.'

'I didn't start it. I just joined in after Moxalan started taking bets. Hey, when I arrived in Turai I didn't even know how to gamble. You encouraged me.'

She has a point there.

'I didn't encourage you to gamble on things like this.'

'Didn't you tell me that you and Gurd once put a bet on how long it would take your commanding officer to die after he caught the plague?'

'That was different. It was in wartime. And no one liked that commanding officer.'

'You're just annoyed because you weren't in on it from the beginning,' says Makri, quite shrewdly. 'If you'd thought of it first you'd have been sending me out to make anonymous bets on your behalf.'

'That's not true. I have a responsibility to my clients. How do you think Lisutaris would feel if she learned that the degenerates at the Avenging Axe are taking odds on how many people are going to be handing in their togas before the case closes?'

'Moxalan is offering fifty to one for the exact total,' says Makri.

'Really? Fifty to one?'

'And twenty to one for a guess to within three of the total.'

'I'm not interested in any odds,' I say, quite sternly.

'Of course not,' agrees Makri. 'Even though you are a man with inside information, and would have a huge advantage when it comes to placing a bet at the very attractive odds of fifty to one…'

I shake my head. 'It would be unethical. And no one has ever accused me of unethical behaviour.'

'That's just ridiculous,' says Makri. 'People accuse you of unethical behaviour all the time. No one in Turai gets accused of being unethical more than you. Just last week–'

'That's enough,' I say, interrupting before Makri can complete whatever damaging story she has in mind. I change the subject and ask if Gurd and Tanrose are showing any signs of making up.

'No. Still arguing.'

It's a worry. If Tanrose left the tavern I'd miss her cooking desperately. I'm still reeling from Minarixa the baker's death last year. Her daughter has taken over the bakery but it's never been the same. Minarixa really understood pastry. It was a rare gift.

Makri looks thoughtful. 'I was champion gladiator. And I taught a puny young Elf to be a champion fighter. And I'm top of the class in every subject.'

'So?'

'So I have natural talents. I've never thought of applying them to other people's problems. If I put my mind to it I could probably help Gurd and Tanrose.'

'You do that, Makri.'

The thought of Makri giving anyone advice on their relationship makes me shudder. I'm still shuddering as I leave the tavern and make my way past the arguing vendors. If Makri puts her mind to fixing the rift between Gurd and Tanrose, God alone knows what disaster will result.

Chapter Seven

Kushni, in the centre of the city, is one of the worst parts of town. Bad things happen here. As I'm stepping over the drunken bodies on the pavement I wonder, as I occasionally do, how exactly I ended up being the person who tries to fix the bad things. There are plenty of other ways of making a living. Dandelion sits on the beach and talks to dolphins. She seems to manage all right.

I check my sword is loose in its sheath, allow a scowl to settle on my features - which it does quite easily - and step into the Blind Horse, home to dwa dealers, gamblers, robbers and murderers.

Whores with red ribbons in their hair mingle with intoxicated sailors looking for an opportunity to spend the money they risked their lives to earn. At the bar two barbarians are arm-wrestling while their companions shout drunken encouragement. I bump into a man I haven't seen for five years but used to know quite well.

'Demanius.'

'Thraxas.'

Demanius is around the same age as me. A lot thinner, and his hair has gone completely grey. Still a tough-looking character, though. We were in the army together. The last time I saw him he was working for the Venarius Investigation Agency, a respectable organisation, liked by the authorities. When I was in Palace Security we'd often find ourselves working alongside Venarius's agents. I ask what brings him to the Blind Horse.

'I felt like a drink,' he replies, not being inclined to tell me his business.

'So did I.'

We make our way to the bar, avoiding the noisy barbarians. The air is thick with thazis smoke. The aroma of burning dwa drifts down from the rooms upstairs. You'd be surprised who you might find upstairs in a tavern like this, partaking of illegal narcotics. Members of Turai's upper classes, not wishing to be found using the substance in their homes, are not above visiting dubious establishments to feed their habit.

The Venarius agency has plenty of money. I let Demanius pay for the beer.

'How's life in Thamlin?' I ask.

The agency headquarters is close to Thamlin, where the Senators live.

'Very peaceful. But they keep sending me here.'

I'm feeling uneasy. Meeting another investigator while out on a case is rare. When it happens I never know quite what to do. If Demanius is working on the same case as me it won't do me any good to have him solve it before me. Bad for my reputation and bad for my income. I drink my beer quickly and then tell Demanius that I'm due upstairs for a private appointment.

'As am I,' says Demanius.

I'm lying. I don't know if he is. As investigators go, I wouldn't class Demanius as sharp as an Elf's ear. There again, he's not dumb as an Orc either. If he's here fishing for information he's not getting anything from me. We cross the room, wary of each other, hardly noticing the whores who flop around the tables, or the Barbarians, who are now throwing knives at a target on the wall. The stairs are dark and narrow with a flickering torch providing insufficient light. We're almost at the top when a door opens and a woman emerges. She's wearing the garb of a common market trader and looks out of place. There's a strange expression on her face but when she recognises Demanius she starts to speak.

'The pendant,' she says.

I might be getting somewhere at last. She opens her mouth again. Then she falls down dead. So no real progress.

Demanius sprints up the last few stairs. I sprint after him. He bends down to examine the body. There's a great wound in the woman's back, still pumping blood. Demanius draws his sword and charges into the room she emerged from. I'm at his heels. Inside we find a man sitting on a chair, staring into space. Demanius starts barking out questions. I hold up my hand.

'He's trying to speak.'

The man's voice comes slowly, from a long way away. 'I'm King of Turai,' he says. Then he slumps forward. It was an odd thing to say. Whoever he is, he isn't the King. I feel for the pulse on his neck. There isn't one. He's dead. There are no wounds on his body. Really he looks tolerably healthy. But he's still dead. I'm becoming very familiar with this scene. More deaths and the pendant still missing. Demanius, lither than me, hauls himself out of the window and drops into the alley below. I don't follow him. Whoever is responsible for this latest outrage is probably long gone. Besides, with my weight I don't fancy the drop. A man doesn't want to break his ankle in this place. I stare at the body still slumped on the chair, trying to figure out the cause of death. I don't believe it was from natural causes. Doesn't look like poison. Is there sorcery in the air? I look around, trying to sense it. With my own sorcerous background I can usually tell if magic has been used, but I can't say for sure. Maybe, faintly.

Outside, a few customers have gathered to look at the dead woman. No one protests as I quickly search the pocket on her market worker's apron. I find nothing, but I notice a tattoo on her arm. Two clasped hands. The mark of the Society of Friends. The Society is a criminal gang, based in the north of the city. They're bitter rivals with the Brotherhood. Last year there was a murderous war over territory and the feud is still smouldering. Whoever this woman is, I doubt she's the market worker she pretends to be. Or pretended to be.

Someone has summoned the landlord. He puffs his way up the stairs with a couple of henchmen, complaining about the inconvenience of always having to carry bodies out of his tavern.

'You could open an establishment in a better part of town,' I suggest. 'But you'd probably miss the excitement. You know who this woman is?'

'Never seen her before. Who are you?'

'Thraxas. Investigator.'

The landlord spits on the floor. 'That's what I think of investigators.' His henchmen get ready to run me off the premises. I save them the trouble by leaving. There's not a lot of point in sticking around. No one in this place is going to answer questions. I'm not certain I could muster any questions. A peculiar feeling of gloom is settling over me. It's starting to seem like I'm never going to find this pendant. Every time I get close all I find is more dead bodies. A man can only take so many dead bodies, even a man who's used to them.

Walking back through Kushni, I try to review the situation, but I have no real idea what's going on. I'm particularly troubled by the death of the man in the chair. Sword wounds are one thing, but a death you can't explain always spells trouble. When I reach Moon and Stars Boulevard I'm uncertain even which way to turn. Should I go back to the Avenging Axe? Possibly I should head north to Truth is Beauty Lane, home of the sorcerers, and report to Lisutaris. But what's the point? She'll only send me out to some other godforsaken tavern where I'll find a pile of dead bodies.

It's hot as Orcish hell. I've been in cooler deserts. My head hurts. Maybe a beer will help. It often does. I look around for a tavern, somewhere where there's unlikely to be anyone being murdered, at least not until I've had a drink. I've just spotted a reasonable-looking establishment across the road when a carriage pulls up in front of me. An official carriage, with a driver in uniform and the livery of the Imperial Palace. The door opens and a toga-clad figure leans out.

'Thraxas. How fortunate. I was on my way to visit you.' It's Hansius, assistant to Deputy Consul Cicerius. He's a smart, handsome young man, son of a Senator, on his way up the ladder in public life. So far he's doing well.

'Cicerius wants you to visit him right away.'

I'm still looking at the inviting tavern across the road. 'Tell him I'm busy.'

'It's an official summons.'

'I'm still busy.'

'Doing what?'

My head hurts more. 'Do I accost you in the street and ask you your business? I'm busy. Tell Cicerius I'll come later.'

'If you require beer I am sure the Deputy Consul can provide it,' says Hansius, which is perceptive of him.

'The Deputy Consul serves wine. And he's miserly with it.'

Hansius looks stern. 'Official summons.'

I climb into the carriage. We ride slowly north towards the Palace. Our official vehicle has right of way but the streets are so crowded it's still a slow journey. Since our King's diplomacy opened up the southern trade routes a few years ago, commerce in Turai has mushroomed and trade wagons roll in all day. At the corner of the street that leads to Truth is Beauty Lane we're held up for a long time by a huge wagon that's trying to manoeuvre its way round a corner it wasn't designed to turn. The driver curses, and shouts at his four horses.

'On its way to Lisutaris's villa, most likely,' Hansius informs me. 'They're building a theatre in the grounds for the performers to use at the ball.'

This worsens my mood. I ask Hansius if he's going. He is, of course. 'I accompany the Deputy Consul to all such events.'

Having learned to be tactful as a young man in public service, Hansius doesn't ask me if I'm invited. He knows very well that since being sacked from my job at the Palace I'm not on the guest list for smart parties. To hell with them. Who wants to go to a masked ball anyway? I can just imagine Deputy Consul Cicerius prancing round in a costume. It's unbecoming. I wouldn't offend my dignity. At the Palace grounds I'm searched for weapons, and before entering the outlying building that houses Cicerius's offices I'm examined by a government sorcerer, checking to see if I might be carrying any dangerous spells or aggressive sorcerous items.

'You can't see the Deputy Consul while carrying a sleep spell.'

I turn to Hansius to protest. 'You expect me to give up my spells? I didn't ask to visit.'

There's no use protesting. Palace Security is very sensitive about anyone bringing usable spells near the King. The official sorcerer holds out a magically charged crystal which I unwillingly take hold of. I feel the sleep spell draining away through my fingers.

'It takes a lot of work to learn these things, you know. Is anyone going to compensate me for my wasted effort?'

Hansius leads me through the marble corridors towards Cicerius's office. Everything here is elegant - pale yellow tiled floors, Elvish tapestries on the walls, each window, no matter how small, decorated with artfully stained glass - and I get a pang of regret for the fine office in a fine building I used to inhabit. The King's residence is one of the finest buildings in the West, full of artwork to rival that of many larger states, and the buildings of his senior officials are likewise well appointed. While I'm not a man who's too concerned with works of art, I can't help feeling a twinge of grief as I realise that everywhere I look there's a bust or statue that would cost more than I'll earn in a year. Even the clerks' desks are made of dark wood imported from the Elvish Isles. Possibly I shouldn't have got so drunk at my boss Rittius's wedding that I was immediately fired for outraging public decency. But Rittius hated me anyway. He was just looking for an excuse.

My visit to the Deputy Consul's office follows a long-established pattern. Cicerius roundly condemns me for my behaviour and I stoutly defend myself. Any time I've worked for

Cicerius there's come a point when he's felt the need to point out that I'm a disgrace to the fair city of Turai. After a little preparatory sarcasm, he starts laying in with the criticism even though, as I point out, I'm not working for his office at the moment.

'But it was this office which gave you the post of Tribune. On the strict understanding that you were not to go around abusing your powers.'

'I wouldn't say I'd been abusing them. Anyway, Professor Toarius abused his first. I had to do something.'

Cicerius points a bony finger at me. 'Any use of your Tribunate powers is an abuse. It was merely a device to let you enter the Sorcerers Assemblage. Look at the trouble you caused when you forbade Praetor Capatius to evict these tenants.' The Deputy Consul is of the opinion that the prospect of a common man from Twelve Seas getting involved in politics is just a step away from complete anarchy.

'Who can say what will happen now? It was never a good idea that Tribunes could hold up public affairs. Their power of referring matters to the Senate was an anomaly. That is why the post was allowed to lapse. I insist you drop your investigation.'

As I suspected, Cicerius shows no sign of providing me with beer. With the heat, my aching head and the intolerable sound of Cicerius lecturing me, I'm close to breaking point, a point at which I shall roundly abuse the Deputy, thereby doing great damage to my career. I interrupt the flow to tell him that much as I didn't want to use my Tribunate powers, I couldn't see a ready alternative. 'As I recall, Deputy Consul, you ran your election largely on an honesty ticket. "Cicerius never takes a bribe and he never prosecutes an innocent man," so your supporters say. Everyone's still impressed by the way you've defended people in court because you believed them to be innocent, even when it meant going against your party.'

This gets his attention. Cicerius never minds hearing good things said about himself.

'So consider things from Makri's point of view. She's completely innocent of the theft. You shouldn't find that hard to believe because you've met her and you know what she's like.

Demented but honest. You also know how hard she works for these examinations. All the while slaving away as a barmaid to support herself and pay for her classes, which don't come cheap. I thought that would impress you in particular.'

Cicerius purses his thin lips. He takes my meaning. Though born into the aristocratic class, Cicerius wasn't born rich. His father died when he was an infant, leaving a family in poverty because he'd invested all his money in a fleet of trading ships which went down in a storm. There was a dispute over the insurance, and Cicerius's mother, outsmarted by her late husband's business partners, ended up in penury. Cicerius had to work extremely hard to make his way through university and up the ranks of government. Though he's wealthy now, his younger years were one long struggle. The reason I know all this, the reason everyone knows all this, is that Cicerius likes to bring up his background any time he needs to remind the Senate that he's a self-made man, and proud of it.

'Are you going to let a citizen of Turai–'

'Makri is not a citizen of Turai. She's an alien with Orcish blood.'

'–who did a good job for you when you needed someone to look after that Orcish charioteer last year. Are you going to let a hard-working young woman be denied her chance to sit her examination because Professor Toarius has taken an irrational dislike to her? And please don't tell me that Consul Kalius has done the poor a great favour by appointing Toarius as Head of the Guild College.'

'Consul Kalius *has* done the poor a great favour by appointing Toarius as Head of the Guild College,' says Cicerius.

'I don't care. He's not stopping Makri from taking the examination. I've forbidden her expulsion. It can't go ahead before it's been discussed by a Senate committee, and by that time I'll have evidence to prove her innocence. Nothing you can say can change my mind. I'm offended that a champion of justice like yourself should be ranged against me.'

Cicerius is almost at a loss for words. I've managed to flummox the great orator, if only because he's honest at heart. An appeal to justice wouldn't have gotten me very far with any other official in this city. The Deputy Consul fixes me with a piercing lawyer's stare. 'You seem extremely concerned for the welfare of this young woman. Is there some understanding between you?'

I'm staggered that the Deputy Consul could suggest such a thing. 'If I prove her innocence she won't slaughter everyone at the college. I suppose you could call that an understanding.'

Cicerius isn't happy but really he's in an impossible situation. He can't bring himself to connive in a blatant injustice, and even if he could, there is no legal way to rescind my Tribune's decree. Only I can do that, and I've made it clear I'm not going to.

'Very well,' he says. 'You may continue with your investigation. When the matter comes to the Senate committee I will ensure that it is looked into thoroughly. But I warn you, if there are any political repercussions of your actions, if Senator Lodius and his opposition party again manage to make you their tool in an action against the government, I will personally rescind your investigator's licence. With your past record, it would be quite in order for me to do so.'

Having nothing more to say, I make to leave.

'One moment,' says Cicerius. 'Why did Lisutaris, Mistress of the Sky, visit you?'

'Why do you ask?'

'Lisutaris is Head of the Sorcerers Guild and an important person in the interests of this city state. If she's in any sort of trouble I would naturally wish to know.'

'If she was in any trouble and she'd consulted me, I doubt I'd tell you. I respect my clients' privacy. But she didn't come to see me, she came to see Makri. She was inviting her to her ball.'

Cicerius is surprised. Fifteen years ago, a woman like Makri would never have been allowed to attend such an event.

'So be careful who you bump into on the night. If it's a crazy-looking woman with an axe, don't ask her about college.' I depart, leaving Cicerius displeased with the laxity of manners in modern-day Turai. As a sorcerer mutters a spell to let me out of the building, I'm wondering what sort of costume our Deputy Consul will be sporting at the ball. I just can't imagine him in fancy dress.

Chapter Eight

Back in Twelve Seas, I take the short cut through St. Rominius's Lane, not caring if the dark alley might be filled with dwa dealers. If they bother me they'll regret it. I don't see any dwa dealers but I do see a unicorn. I stand and stare in amazement. You don't find unicorns in Turai. You find them mainly in the magic space, which can only be visited by sorcery. As for the real world, unicorns only appear in a very few places, each of these places being of some mystical significance. The Fairy Glade, for instance, deep in the forests that separate Turai from the wastelands, has its share of the one-horned animals, and there's reputed to be a colony way out in the Furthest West. Other than that, you'd have to go to some of the remoter Elvish Isles to see one. Wherever you might expect to find a unicorn, it wouldn't be in a noisy, busy, dirty city like Turai. Absolute anathema to the refined breed. Yet here it is, snowy-white, golden-horned, standing in a grimy little alleyway looking at me like it hasn't a care in the world. Faced with the fabulous creature, the thought quickly flashes across my mind that if I could capture it, I might be able to sell it for a healthy profit to the King's zoo. He's been short of fabulous creatures since his dragon was chopped up a year or two back.

'Nice unicorn,' I say, holding out my hand in a reassuring manner and stepping forward carefully. The unicorn turns and bolts round the corner. I fly after it but it's vanished.

'Stupid beast,' I mutter, and hurry on. Now it will have plunged into Quintessence Street, where it will be apprehended and sold for profit by some person far less needy than me. If I get there quickly I still might be up for a share. I rush down the alley, oblivious to the heat and dust, and burst into the main street, eagerly looking in every direction at once.

'It's mine, I saw it first, you dogs!' I cry, and brandish my fist to discourage anyone from muscling in on the deal.

Two women at a watermelon stall look at me, puzzled. 'What's yours?' they ask.

'The unicorn. Which way did it go?'

The women burst out laughing, and keep laughing for a long time. It is apparently the funniest thing they've ever heard. And yet I'm right next to the mouth of the alley. It had to have emerged here. I confront the watermelon sellers.

'Didn't a unicorn come out of that alleyway?'

They look at me with what might be pity.

'Dwa,' says one.

'A serious addiction,' agrees her friend.

I look round. Apart from a few people staring at the mad person shouting about unicorns, no one in Quintessence Street is showing signs of abnormal activity. It's quite obvious that no single-horned fabulous creature has featured here recently. So it just ran round the corner and vanished from sight. I realise someone has been playing a trick on me. A sorcerer's apprentice with nothing better to do, most probably. He'll regret it if I catch him.

'I'll take a watermelon then,' I say to the women.

I eat it on the street, cooling down from my exertion. What was I thinking, chasing after an obvious illusion? I must be getting foolish. Flocks of stals - unfortunately real - are perched listlessly on the roofs. These small black scavenging birds spend their time picking up scraps from the market, but in the deadening heat even they're finding it tough to make a living. Makri is waiting for me in my office. I'm not mentioning the unicorn to her.

'You know I have to stand up and talk to the whole class?'

'I believe you mentioned it.'

'I have to walk out in front of everyone and declaim in public.'

'So you said.'

'It's worse now. I have to stand up and talk to a class of people who all think I'm a thief! Is that fair?'

When Makri is in a bad mood her hand has a tendency to stray towards where her sword would be, if she was wearing one. She's doing it now, but is clad only in her chainmail bikini, without weapons. In the sweltering heat, perspiration makes her body shine. I'm given to believe that the ill-bred, lower-class elements in Twelve Seas like the effect.

'Have you proved me innocent yet? No? Why not?'

'I've been busy.'

'Will it take long?'

'I'm involved in a very important case, Makri. Vital for the city. With bodies everywhere.'

'How many bodies?'

'Nine.'

Makri purses her lips. 'I've bet on fourteen. Do you think I should up it?'

'Don't talk to me about that.'

She frowns. 'So don't I matter as much as this other case?'

'No,' I say.

'Why not?'

'Because the other case involves a matter of national importance!' I explode. 'And also I'm being paid.'

'Fine,' retorts Makri. 'Of course when I was saving your neck last winter from that man with the magic sword I didn't stop to ask if I was being paid or not. I just saved your life. I didn't wait around to check on any possible remuneration, just weighed in there and risked my own life to save yours. But hey, I'm only a barbaric gladiator. When I was growing up I didn't learn all the rules of civilised society. I just did what I thought was the right–'

'Makri, will you shut the hell up!'

When Makri arrived in Turai I swear she wasn't capable of these sustained bursts of eloquence. I blame the rhetoric classes.

'I'll sort it out for you. And meanwhile you can still take the examination.'

'In front of people who think I'm a thief.'

I ask Makri what she's doing in my office when she should be working downstairs. She looks uncomfortable.

'Gurd and Tanrose are still arguing. The atmosphere's bad.'

I'm still curious as to why she's in my office instead of her own room.

'Dandelion's there. I said she could stay a while.'

'Why do you put up with that woman? Sling her out.'

Makri shrugs, and when I press the point she becomes agitated. I drop it. Makri has to return to her work anyway so I accompany her downstairs. I should send another message to Lisutaris letting her know what happened at the Blind Horse. I'll do it after a beer or two. At the bar I'm accosted by Parax the shoemaker, who, in keeping with his normal practice, is not making shoes at this moment. He asks me how my day has been.

'Bad.'

'Any dead bodies lying around?'

'Since when would you care, Parax?'

'Can't a man worry about his friends?'

It's news to me that Parax is my friend. Telling him that he can look elsewhere for his inside information, I take a beer, a bowl of venison stew, a plate of yams and a large apple pie to a table, where I read the latest copy of The Renowned and Truthful Chronicle of All the World's Events, a fertile source of information on the city's many scandalous occurrences. There doesn't seem to be much scandal today apart from a report that Prince Frisen Akan, heir to the throne, has extended his holiday at his country retreat, which, as everybody knows, is a coded way of saying the King has sent him out of town in an effort to get him sober. The Prince is degenerate even by royal standards. At one time it would have been a better-kept secret, but these days, with Senator Lodius's opposition party grown so powerful, fewer people are feeling it necessary to revere the royal family. When I was a boy no one would have dared speak a word against the King, but these days you can hear talk about how we might be better off as a republic. Certain other members of the League of City States have already been riven by civil war as the power of their kings waned. If Senator Lodius and his Populares party get their way, it'll happen in Turai sooner rather than later.

Gurd sits down heavily beside me. 'I can't take any more of this,' he confides. 'That fishmonger was here again today and Tanrose was all over him.'

'Gurd, you're exaggerating.'

'Does it take two hours to order fish for next week's menu? It's not that popular an item.'

'I don't know. A lot of dockers like it.'

'I'd say dockers usually go for stew,' says Makri, appearing next to our table with a tray of drinks in her hand.

'No, I think they prefer fish.'

'How would you know? It's me that takes the orders.'

'I'm an investigator. I notice things.'

'Tanrose didn't have to–' begins Gurd.

'There's definitely more stew sold to dockers than fish,' states Makri emphatically.

'I beg to differ. Fish is still the staple diet of the dockers in Twelve Seas.'

'How can you say that, Thraxas? It's just not true. No wonder you're always having trouble solving your cases if you can't observe a simple thing like who eats–'

'Enough of this!' yells Gurd, banging his fist on the table.

'Is Tanrose still upset at you?' asks Makri.

'Yes. No. Yes. I don't want to discuss it.'

Seeing my old companion-in-arms looking as miserable as a Niojan whore, I wish there was something I could do to help.

'Maybe it's time for some action,' I suggest. 'Remember when we spent five days in that mountain fort waiting for the Simnians to attack? And eventually Commander Mursius said he'd be damned if he was going to wait any more than five days for a Simnian and he led us out and we drove the Simnians way back over the border?'

'I remember,' says Gurd. 'What about it?'

'Well maybe it's time you asked Tanrose to marry you.'

There's a slight pause.

'Did I miss something?' says Makri.

'I don't think so.'

'Well how did you get from attacking the Simnians to Gurd asking Tanrose to marry him?'

'It's obvious. There comes a time when it's no good sheltering behind the walls any longer. You have to attack. Or, in this case, get married.'

Makri considers this. 'What if the Simnians had brought up reinforcements?'

'We'd have beaten them as well.'

'What if they'd made an alliance with the Orcs and had some dragons lying in wait?'

'Very unlikely, Makri. The Simnians have never been friends with the Orcs.'

'So you're saying I should ask Tanrose to get married?' says Gurd, looking quite troubled at the thought.

'Perhaps. But you know I've always been useless with women.'

Makri nods her head. 'Tanrose tells me you treated your wife really badly.'

'Tanrose should keep her mouth shut.'

Gurd looks offended.

'About certain subjects only,' I add.

'That fishmonger has always been in pursuit of Tanrose. I'm banning him from the tavern from now on.'

'Most people prefer stew anyway,' says Makri. 'And Thraxas eats enough of it to keep you in business.'

But by now Gurd has raised his brawny figure and departed, looking thoughtful. Makri takes his seat.

'Why have you always been so bad with women?' she asks.

I shrug. 'Don't know. Just never learned what to do, I suppose.'

'I thought it might be because you drink too much.'

'Yes, also I drink too much. But at least I don't take dwa.'

Four dock workers, waiting for the drinks presently marooned on Makri's tray, call loudly for their beer. Makri ignores them.

'I don't take dwa. Well, not for a while. Don't start criticising me. I'm not the one who's useless at relationships.'

Makri is useless at relationships. She spent all last winter snivelling about some Elf she met on Avula because he didn't keep in touch with her. I don't bother to point this out. The dockers call for their beer. Makri curses them and tells them to wait. The front door opens and Lisutaris, Mistress of the Sky, strides majestically into the tavern. This time, she hasn't bothered to disguise herself. 'We need to talk,' she says, and heads for the stairs.

'Thanks for the invitation,' says Makri, but Lisutaris doesn't reply, obviously having more important things on her mind than social functions. I follow Lisutaris upstairs while Makri takes her tray of beer to the thirsty dockers. As I'm climbing the stairs I can hear them arguing. It's a while since Makri punched a customer but she seems to be working up to it again.

In her full costume Lisutaris stands out strikingly in my shabby office. Her official sorcerer's rainbow cloak positively vibrates with colour. Unusually for her she doesn't take a seat but paces up and down nervously, lighted thazis stick in hand.

'Things taken a turn for the worse?' I enquire.

'They have. Consul Kalius suspects that the pendant is missing. He sent his representative to my villa this morning specifically to ask if it was still secure in my hands.'

'How did the Consul learn of the affair?'

Lisutaris glares at me. 'How? I thought it might have something to do with you barging your way all over town leaving a trail of dead bodies in your wake. I appreciate you're not famous for your subtlety, but when I hired you I wasn't expecting you to start slaughtering the city's inhabitants. It was bound to cause comment eventually.'

I'm astonished by her effrontery. 'I haven't killed anyone. The way people have been after this pendant it's no wonder the Consul's got wind of it. I can't believe you'd blame me.'

'Why not? You're supposed to be an investigator. And yet on the simplest of cases you have notably failed to produce any results. Tell me, Thraxas, on most of your cases do you have exact information as to the whereabouts of the stolen item?'

'No.'

'Yet I have three times told you precisely where the pendant is and on each occasion you've failed to retrieve it. Instead, all I get is messages telling me that some brutal massacre has occurred and the gem is missing again. Don't you think it would be a good idea to arrive in time to locate the item I'm paying you to find?'

Lisutaris halts in the middle of the room and fixes me with a hostile stare. Coming from the Head of the sorcerers Guild, this is quite disconcerting. Lisutaris is one of the most powerful magic users in the world. I'm wearing a fine spell protection necklace but no such item could hold out against the might of Lisutaris for long. That being said, I don't allow anyone to enter my room and abuse me. I meet her gaze and inform her coldly that if I'm not given enough time to do the job then the job won't get done, and besides, it would be a help if she'd told me the full facts of the case.

'Are you implying I have withheld information?'

'Most clients do. You said that no one knew the power of this pendant. That's obviously not true. From the way people have been killing each other to get hold of it, I'd say its importance was well known to someone. When you first arrived here the job looked simple and we were in a hurry so I didn't get the full background to the case. Maybe I should have. Who else in your immediate circle knew you had the pendant, for instance?'

'No one but my secretary.'

'Then maybe we should have a few words with your secretary.'

'You will not investigate her,' says Lisutaris, quite emphatically.

'I think I should.'

'You will not speak to my secretary and that is final. If knowledge of the pendant's true significance has somehow been learned, it is unfortunate but no longer relevant. I don't care how it came to happen; the point is I must have the pendant back immediately. Consul Kalius will be at my house in two days' time. He's suspicious already. He's bound to ask to see the pendant.'

'Can't you fob him off with an imitation?'

'If it were only the Consul, yes. But he'll have government sorcerers with him. No imitation jewel I could fabricate would fool Old Hasius the Brilliant. Hasius is still seething with jealousy over my election as Head of the Guild. He'd take one look at an imitation pendant and squawk so loud they'd hear him in Simnia.'

Lisutaris finishes her thazis stick and lights another. 'This is such a mess! Damn it, I never asked to be put in charge of items vital for the defence of the city. The Consul's going to be down on me like a bad spell when he learns I've lost the pendant. Only last month he was telling me that some Orcish prince or other had just conquered a neighbouring country and was looking to set himself up as war leader.'

'Prince Amrag?'

Lisutaris nods. Already in the west we've heard quite a few reports about this prince. The Orcs hate us as much as we hate them but they're often riven by internal warfare which prevents them from mounting a concentrated attack on us. But every now and then a leader comes along capable of unifying the Orc nations, and when that happens it's but a short step to an invasion of the Human lands. Prince Amrag looks like he might be the Orc to do it, and it might not be too far in the future.

'Maybe it's time to call in someone else.'

'What do you mean?' demands Lisutaris.

'If this is so important for Turai, maybe Palace Security should be involved.'

'Absolutely not,' says Lisutaris, shaking her head and lighting another thazis stick. Lisutaris's substantial use of thazis often sends her into a happy dream world, and it's a sign of how deep the crisis is that she shows no signs of relaxing, no matter how many sticks she smokes.

'I cannot own up to the loss of the pendant. I'd be ruined. The King would expel me from the city in disgrace. My family has been in the leading tier of Turanian society for as long as the city's been here, and I refuse to end up a mad old hermit in the wastelands casting horoscopes for travellers.'

I break open a new bottle of klee. Lisutaris downs a glass in the blink of an eye and holds out her glass for more. I pour her another glass and ask her if she knows of any reason why an operative from the Venarius Investigation Agency might also be on the trail of the pendant.

'I've no idea. Surely it's not possible?'

'I'm pretty certain that's what Demanius was doing in the Blind Horse. Before the woman died she seemed to recognise him, and she mentioned the jewel.'

'This is a disaster,' says the sorcerer, and starts pacing again.

'It is. Whoever stole the jewel probably knew exactly what they were getting, and probably tried to sell it to someone who also knew all about it. Since then it's come to the attention of both the Brotherhood and the Society of Friends. It's pretty clear the matter is no longer much of a secret. We might as well assume that everyone knows about it. Are you sure you don't want to call in some outside help?'

Lisutaris doesn't. 'The moment I admit the loss, I'm ruined. We have two days left. You must find the pendant.'

'I'll do my best. I'll do better if you fill me in on a few missing details.'

'Like what?'

'Like why so many people are dying. It's not credible that they all just happened to kill each other. Thieves don't suddenly kill each other. If one is dominant the others back down after the first sign of violence. None of these crime scenes looked like the scenes I'm used to. It looked like something had affected the people in a way that drove them insane. Which would be backed up by some of their dying words. One man told me he was on a beautiful golden ship and another one thought he was King of Turai. Any particular reason why they might be thinking that?'

'Yes,' says Lisutaris. 'Looking into the green jewel could drive an untrained mind insane. Four people who had all looked into it would be quite likely to kill each other as their dreams took over their reality.'

'You're telling me this now? Don't you think you could have mentioned it earlier?'

'I did say that it was a dangerous object,' protests Lisutaris.

'Not so dangerous that it was going to lead to such slaughter. So it's quite likely that every time someone gets hold of this pendant they'll go mad, kill their companions and make off with it?'

'Yes. But they won't get far. If they stare deeply into it themselves, they'll probably die even without violence being inflicted on them. It will just break their minds.'

Lisutaris really should have given me more information when she hired me. There's not much point in complaining now. I'm stuck with it. 'So we now have two problems. One, lots of people seem to know about the jewel. Two, it's going to drive them all murderously insane.'

Lisutaris studies her glass. 'This klee is disgusting. My throat is burning. Where do you buy it?'

'It's supplied to Gurd by a monastery in the hills. The monks distil it in their spare time.'

'Do they have a grudge against the city?'

'I find it bracing.'

Lisutaris drains her glass and winces again as the fiery spirit trickles down her throat. 'It's poisonous. This liquid would kill you.' She holds out her glass. 'Give me more.'

I fill her glass.

'I could send you a few bottles for your masked ball.'

'I don't think the Senators could take it,' replies Lisutaris, completely failing to catch my hint that she ought to be inviting me. Not that I want to go. The sight of Turai's aristocracy disporting themselves in costume is not one that appeals to me. But it still rankles that Makri has an invitation. All she did for Lisutaris at the Assemblage was walk around behind her pretending to be a bodyguard, meanwhile getting so wrecked on thazis, dwa and klee that I had to carry the pair of them home in a carriage. I did all the hard work. Her ingratitude is simply appalling. I realise that Lisutaris has been talking to me for some time.

'What were you saying?'

'Have you not been listening?'

'I was contemplating some aspects of the case. Tell me again.'

'I can no longer locate the pendant.' Lisutaris is frustrated at having to repeat herself. Apparently after I failed to find the gem in the Blind Horse she repeated her sorcerous procedure for tracing the pendant but was this time unsuccessful. Someone has now succeeded in hiding the jewel from sorcerous enquiry, no mean feat against the power of Lisutaris. It might mean that it's now in the hands of someone capable of providing some heavyweight sorcerous protection themselves.

'There aren't too many rogue sorcerers around who could do that,' I say. 'There's Glixius Dragon Killer of course, he might have the power. I haven't seen him for a while but he's been on my mind ever since I saw that woman's Society of Friends tattoo. He used to work with them.'

Another possibility is that whoever now has the jewel has wrapped it in red Elvish cloth, which would have the effect of casting an impenetrable shield over the object. No sorcerous enquiry can penetrate the cloth. However, red Elvish cloth is fabulously expensive and hard to come by. It's illegal for anyone but the King and his ministers to own it.

'But someone might have got their hands on some. Another possibility is that the pendant might have left the city. It might be on its way east right now.'

Lisutaris looks alarmed. 'Surely no one would be so base as to sell such an item to the Orcs?'

'You'd be surprised how base some people in this city can be.'

'You may be right. But not much time elapsed between when the pendant last went missing and the time of my enquiry. I think I'd have picked up traces were it close to the city. I think it most likely that it's still in Turai, concealed in some manner. Where do you suggest we look?'

'I've no idea. It could be anywhere. If you can't locate it with sorcery, I'm stuck.'

'I thought you were an investigator,' says Lisutaris, drily.

'Number one chariot in the field of investigation. But we don't know who took it and Turai's a large city. I'll start making enquiries but it'll take time.'

Lisutaris clenches her fists. 'I have no time.'

There's a knocking at the door. I open it. Sarin the Merciless is standing outside. Sarin is one of the deadliest killers I've ever met. She has a loaded crossbow in her hand. She points it at my heart.

'I'm looking for a pendant,' she says.

Chapter Nine

Sarin the Merciless is as cold as an Orc's heart. Not a woman you can take lightly. She learned her fighting skills from warrior monks and is as ruthless a killer as I've come across in all my years of investigating.

'You know it's illegal to carry a weapon like that inside the city walls?'

'Is that so?'

'It is. But don't get the impression I'm not pleased you visited, Sarin. There are enough warrants out for you for murder and robbery to make a man wealthy.'

'Only if he was alive to collect the reward.'

Sarin is rather tall. She wears a man's tunic - unusual enough - and, uniquely for a woman in this city, has her hair cut very short. This is next door to taboo, and quite unheard of in civilised society. For some reason I've never been able to fathom, she wears an extraordinary number of earrings, an odd indulgence for a woman whose image is otherwise so severe. She's added a few since I last saw her and the piercings now travel the full semicircle of each ear. She looks at Lisutaris, meanwhile keeping the crossbow pointed at my chest. A bolt at this range would pin me to the wall. Sarin once shot Makri and it took the power of a magical healing stone to save her life. Round about the same time she killed Tas of the Eastern Lightning, one of Turai's most powerful sorcerers.

'Who are you?' she demands.

'Lisutaris, Mistress of the Sky,' replies the sorcerer coldly. 'Put that crossbow down.'

Showing no desire to put the crossbow down, Sarin points it instead at Lisutaris, which is a mistake. Lisutaris makes a slight movement of her hand and the weapon flies from Sarin's grasp to clatter on the floor, ending up under the sink. If Sarin is perturbed she doesn't show it. She steps forward so her face is only a few inches from that of Lisutaris.

'I don't like sorcerers,' she says.

'I don't like you,' counters Lisutaris.

Lisutaris is not a woman you can intimidate easily. She fought heroically in the last war against the Orcs, bringing down war dragons from the sky and blasting Orcish squadrons with powerful destructive spells. When her supply of sorcery eventually ran out, she picked up a sword and hewed at the Orcish invaders as their heads appeared over the city walls. I was beside her at the time.

'You might believe that the spell protection charm I sense on your person will protect you against me. You are mistaken. Remove your face from mine or I will engulf you in flames.'

'Will you?' says Sarin, not removing her face. 'Before you wore down my protection spell I'd break your neck.'

As a sporting man, I wouldn't mind seeing Sarin and Lisutaris squaring off against each other, but it would probably mean my rooms getting wrecked, and when that happens Gurd is never happy about it. So I interrupt. 'Did you come here just to pick fights with my guests? That's something I can usually do myself.'

Sarin draws back a few inches. 'No, Thraxas, I came here looking for a pendant. I thought you might have it. Not an unreasonable assumption, given that you were seen at the green jewel's last known location. Do you have it?'

'I don't know what you're talking about.'

'The pendant. For far-seeing. Lisutaris hired you to retrieve it. Just as I hired men to retrieve it for me. My men ended up dead. I see you fared better.'

'I'm a hard man to kill.'

An expression of withering contempt flickers over Sarin's features. 'Hard to kill? I've passed by you drunk in the gutter, Thraxas. I could have gutted you had I wished.'

'When was this exactly?'

'On one of the many occasions I've been in this city, undetected. There are plenty of unsolved crimes which could be laid at my door, investigator. Some of them investigated by you, without result. The few successes you brag about are as nothing compared to your multitudinous failures.'

I don't believe her. Sarin is just angry at me because I've thwarted her in the past. But I notice Lisutaris is looking at me with a new lack of respect. No client likes to hear their investigator being mocked by a criminal.

'Me lying drunk in the gutter notwithstanding, Lisutaris hasn't lost any pendants that I know about. The Mistress of the Sky merely called in to invite me to a masked ball she's holding in a couple of days. And I'm very gratified to receive the invitation, Lisutaris. I shall be delighted to attend.'

'Stop this buffoonery,' says Sarin, loudly. She studies my face. 'You don't have the pendant,' she says. She turns her head to Lisutaris and regards her for a few seconds. 'And neither do you.'

'So you can read minds?' I ask, intending it to be sarcastic.

'Not exactly,' replies Sarin, taking my statement at face value. 'But I trained with warrior monks. I can read emotions.'

She picks up her crossbow. 'A puzzle,' she says, softly. 'I knew that the pendant had been intercepted by the Society of Friends. I intended to take it from their operative at the Blind Horse. Someone beat me to it. I thought it might have been you, but apparently I was wrong. No matter. I'll find it again. If you get in my way I'll kill you.'

Sarin the Merciless departs, closing the door quietly behind her.

'At least we're not the only ones who don't know where the pendant is.'

'That is little comfort,' says Lisutaris. 'Who was that woman?'

'Sarin the Merciless. Ruthless killer. She almost killed Makri and she did kill Tas of the Eastern Lightning though it could never be proved against her. She once blackmailed the Consul's office and made off with enough gold to last her a lifetime, but it hasn't induced her to retire from crime. I get the impression she enjoys it. Of course, she's mentally unwell. That whole part about seeing me drunk in the gutter was obviously a hallucination.'

'Obviously. Who are her associates?'

'She has no fixed alliances. She did work with Glixius Dragon Killer and the Society of Friends one time, but they fell out. She was all set to rob the Society but someone beat her to it.'

'Might we use her as a means of finding the pendant?'

'Perhaps. Can you track her with sorcery?'

'I can,' says Lisutaris. 'I'll trace her movements round the city and keep you informed. Meanwhile I must urge you to spare no effort in your own search.'

I speak some words of caution to Lisutaris. 'Sarin is a very dangerous woman. If she can't find the pendant herself she might just decide to search for it at your villa. Perhaps I really should come to the ball.'

'Do not trouble yourself,' says Lisutaris. 'I have adequate security.'

She departs. I march straight downstairs for a beer.

'Good meeting?' asks Makri, at the bar.

'Stop talking and give me a beer.'

'So what are you as miserable as a Niojan whore about?'

'Nothing.'

'Nothing?'

'That's right, nothing. Also, Sarin the Merciless just paid a visit.'

Makri is agitated. Sarin once put a crossbow bolt in her chest and Makri would like the opportunity to return the favour.

'I think Sarin must be the only person ever to wound me that I haven't killed in return.'

I tell Makri she'll probably get her chance. 'Sarin has a way of appearing when she's not wanted.'

'Does this mean you can't investigate at the Guild College?'

'It might have to wait a while.'

'It can't wait. If you don't find the thief soon I'm going to have to do the examination with everyone thinking I'm a criminal.'

'Well you'll just have to make the best of it.'

'Make the best of it?' says Makri, flushing. 'Make the best of it? Is that your advice? I didn't ask you to get involved in the first place. I was quite happy to go there and kill Professor Toarius. You persuaded me not to and now you're saying I just have to make the best of it?'

Seeing Makri getting angry, the drinkers around us draw back nervously.

'That's right, you'll just have to make the best of it. Just because Lisutaris invited you to her smart party doesn't mean the whole city has to start jumping around for your convenience.'

'Aha!' yells Makri. 'So that's why you've been acting like a troll with toothache. You're jealous because you can't go to the ball.'

'I am not jealous.'

'Just like the Elvish princess in the story,' says Makri.

'What story?'

'The Elvish Princess Who Couldn't Go to the Ball.'

'There's no such story.'

'Yes there is. I translated it last year.'

I glare at Makri with loathing. 'Fascinating, Makri. I'm gratified to learn that while I'm fighting desperate criminals you're safe in a classroom translating Elvish fairy stories.'

Makri takes her sword from behind the bar. 'I'm off to kill Professor Toarius,' she mutters.

I move swiftly to cut off her exit. 'Fine. I'll go investigate at the College.'

I grab a bag of food from Tanrose and eat on the hoof. Possibly Makri was right. I should be paying more attention to her problem. It's just that with bodies everywhere, Lisutaris's case was hard to ignore. Till the sorcerer sends me another lead, however, I've got time to investigate the theft at the college. I can't help resenting all the work I'm having to do over a lousy five guran crime. I still have some students left to visit, people who were close to the scene on the day in question. I set about tracking them down. It takes a lot of trudging round the streets and a lot of knocking at doors where no one is pleased to see me. I work my way northwards through the city and as the houses become smarter the replies get briefer. Several families flatly refuse to let me in, and only succumb eventually to the threat of a court order from the Tribune's Office. There isn't actually a Tribune's Office, but they're not to know that.

'When I heard that the Deputy Consul had reinstated the post of Tribune I didn't realise it would lead to the harassment of honest people,' says one angry master glassmaker, upset at me interrupting the family dinner to question his son.

'Just a few questions and I'll be on my way.'

This is the eighth house I've visited, so far with no results. I'm shown into an elegant front room which is sufficiently well furnished to make me think that a master glassmaker can't be that bad a thing to be. I wait a long time, and no one offers me a drink; bad manners towards a guest. Even the Consul would offer me wine, and he's never pleased to see me. Eventually the glassmaker's son, Ossinax, appears. He's around nineteen, small for his age, with long hair tied back in a ponytail like most of the lower-class sons of the city. My own hair has trailed down my back since I was young. These days I notice some grey streaks.

'I'm glad you've come,' he says, taking me by surprise.

'You are?'

He lowers his voice as if fearful that his father might be listening outside. 'I don't think Makri stole that money.'

'Why not?'

'Because once I asked her to look after a quarter-guran for me and she gave it right back when I asked.'

'Why did you need her to look after a quarter-guran?'

'I didn't. It was a bet with some other students. To see how long she'd keep it without stealing it. But then she didn't steal it at all. We were surprised.'

'I see.'

'I like her,' says Ossinax. He looks a little downcast. 'Though she did punch me after she learned about the bet. But I never told anyone. I didn't want to get her into trouble.'

From the tone of Ossinax's voice, I get the impression that he might be harbouring more than friendly feelings towards Makri.

'So who else might have taken the money?'

'I don't know. There were a few people around.'

Everyone he can remember is on my list, and I've checked them all out. 'Are you sure there was no other student around?'

'Not that I can remember.'

'No members of staff?'

'Why would a member of staff steal five gurans?'

'You never know who might need money urgently.'

Ossinax doesn't remember seeing any members of staff anywhere near the room in question.

'Professor Toarius was there earlier, but he often walks round the building.'

'How much earlier?'

'Around an hour. It was before my philosophy class. He walked along the corridor with Barius, his son.'

'What was he doing there?'

'I don't know. He's a student at the Imperial University. I only saw him once before, when he came down to visit his father. But I'm sure it was him.'

No one has mentioned anything about the Professor's son before. That's probably not suspicious. After all, this was more than an hour before the theft. But I'm curious anyway. The Professor didn't say that his son had been there earlier in the day. There again, the Professor didn't mention much before he stormed out of the room.

I ask Ossinax if he can tell me anything more about Barius. He's surprised I'm interested.

'The family is rich. Barius wouldn't need to steal five gurans.'

'I suppose not.'

I let him have my address and tell him to get in touch if he thinks of anything else that might interest me.

'The Avenging Axe? Is that where Makri works?'

'It is.'

'Is it a dangerous place?'

'Any place Makri works is a dangerous place.'

'Did she really slaughter an Orc lord and all his family when she escaped from the gladiator pits?'

'She did.'

'Did she really fight a dragon in the arena?'

I see Makri has not been above doing a little bragging.

'Yes, she did,' I tell him. 'And she helped me fight another one, much bigger,' I add, not wishing young Ossinax to get the impression that Makri's the only one capable of epic feats in battle. We didn't kill the dragon but we defeated the Orcish forces that accompanied it. Makri dealt the fatal blow by hewing her way through their ranks to kill their commander.

I leave Ossinax looking thoughtful. A servant shows me out under the watchful eye of his father. Outside I can hear the sound of hammering coming from the workshop at the rear. I gaze at the front of the house. 'Nice windows. You make them all yourself?' The glassmaker shuts the door. It's hot as Orcish hell. I take a drink from a fountain and look around for someone to sell me a watermelon. I have an urge to visit Barius, son of Professor Toarius. After eating two large watermelons, I still have the urge, so I wave down a landus and tell the driver to take me to Thamlin.

Chapter Ten

It's surprisingly difficult to find Barius. He's not at the Imperial University and no one there has seen him for several days. I traipse uncomfortably around the huge marble halls, asking questions of students and members of staff, but the young man's friends don't know where he is, and the tutors and professors aren't keen to give information to an outsider, Tribune or not. When I find myself being lectured on the historical duties of the Tribunate by a Professor of Theology, I realise it's time to leave the University. So much learning is making me feel ignorant. The sight of ranks of well-dressed, attentive students sitting in vast lecture halls makes me wonder what they'll make of Makri if she ever manages to force her way into the place. Deputy Consul Cicerius did once hint that he might help her, if circumstances allowed, but he needed a favour from her at the time. I doubt he'd come through with any real assistance if it came down to it.

Barius still lives in the family home, so that should be my next destination, though I'm not looking forward to another encounter with Professor Toarius. The Professor will be down on me like a bad spell if I start bothering his household. Toarius belongs to an important family and has influential friends. Being a professor doesn't by itself give a man high status, but Toarius's family own a lot of land outside the city and have been wealthy for a long time. Too bad, I muse, as I head towards his villa. During my career as an investigator I've already offended most important people in the city. Another one probably doesn't matter that much.

Which reminds me. I've been meaning to make enquiries about Lisutaris's secretary. I'm curious as to why the sorcerer is so protective towards her. I break off my mission to call in on a tavern owner who used to be employed as head of stables by Tas of the Eastern Lightning. When that sorcerer handed in his toga a year or so back, the stableman found himself out of a job and ended up putting his savings into a tavern, which suits him well enough. I once got his son off a charge of assault after a street fracas and he's helped me once or twice with his knowledge of the staff and servants of our city's sorcerers.

'Lisutaris's secretary? Sure I remember her. Avenaris. Nervous little thing. Daughter of Lisutaris's older brother. When he was killed in the war, Lisutaris took her in. Looked after her ever since. What's she been up to?'

'Nothing that I know of. What does she have to be nervous about?'

'Who knows?'

He can't tell me any more. Avenaris has never been in trouble and is a loyal employee. No scandal, no boyfriends. Just nervous. I thank him, leave him enough money for a few drinks, and get back to my quest.

Professor Toarius lives in Thamlin. As always, I'm amazed at how neat and clean everything is. No rubbish on the streets, no beggars on the corners, no stray dogs looking hungrily for food. The pavements are covered in the pale yellow and green tiles that are a distinctive feature of Turai's wealthy areas, and every large house is set well back from the road, fronted by extensive gardens. The streets are quiet, with well-behaved servants carrying provisions home to their employers, and a visible presence of Civil Guards, here to keep out undesirables. When an official-looking carriage pulls up alongside me, my first thought is that I've been deemed undesirable. I'm astonished when the curtains of the carriage open and the Consul himself beckons to me. I've met Kalius before but I wouldn't expect Turai's highest official to be searching the streets for me.

'Get in,' instructs Kalius.

I get in. 'Where are we going?'

'We're not going anywhere.'

Kalius must be sixty. His toga is lined with gold as befits his rank, and he wears it with pride. As Turanian Consuls go, he's moderately well regarded. If he's not exactly as sharp as an Elf's ear, then neither is he the most foolish we've had. While he lacks Cicerius's reputation for incorruptibility, at least he hasn't been flagrant in taking bribes, and he's more charismatic than his deputy. 'I wish to talk with you. Here will do as well as anywhere.'

I'm puzzled by the meeting. I ask the Consul if he just happened to be riding by.

'I was searching for you. My sorcerer located you and I rode quickly to intercept you.'

If the Consul has actually used a sorcerer to locate me, I have to be in trouble over something. The authorities generally don't use their sorcerers for trivial matters.

'What task are you performing for Lisutaris?'

I'm not sure what to say. I can't possibly reveal Lisutaris's reason for hiring me. It strikes me fully for the first time that Lisutaris is withholding some tremendously important information from the state, information that really should not have been withheld, and I'm now implicated. If disaster strikes Turai because the errant sorcerer has lost the pendant, and I'm held to have been responsible for its non-recovery, I'll be lucky to avoid spending the rest of my life on a prison galley. I consider denying that Lisutaris has hired me but reject it as too risky, given the Consul's many sources of information. It's time to lie, something I pride myself on my talent for. 'She hired me to find some personal papers.'

'What sort of papers?'

'Her diary.'

Kalius regards me coolly for some moments. 'Her diary?'

'Yes. She lost it at the chariot races. Naturally it's a sensitive matter. No important sorcerer wants details of her daily thoughts placed before the public. You know how cruel people can be. The Renowned and Truthful Chronicle would probably publish the whole thing if it fell into their hands.'

Kalius isn't looking convinced. 'Lisutaris hired you to find her diary? I find that hard to believe.'

'Diaries are sensitive objects, Consul. I believe hers may contain several love poems. She's anxious that no one should see them.'

'Are you telling me that Turai's most important sorcerer has been wasting her time writing love poems?'

I raise my palms towards the sky. 'Are love poems a waste of time? Who can say? In the tavern where I live there are various persons deeply enmeshed in affairs of the heart.'

'I am not interested in the squalid affairs that go on in the Avenging Axe,' says Kalius, acidly.

It's gratifying to realise that the Consul actually remembers where I live. He did come there one time, to harangue me, but I thought he'd probably have forgotten. I struggle on with my story.

'Lisutaris needed a man of discretion to work on her behalf. I'm sure you understand. Really I shouldn't be telling you this and must ask you to make sure the information goes no further.'

'I have been informed that you've been involved in a great many deaths in recent days. Are you aware that earlier today six men were found hacked to death near to the pleasure gardens?'

'I wasn't. Does it concern me?'

'It concerns Lisutaris. An investigator named Demanius was quickly on the scene and I've learned that Demanius is involved in some matter concerning Lisutaris.'

'Demanius? The name is vaguely familiar. Who hired him?'

Kalius won't tell me who hired Demanius. Nor will he tell me how he knows that Demanius is working on anything that concerns Lisutaris, but I take his information as reliable. The Consul's office has its own efficient intelligence services. It's distressing to learn that another six men have died. More distressing that Demanius was on the scene and I knew nothing about it.

'It seems unlikely that so many murders would have occurred during the pursuit of a diary, no matter how many poems it contained,' says the Consul.

'I haven't actually been involved in these deaths, Consul. They just happened while I was there. Following up leads on the diary led me into several insalubrious venues. I believe there may have been some violence but it was nothing to do with me. Or Lisutaris.'

Kalius wears a small gold ring on his right hand, an official seal, one of the emblems of his office as chief representative of the King. He fingers it and looks thoughtful. 'If I learn that you are lying to me, investigator, you will be punished.'

I assure him I'm not lying. I'm eager to be on my way but Kalius hasn't finished with me. 'When Cicerius made you a Tribune, I understand he made it clear that the appointment was honorary.'

'He did.'

'And yet you are using the historical powers of the Tribunate against the express will of the government.'

There's no point lying on this one. 'I felt it was justified.'

'Last time you foolishly used these powers was there not an attempt to kill you?'

'There was.'

'I would have thought that would have been sufficient discouragement,' says Kalius. 'Politics in this city can be dangerous. Be warned. Your powers are purely notional. If you find yourself in trouble because of your actions, the government will not support you.'

Kalius dismisses me from his carriage. His driver takes up the reins and canters off. I wonder what sort of punishment Kalius has in mind. I wonder if I should just pack a bag and leave the city. I wonder why they don't build more taverns in Thamlin. I really need a beer. I can't find a landus for hire anywhere so I have to walk a long way back towards the centre of the city. Here the streets are unpaved and I'm soon choking on the dust and cursing the heat. Halfway along Moon and Stars Boulevard another carriage pulls up. It's a big day for finding Thraxas in your carriage. Lisutaris opens the door and beckons me in. Her conveyance is luxuriously furnished but smells strongly of thazis.

'Find me with a spell?'

She nods. 'I think I've located the pendant.'

'Just as well. The Consul suspects you've lost it.'

I describe my recent encounter. Lisutaris is greatly disturbed, not least by my informing the Consul that she's been writing love poetry. Her elegant features take on a rather piqued air.

'Couldn't you think of anything more convincing?'

'I didn't have time to think. Anyway, it's not that unbelievable. Sorcerers are occasionally poetic. And you've never married. Who knows if you might be pining for someone?'

'I'm starting to believe Harmon Half Elf was right about you.'

'Harmon? What's he been saying?'

'That you're an imbecile.'

Lisutaris looks like she more to say on the subject, but at this moment the call for afternoon prayers rings out over the city. It's a legal requirement for all Turanian citizens to pray three times a day, and while the last thing I want to do right now is get down on my knees, I don't have a choice. It's illegal even to remain in a carriage, so, muffling our frustration, Lisutaris and I both clamber out into the street to join those others also unfortunate enough not to be indoors. Lisutaris frowns at the prospect of kneeling in the dust and getting her gown dirty.

'Perhaps I could do with some divine help,' she mutters, shooting me a glance which may imply that she no longer has total confidence in me as an investigator. We pray in silence. Or rather pretend to pray. I'm too busy seething with resentment over Harmon Half Elf calling me an imbecile. He might be a powerful sorcerer but I've never considered him that intelligent. The call goes up for prayers to end.

'I'm going to have something to say to Harmon Half Elf,' I say, hauling myself to my feet.

'You would be unwise to offend Harmon,' replies Lisutaris.

'Unwise? You think I'd worry about offending that pointy-eared charlatan? He wouldn't be the first sorcerer I've punched in the face before they had time to utter a spell.'

Lisutaris starts hunting in her bag for some thazis.

'If I'd realised you were so unstable I'd never have hired you.'

'I'm not unstable. I just don't like sorcerers calling me a moron.'

'The word was *imbecile*.'

'Or imbecile.'

We set off at a fast pace through the city. Lisutaris tells me that though she's still unable to locate the pendant directly, she has tracked Sarin to a warehouse at the docks. 'I've also traced a powerful user of magic heading there. It must be connected to the pendant.'

'Probably. Any idea who the powerful user of magic is?'

Lisutaris shakes her head. 'An aura I'm not familiar with.'

We're making good progress down the boulevard, and cross the river at a brisk pace. Lisutaris's driver is an experienced hand and wends his way through the crush of delivery wagons with a skill I can admire.

'Does Kalius really think I've lost the pendant?'

'I'm not certain. He suspects you're in some deep trouble. He may know nothing more. But that would be enough to worry the government, with you being Head of the Sorcerers Guild.'

'He's bound to ask to see the pendant at my ball,' moans the sorcerer.

'Perhaps if I was there I could divert him in some manner?'

'I doubt it,' says Lisutaris, and lights another thazis stick.

I sit in silence for the rest of the journey. Lisutaris idly wipes the dust from her gown. Like her rainbow cloak, it's of the highest quality. The Mistress of the Sky is an extremely wealthy woman. She inherited a vast fortune from her father, a prosperous landowner who greatly increased his fortune after he entered the Senate, as Senators tend to do. It's unusual for Turai's sorcerers to come from the very highest stratum of society - sorcery, like trade, is generally thought to be beneath their dignity - but Lisutaris, as the youngest child in the family, was left free to choose her own path while her older brothers were groomed for their roles in society. Her father may not have been overly pleased when she began to show an aptitude for sorcery, but with two male siblings already growing up respectably he didn't forbid her to carry on with her studies.

In normal circumstances, Lisutaris would have ended up as a working sorcerer with a modest income, but both her brothers were killed in the last Orc war, leaving her as sole heir to the family fortune. Since then she's carried on her dual role as member of the aristocracy and powerful sorcerer without causing too much scandal in a city which frowns on the unusual. Her fine record during the war still protects her from criticism, even though her enormous appetite for thazis must be widely known to her peers. The Renowned and Truthful Chronicle of All the World's Events has occasionally made some snide references to her remaining unmarried, but even that is not regarded as too outlandish for a sorcerer. They're allowed a degree of eccentricity, particularly a sorcerer who hurled back regiments of Orc warriors. Furthermore, her recent election as Head of the Sorcerers Guild, an organisation covering most of the sorcerers in the west, brought honour to Turai, and a degree of security.

Our carriage pulls up alongside a tall warehouse not far from the harbour. 'Sarin is inside,' says Lisutaris.

I don't ask her how she knows. Lisutaris has powers of seeing I could never aspire to even if I'd studied all my life.

'Fine,' I say. 'How do we get past the centaurs?'

'Centaurs?'

Three centaurs are currently walking round the corner, these being half man, half horse, and absolutely never seen in Turai. They're even rarer than unicorns. I met some in the fairy glade, but apart from that I'm not sure they exist anywhere in the world. We stare at them, more or less open-mouthed in surprise.

'They just cannot be here,' says Lisutaris. 'A centaur would never visit this city. The human environment is anathema to them.'

As we watch the centaurs pause in front of the warehouse, I wonder if I should draw my sword. Centaurs can be tough creatures when they're roused. I know, I've seen them fight. However, they pay us no attention but carry on round the warehouse, disappearing around the far corner, human heads held high, horse tails flapping behind them. We walk cautiously to the corner of the warehouse and peer round. No centaurs are in sight.

'They can't have disappeared,' mutters Lisutaris. 'I should alert the authorities.'

'No footprints.'

'What?'

'No footprints. Real centaurs would have left marks in the dust. It was some sort of apparition. Is there sorcery being used here?'

'Yes,' replies Lisutaris. 'But I'm not sure what type, or by who.'

Three mysterious centaurs are interesting enough, but we have business to attend to. I suggest we check out the warehouse before Sarin also disappears. Inside it's dark. Lisutaris draws a short staff from her cloak and mutters a word of power. Light floods to the furthest corner of the building. All around are crates and boxes.

'Upstairs,' says Lisutaris.

I follow her up the wooden stairs, all the time keeping a sharp look-out for Sarin the Merciless.

'She's deadly with a crossbow,' I whisper.

'I'll protect you,' says Lisutaris.

I'd meant it more as a warning than a plea for protection but I don't argue. I'm concerned about the powerful user of magic

Lisutaris detected heading our way. You never know who might just be carrying the spell that will pierce your protection. We climb up a long way. Inside the warehouse it's hot as Orcish hell, and by the third flight of stairs sweat is pouring down the inside of my tunic. My senses, already buzzing after the centaurs, start going into overdrive. Danger is close. Lisutaris dims her illuminated staff and steps carefully through the doorway that leads on to the top floor. Suddenly there's a humming sound in the air. I duck instinctively but Lisutaris remains upright, hand in the air. A crossbow bolt bounces off her magical energy field and clatters harmlessly on the floor.

Lisutaris boosts her illuminated staff to full power again, and there in the far corner I see Sarin urgently loading another bolt into her weapon. I raise my sword and charge at her with the intention of running her through before she can fire again. Which I'm confident of doing. I might not be able to magically deflect a crossbow bolt, but when it comes to street fighting Thraxas is number one chariot. I aim a blow at Sarin's neck and I swear my sword is no more than two inches away from her when I'm suddenly picked up bodily as if by an invisible hand and flung across the warehouse, where I land in a breathless heap, bruised and confused. As I haul myself to my feet, two things catch my eye. One, Sarin has now reloaded her crossbow. Two, Glixius Dragon Killer has ascended the stairs behind us. Glixius is a really powerful sorcerer, the most powerful criminal sorcerer I've ever encountered, at least of the Human variety. He motions with his hand and Lisutaris goes flying through the air.

Trusting that Lisutaris can look after herself, I throw myself sword first at Sarin just as she's pulling the trigger of her crossbow. My blade connects with the tip of her weapon, sending the bolt upwards into the ceiling but in the process wrenching my blade from my hands. Sarin immediately drops the crossbow and kicks me in the face, giving me a painful reminder that the last time I encountered her she proved to be a formidable opponent in hand-to-hand combat. I can feel blood spurting from my nose. I ignore it and step forward with my fists raised. I've nothing fancy in mind, just use my bulk to overwhelm her. Sarin kicks me again and leaps backwards but I keep on going till she's up against the wall, and then I connect with a punch which drops her like a drunken Elf falling from a tree.

I pick up my sword, and gaze down at her prostrate form with some satisfaction. I owed her that. Suddenly the invisible hand again picks me up and hurls me backwards through a window, sending me, several boxes and a great deal of broken glass plummeting to earth from a height of more than a hundred feet.

Chapter Eleven

Fifty feet from the ground, I'm not feeling confident. There's a paved road outside the warehouse and I'm hurtling towards it at an ungodly rate. I curse Glixius, Sarin, Lisutaris and the hostile fates who've had it in for me since the day I was born. This takes me down to about ten feet. I close my eyes. I come to a gentle halt. Benevolent sorcery, presumably from Lisutaris, has rescued me. I land lightly on my feet, sword still in hand, and immediately charge back into the warehouse, ready to show Glixius Dragon Killer that I'm not a man you can toss out of a high window without suffering the consequences.

Inside the situation is confused. More people have entered the building. There's a full-scale battle going on all up the wooden staircase. I recognise several local Brotherhood men struggling with opponents whom I guess to be from the Society of Friends. Approaching fast are five or six uniformed men from Palace Security, the King's own intelligence service.

'Quite a commotion, Thraxas,' says a voice behind me.

It's Demanius, from the Venarius Investigation Agency.

'What are you doing here?' I demand.

'Same as you,' replies Demanius.

'I'm not doing anything.'

'Then neither am I.'

Above our heads the fight intensifies. Some of the struggling figures are forced off the staircase onto the floors that lead off to either side, and I make an effort to fight my way through. My client is upstairs, currently in combat with Glixius Dragon Killer and Sarin the Merciless. I should be at her side. When four men from the Society of Friends appear before me, swords raised, I get the fleeting feeling that I wish Makri was here to lend her strength to mine. Though if she was, she'd probably end up killing the men from Palace Security as well as my opponents and things would only get worse. Makri has no self-control once she gets her axe out. As it turns out, I'm not alone. Demanius arrives and we confront our foes together. The Society of Friends men are far from their home territory. It's dangerous for them to venture south of the river where the Brotherhood hold sway. I'd guess these thugs, seeing their mission go wrong, are keen to depart as swiftly as possible. I'm about to offer them the opportunity to do just that, thereby avoiding a messy conflict, when from behind me comes the sound of a Civil Guard's whistle. I risk a swift glance backwards. Twenty or so Guards, led by Captain Rallee, are streaming into the warehouse. Intent on not being captured by the Guards, the Society of Friends men lose interest in me. They turn and flee up the stairs. I follow them with Demanius at my heels.

With the warehouse now full of the Brotherhood, the Society of Friends, Palace Security, Civil Guards, plus assorted investigators, sorcerers and murderous adventurers, I'd say that I've finally blown it as far as keeping Lisutaris's problem a secret goes. When I reach the second floor and find Harmon Half Elf floating in through an open window, rainbow cloak billowing in the breeze, it strikes me that Lisutaris, Mistress of the Sky, might be in for some tough questioning from the Sorcerers Guild if she ever finishes her session with Palace Security. All this is dependent on Lisutaris remaining alive, of course. I ignore the struggling masses and keep heading up the stairs.

I'm just beneath the top floor when a shattering explosion rips through the building. Wood and stone rain down on my head. The floorboards groan in protest as mystical forces start to rip the place apart. Voices are raised in panic as the warehouse starts to sway.

'Get out of here!' yells Demanius.

I keep on going. I have to rescue my client. Her sorcerous conflict with Glixius Dragon Killer has brought about the destruction of the warehouse, and for all I know she might be lying unconscious with Sarin the Merciless standing over her, crossbow in hand. The walls are starting to buckle. Strips of wood fall around my shoulders as I rush into the room at the very top of the warehouse. Fire has broken out and smoke is now pouring from the walls, quickly taking hold. As I reach the final room the roof starts caving in and I'm knocked off my feet by a great beam which pins me to the floor. I struggle to free myself, vainly.

'Thraxas?' Lisutaris is standing over me, looking calm and untroubled. 'I gave you a safe landing. Why did you come back?'

'To rescue you.'

I think Lisutaris smiles. In the ever-thickening smoke, it's hard to tell. 'Thank you,' she says.

The Sorceress waves her hand. The beam flies off me. I haul myself to my feet, with some difficulty.

'We have to get out,' I gasp. 'Building's coming apart.'

There's a blast that sounds like a squadron of war dragons crashing to earth and the warehouse caves in. For the second time in the space of a few minutes I find myself one hundred feet off the ground with nothing in the way to break my fall. Lisutaris is beside me in mid-air. We're both hovering gently. It's quite a pleasant sensation.

'Did you really come back to rescue me?'

'Yes.'

'But the building was collapsing. It was foolish.'

'I have a duty towards my clients.'

The breeze blows smoke from the wreckage around our faces. From this elevation I have a really good view of Twelve Seas. It doesn't look any better. We start to sink, very gently.

'Are those Civil Guards?' asks Lisutaris.

'I'm afraid so. Palace Security is here as well. And Harmon Half Elf.'

'What does he want?'

'Maybe the Sorcerers Guild is getting curious.'

Lisutaris frowns. Her long hair flutters in the wind. 'Are you saying my secret is out?'

'They have their suspicions. What happened to Glixius and Sarin?'

Lisutaris didn't find it difficult to defeat Glixius in a contest of sorcerous strength but she was unable to prevent him from bringing down the building with a blasting spell which allowed him to escape.

'As for Sarin, I don't know.'

With any luck she'll have perished horribly. By this time we're almost at ground level. A lot of people are waiting for us to land.

'What am I going to say?' asks Lisutaris.

'Say nothing.'

'Nothing? That's hardly going to convince anyone.'

'You outrank all these people. Till the Consul himself has you under oath in a courtroom, deny everything. Let me do the talking.'

The corners of Lisutaris's mouth turn downwards. 'I fear I'm doomed. But thank you again for your rescue attempt.'

We land a short distance away from the burning warehouse and are immediately surrounded. Everyone is asking questions at once. Captain Rallee is particularly insistent. This is his patch and he doesn't like having it disturbed by armed gangs burning down warehouses.

'Or did you destroy the warehouse with sorcery?' he says, directing his gaze towards Lisutaris.

Harmon Half Elf stands to one side, waiting his turn. As far as I know, Turai's senior sorcerers have no power to officially censure the Head of the Guild, but it's going to destroy Lisutaris's reputation if they turn against her. The man in charge of the operatives from Palace Security adds his voice to the others. Everyone looks to Lisutaris, waiting for an explanation. Desperate measures being called for, I step to the fore and hold up my hand.

'Thraxas, Tribune of the People, carrying out official Tribune's business,' I state, loudly. 'Lisutaris is here at my request, helping me with an inquiry. As such, I forbid her to talk of today's events. A full report will be presented to the Consul in good time.'

There's something of a stunned silence. Civil Guards and Palace Security don't expect to be given orders by private investigators.

However, for some reason which would take a historian to explain, the Tribune's powers were great, and could only be overruled by a full meeting of the Senate. It's little wonder the authorities eventually let the institution fall into disuse. Their powers were never legally rescinded, however, which means that as long as I'm a Tribune they're stuck with it. Captain Rallee knows enough about the law not to argue, but as I lead Lisutaris away from the scene he draws me to one side.

'You're digging yourself a pretty big hole, Thraxas. I don't know what's going on, but if you're covering up for Lisutaris, the government is going to come down on you like a bad spell. Don't expect her to stick up for you when you're being indicted before a Senate committee.'

'I won't.'

'You know anything about any centaurs? We got a report from some crazy person that three of them were wandering around.'

'They were. I saw them.'

The captain doesn't like this at all. 'Yesterday it was unicorns, now it's centaurs. At first I thought it was the dwa talking, but now I'm not so sure.'

He turns to Lisutaris. 'You know of any reason why strange magical creatures might be suddenly appearing all over the city?'

'I have no idea,' responds Lisutaris, which ends the matter. A Guards' Captain can't get tough with the Head of the Sorcerers Guild. Lisutaris turns to go and I follow her. Captain Rallee calls after us.

'I made a quick body count in the warehouse. Six men dead. How many more before it ends?'

'I have no idea,' I call back, uncomfortably.

'I've got a bet down on twenty; how's that looking?'

Declining to reply, I usher Lisutaris up the paved road onto which I almost plunged from a great height. Behind us the fire wagons have arrived and are doing good work putting out the blaze. They train their horses not to fear fire. It's a marvellous institution. The Civil Guards are arresting every remaining gang member, and Harmon Half Elf stares after us. Let him stare. I haven't forgiven him for calling me an imbecile. We leave the scene in Lisutaris's carriage.

'I believe there is no extradition treaty between Turai and Abelasi,' says Lisutaris.

'So?'

'I'm just wondering where the best place to flee might be.'

'Flee? Put the thought out of your mind. We're not beaten yet.'

'We have less than two days to retrieve an item which has so far eluded all our efforts. And even if we do find it, I'm still ruined. There's no way of keeping it secret now.'

Lisutaris draws a thazis stick from a pocket inside her gown.

'Don't despair. I don't give up easily,' I tell her. 'Besides, none of these people really know what's going on. Till you admit you've lost the pendant, everything is rumour and supposition. The Head of the Sorcerers Guild doesn't have to answer to rumour. Just keep denying everything.'

'And what if someone else retrieves the pendant?'

'Then I'll be joining you in Abelasi. But it's not going to happen. I'll find it.'

Lisutaris isn't convinced. Neither am I, but I am stubborn.

'Any theories regarding the centaurs?' I ask.

'No. I can't explain their appearance, What did Captain Rallee mean when he asked you about how many bodies?'

'I expect he was just wanting information for his report. You know these guards, always like to get their figures correct.'

Lisutaris turns her gaze fully upon me. 'I am Head of the sorcerers Guild,' she says.

Meaning, I think, that you can't fob her off with a lie. 'Word got out I was on a big case,' I admit. 'It was the fault of this weird young woman called Dandelion who talks to dolphins. She read in the stars that I was about to be involved in a bloodbath, and ever since then the regulars at the Avenging Axe have been placing bets on how many bodies there will be before it ends.'

Lisutaris's eyes widen. I get ready to leap from the carriage. Unexpectedly, she starts to laugh.

'They're placing bets?' She seems to find this funny. 'Here we are, trying to keep the news from the Consul, and down in the Avenging Axe they're placing bets.'

'I strongly advised them to desist.'

'Why? How much has Makri gone in for?'

'Fourteen bodies.'

'Too few, I fear,' says Lisutaris.

'It is. I think we're up to twenty-one now.'

'What odds are being offered?'

'Fifty to one for the exact total, twenty to one if you get within three.'

'You still have the money I gave you to retrieve the pendant? Then put me down for thirty-five,' she says.

'Are you sure?'

'After my recent losses at the chariot races, why should I pass up this opportunity?'

'Because the whole thing is unethical.'

'A bet is a bet,' says Lisutaris.

I feel a great weight lifting off me. I realise why I've been so angry about the whole thing. It's because I've felt unable to place a bet. Here am I, Thraxas, number one chariot among Twelve Seas gamblers, caught up in a sporting contest yet unable, for reasons of ethics, to participate. No wonder I felt bad. Now, with the sanction of my client, I'm free to join in. It's a relief.

'Fine. But do you really think we'll reach thirty-five?'

'At least,' says Lisutaris. 'I can feel it.'

I'll show these scum at the Avenging Axe what a real gambler is capable of. Young Moxalan will regret ever entering the bookmaking business by the time I've cleaned him out. Lisutaris drops me off at Quintessence Street. The woman who sells fish and the man who's set up a stall for sharpening blades are arguing again. I've more to worry about than bad-tempered vendors. Like Makri, for instance, who once more is sheltering in my office.

'Are you going to spend every meal-break in here till Dandelion leaves?'

'I might.'

'You see, that's one of your problems, Makri. You tolerate these weird sort of people and where does it get you? They take advantage. In a city like Turai it doesn't pay to tolerate people. You have to be tough.'

'I am tough.'

'With a sword, yes. With down-and-outs, not nearly tough enough.'

'Doesn't your religion say you should be kind to the poor?'

I shrug. 'Probably. I never learned much about it.'

'What about your three prayers a day? What are you praying for?'

'Self-advancement, same as everyone else.'

'I'm glad I don't have a religion,' says Makri.

'That's because you're a barbarian who grew up without the benefit of a proper education.'

'I'm educated enough not to continue with this conversation, you hypocrite,' says Makri.

She produces two thazis sticks she's stolen from behind the bar. We light one each and smoke them in silence. Relaxed from the effects of the thazis, I describe today's events.

'All in all, another disaster.'

'How many dead does that make?' asks Makri.

'Twenty-one. But there's every indication that there's more to come. So I figure we should place a few bets somewhere around the thirty mark, and maybe take a punt at forty, just in case things really get rough.'

'Pardon?' says Makri.

'You'll have to put the bet on for me. Moxalan isn't going to accept a wager from me, he'd disqualify me for having too much inside information.'

Makri is looking baffled. 'I'm getting the feeling I've missed something. You've spent the last two days berating me for gambling on your investigation, and now you're telling me I have to place a bet on your behalf? What changed?'

'Nothing.'

'What about the ethical problems?'

'I leave ethics to the philosophers. Lisutaris wants to put money on, you'd better do that as well.'

'All right. As long as I can hide in your rooms from Dandelion.'

'If you must. I may need to borrow a little money.'

'What about all the money Lisutaris gave you?'

'I used it to pay the rent and buy a case of klee.'

'I don't have any money to spare,' claims Makri.

'Yes you do. You've been putting away your tips to pay for your examinations and I happen to know you've more than a hundred gurans secreted in your room for that purpose.'

'How dare you–'

I hold up my hand. 'Before you launch into a diatribe, I might remind you that it wasn't too long ago I found you trying to steal the emergency fifty-guran coin I was hiding under my couch. Furthermore, I've helped you out with money on numerous occasions, not to mention steering you in the right direction when it came to placing several astute wagers, so lend me the money. With my inside information and your cash we're onto a certainty. You'll win enough money to pay for your examinations this year and next year and probably buy a new axe as well.'

'Well, all right,' says Makri, 'but don't ever lecture me about anything again.'

'I wouldn't dream of it.'

'Are you any closer to actually recovering the pendant?'

'No. It's frustrating. I thought it was going to be easy. Sorcerers. You can't trust them.'

The heat makes me drowsy. When Makri goes back to work I don't fight the urge to go to sleep. I waken hungry and head downstairs to fill up with Tanrose's stew. I hope she's patched things up with Gurd. I depend so completely on her cooking that I dread her leaving the tavern. Moxalan is in the bar and Makri gives me a discreet nod, indicating that she's placed our bet.

Despite the usual hubbub from the early-evening customers, something seems to be missing. No friendly aroma of stew. No smell of food at all. A strange sensation washes over me and I find myself trembling, something that's never happened even in the face of the most deadly opponent. I fear the worst.

'Where's Tanrose? Where's the food?'

'Tanrose left,' says Gurd, and draws a pint with such viciousness that the beer pump nearly disintegrates in his hand.

'What about the food?'

'Tanrose left,' repeats Gurd, slamming the tankard down in front of an alarmed customer.

'Did she leave any food?'

'No. She just left.'

'Why?'

'Makri told her to.'

'What?'

'I did not tell her to leave,' says Makri.

My trembling is getting worse. 'Someone tell me what happened!' I yell. 'Where has Tanrose gone?'

'Back to her mother,' says Gurd, flatly. 'Makri told her to.'

'This is a really inaccurate description of events,' protests Makri. 'I merely suggested that she take a little time to sort out her feelings for Gurd and then speak to him frankly.'

Gurd sags like a man with a fatal wound. I get the urge to bury my face in my hands.

'What happened then?'

'She told me she was fed up with working for a man who was too mean-spirited to appreciate the things she did for him,' groans Gurd. 'Then she packed her bags and left.'

Makri studies the floor around her feet. 'It wasn't the result I was expecting,' she says.

'Why couldn't you leave well alone?' I yell at her. 'Now look what you've done! Tanrose has gone!'

Makri looks exasperated. 'I was only trying to help. Like you suggested.'

'Thraxas suggested it?' says Gurd.

'I did no such thing. Makri, you vile Orcish wench, do you realise what you've done?'

Makri's eyes open wide in shock. 'Did you just call me a vile Orcish wench?'

'I did. Of all the ridiculous things you've done since you arrived here to plague us, this is the worst. Now Gurd will be as miserable as a Niojan whore for the rest of his life and I'll starve to death.'

'Why couldn't you leave things alone?' cries Gurd.

After my Orcish slur Makri's first impulse was to reach for her sword, but faced with fresh criticism from Gurd she's confused.

'I was just trying to–'

Dandelion suddenly arrives and throws herself into the conversation. 'Thraxas, I have terrible news.'

'I've already heard,' I say. 'We have to bring her back.'

'Who?'

'Tanrose, of course.'

'Has she left?' says Dandelion.

'Of course. It's terrible news.'

'Why?'

'What do you mean, why? She cooks the best stew in Turai.'

Dandelion sniffs. 'I do not partake of the flesh of animals.'

I raise my fist.

'Don't you dare punch Dandelion,' says Makri, getting in between us.

'Maybe I should punch you.'

'Just try it.'

Makri raises her hands and sinks into her defensive posture.

'I can't live without Tanrose,' says Gurd. I've never heard him sounding so distressed. I once pulled three arrows out of his ribs and he never so much as complained.

'You're not listening to my news,' says Dandelion.

'If it's something to do with the stars, I'm not interested.'

'But the stars are sacred!'

'I'm not interested.'

There's no putting the woman off. Dandelion is practically jumping up and down in her frenzied eagerness to tell me something. 'The most serious of warnings! Last night there were flashes in the sky the like of which I've never seen! It was as if the skies above the beach were on fire!'

'Will you stop giving me warnings? They've already caused enough trouble.'

Dandelion looks hurt. She fingers her necklace - a ridiculous affair made of seashells - and mumbles something about only trying to help. Voices are raised everywhere as people in the bar now seek to give their opinions on the various topics on offer. Gurd, Makri and myself all find ourselves bombarded with suggestions. Most people seem to think that Gurd should go and propose marriage to Tanrose immediately, but there's a vocal faction who want to know if it's true that Lisutaris has promised to kill anyone who gets in the way of her illicit love affair.

'Lisutaris is not having an illicit love affair.'

'Then why has she hired you to retrieve her diary? Word is it's full of incriminating poetry.'

'How many people are likely to get in her way?' asks Parax. 'Are we talking three figures?'

'If she's been spurned,' muses a docker, 'she might get violent. You know what women are like when they're spurned.'

Gurd abandons all hope and sits down heavily behind the bar, unwilling or unable to even draw a jar of ale. Makri, remembering that I called her a vile Orcish wench, is now threatening to kill me. I inform her I'll be happy to send her head back to her mother, if she has a mother, which I doubt. It would seem that things could hardly get worse when a young government official in a crisp white toga strides into the bar. He hands me a document.

'What's this?'

'Citation of cowardice.'

'What?'

'You've been called before a committee of the Senate to account for your behaviour at the Battle of Sanasa.'

My head swims. The Battle of Sanasa was seventeen years ago.

'What are you talking about?'

'It is alleged that you discarded your shield and fled the field.'

There's a gasp from the assembled drinkers in the tavern. Discarding one's shield and fleeing the field of battle is one of the most serious charges that can be faced by a Turanian citizen. Never did I imagine that I could be accused of such a thing. The world has truly gone insane.

Chapter Twelve

I erupt in a volcanic fury. 'Discarded my shield? Me? I practically won the Battle of Sanasa single-handed, you young dog. If it wasn't for me you wouldn't be walking round this city in a toga. You wouldn't have a city to walk around. Who makes this allegation?'

'Vadinex, also a participant in the battle,' answers the official.

'We'll see about that,' I roar, and head for the door, sword still in hand. I wave it for extra effect. No one accuses me of cowardice. Gurd brings me to a halt by placing his arms around me and wedging his foot against a table.

'Where are you going?' he demands.

'To kill Vadinex. No one accuses me of discarding my shield.'

'Killing Vadinex won't help.'

'Of course it will help. Now get your arms off me. I have some killing to do.'

'They'll hang you.'

Makri is looking on, amused. 'Not that I mind you being hanged for murder, Thraxas, what with you calling me a vile Orcish wench, but isn't this similar to when you told me not to kill Professor Toarius?'

'It's not the same at all. Vadinex has impugned my honour.'

'Toarius impugned mine.'

'I don't care!' I roar, and renew my struggle with Gurd.

'You'll be arrested and then you won't be able to help Lisutaris.'

I cease struggling. In truth, I'm finding it hard to break free of Gurd's grasp. He always was an unusually strong man, and he's kept himself in better shape than me. He starts hauling me back towards the bar.

'Would they really hang Thraxas if he killed Vadinex?' asks Makri.

'Yes,' replies Gurd.

'Then it sounds like a good plan. Let him go.'

Gurd shoots a fierce scowl in Makri's direction. 'We don't need any more advice from you. Go and serve customers.'

Throughout all this the government official has remained calmly waiting for an opportunity to speak, and when he does so the tavern falls silent. There's still something about a man in a toga that induces respect. 'I must inform you that a man facing such a charge can no longer participate in any official duty. So you are forbidden by law to use the office of Tribune. Furthermore, your investigator's licence is temporarily suspended until such time as you be either cleared, in which case it shall be renewed, or convicted, in which case it will be revoked.'

'Are you saying I can't investigate?'

'That is correct.'

'How long for?'

He doesn't know. Until my case is heard by the Senate committee. That could take months. Possibly years. Unless you're a man with influence, legal cases can take a very long time to come to court. The official departs, leaving me to contemplate the terrible baseness of the accusations. Gurd directs Makri to look after the bar and leads me into the back room, where he pours me a hefty glass of klee. I drink it in one and he refills the glass.

'Thanks, Gurd. For stopping me going to kill Vadinex. It would have been foolish. Though I still want to do it.'

'Of course,' says Gurd. 'That's what I'd want to do if anyone accused me of cowardice. Back in the north I'd have killed him already. But things are different here.'

I look at Gurd with some surprise. 'When did you become the responsible citizen?'

'When I bought this tavern and started paying taxes.'

I've known Gurd for so long. I always think of him with his axe in his hand, hewing at the enemy. Somehow it hadn't quite struck me how much he's changed. Matured, I suppose. Not that he's a man who'd avoid a fight if it came along, as he's demonstrated various times on my behalf in the past few years. Gurd senses my thoughts.

'Don't worry. If you can't clear your name by the law, I'll help you kill Vadinex and we can flee the city together.'

I take another glass of klee. The way things are going we might find ourselves heading south with Lisutaris. She'd be a good companion for an outlaw. No problem lighting campfires in the wilderness. Gurd asks me if I know what's behind this unfortunate turn of events.

'I used my Tribune's powers to protect Lisutaris. It meant putting a block on the Civil Guards and Palace Security. Now someone's out for revenge. Probably Rittius, head of Palace Security. He's had it in for me for years. It was bound to happen.'

'No one who knows you would ever believe you threw away your shield and fled the battlefield.'

'What about people that don't know me? This will be all over the city. Some people will believe it.'

In a place like Turai where every man is glad to hear something bad about his neighbour, accusations of this sort tend to stick. A man's name can be ruined, even if the case never comes to court. Just the association with cowardice in war is a terrible taboo. Throwing away your shield is punishable by law, but the stigma is worse. It's so grave an accusation that it's rarely levelled against any of the hapless men who might actually be guilty of it. Most times the commander of a cohort, faced with a soldier's cowardice, would simply beat the soldier, make sure he was full of drink when the enemy next approached, and send him back into the field. Actually taking a man to court for cowardice is the sort of thing normally reserved for politicians whose enemies are seeking a means of ruining them. Either that, or a rich man whose relatives are looking for a way to part him from his fortune. Once it's proved against you, you lose all rights as a citizen.

'Why Vadinex?' wonders Gurd.

We both know Vadinex. A huge, brutal man. An effective soldier, but dumb as an Orc; vicious and bad, even in peacetime.

'I crossed him last winter,' I say. 'He'd willingly play along if Rittius offered him enough.'

I'm certainly not giving up my investigation on behalf of Lisutaris. Not even the King can prevent a citizen of the city walking around asking questions, though it could lead me into difficulties. I no longer have any legal status to protect my clients and could be forced by the Civil Guard to tell them everything I knew about any case I was working on. In theory anyway. In practice, the Guard can go to hell.

'Everyone can go to hell. If I run into Vadinex I still might kill him. Otherwise it's business as usual. I'm going to rescue Lisutaris. And I'm going to clear Makri.'

'What will I do about Tanrose?'

'Go and visit her. Take flowers. Apologise for criticising her bookkeeping. And make sure Makri doesn't interfere. She's not qualified to advise normal people about how to run their lives.'

'Do you think I should ask her to marry me?'

My own marriage was such a disaster, I'm loath to answer this. 'Gurd, you know I'm about as much use as a one-legged gladiator when it comes to relationships.'

Unfortunately Gurd is unwilling to let me off the hook. He demands to know what I think. I seem to owe him a proper answer.

'Yes. Get married. After all, you're paying taxes. It's probably the next step.'

Gurd pours himself a glass of klee. Probably he's thinking that the prospect of marriage is more frightening than facing an enemy force who outnumber you twenty to one. Which we've done, of course. More than once. Gurd realises that he's left Makri to look after a busy tavern and goes off to assist her. Makri's coping with the situation, aided by Dandelion, who's decided to help and is currently fumbling with a beer tap, wondering how it works. Several recently-arrived regulars are looking puzzled at the sight of the bar at the Avenging Axe being run by the odd pairing of Makri and Dandelion. As a respectable local drinking establishment, the Avenging Axe doesn't generally go in for novelty attractions.

'Is this something to do with it raining frogs outside?' asks a docker, a regular customer not noted for drunkenness.

'Raining frogs?'

We all troop outside to look. It is indeed raining frogs. They bounce on the dusty road then hop off sharply. After a minute or so it stops, and the frogs disappear.

'I've never seen that before,' says another dock worker.

'Yesterday I saw a unicorn,' says his companion. 'But I didn't like to tell anyone.'

No one can explain the downpour of frogs. The general consensus is that it's a bad sign and the city is doomed. I shake my head. Unicorns, centaurs, frogs. Let someone else sort it out. I'm still livid about the accusation of cowardice. I head up to my office, ready to make someone suffer for the indignity which has been inflicted upon me. You can't expect to accuse a man like Thraxas of deserting the battlefield and not suffer some consequences. The next person who gives me so much as an unfriendly look is going to find himself at the wrong end of a hefty beating, and maybe worse.

Unfortunately, the next person I encounter is Horm the Dead, and he's not a man to whom you can just hand out a beating. He's one of the most malevolent and powerful sorcerers in the world, an insane half-Orc from the wastelands who almost destroyed the entire city a year ago. He's strong, he's evil, he hates Turai and he hates me. It's a surprise to find him sitting in my office.

'Make yourself comfortable, why don't you?' I growl at him.

Powerful sorcerer or not, I'll have a good attempt at plunging my sword into his ribs before he can utter a spell. I demand to know what he's doing here.

Horm the Dead is a sorcerer of striking appearance. Black clothes, pale skin, long dark hair, high cheekbones, eagle feathers in his hair and a fistful of silver rings, most of them bearing impressions of skulls. His long black cloak trails over the chair like a great pair of bat's wings.

'Are you always so uncivil to your guests?' he asks, and laughs. His laugh sounds like it comes from somewhere on the other side of the grave. The last time I heard it he was riding a dragon over the city, having just intoned a spell which drove the entire population insane. Turai would have consumed itself in a bloody orgy of fire and violence had Lisutaris, Mistress of the Sky, not managed to neutralise the spell at the very last moment. Even so, the destruction was widespread, severe enough to make Horm an eternal enemy of Turai.

'I'm famous for my incivility. Now get out of my office.'

Horm ignores the suggestion. 'I am not impressed with this city,' he says.

'We're not impressed with you.'

'I really thought my eight-mile destruction spell would wipe you out. I was terribly disappointed when it didn't.'

'So you decided to bombard us with frogs?'

'Frogs? The unusual downpour? Nothing to do with me.'

Despite being half Orcish, Horm speaks very elegant Turanian. Coupled with his languid malevolence, it has an unsettling effect. As there seems to be no prospect of banishing him from my office without using violence, I ask him again why he's here.

'I thought I might hire you, investigator. Perhaps to find a certain pendant for me?'

'I'm busy,' I reply curtly, and don't let it show that I'm perturbed. With Horm now looking for the pendant, the stakes have moved up a notch, and they were already far too high.

'You know Prince Amrag will destroy you soon?' says Horm.

I'm thrown by the sudden change of subject. 'He will?'

'The young Prince is proving to be a surprisingly charismatic leader. He's quickly uniting the Orcish lands. I imagine that before too long he'll be in a position to lead an army from the east.'

'Then there will be a lot of dead Orcs for burning.'

Horm shrugs. 'No doubt. But he'll wipe you off the map, and every other Human nation. You're not as strong as you used to be, and neither are the Elves. How strange that they too should now be suffering from the ravages of dwa.'

Horm seems to have some very up-to-date information. It's not too many months ago that I was far down south on the Elvish Isles. It's true that dwa had found a foothold among the Elves, but I wouldn't have thought that news of this could have travelled to the Wastelands. Unless Horm had something to do with dwa reaching the Elves in the first place. He's a user and purveyor of the drug himself, and makes money by supplying it to the Human lands, including Turai. We're all conspiring in our own downfall and seem unable to do anything about it.

'Turai has few allies,' he continues. 'There is little cohesion left in the League of City States. And the larger countries will look to protect their own borders. No one will help Turai when the Orcs next attack.'

'Did you just come here to lecture me on politics? Because I'm a busy man.'

'Of course, I am not under the sway of Prince Amrag. My kingdom has never been subject to rule by any of the eastern Orcish nations, and so it shall remain. But I will probably add my might to their forces. One gets so bored sometimes. In truth, I've been looking forward to the emergence of a new warlord.'

He sits forward in his chair. 'But I digress. Turai still has a little time left. It also has something I want, namely the pendant.'

'So you can hand it over to Prince Amrag? If you think I'd help you with that, you're madder than you look.'

Horm leans forward. 'Perhaps I should just kill you now.'

'Perhaps you should just bounce a spell off my fine protection charm while I stick my sword in your guts.'

Horm sits back, perfectly relaxed. 'You're really not scared of me, are you? It's foolish, but admirable in a way. Tell me, why do you wish to protect this city?'

'I live here.'

'You could live anywhere. Turai doesn't like you. I was concealed downstairs when that unpleasant official arrived carrying the allegation that you had once fled from the field of battle. An allegation I would judge unlikely to be true. In my kingdom I would not allow such an accusation to be made. Of course, such things are commonplace in these lands you call civilised. A true warrior will always be brought down by his jealous, cowardly enemies.'

Not liking the way Horm the Dead is starting to make sense, I ask him directly about the pendant. 'What's your involvement?'

'It was offered to me for sale.'

'By Sarin the Merciless?'

'Indeed.'

'I remember you fell out last time you worked together.'

Horm waves his hand rather grandly. 'We may have argued. However, that was not the last time we worked together. Merely the last time you are aware of. Since then we have collaborated on various pieces of profitable business.' Horm smiles. 'I see this perturbs you, investigator. Did you really think everything that happens in this city is known to you?'

'I know that Sarin doesn't have the pendant.'

'Unfortunately she does not. Having gone to some trouble to visit this miserable city - I am of course obliged to use a variety of disguising spells - I find that the item has gone missing. The transaction was disturbed by Glixius Dragon Killer, who I look forward to removing from this world. Really, Thraxas, it has been farcical. The pendant travelling this way and that around Turai, pursued here and there by either Sarin or Glixius's men, none of whom were able to resist staring into the jewel, which, of course, drove them insane. Whoever has the pendant now seems to have hidden it very successfully. And I do so want it. As a tool for farseeing it's unmatched in the East or the West. Only the Elvish glass of Ruyana can compare, and the Elvish glass is, for the moment, beyond my reach.'

'How did Sarin learn of its existence?'

'I have no idea,' says Horm, sounding bored. 'When she offered it to me for sale, I did not trouble myself with the petty details.'

'Careless of you, Horm. If you'd paid attention to details you might have the pendant.'

'I might. But I was not to know that Glixius Dragon Killer would become involved. I watched that rather ridiculous melee at the warehouse. The pendant was taken swiftly from the scene by a man I didn't recognise. I traced him by sorcery and would have intercepted him last night had Glixius not interfered. By the time I had driven off Glixius, the pendant was again gone.'

'So you expect me to find it for you?'

'Why not? I will pay you a good deal more than Lisutaris, Mistress of the Sky.' Horm sneers as he pronounces her name. 'I laughed when she was elected as Head of the Sorcerers Guild. I understand you had a hand in it. I misjudged you when we first met. You are a man of considerable competence, Thraxas.'

I can't explain it, but there's something persuasive about Horm's deathly compliments. I have to throw him out before he starts winning me over.

'Perhaps,' continues Horm, 'you could bring me the pendant? I'd pay you very well. Though your own city seems to place no value on your talents, my kingdom could offer you a very comfortable home...'

I wonder what that would be like. Thraxas, Chief Investigator of the Wastelands. It doesn't sound too bad.

'Though many of my subjects are regrettably primitive, I have a splendid palace in the mountains. Quite unassailable, and considerably better appointed than this—' He struggles to find the right word. '—this place you call home.'

I look round at my office. It's very unpleasant. No place for a man to live really.

'Is it not true that the upper classes in Turai have conspired to crush you, Thraxas? Frustrated you at every turn, used their malign influence to keep you down, when in reality a man of your talents should be in a position of authority high above those fools?'

'It's true.'

'Not content with that, they're now assaulting the very core of your being with this outrageous accusation of cowardice. Over the years you've served this city better than any man, but will your leaders now come to your aid?'

'They won't.'

There's a lot of sense in what Horm says, I slam my fist angrily on the table, raising dust. 'The Turanian aristocracy are a foul, perfidious bunch of cowards who've been conniving at my downfall from the moment I was born. Well, I've had enough!'

The inner door opens and Makri walks in. At the sight of Horm the Dead, she halts and takes out the knife she keeps concealed in her boot.

'No need to arm yourself, Makri,' I say. 'Horm has come to offer me a job.'

'What?'

'He's on our side. We must help him find the pendant.'

'Are you crazy? Last time we met this guy he tried to kill us.'

'A misunderstanding. Our King is our real enemy.'

Makri puts the knife back in her boot, marches straight up to me and slaps me in the face. 'Slap' doesn't do the blow justice. It's the sort of open-handed strike she used in the arena to knock the head off a troll. So fierce and unexpected is the assault that even with my considerable bulk I sag to my knees, my ears ringing and my head full of shooting stars. I look up, surprised, just in time to see Makri land another mighty blow on the other side of my face, leaving me sore, confused and generally dissatisfied with events.

'Thraxas!' yells Makri, and starts shaking me. 'Don't you recognise a persuasion spell when you encounter it? You're meant to know about sorcery, for God's sake. Stop making up to this half-Orc madman and get back to being your usual oafish self.'

Faced with Makri's fury, my head starts to clear. I realise that Horm was indeed using a spell of persuasion on me, one powerful enough to seep past my protection charm. It's unbelievably stupid of me not to have noticed. I haul myself to my feet.

'Don't worry, I'm fine. A lesser man may have succumbed.'

I turn to Horm and order him out of my office. Horm is no longer paying any attention to me. Rather, he's transfixed by Makri. So transfixed that he rises from his chair, treads softly across the room then kisses her hand, something you don't often see in Twelve Seas.

'You are magnificent,' he says, and stares at her.

'Don't try your persuasion spell on me,' retorts Makri.

'I never imagined to meet such a woman in the west.'

Makri abruptly strikes Horm in the face. So fast is her movement that Horm is lying in a heap on the floor before he knows what's happening. I look down at him. I wish I'd done that.

Chapter Thirteen

Now I have a really powerful sorcerer lying dazed on the floor of the office. In a few seconds he'll wake up and start destroying everything in sight.

'We have to kill him. We need a powerful weapon. Where's your axe?'

'I didn't bring it,' says Makri.

'Why not?'

'What do you mean, why not? You're always complaining about me bringing my axe places.'

'That's only when you bring it at inappropriate times. Right now we need it.'

Makri is not satisfied with this. 'That's what you say now. But next time I walk in here with my axe I guarantee you'll start complaining again. You can't just pick and choose when a woman carries an axe, Thraxas. Either she does or she doesn't.'

Horm the Dead rises to his feet. 'Please stop this argument,' he says. 'It's making my head ache.'

I point my sword at him. Makri raises her knife. Horm motions with his hand and the room cools slightly as a spell takes effect.

'Very careless of me to neglect my personal protection spell,' he says, almost apologetically. 'But I was not expecting to meet such a fierce warrior in this tavern. You really are magnificent.'

'Stop saying that,' says Makri, and shifts uncomfortably under his gaze. Makri is clad in her chainmail bikini, one of the smallest garments ever seen in the civilised world. It seems to be having an effect on Horm.

'And stop staring,' says Makri.

'Forgive me.'

Horm regards her for a few moments more. As a skilled practitioner of sorcery, he can learn much from the study of a person's aura. 'Orc, Elf and Human? A very rare mixture indeed. Impossible, according to most authorities. It accounts, I suppose, for your unusual rapidity of action. Though not necessarily your beauty. How can it be I have never heard of you before?'

'We did meet,' answers Makri. 'In the fairy glade. You were on a dragon and I killed the commander of your troops. I'd have killed you too but you flew away.'

'That was you? In the heat of battle, I'm afraid I failed to register you properly. I believed you to be one of the magical characters who inhabit the glade.' He bows formally. 'Allow me to introduce myself. I am Horm, Lord of the Kingdom of Yal. And you are - ?'

'Makri.'

Horm raises his eyebrows. 'Makri? The champion gladiator?'

'Yes.'

Horm laughs, quite heartily by his standards. 'But this is splendid. The tale of the carnage you wreaked when you escaped the slave pits is known all over the East. You killed an Orc Lord and his entire entourage in a savage fury that has become legendary. Only last month I heard a minstrel sing of it. And of course your exploits in the arena were already legendary. I am honoured to meet you.'

Makri looks confused. Horm himself looks puzzled.

'How can it be that such a woman as yourself is reduced to working in a tavern?'

Not having a good answer to hand Makri remains silent, regarding Horm with suspicion, wondering if he's trying to baffle her with a persuasion spell. As far as I can tell Horm is no longer using magic and has switched to standard flattery, something at which he seems quite proficient.

'A strange city indeed,' continues Horm. 'That makes the greatest swordsman it has ever seen work in a tavern.'

'It's my choice.'

'Come with me to my kingdom. I'll make you a general.'

Makri shakes her head.

'Captain of my armies.'

I'd better interrupt before he offers to make her Queen. 'We're not helping you find the pendant, Horm. You'd best be on your way. Sarin the Merciless is probably missing you.'

'Sarin. Another interesting woman. Were I in the mood for bragging I could tell you much of value that she has brought to me from Turai and other cities, all unsuspected by your authorities. However I am not in the mood for bragging. I am in the mood for finding the pendant which Lisutaris, Mistress of the Sky–'

He breaks off.

'Not that she deserves such a title. Bringing down a few dragons does not give her control of the sky. Personally I count myself as far more powerful in aerial magic.'

Sorcerers are always jealous of each other. I once heard Harmon Half Elf going on at length about the injustice of Tirini Snake Smiter claiming such a title when she'd never smited a snake in her life, or at the most one snake, and only a small, harmless specimen at that. But Tirini is very beautiful and she'd just rejected Harmon's advances, so that probably accounts for it.

'I have a low opinion of Lisutaris,' continues Horm. 'Her dependence on thazis sickens me. A very poor drug for a sorcerer.'

Horm the Dead presumably regards dwa as an acceptable drug for a sorcerer. He wouldn't be the only one.

'Lisutaris was smart enough to negate your eight-mile terror spell,' I tell him.

'Sheer good fortune on her part, I'm sure. The woman has no talents. No doubt her masked ball will be a dreary affair.'

'Fortunately she hasn't invited you.'

'True,' admits Horm. 'She has neglected to send me an invitation. But as I'm already in Turai, and so adept at disguises, I am intending to attend the function. In the Wastelands, one rarely finds the opportunity to dance. I regret that you, Thraxas, are not among those deemed worthy to attend.'

I don't catch any flicker of emotion on Makri's face but Horm does. 'You are going, Makri? Excellent. Perhaps we may converse more regarding my offer of employment.'

He turns to me. 'I see you have nothing to tell me regarding the pendant, so I will now depart. I had intended to kill you, because I've always resented the role you played in the failure of my spell to destroy this city. I worked long and hard on that incantation. I've now changed my mind. I do not wish to upset your companion Makri, who I judge to be the finest flower in all of Turai.' He studies her for a while more. 'Your hair. So extremely luxurious yet not sorcerously enhanced. I have never seen its like. Who, may I ask, were your parents?'

Makri's face sets into an expression of malign hostility and she raises her knife a fraction.

'Forgive me,' says Horm. 'I did not mean to intrude. Thraxas, we shall no doubt meet again. Till then, farewell.'

Horm steps lightly towards the outside door, but he hasn't finished yet. He pauses and turns his head, causing his long dark hair to sway quite dramatically. He may have worked on the effect.

'Your trouble at the College. Have you looked into the role of Barius?'

'Professor Toarius's son? What about him?'

'A dwa addict. So I understand from my business contacts.'

Horm makes a formal bow, then slips quietly out of the door.

'That was unexpected,' says Makri.

'It was. At least he didn't destroy my room this time.'

'Shouldn't we follow him?' asks Makri, eager for action.

'I can't believe he's going to Lisutaris's ball. Everyone is going except me.'

'Stop complaining about the ball, Thraxas.'

I hunt around for a beer. 'It's annoying. Horm's going. Cicerius is going. You're going.' I stare at Makri balefully. 'I mean, what did you really do for Lisutaris? All right, you were her bodyguard, but who did all the work? Me. She would never have been elected Head of the Sorcerers Guild without me.'

I take a heavy slug of beer. Makri is regarding me with a curious expression.

'Thraxas. Every time I think I've discovered the true shallowness of your character, you manage to surprise me with some further outrageous lack of depth. Have you forgotten what's going on around you? Lisutaris is missing an important pendant and most of the bad guys in the world are after it at this moment, including several powerful sorcerers and a killer who once put a crossbow bolt through my chest. Not only is this bad for Turai, it's also bad for your client, because Kalius will be down on her like a bad spell when he gets proof of the loss. Apart from that, I've been expelled from college and you've promised to put that right, and apart from that, you've been accused of cowardice at a battle that took place seventeen years ago and are no longer allowed to investigate pending a Senate inquiry. Also, it's raining frogs.'

'I am aware of these matters.'

'Then stop whining about Lisutaris's masked ball like a spoiled young princess and do some investigating.'

I sit down at my desk and drag a new bottle of beer from the drawer. 'I thought I'd just drink beer instead. You investigate. *Finest flower in Turai* indeed. After you've investigated you can go and be Captain of Horm's armies. Have a good time.'

'It couldn't be worse than listening to you.'

'Maybe not. But if he tries to make you his bride, watch out. You might have to be dead first.'

'What do you mean?' says Makri, curiously.

'Horm the Dead is rumoured to actually have been dead. Died by his own hand then returned from the grave in some evil ritual known only to himself.'

'Why would anyone do that?' wonders Makri.

'Presumably the death-ritual gave him unearthly powers. I don't know if it's really true. He might just be pretending to have been dead to impress people.'

'He does look very pale,' says Makri.

'Not too pale to clutter up my office and go around kissing people's hands.'

'Thraxas, that barely makes sense.'

'Not too pale to go to Lisutaris's ball and spend the night dancing with a bunch of senators who've never done an honest day's work in their lives.'

Makri wonders out loud at my intransigence and stupidity. I continue to drink beer. After a while she departs. It's hot as Orcish hell in here. I detest this city and everyone in it. It's intensely annoying the way everyone is always playing up to Makri. The finest flower in Turai! It's ridiculous. An Orcish savage in a ludicrous chainmail bikini more like. Unable to find any more beer in my desk, I go through to my only other room and hunt under the bed for my emergency supply.

Chapter Fourteen

The city is full of mythical creatures and dead Humans. Reports from all sides indicate an inexplicable outbreak of unicorns, centaurs, naiads, dryads and mermaids. No harm is caused by these creatures - they tend to vanish when pursued - but it makes the population edgy. The fear of Orcish invasion is never far below the conscious thoughts of the citizenry, and anything strange or unexplained tends to be regarded as an evil portent.

I've been chasing round the city looking for a powerful sorcerous item. Strange sorcerous events are now happening. It doesn't take a genius to think they might be connected, but if they are, no one knows why, not even Lisutaris. Furthermore, there seem to be too many of these occurrences for them all to be linked to one missing green jewel, even if the green jewel could produce these events, which it can't. As for the dead Humans, it's another epidemic. Everywhere the authorities look, they find more corpses. Some with wounds, some just dead for no apparent reason. Again, it's hard to link this exactly to the missing pendant. At the same time as three market workers are found dead in the centre of town, four aqueduct maintenance men are found slaughtered in Pashish. Lisutaris's pendant can't be causing it all, and in a city where death is a common occurrence, it's impossible to work out which of the fatalities might be linked to the jewel.

After waking with a headache, and visiting the public baths to cleanse myself of the accumulated filth of several days' activity in hot weather, I go to see Cicerius at the Abode of Justice. He's already aware of the charge which has been laid against me.

'I don't sympathise in the slightest,' he says.

'Thanks for your support.'

'You were clearly warned that trouble would arise from your use of the Tribunate powers.'

'But I did it anyway. And now I'm in trouble.'

'You are, though personally I don't believe the charge of throwing away your shield and fleeing the battlefield,' says Cicerius. 'I studied your record quite carefully before I first hired you. You were an insubordinate soldier but your valour was never questioned. But I cannot have the charge dropped. The matter must go before a Senate committee, and until then your Tribune's powers are revoked, as is your investigating licence.'

'Can't you use your influence? My accuser is Vadinex and he works for Praetor Capatius.'

Cicerius knows Capatius very well. Not only is the Praetor the richest man in the city, he's a senior member of the Traditionals, Cicerius's party.

'Last year I got in Capatius's way and now he's getting his revenge. Can't you get him off my back?'

The Deputy Consul is unenthusiastic, though he knows I'm speaking the truth when I claim he owes me a favour.

'Were you with Vadinex at the Battle of Sanasa?'

'We were in the same regiment. I don't remember ever being close to him on the battlefield. But I was with plenty of other men who are still alive today who'll testify on my behalf.'

'So you hope, Thraxas. My experience as a lawyer has taught me that men's memories can be strangely affected by the passage of seventeen years. They can be affected a good deal more by bribery. A charge of this sort, brought after so many years, will not be easy to defend in court if your opponents have planned it well.'

Cicerius muses for a while. 'I really doubt that Capatius is behind this charge.'

'He has to be. Vadinex is his man.'

'Even so, I doubt it. It's true you inconvenienced Praetor Capatius last year, but the inconvenience was minor by his standards. A mere blip in his considerable income. I have seen the Praetor many times since then and he's never given me the impression he holds any strong grudge against you. I am aware you don't trust him, but I believe him to be far more honest than you give him credit for. Like many rich men, he has suffered at the hands of the Populares, who are always keen to accuse any worthy supporter of the King of corruption. Capatius himself fought bravely in the war, with a cohort he equipped at his own expense. In my experience, it's rare for a man who fought in that campaign to raise a false charge against another who also fought. It would go against his sense of military honour.'

I'm not convinced. Capatius is obscenely wealthy. I can't believe anyone could get to be so rich and still have a sense of honour.

'You offended many people when you prevented a full investigation of Lisutaris's actions at the warehouse,' points out the Deputy Consul. 'More likely one of them would want to see you punished. The head of Palace Security has long disliked you.'

'Yes, it's possible it's Rittius. But my instinct tells me that Capatius put Vadinex up to it. So I appeal to you to make efforts on my behalf. Because, Deputy Consul, if I'm dragged before a Senate committee on a charge of cowardice, I'll be obliged to kill my accuser and flee the city.'

Cicerius looks shocked. 'You will obey the law of Turai,' he informs me sternly.

'Absolutely.'

'Would you care to tell me the precise nature of the difficulties that Lisutaris finds herself in?'

'A minor matter of a missing diary.' I intimate that I'm unable to say more due to investigator-client privilege.

'You have no such privileges. Your licence has been suspended.'

'Then I've suffered a sudden loss of memory.'

'Yesterday a unicorn wandered through the Senate while I was speaking,' says Cicerius.

'That must have livened things up.'

'My speech did not need to be livened up. Do you have any idea why these creatures should suddenly be infesting the city?'

'None at all.'

'Nothing to do with Lisutaris?'

'Not as far as I know.'

Cicerius dismisses me. I'm fairly satisfied with the meeting. He might help. I've ascended the social ladder a fraction in the last year. Not too long ago I'd never have been granted permission to see the Deputy Consul, never mind ask him for a favour. Halfway between Cicerius's office and the outskirts of Thamlin, I encounter a figure walking briskly up the road in a cloak and hood which partially hides her features.

'Makri?'

Makri pulls back her hood a little. 'I'm in disguise.'

'I can see that. Why?'

'I'm going to kill Vadinex.'

'What? Why?'

Makri shrugs. 'I thought I'd help you.'

'How are you going to find him?'

'Call in at Praetor Capatius's mansion and find out from someone there where he was likely to be.'

'And then go and kill him?'

'That's right. If he was dead, there wouldn't be a charge against you, would there?'

I'm touched by Makri's concern. 'It's not a bad plan. But I've just asked the Deputy Consul to intervene on my behalf and I don't want to offend him by killing Vadinex before it's absolutely necessary.'

Makri shrugs. She hasn't asked me a single question about the Battle of Sanasa because, I know, she does not regard it as possible that I fled the field. I remember I'm friends with Makri and feel bad about giving her a hard time.

'I'm about to hunt through some taverns in Kushni for Barius, Professor Toarius's son. If we apply some pressure we might get to the bottom of this theft at the college.'

Makri wants to come along, so we set off towards the centre of the city. 'Was it a bad disguise?' she asks.

'Not too bad. But I recognised your walk.'

'I thought if I killed Vadinex it would be better if people didn't know it was me that did it. You know, with us living in the same tavern. It might have cast suspicion on you.'

'I appreciate you making the effort. I'm sorry I moaned at you.'

'It was more than moaning. It was vilification and character assassination.'

'Surely not?'

'You called me a vile Orcish wench.'

'Then I apologise for any offence. As always, I meant it in a positive sense.'

The heat is stifling. Makri removes her cloak as we walk through the dusty streets. 'I did mess things up with Tanrose. When I suggested she take some time to think about her feelings, I wasn't expecting her to leave the tavern.'

'It's not really your fault, Makri. The problem is with Gurd. He's been a bachelor so long, he's scared to acknowledge any sort of affection for her. That's why he criticised her bookkeeping.'

'To disguise his affection?'

'Yes.'

Makri nods. 'I've encountered this sort of thing in the plays of the Elvish bard Las-ar-Heth. The great Elvish lord Avenath-ir-Yill once made his queen cry by accusing her of infidelity, but really he was just upset because she no longer played the harp to him at bedtime. The reason for this was her hands were sore from plaiting a unicorn's mane, which she had to do to keep her son alive, but of course she couldn't explain this to her husband without letting him know about the curse which hung over her family.'

My head is starting to spin. 'This is similar to Gurd and Tanrose?'

'Very. A frank exchange of views would have resolved the problem, but they both had secrets they didn't want to reveal. Eventually, of course, it led to the great schism between the tribes of Yill and Evena, which is not fully resolved even now.'

'You read all this in a play?'

Makri nods. She is apparently a great enthusiast for the plays of the Elvish bard Las-ar-Heth.

'Quite an unconventional rhyme scheme, and rather archaic in tone, but very stirring.'

'I'll read some at the first opportunity,' I say, which makes Makri laugh, which she doesn't do that often.

'Is that a mermaid in that fountain?'

We stare across the road at the large fountain. Sitting at the feet of the statue of St. Quatinius there is indeed a mermaid. Children laugh and point. The mermaid smiles seductively, then fades away.

'Turai is becoming a very interesting place. Are we all going mad?'

'I don't know. At least it's only friendly creatures who've been appearing. It's not going to be much fun if dragons start roaming the streets.'

'I liked the frogs,' says Makri.

By this time we're passing through the royal market, just north of Kushni, one of Turai's main concentrations of goods for sale. The shops here sell clothes, jewellery, wine, weapons, expensive items mainly. The market stalls sell food but are very different from the cheap markets of Twelve Seas. Here the servants of the rich come to order household provisions from traders whose stalls are full of the highest-quality fare, often imported from the nations to the west, or even the Elvish Isles.

Makri stares through the window of a jeweller's shop.

'Who earns enough to buy these things?' she wonders out loud.

A young woman emerges from the shop, followed by two servants. When she sees Makri she gives her the slightest of nods before passing by. I ask Makri who the young woman was.

'Avenaris. Lisutaris's secretary.'

I'm already in pursuit. I've been forbidden to question this young woman. Always makes an investigator suspicious. I cut her off with my bulk. She regards me rather nervously. I introduce myself.

'I was wondering if you could help me with a few questions.'

'Lisutaris wouldn't want me to talk about her business with anyone,' says Avenaris. 'Even an investigator she hired. Excuse me.'

She tries to walk past. I get in the way. She's looking very, very nervous. More nervous than she should be. I'm not that frightening, not in daylight anyway. Not frightening enough to make a person develop a facial tic within seconds of meeting me, yet Avenaris's eyelid is starting to tremble violently.

'Maybe you could just tell me a little about what happened that day at the stadium–'

'What is going on here?'

It's Lisutaris, Mistress of the Sky.

'Did I not specifically tell you to leave my secretary alone?'

'He stood in my way,' says Avenaris, making it sound like a major crime. She's now close to tears.

'I'm sorry,' says Lisutaris, attempting to pacify her. 'He had no business bothering you. Go home now, I'll make sure he doesn't trouble you again.'

Avenaris walks off swiftly, still attended by the servants. The Sorceress regards me with fury. 'How dare you harass my staff!'

'Save the lecture, Lisutaris. What's the matter with her? I asked her a polite question and she practically broke down in tears.'

'She is a young woman of nervous disposition. Far too delicate to be confronted by the likes of you. I must insist–'

'You should've let me talk to her. I get the strong impression she knows something.'

'Must I remind you that Avenaris is my niece? I didn't hire you to harass my family. For the last time, stay away from my secretary.'

Lisutaris looks genuinely threatening. I drop the subject, for now anyway. I'll pursue it later, no matter what Lisutaris says.

'Encountered any unicorns?' I ask.

'No. But there were two mermaids in my fish ponds, albeit briefly. I'm baffled. They're obviously sorcerous apparitions but I can't trace their source.'

'Did you get my message about Horm the Dead?'

Lisutaris nods, and frowns. 'Horm the Dead is a very dangerous individual. Consul Kalius should be informed that he's in the city.'

'And has he been?'

'No,' admits Lisutaris. 'I'm still trying to keep things quiet.'

In the past few days Lisutaris has been subjected to much questioning from fellow sorcerers and government officials. So far it has remained informal. 'Deputy Consul Cicerius visited to ask me about some aqueduct renovations. I wasn't aware that he valued my opinion on the city's water supply. Harmon Half Elf happened to find himself in the vicinity and dropped in to share an amusing story about some Elvish sorcerers.'

Given Lisutaris's status, it's difficult for anyone to come right out and demand to know what's going on, though it's obvious that something is. However, having moved heaven, earth and the three moons to get her elected as Head of the Sorcerers Guild, no one in Turai wants her to be plunged into disgrace only a few months later. Turai would be severely damaged in the eyes of all nations.

'They're hovering round the subject. I've been keeping quiet like you suggested, but I can't hold out for ever. Tilupasis was sniffing round for information and you know what a cunning operator she is. I was reduced to telling her that I really had to ask her to leave because I needed privacy to smoke my thazis pipe, so there goes my reputation among Turai's aristocratic matrons. Now it'll be all over Thamlin that Lisutaris can't grant you more than a half-hour audience before she has to smoke thazis.'

'Didn't everyone know that already?' asks Makri, who has not yet learned how to be tactful.

'I am not completely reliant on thazis,' says Lisutaris, coldly.

'Oh,' says Makri. 'Sorry. I thought you were. I remember when you collapsed at the Sorcerers Assemblage and you were gasping about how you needed thazis, so I just naturally assumed–'

'Could we discuss this another time?' says Lisutaris, shooting her an angry glance. She turns the angry glance in my direction. 'Not that I had much reputation left after word got around that I'd hired you to buy back my diary, which I was desperate to retrieve due to its being full of intimate love poems. Guessing the identity of my secret lover is now a popular game at dinner parties.'

'I'm shocked, Lisutaris. When I told Kalius about your diary, I thought he'd keep it a secret.'

'Who is it?' asks Makri.

'Who is who?'

'The person you're in love with?'

'I'm not in love with anyone. Thraxas made it up.'

Makri looks puzzled. 'Why?'

'I needed a cover story. It was all I could think of.'

Makri is of the opinion that I could have done better. 'After all, people say you're one of the finest liars in the city.'

Lisutaris is certain the Consul is going to ask to see the pendant when he comes to the ball. 'Kalius might not be sharp as an Elf's ear, but even he must know by now I've lost the pendant. Damn it, I wish I hadn't chosen this moment to hold a social function.'

'Talking of your social function,' I say, 'Horm the Dead mentioned that he might be paying a visit.'

'Really?'

'Yes. And Horm is a very dangerous individual. I think it would be wise for you to have some extra personal protection at the ball.'

'You may be right,' says Lisutaris.

I wait for my invitation. Lisutaris turns to Makri.

'Would you mind being my bodyguard again?'

'I'd be delighted,' answers Makri.

I stare morosely at the jeweller's window. Lisutaris is a disgrace to the city. Her abuse of thazis is a scandal. She deserves to be exiled.

'What do you suggest we do now, investigator?'

'I've no idea.' I've started to believe that there is no point investigating. Either someone is deliberately leading us on and mocking us at every turn, or the situation has become so chaotic there's prospect of repairing it. Either way, I'm beaten.

'If no one has any plans for saving the city, how about going to see Barius?' suggests Makri.

'Who is Barius?' asks Lisutaris.

'Professor Toarius's son. I think he might be able to shed some light on Makri's expulsion.'

Lisutaris offers to take us there in her carriage, which is waiting nearby. She doesn't feel like going home, fearing that she'll once more be confronted by an inquisitive sorcerer or curious government official.

'Six more deaths in the city today,' I say. 'Brings the total to twenty-seven, near as I can count. For that many unexplained deaths the Abode of Justice will call in a sorcerer. Old Hasius the Brilliant will learn every detail of the affair.'

'Not for a long time,' says Lisutaris. 'The moons are way out of conjunction.'

For a sorcerer to look back in time, it's necessary for the three moons to be in a particular alignment. According to Lisutaris, we're in the middle of one of the longest blank periods of the decade. I'd have known that if I wasn't so hopeless at sorcery.

'It'll be months before sorcerers can look back in time. If that wasn't the case I'd have been looking back myself.'

The carriage takes us towards Kushni. The driver shouts at some revellers who are blocking the street. They look like they might be inclined to argue, but when they recognise Lisutaris's rainbow livery on the side of the carriage, they hastily move, not wishing to be blasted by a spell.

'Do you think we should revise our bet?' asks Makri. 'We bet on thirty-five deaths. But it's twenty-seven already, and going up.'

Lisutaris manages a grim laugh. 'True. And if the Consul freezes my assets before bringing me to trial, I may be in need of money to pay for a lawyer. What's the cut-off point for this wager?'

Makri looks uncomfortable. 'When the case comes to an end...'

'And when would that be?'

'When Thraxas solves it. Or gets killed. Or you get arrested.'

Lisutaris is shocked. 'The Turanian masses are gambling on me being arrested?'

'Only tangentially,' says Makri.

'Have they no respect for the Head of the Sorcerers Guild?'

'Don't complain,' I say. 'It's not as bad as betting on me dying.'

'I think Lisutaris dying also brings the betting to an end,' says Makri, helpfully. 'But no one is really expecting that to happen. Apart from Parax the shoemaker; I think he wagered a little on Lisutaris's death. And maybe one or two others. But not many. It's definitely not as popular an option as Thraxas handing in his toga. Do you have any thazis?'

We smoke Lisutaris's thazis sticks as we make our way through the busy streets. Even in the tense situation I appreciate the high quality of her narcotic.

'Grown in your own gardens?'

'Yes. Or rather, in the glasshouse I built last year.'

'A house made of glass?'

'A special construction,' explains the sorcerer. 'For protecting plants from the elements and maximising the sunlight that feeds them. They were developed in Simnia. I believe mine is the first in Turai.'

I've never heard of such a thing, and once more marvel at Lisutaris's dedication to her favourite substance. Thazis is imported into Turai from the southeast, where it's extensively cultivated. Though I've known people to produce their own plants, I don't think anyone else in the city is capable of growing it in volume. A *glasshouse*. I would hardly have believed it possible. It must have been extremely expensive.

'Fabulously expensive,' agrees Lisutaris. 'But with the amount of bad weather we have in Turai, nothing else would do.'

Lisutaris turns sharply to Makri. 'Why have people bet on me dying? Is there some inside information?'

Makri doesn't think so, but Lisutaris is troubled. Maybe it's the thazis. Overuse can lead to feelings of paranoia. I ask Makri casually if many people are betting money on me dying.

'Lots of people. It's a strong favourite. The moment the Brotherhood got involved, money started pouring in.'

'I'm damned if I'm going to die just to win money for a lot of degenerates in the Avenging Axe. The Brotherhood won't get me. I thought this betting was just on the body count?'

Makri shrugs. 'It sort of grew. Moxalan was getting so many enquiries he had to take on an assistant and widen his range.'

The carriage pulls up and we climb out into the dusty street. Lisutaris is clad in her rainbow cloak. Perhaps fatalistic by now, she makes no attempt to disguise herself as we stride into the Rampant Unicorn, a tavern on the outskirts of Kushni. It's yet another appalling den of iniquity. At the sight of the Head of the Sorcerers Guild striding through the doors, the place goes quiet. Several customers, presuming that Lisutaris must be here on official business, scurry for cover as the Mistress of the Sky heads towards the bar.

'I am looking for a young man by the name of Barius,' she says.

'He's upstairs,' blurts the barman, quaking as he imagines the effect a spell from a disgruntled sorcerer might have on him.

'This way,' says Lisutaris, leading myself and Makri up the stairs. She's looking pleased with herself. 'I've never investigated anything before. It does not seem to be overly difficult.'

I stifle a sarcastic response, and follow Lisutaris to one of four doors that lead off the upstairs corridor. Lisutaris tries the first door. Finding it locked, she mutters a minor word of power and it springs open. Inside the private room we find a stout man in a toga in the embrace of a woman who's young enough to be his granddaughter, but probably isn't a relation.

'I beg your pardon, Senator Alesius,' says Lisutaris grandly, and leads us back into the corridor.

'That's spoiled his afternoon's entertainment,' I say. 'The thing about investigating, you don't just barge through the first door you come to.'

'How did you expect me to choose?'

'Experience and intuition,' I explain. 'You develop it after a few years in the business.'

'Very well,' says Lisutaris, motioning to the three remaining doors. 'Which do you recommend?'

I select the door on the left. Lisutaris again mutters a word of power and it springs open. Inside we find a well-dressed middle-aged woman with plenty of jewels and a younger man, naked, who looks like he might be a professional athlete, both of them very busy with a pipe full of dwa.

'I beg your pardon, Marwini,' says Lisutaris, and withdraws from the room, quite elegantly. Makri and I stumble out after her, rather embarrassed at the whole thing.

'Who was that?'

'Praetor Capatius's wife,' says Lisutaris. 'Really, I had no idea. One understood that they were a contented couple. Only last week she informed me over a glass of wine that she'd never felt happier with her husband.'

'Probably because he's coming home less.'

'Is this sort of behaviour standard all over Kushni?'

'Fairly standard,' I reply. 'Though they might have to find a new place to misbehave if you keep using spells to open doors.'

'I want to pick the next room,' says Makri.

Inside the next room we find Barius. He's lying semiconscious on a couch. The room stinks of dwa. From the overpowering aroma and general squalidness of the situation, I'd say he'd been lying here for a few days.

'I picked the right room,' says Makri, happily.

'You only had two doors to choose from.'

'That's not the point. You were wrong and I was right.'

'It's completely the point. The odds were entirely different.'

'Do you two never stop bickering?' says Lisutaris. 'Here is your suspect. What do you do now?'

'Wake him up, if that's possible.'

There's a pitcher of stale water beside the couch. I take a lesada leaf from the small bag on my belt and try getting Barius to swallow it. It's a difficult process and I'm careful in case Barius chooses this moment to vomit. Finally I succeed in making him swallow the leaf.

'Now we wait. Lisutaris, please lock the door again.'

Elvish lesada leaves are extremely efficient in cleansing the system of any noxious substances. They're hard to get hold of in the Human lands. Normally I'd be reluctant to waste one on a dwa addict who's only going to fill himself full of dwa again at the first opportunity, but I don't have time to wait for Barius to come round naturally. A few minutes after he's swallowed the leaf, the colour is returning to his skin and his pupils are reverting to their normal size. He coughs, and struggles to rise. I give him more water.

'Who are you?'

'Thraxas. Investigator.'

'Investigator...from Ve...Vee...' he gasps.

'No. Not the Venarius Agency. I'm independent. I can help you.'

'What do you want?'

'I want to ask you a few questions.'

Possibly the lesada leaf has done its job too well. Barius has regained some youthful vigour and defiance.

'Go to hell,' he says, and struggles to rise from the couch. I place my arm on his shoulder and hold him down. Makri is by my side. I can sense her impatience. If Barius has any information that can help to clear her name, she's not going to let him leave the room without imparting it. I ask him if he knew about the theft of the money at the Guild College. He gives an impression of a young man too confused by dwa addiction to know much about anything. I'm about to make some threats about telling his father just what he gets up to in his spare time, when Makri's patience snaps.

Makri has two swords with her, one Elvish and gleaming, and one Orcish and dark. She brought the Orcish blade from the gladiator pits and received the Elvish sword as a gift from the Elves on Avula. Both fine weapons, as fine as any held by anyone in Turai. She draws both of her swords. The light from the torch on the wall reflects brightly off the Elvish blade, but the grim Orcish sword seems to absorb light. It's a vile weapon, and caused offence to the Elves when Makri took it to their islands. She deftly positions the black Orcish sword under Barius's chin.

'Tell us about the money or I'll kill you right now,' she says.

Barius realises she's serious. He looks at me fearfully, waiting for me to protect him. I look up at the ceiling. Makri pushes her sword forward. A spot of blood appears on Barius's throat. Barius cringes backwards, then tries to shrug as if unconcerned.

'So I took five gurans from a locker. Who cares?'

'I do, you cusux,' says Makri, raising her sword. 'For the price of some dwa, you'd ruin my life?'

I raise my hand to block Makri's arm. 'It's okay, we've got what we came for. We can go.'

'Have you got what you came for?' enquires Lisutaris. 'Will such a confession under duress stand up in court?'

'There isn't going to be a court case. Professor Toarius is going to quietly reinstate Makri when I tell him that his son stole the money for dwa and I have witnesses to that effect. The Professor is keen to protect the family name, which is no doubt why he was so quick to pin the rap on Makri in the first place.'

Barius is shaking. I place my arm round him and lower him back on to the couch. He can sleep it off. Then he should go home, but I doubt he will. It's not my problem. I'm concerned to learn that the Venarius Investigation Agency has already got to him. I still don't know who hired them.

Outside the Rampant Unicorn, Lisutaris shudders, rather delicately. 'What an awful place. I am astonished that Marwini should choose to have an assignation in such a location. Who on earth was that naked young man?'

'One of the King's athletes, I think. On his way up in the world. Or down, maybe, if Praetor Capatius catches him.'

'It's all rather embarrassing,' says Lisutaris. 'Marwini is one of my guests at the ball tomorrow. As is Senator Alesius. I'm not so surprised to find him here, of course. His behaviour is well known in certain circles.'

'Will my name be cleared before my examination?' asks Makri.

'I'll see Toarius tomorrow. It'll be fine.'

'When is this examination?' asks Lisutaris.

'The day after tomorrow.'

'So soon? Will you still be able to attend my ball as my bodyguard?'

'Of course. I've already completed my studies. Did I tell you I have to stand up and speak to the whole class? It's really stressful.'

Makri is still complaining as we climb into Lisutaris's carriage. One problem solved, more or less. Now we only have the matter of an important pendant to find, followed by Thraxas being hauled before a Senate committee on an allegation of cowardice. Somehow I can't concentrate. It's just so annoying the way Lisutaris, so-called Mistress of the Sky, flatly refuses to invite me to her masked ball. I suppose it's only to be expected. The upper classes of Turai are notorious for their degeneracy and ingratitude. Adultery. Dwa. Corruption. All manner of sordid behaviour. An honest working man like myself is far better off not associating with them.

Chapter Fifteen

At the Avenging Axe there's a summons waiting, ordering me to report to the Consul, and another message, from Harmon Half Elf, requesting a meeting. I throw both messages in the bin and head downstairs for a beer. There I find Dandelion behind the bar being irritating, Gurd still looking as miserable as a Niojan whore, no food on offer, and a great cluster of dock workers all keen to know if there have been any more deaths recently. The front door opens. A government official in a toga walks in, swiftly followed by another official in a toga, and they each beat a path towards me, bearing scrolls. The togas are hitting the Avenging Axe thick and fast these days. It's a while since I've worn one. I used to when I worked at the Palace, for official duties. They're expensive garments. Quite awkward to wear, but it lets everyone know you're not the sort of person who wastes his time doing manual labour.

'Rittius, head of Palace Security, commands that you visit him immediately,' says the first official.

'The senate licensing committee, finding you in violation of an order prohibiting you from investigating, requires you to attend a–'

'I'll be right there,' I say, finishing my beer in one swift gulp. 'I just have to change my boots.'

I only have one pair of boots. They're not to know that. Once in my office I head straight for the external door and down the outside stairs, pausing only to mutter the minor incantation I use for a locking spell. The two rival vendors have now come to blows. I use my body weight to send them flying in opposite directions then start walking, heading for anywhere that's free of summonses, enquiries and other oppressive instruments of state.

The situation is now disastrous. I've abandoned all hope of successfully bringing matters to a conclusion. Lisutaris is going to be unmasked at her own masked ball, revealed to the world as an intoxicated incompetent who's lost the pendant, thereby endangering Turai. This will swiftly be followed by a general round-up of all guilty parties, which will certainly include me. I'm going to be charged with failing to report a crime, obstructing the authorities, lying to the Consul, going against the wishes of the Senate and God knows what else. Even the claim of investigator-client confidentiality - dubious at best in matters of national security - won't do me any good, because I've been stripped of my licence and can no longer claim to be an investigator in the legal sense of the word. My most likely destination is a prison galley.

I strain to think of some way out. A golden tree erupts from the road in front of me and stands there looking pretty. This is now becoming seriously disconcerting. There's a time and a place for sorcery and it's not in the middle of Quintessence Street while I'm trying to concentrate. Attractive as the tree is, no one is pleased to see it. Onlookers mutter alarming comments about portents for the destruction of the city, and the more nervous among them start wailing and kneeling down to pray.

I have some experience of this sort of thing. In the magic space, a kind of sorcerous dimension, things appear and disappear all the time. When it's flowers and unicorns it's fine, but last time I was there a volcano erupted and I was lucky to escape with my life. If the magic space is somehow breaking through into Turai - which is impossible, but I can't think of any other explanation - then it could mean the destruction of the city. Now I think about it, it could mean the destruction of everything. The tree disappears as swiftly as it arrived. Hoping that the Sorcerers Guild is currently working on the strange apparitions, I get back to my own problems.

I could go to Kalius and tell him everything I know, but it might be too late for that. Once Kalius learns I've known about the missing jewel for a week, he'll be down on me like a bad spell. I'll be turned over to Palace Security and Rittius will positively dance with glee as he's locking me up. So telling the truth seems to be out of the question. Unfortunately, keeping silent doesn't hold out much hope either. Everything is going to come out at the ball tomorrow. I wonder if it might profit me to actually find out how the pendant went missing in the first place. Lisutaris has consistently prevented me from properly investigating this, claiming that only the recovery of the pendant is important. If I actually turned up at the Consul's office with full details of who took the pendant and why, I might be able to bargain for a lesser sentence. It goes against the grain. I'd be acting against my client's wishes. I keep this in reserve, though it's a weak plan at best.

The only thing which would really help would be if I found the pendant right now and returned it to Lisutaris. She could show it to Consul Kalius and then just clam up about everything. Completely deny it had ever been missing. Who could prove her wrong? It might still get us off the hook. It strikes me that I may have been mistaken in following Lisutaris's so-called leads all around the city. Naturally, when a man is looking for a lost pendant, and the Head of the Sorcerers Guild tells him she has located said pendant, the man goes along with it. But where has it got me? Precisely nowhere. A lot of dead bodies and a headache from rushing around in the heat. For all I know the jewel might never have been in any of these locations. Someone could have been leading Lisutaris on. Just because Lisutaris is extremely powerful it doesn't mean she's always right. Maybe if I'd just stuck to my own methods of investigation I might have made better progress. I've solved a lot of crimes by trudging round the city asking questions.

By this time I've walked clear down to the southern wall of the city. I pass through a small gate that leads on to the shore, a rocky stretch of coastline some way from the harbour. Further along the coast there are some stretches of golden sands, but this close to the city the sea washes up against a barren patch of rocky pools. The area stinks from the sewage which flows out of Turai, making it a place which few people visit. Even the fishermen who take crabs from the pools tend to stay clear of this polluted part of the landscape, particularly in the heat of summer. The offensive odour makes me wrinkle my nose. I wonder why I've walked here. I should have made for the harbour and checked out the ships. I might have found a trireme heading south and asked for passage.

I spot a figure in the distance, half hidden behind a tall spur of rock. I'm about to leave when something about his movements strikes me as familiar. My curiosity piqued, I stroll over, taking care not to slip on the slime that clings to the rocks. When I reach the spur I find Horm the Dead scrabbling around in a small pool.

'Looking for crabs?'

He looks up, surprised at the interruption. 'I sent the pendant here for safekeeping after I took it from Glixius,' he announces. 'But it's gone.'

Before I can deny any involvement, Horm states that he already knows I haven't taken it.

'I've long since stopped worrying about your investigative powers. It is your fate to be always too late. But who can have found the pendant here?' Horm withdraws his hand from the water, shaking off the dark liquid with some disgust. 'It really is too bad. I'm now heartily sick of this whole affair.'

'Everyone is sick of it.'

'And yet I must have the pendant.'

'Why not give it up? You probably don't really need it.'

'I am afraid I do,' says Horm. Unexpectedly he smiles. 'I promised it to Prince Amrag. Rash perhaps, but true. Our new Orcish warlord seems to have taken offence at comments I made that were reported to him by his spies. Comments taken out of context, of course. Still, I really must have the pendant.'

'You mean your neck is in danger if you don't deliver the goods?'

'I would not go as far as that,' says Horm. 'But it will certainly help to smooth out the misunderstanding.'

I gather from this that Horm the Dead has managed to get himself quite seriously on the wrong side of Prince Amrag. A sorcerous lord like Horm doesn't go around dipping his hands into polluted water unless he has a lot of smoothing-over to do.

'Yes, Horm, it's a problem. You offend someone in authority and they make your life hell. Happens to me all the time.'

'Prince Amrag has no authority over me.'

'True. But he's soon going to have the biggest army in the East.'

We walk up the beach together. By his standards, Horm the Dead is being positively convivial, and he's not even using a spell of persuasion. He simply regards me as so little threat he's unconcerned about how much I know of his affairs. In fact he seems eager to discuss them.

'I presume Lisutaris has not recovered the pendant?' he says.

'Not to my knowledge.'

'Glixius Dragon Killer doesn't have it. As for the criminal gangs of Turai, I feel that neither of them has it either. I have enough contacts in the Turanian underworld to have learned if they had. Do you think your Sorcerers Guild might have recovered the jewel?'

I shrug. I've no idea.

'I find this all very unsatisfactory,' complains the sorcerer. 'In a matter such as this I'd have expected discretion. It is amusing that so many people know of the theft, but it's hardly convenient.'

'I thought it might have been you that spread the word, Horm. You must be enjoying seeing Lisutaris heading for a fall.'

'I am indeed. But it was not me that spread word throughout the city that she'd lost the pendant.'

Melodious singing interrupts our conversation. Close to the shore, mermaids are forming a chorus.

'Are you responsible for this?' I ask.

Again Horm the Dead denies it. 'Why would I waste my time? Yesterday I was almost knocked over by a centaur. I presumed it was some sort of Turanian custom till children started screaming in alarm. I suspect the magic space may be breaking through into the real world.'

'I thought the same. Any idea how that might be happening?'

'None whatsoever. If it happens, it will certainly hasten your destruction.'

'If it keeps spreading it might hasten yours.'

The mermaids disappear. I'm not entirely certain where mermaids live, or if they really live anywhere. Unlike unicorns, centaurs, dryads and naiads, I've never actually met any.

Horm frowns. 'This should all have been simple. Sarin the Merciless receives the pendant and passes it to me. I leave the city bearing a gift for Prince Amrag. I'm still not certain what went wrong. Glixius, possibly. He knows Sarin the Merciless. He might have learned of the affair earlier than I imagined.'

'Possibly Sarin thought Glixius might pay more.'

'Possibly. She is an efficient woman, but I have had occasion to criticise her for her venality.'

'Who was Sarin meant to receive the pendant from?'

'That, I imagine, is the crux of your investigation,' says Horm. 'So I would not wish to spoil it for you by telling.'

We've now walked back to the outskirts of the city, to the small gate in the walls, which is manned by a bored-looking guard.

'People are dying all over Turai, I believe,' muses Horm. 'Which is puzzling. When I learned of the first deaths I presumed they were connected to the pendant. It would certainly have that effect on the untrained mind. Yet the deaths are now so widespread that the jewel cannot be causing them all. It is a sorcerous item but it can't be in more than one place at the same time.'

'Yes, Horm, it's a mystery. And you saying you know nothing of the matter doesn't convince me.'

Horm raises his eyebrows, just the slightest bit perturbed by me implying he may be lying. 'Tell me, investigator, if you had by any chance stumbled across the jewel, what makes you think it would not have driven you mad?'

'Strong will power.'

'You think so? Sarin's description of you rolling around drunk in the gutter would not seem to fit a man of strong will power.'

'Sarin is a liar.'

Horm stares back down towards the sea. He points over to some rocks further along the coast. 'Another three bodies.'

'Really?'

'From the Society of Friends, I believe. Probably followed Glixius and ended up killing each other.

'Glixius Dragon Killer,' muses Horm. 'Three times I have defeated him in combat, yet he seems undeterred. One could admire that, but really I find it tedious. Next time we meet I'll certainly have to kill him.'

'You're fond of promising to kill people, Horm.'

Horm looks surprised. At the foot of the city walls a slight breeze makes his cloak wave in the air. I'm sweating in the heat but the half-Orc sorcerer seems unaffected.

'Am I? Who else have I threatened to kill?'

'Me, for one.'

'I hardly think that likely,' says Horm. 'Why would I threaten to kill you? There is not, and has never been, the slightest chance of you preventing me from carrying out my plans. You are beneath me, Thraxas, beneath me by a distance you cannot comprehend, investigator who failed his sorcerous apprenticeship.'

Horm smiles his malevolent smile 'Please give my regards to your fair companion Makri. If I'm obliged to leave Turai without encountering her again, kindly inform her that when Prince Amrag sweeps this city away, I'll try to save her.'

Horm the Dead makes a formal bow and walks off along the foot of the city walls. I go through the gate into the bustle of Twelve Seas. It was an informative conversation. And polite. When Horm dismissed me as not worth bothering about he used only the most reasonable language. I'm thoughtful as I walk back towards the Avenging Axe. For all his superior power, Horm has no idea where the pendant is. He can't find it by sorcery. That gives me just as good a chance as him. Better, in fact. I'm an investigator. Number one chariot when you need something investigated. He's just a hugely powerful sorcerer who happens to rule his own kingdom. I wonder again about the rumours of Horm having been dead. I should have asked him about it. Difficult to work into the conversation, I suppose. I notice he mentioned Makri again. He was obviously quite taken by her. Probably it's been a long time since a woman punched him in the face. Might be the very sort of thing he's looking for in a relationship.

Whether Horm is living, not living, or somewhere in-between, I'll find the pendant just to spite his arrogant face. As I reach the hot, choking stretch of dirt that is Quintessence Street, I remember what Dandelion told me yesterday. She'd seen flashes of light over the beach. I wonder if she might have had anything else of interest to impart before I shut her up. I seek her out in the tavern and learn that she's upstairs in Makri's room. I knock on the door, with no results, so I walk in and find Dandelion sitting on the floor, dangling a pendant in her hand. Hanging from the pendant is a green jewel, and the young woman is staring at it, transfixed.

'Give me that!' I yell.

She's lost in some other reality and shakes her head and blinks her eyes as I grab the pendant from her and cram it in my bag. I get ready to slug her in case she wakes up insane, not that it's going to be easy to tell.

'Pretty colours.'

'Yes. Very pretty.'

Dandelion smiles and lies down on the floor to sleep. She doesn't look like she's going to do anything violent. I'm puzzled. Everyone else who's looked through this jewel turned into a violent lunatic. Maybe you have to be that way inclined. Perhaps the jewel doesn't make you mad if you're the sort of person who likes flowers and dolphins. Leaving Dandelion to sleep it off, I take the pendant along to my room and wonder what to do with it. I have an almost overpowering urge to risk a glance, just to see what it's like. I overcome the urge and cram it in my desk drawer.

I've recovered the pendant. A huge stroke of luck, really, though I'm not going to admit that to anyone. Trust Dandelion to wander down to the polluted part of the beach and pick up the pendant from under the nose of Horm the Dead. I wonder what to do now. The pendant can't stay here. It's too much of a risk. I'd best get it back to Lisutaris as quickly as possible. I risk a quick trip downstairs to pick up a beer and I ask Gurd to look in on Dandelion to check she's okay.

'Trouble?'

'Probably not. She looked at something she shouldn't but I don't think it's done her any harm. Where's Makri?'

'Hunting for money.'

'Huh?'

'She's getting another bet down with Moxalan.'

Good point. With the three recent deaths I make the total thirty, and the case will end when I get the pendant back to Lisutaris. We ought to get some money on quickly. Suddenly life looks brighter. I can save Lisutaris, completing my case satisfactorily, then make a healthy profit from Moxalan. I go back upstairs to look for Makri. I find her in my room, standing next to my desk. She has the pendant in one hand, her black Orcish sword in the other, and a glazed look in her eyes.

'I am Makri, captain of armies,' she says.

'Put the pendant down, Makri.'

'Prepare to die,' snarls Makri, and raises her sword.

Chapter Sixteen

About twenty years ago, I won the great sword-fighting contest in far-off Samsarina. This competition attracts the best fighters from all over the world. I had to defeat a lot of good men. The savagery of the competition was legendary but I took on the best and beat them. Of course I was a lot younger then; a lot leaner, a lot hungrier. Even so, in the intervening years I've never met a person who could best me in close combat. But I'm thinking that Makri probably can. I've seen her fight too often to think otherwise.

Makri's under the influence of the jewel. It might slow her down. If so, I might defeat her, but a dead Makri doesn't seem like a great outcome either. I could try fleeing the room but Makri would probably have a knife in my back before I made it through the door. So I raise my sword to defend myself, curse the heavens, and hope the effect of the jewel wears off quickly. With my sword in my right hand and a knife in my left, I'm better armed than Makri. She's only carrying one sword, which is fortunate for me, as her own twin sword technique is something between a hurricane and a scything machine. Even so she quickly forces me back against the wall.

'Stop fighting, it's the jewel!' I scream, to no effect. Makri continues her attack. From the blank look in her eyes and a certain unfamiliarity about her movements, I'm pretty sure she's fighting below her usual capacity, but even so I'm very hard pressed to hold her off. There's a fraction of a second where I see an opening, but I pull back from a lethal stroke and after that I'm pressed further and further back. Makri takes my blade on her own and with one smooth movement runs her sword down it. Such is the force of her black sword that the finger guard on my weapon is sliced off. Blood pours from my hand. I'm screaming at Makri to regain her senses but nothing is getting through. Damn this woman. I always knew she'd end up killing me somehow.

Desperation makes me forget my scruples and I fight with my full intensity, deciding that a dead Makri is better than a dead Thraxas. Still she forces me back till I've retreated the full length of the wall and am trapped against my desk. I'm about to make a desperate attempt at throwing my dagger into her unprotected torso when, with a movement I don't really see, Makri takes my dagger on the point of her sword and sends it spinning across the room. In another blinding movement she slashes downwards. I attempt to block the blow and my sword shatters into a thousand pieces.

She raises her weapon.

'It's time for your examination,' I say.

Makri hesitates, confused. 'What?'

'Your examination. You have to get up and talk to the class. Right now. It's very important.'

Makri's sword arm drops a few inches. 'I don't want to stand up in front of the class,' she says. 'It's scary.'

'You have to do it. Right now.'

Makri lowers her sword. She slouches across the room and sits down heavily on the couch.

'I won't do it,' she says. 'It's not fair.'

I'm panting for breath. I feel like I'm about to die for lack of air. I pick up my water ewer and take a great draught. It's stale and warm. I offer some to Makri. She drinks it awkwardly.

'Did I pass the examination?' Some of her natural expression has returned to her face. Abruptly she shakes her head and looks alert. 'What happened?'

I pick up the pendant. 'You looked into the jewel.'

An expression of disappointment settles on her features. 'Am I not really captain of the armies?'

'I'm afraid not.'

'Oh. I thought I was. It was good. We destroyed everything.'

Makri drinks more water and pours the last of it over her face.

'Did I pass the examination?'

'You haven't taken it yet. You've been confused from the jewel.'

'I haven't taken it yet?' Makri's shoulders droop. She looks almost comically glum. 'No examination pass. No captain of the armies. Of course. I'm just a waitress. What a lousy day.'

By now I'm busy putting lotion on my cut fingers, a preparation made by Chiaraxi the local healer which is good on wounds.

'Did I do that?' asks Makri.

'Yes. But I wasn't really fighting properly. I was just letting you burn yourself out. I didn't want to take advantage of your weakened state.'

'I think I have an accurate memory of our combat,' says Makri. All over the floor are the shards of my broken sword. I change the subject.

'Why were you looking in the drawer?'

'For money,' says Makri.

'Of course. I should have known. Feel free to regard my money as your own.'

'I was putting on a bet for both of us,' says Makri, but she doesn't seem inclined to engage in our normal bickering. Instead she hauls herself to her feet, heavily, worn out from the effect of the jewel. Perspiration has dampened her huge mane of hair and her pointed ears show through.

'Thanks for not killing me anyway,' she says. Then she kisses me lightly on the cheek and slips out of the room.

'You're welcome,' I say, to the door.

The pendant is dangling in my hand. It's a pretty thing, Elvish silverwork and a green gem of moderate size, well-cut and sparkling in the few rays of sunlight that penetrate the drawn blinds of my office. This jewel is deadly. Anything other than a quick glance can suck you in. I'm tempted, but I don't succumb. I tear a scrap of cloth off an old tunic that serves as a towel, wrap it round the jewel then put it in my bag. It's time to take it to Lisutaris before it does any more harm.

As the rush of excitement brought on by combat fades, I find myself feeling satisfied. You hire Thraxas to find a missing pendant and what happens? He finds your missing pendant. Whilst malevolent sorcerers, evil killers, gangsters by the score and a whole army of government lackeys waste their energy in a fruitless search, I, Thraxas, have located the pendant without the help of sorcery or the assistance of a well-staffed intelligence service. Just solid, professional investigating and the willingness to do an honest day's work. It was bound to happen. You have a problem? Call on Thraxas. This man delivers. In all of Turai, I doubt there's another person who could have retrieved the pendant.

There's a knock on my door. Avenaris, Lisutaris's secretary, walks into my office.

'Lisutaris has retrieved the pendant,' she says.

I raise my eyebrows a fraction. 'Really?'

'Yes. This morning. She sent me to tell you to stop looking. And to pay you.'

Avenaris lays some money on my desk. As always, behind her small, measured movements I can sense tension. She wants to get out of here as quickly as possible.

'How did Lisutaris locate the pendant?'

'She didn't tell me.'

'Weren't you curious?'

'I should leave now. Be sure not to mention anything to anyone.'

As ever, I'm curious about this nervous young woman whom Lisutaris is extremely keen to protect. 'You know anything about how the pendant went missing in the first place?'

'Pardon?'

'You heard me. One minute you're looking after Lisutaris's bag, the next the pendant's missing. That always struck me as odd.'

'I don't know why Lisutaris hired such a man as you,' blurts Avenaris.

'Because I'm good at noticing things. I notice when people are more nervous than they should be. Why is Lisutaris so keen to protect you? Do you need protecting?'

'No.'

'Does Lisutaris treat you well?'

'Lisutaris has always been very kind to me. I have to go now.'

The tic on her face has started up again. I notice how skinny she is. Skinnier than Makri even. Not a young woman who enjoys her food. Not a woman who enjoys anything much, from the look of her. A memory floats into my mind. Young Barius, lying on the couch, gasping.

'Anyone ever call you Vee, Avenaris?' I say, abruptly.

The tic goes into overdrive. Avenaris puts her hand to her face to cover it. For a second I think she's going to faint.

'No!' she says. 'Stop questioning me! Lisutaris told you not to.'

With that she runs from my office. I'm still weighing up the implications of our encounter when Sarin breezes in, this time not pointing a crossbow at me.

'I'm disappointed,' I say.

'At what?'

'I hoped you'd died when the warehouse collapsed.'

'I didn't,' says Sarin. She's not one for banter.

'What do you want?'

'I have a pendant to sell.'

'A pendant?'

'Belonging to Lisutaris. I recovered it. I had planned to sell it to Horm. Circumstances have now changed and I am prepared to sell it to either Lisutaris or the government, using you as an agent.'

Lisutaris has the pendant. Now Sarin also has the pendant. Obviously they're both lying because I have the pendant. I spin Sarin along a little, trying to find out what she's up to.

'Circumstances have changed? Let me guess. Horm the Dead suspects you of double-crossing him and offering the pendant to Glixius Dragon Killer. Now you're worried you might find yourself on the wrong end of a heart attack spell.'

No reaction from Sarin.

'What makes you think I'd act as your go-between?'

'You did before,' says Sarin, which is true, though circumstances were different.

Sarin's price is five thousand gurans.

'Worth it to Lisutaris, to save her skin.'

'Maybe, Sarin. But one day you're going to come to grief, meddling in the affairs of sorcerers. They're not all going to fall for you like Tas of the Eastern Lightning. What did you do to him? A simple stab in the back?'

'Something like that,' replies Sarin the Merciless. 'Lisutaris has till tomorrow to come up with the money. Which she'd better do. My next approach will be to the Palace. They'll pay well to keep the pendant from the Orcs.'

'It doesn't worry you, selling state secrets to the enemy?'

'Not at all.'

'If the Orcs invade, I doubt they'll spare you.'

Sarin looks at me quite blankly, and I get the sudden odd impression that she'd welcome death. Unwilling to engage in further conversation, she slips quietly from my office, leaving me to mull over her offer. I find myself admiring her nerve. She doesn't even have the pendant, yet here she is, still trying to profit from the affair. I need beer. I head downstairs to get myself around a Happy Guildsman jumbo-sized tankard. Gurd is still as miserable as a Niojan whore, and Makri is resting upstairs, leaving the incompetent Dandelion to struggle with the task of pulling the ale. By the time she finally plants my Happy Guildsman in front of me, I could have walked to the next tavern and downed a few.

'You're looking thoughtful,' says Dandelion, who, I think, has learned from Gurd that the clientele often enjoy a word with the bartender.

'Too many pendants.'

'What?'

I shake my head. If I ever reach the stage of discussing my work with Dandelion, it'll be time to retire.

'What did you see when you looked in the jewel?'

'Lots of nice colours. And flowers.'

It didn't do her any harm. Everyone else it drove mad. Dandelion just saw some pretty colours. Maybe there's something to be said for walking around in bare feet. I warn her not to relate her experience to anyone, and tell her I'd like another tankard as soon as she's finished struggling with the order from three sailmakers who are shouting for drinks from the far end of the counter. They've just completed the re-sailing of a trireme and they have a lot of money to spend. More sailmakers arrive, demanding ale and bragging about the work they've done and the money they've earned. It's not a bad life being a sailmaker if the city's merchant trade is healthy, which it is. Plenty of ships, plenty of work.

I secure another beer and leave them to it. I'm unsure of what to do now. Visit Lisutaris, I suppose. She claims to have the pendant. But she can't have it. I've got it. But why send me the message? I can understand why she might be faking something for the benefit of the Consul, but there's no point lying to me.

Casax, the local Brotherhood boss, appears before I have time to sit down. It's surprising how busy my office can be at times. You'd think I'd earn more. 'You want to buy this pendant everyone's been looking for?' he asks.

'Why do you want to know?'

'Because I have it,' says Casax. 'One of my men found it in Kushni. But I'm a patriotic guy. I'm not going to let it fall into the hands of one of these outsiders. I'll let it go back where it belongs, so long as there's a profit in it for me.'

'I know nothing of any missing pendant.'

'I know you know nothing of any missing pendant. But if you did know anything about a missing pendant which contains a jewel which will give our top sorcerer some advance warning about when the Orcs might attack, would you want to buy it back?'

'When you put it like that, maybe. What's your price?'

'Three thousand gurans. In gold.'

'That's a lot of gold for a patriotic guy.'

'I have to make a living.'

I ask to see the pendant.

'It's in a safe place,' says Casax.

He expects me to trust him. I probably would, normally, in a matter like this. The Brotherhood boss would not waste his time trying to sell me an item he didn't have. So why is he trying to do it now? I can't figure it out. The pendant is in my bag. I know it is. I checked just a moment ago. Are these people all trying to work some scam, or is this some effect of the sorcerous madness that's been breaking out all over? Maybe Casax really thinks he does have the pendant. Maybe he thinks he can talk to the unicorns.

'There was a centaur in my tavern last night,' he says, which makes me think that my guess might not be so far off.

'Really?'

'Yes. I've never seen one before. You think it would be strange, being half man, half horse, but the centaur didn't seem to mind.'

'What happened to it?'

'It drank some beer then disappeared. Is all this stuff going to end now the pendant's been found? It's bad for business, strange things happening all over the city. Makes my men forget what they should be doing. I sent two guys out last night to pick up a debt and they came back spouting some nonsense about mermaids in fountains. I'd have killed them on the spot if the centaur hadn't showed up, which did give their story some credibility. Bad for business, though.'

I admit to Casax that I don't know if the strangeness will end. I don't know if it's really connected to the pendant.

'The Sorcerers Guild should sort it out. Normal people shouldn't be coping with this sort of thing.'

I tell Casax I'll put his offer to Lisutaris. I wonder what Lisutaris will say when I do. I don't know why they're all lying. I can't think straight. At least I know why I can't think straight. It's because I haven't had a decent pie or portion of venison stew for days. Since Tanrose left, I haven't eaten one thing that truly satisfied me. A man can't be expected to do his best work in these circumstances. I decide to visit Tanrose. I might be able to persuade her to come back to the Avenging Axe. Failing that, she might offer me dinner.

I disturb Makri's rest. 'I have to go out. Stake some money on forty. It's still going up.'

'All right.'

'I'm going to see Tanrose. Should I bring you back a pie?'

Makri shakes her head. She has little enthusiasm for food.

Chapter Seventeen

Tanrose is living with her mother on the top floor of a dark stone tenement on the border of Twelve Seas and Pashish. Five flights up, with a stairway that could use some cleaning and a few more torches to light the way. As I arrive, Tanrose is laying dinner out on the table, one of the few strokes of good fortune I've had all summer. Not wishing to be impolite, I accept her offer of a meal. Once at the table, I lose all self-control and take second and third helpings of everything. Tanrose is amused, as is her mother, an elderly woman with white hair who already knows my appetite by reputation.

'I like to see a man eat well,' she says, and brings me another pie from the larder. I hesitate. With Tanrose no longer bringing in her wages from the Avenging Axe, there might not be much money to go around. There again, I don't want to appear impolite. I eat the pie.

'Tanrose, you have to come back to the Avenging Axe. The population of Twelve Seas is starving to death. There's misery everywhere, particularly in my rooms.'

Tanrose asks if Gurd sent me.

'No.'

'So he's too useless even to send a message,' says Tanrose, which is true, I suppose. I try to excuse him.

'He spent his life fighting. There was no finer companion for killing Niojans. It's not easy for a warrior to settle down. He has trouble saying what he feels.'

'He doesn't have any trouble saying he doesn't like my bookkeeping.'

I contrive to look hopeless. A few minutes of this sort of conversation is all I can ever manage. I've no idea how to bring together sundered couples. I don't remember ever caring about a sundered couple before.

'What will it take to bring you back? An apology? A marriage proposal? Or would a bunch of flowers do it?'

'It would help.'

'I'm always surprised how much you like flowers, Tanrose.'

Tanrose smiles. 'It's the thought behind them.'

'Is it such a great thought?'

'It worked with Makri, didn't it?'

On several previous occasions when Makri has taken offence at some of my wilder outbursts of invective - criticism of her morals or her ears or her clothes, or maybe a few other things - I've managed to calm the troubled waters with flowers, not something I would ever have thought of myself unless prompted by Tanrose. Naturally this entire process was humiliating to a man such as myself, involving much mirth from the flower sellers, Gurd, and the assembled drunks at the Avenging Axe, but it seemed preferable to the terrible atmosphere caused by Makri storming round in a bad mood for weeks on end.

'It did work. But only because Makri is too naive to realise I was faking it.'

'Faking it?'

'Sure. I don't care if the woman is upset or not. It just makes it difficult getting a quiet beer. Have you noticed how much more annoying she's got recently?'

'No, I don't think so.'

'There's definitely something different,' I say.

'Maybe the difference is with you,' suggests Tanrose.

I look at her suspiciously. 'What do you mean by that?'

'Ever since last year when Makri had her first romantic encounter with that Elf on Avula you've been in a bad mood. And I notice you're really giving her a hard time as well.'

'So?'

'So I'm beginning to think the gossips might be right.'

I'm not liking the way this conversation is going.

'Right about what?' I demand.

'Maybe you wouldn't mind ending up with a young companion to keep you warm in winter.'

I practically choke on my pie. 'Tanrose! Have you lost your mind?' I rise to my feet. 'I came here to try and smooth things out between you and Gurd, and now you're making crazy insinuations. Of course I give Makri a hard time. She's an insane half-Orc menace to society who'll probably get me killed one of these days. Kindly never insinuate anything again.'

Tanrose is laughing. 'Sit down and finish your pie. You know I can't just arrive back in the Avenging Axe. Might as well send Gurd a message saying he's welcome to walk all over me. He has to make the first move.'

'What if Gurd thinks you have to make the first move?'

There doesn't seem any ready answer to this. It's the sort of insoluble problem that led to my marriage falling apart a long time ago. I'm grateful for the food, but even a brief conversation about Tanrose and Gurd's relationship has made me feel very uneasy. I leave after expressing my profoundest wishes that Tanrose hurry back to the Avenging Axe where she belongs.

Outside the tenement, magical silver doves are fluttering around gaily. I bat them out of the way, not being in the mood for magical silver doves. Further down the street I come across a detachment of Civil Guards and at the next corner a squadron of the King's troops. The city is becoming nervous. Alarm is spreading at the widespread reports of mysterious apparitions and unexplained deaths. Personally I'm more alarmed at Tanrose making a joke about me desiring Makri to keep me warm on a winter's night. It was in very poor taste. I hurry into a tavern to wash away the bad taste with beer. Inside the tavern I pick up a copy of the Renowned and Truthful Chronicle, freshly printed. One side of the single sheet is taken up with reports of sightings of magical creatures, golden trees and such like, and the other details the surprising number of deaths in the city in the past few days. Even by Turai's standards, the population is decreasing at a disturbing rate.

Who is responsible for this? thunders the Chronicle. *And why has no attempt been made to arrest the renegade Tribune Thraxas?*

What? I shake my head, barely able to believe what I'm reading. I find myself shrinking in my seat, hoping no one recognises me, as I hurriedly scan the rest of the article.

All signs indicate that Thraxas, a so-called investigator of whom we have had reason to complain before, is heavily involved in the affair. Our enquiries show that in the space of three days this man has been at the scene of a great many unexplained deaths. Several landlords, for instance, report that Thraxas - a huge man of bestial appetites - visited their taverns only minutes before a series of savage murders were committed, leaving swiftly after searching the bodies for valuables.

Furthermore, Thraxas, a known associate of several renegade sorcerers, has been repeatedly questioned by the Consul and his deputy after an attempt was made to blackmail Lisutaris, Mistress of the Sky. While we have no absolute proof that Thraxas was behind this attempt, he has reportedly been trying to sell various personal items belonging to the sorcerer, including a diary and items of jewellery. Reports from other sources indicate that guards at the Guild College were forced to eject him after he menaced Professor Toarius over a sum of five gurans.

Although it cannot yet be established that Thraxas is responsible for the mysterious apparitions that have been troubling the city, he is known to have dabbled in the sorcerous arts, and may be in possession of devastating Orcish spells (He is fluent in the Orcish language, and is rumoured to have Orcish associates). It has recently come to light that he once threw down his shield and fled the field of battle, an offence for which he will shortly face charges in court. Why is this man still at liberty? And why, we would like to know, was he ever granted the office of Tribune? Even in a city as corrupt as Turai, surely a man of such reputation should not be able to bribe his way into lucrative government positions...

It goes on in a similar manner. I've been denounced by the Chronicle before, but never so damagingly. Reading the remarks about throwing down my shield, I feel a rage swelling up inside me the like of which I can rarely remember. I wonder why I haven't killed Vadinex yet. Kill him, then pay a visit to the Chronicle and beat the editor. Damn these people, no one says things like that about me and gets away with it. I throw back my beer and storm out of the tavern, intent on doing some violence to someone, and quickly. I'm intercepted by Makri in Quintessence Street.

'Thraxas, I've been looking for you.'

'Did you see the article?'

'Everyone saw it. You can't come back to the Avenging Axe. The Civil Guards are waiting to arrest you. They have a warrant.'

'The Guards? Damn them. Every time the Chronicle criticises them they think they have to do something about it. When I get hold of that editor I'm going to–'

'What about the pendant?' asks Makri.

'I've still got it.'

'Then why did three men die in the next street just an hour ago for no good reason? I thought the strange deaths were all related to the pendant, but it's been with you. They can't have looked at it.'

I admit I'm baffled. 'I thought it was all pendant-related too. Maybe it's some madness unleashed by Horm the Dead. Anyway, I have to get the pendant back to Lisutaris. Once that's done, she can get back to looking after the sorcerous requirements of the city. She can sort out the unicorns and all the rest.'

'How are you going to get it back to Lisutaris? It's not safe for you to travel around the city.'

Four Civil Guards are heading in our direction. I withdraw into the cover of a shop doorway as they pass. In the dim evening light they don't pay much attention to me.

'I'll just have to make my way there by the back streets.'

Makri points out it's not going to be easy for me to even approach Lisutaris's house. 'They're bound to be watching.

Everyone knows there's something going on with Lisutaris. If you turn up at her door, they'll just haul you away.'

'You're right.'

I try to think.

'Do you have any idea what sort of costume I should wear?' asks Makri.

'What?'

'For the masked ball tomorrow. Lisutaris says I have to wear a costume. I'm not familiar with this concept. I was going to look it up in the Imperial Library but I didn't have time, what with everything that's being going on.'

'This is no time to be discussing costumes.'

'But I don't know what to wear,' says Makri, sounding unhappy. 'I don't want everyone to laugh at me.'

It's really too much. A man can only stand so much harassment in his own city. I resolve to slip out of the city under cover of darkness and never come back.

'All the rich people will have really fancy costumes, I expect,' continues Makri. 'How am I meant to compete with that?'

'Wear your armour,' I suggest.

'My armour?'

Makri brought a fine suit of light body armour with her from the Orc gladiator pit. Made of chainmail and black leather, it's an arresting sight, and the Orcish metalwork is not something you see in Turai every day.

'Why not? You're meant to be going there as Lisutaris's bodyguard, so it would be appropriate.'

'But am I meant to be appropriate?' says Makri. 'Don't Senators go dressed as pirates and things like that?'

'I believe so.'

'So if I'm really there as a bodyguard, shouldn't I be dressed as maybe a philosopher?'

Night is closing in. I should probably flee the city soon. I explain to Makri that while it is common for people to attend a masked ball in costumes that may bear no relation to their normal station in life, it's not something that's governed by rules.

'I doubt if Cicerius is going to dress up as a pirate. Probably he'll go as the Deputy Consul, but wear some discreet little mask. Only the more extrovert Senators will turn up in outlandish garb.'

Makri nods her head. 'I see. So really, any costume is fine?'

'I expect so.'

'I suppose a person might gain some social status by turning up in an especially fine costume. It would get noticed, I imagine.'

'Yes, Makri, you seem to be getting the hang of it. Could we stop discussing it now? I have other pressing matters to attend to.'

'Okay,' says Makri. 'I just wanted to get it clear. My armour should do fine. After all, how many people will be there in a full set of light Orcish armour? None, I'm sure. And I don't often get the chance to wear the helmet. Thanks, Thraxas.'

Makri now looks happy. Obviously the costume problem was preying on her mind. Despite my numerous other problems, I still manage to feel annoyed that I'm not invited. It strikes me that the masked ball does present an excellent opportunity for getting myself unnoticed into Lisutaris's house.

'Of course,' I exclaim. 'I'll dress up as something and just waltz in tomorrow evening. I give the pendant back to Lisutaris, she shows it to the Consul and the main problem disappears. Once the threat to national security is out of the way, I can start proving I haven't been going round killing or blackmailing people. Lisutaris will speak up for me once I've solved her problem.'

Makri purses her lips. 'But you're not invited.'

'So what? I'll forge an invitation.'

'You just can't stand it that I'm going to the ball and you're not invited,' says Makri.

'That has nothing to do with it.'

'Admit it, Thraxas, you've been plotting to go to Lisutaris's ball from the moment you learned I was going. It's really not mature behaviour.'

'Will you stop this? I don't give a damn that you're going to some party. I have no wish to attend and am merely planning to do so in order to bring the case to a conclusion.'

'You don't fool me for a moment,' says Makri, and looks cross. 'What if you're found out? People will think I let you in.'

'Who's going to think that?'

'Everyone.'

'Well so what? Since when did you care what Turai's aristocracy thought of you?'

'I don't want to be humiliated at my first major social function.'

I clutch my hand to my brow, something I don't do that often. 'I can't believe we're having this conversation. Are you still dazed from the jewel? I have important business to take care of.'

Makri remains convinced that I merely wish to attend the ball.

'You'd better not embarrass me.'

'Me embarrass you? Who was it got so intoxicated at the Sorcerers Assemblage that I had to pick her up and carry her out of the hall? Who threw up in front of the Deputy Consul?'

'That was different. The Sorcerers Assemblage was full of people getting drunk and throwing up. Almost every sorcerer, from what I remember.'

In the next street a huge mushroom of flame suddenly spurts from the rooftops. Whistles sound and Guards appear from every direction. I shrink further back in the doorway. The flames turn green then disappear.

'Another apparition. They're getting worse. I have to get moving. I'm going to hide down by the docks. I have the pendant safe with me. Providing Horm or Glixius don't find me, I'll meet you at Lisutaris's house tomorrow. See what you can find out about the secretary.'

'What?'

'Avenaris. I'm suspicious about her. I think she had some involvement with Barius.'

'Why?'

'Investigator's intuition. One other thing. The body count is way out of control. People are dying everywhere. I don't know how Moxalan is going to prove which deaths are connected to me, but in case it turns out they all are, get the last of the money and put a bet on sixty.'

'Sixty?'

'That's right. See you tomorrow.'

'What are you going to do for a costume?'

'Good question. You'll have to find something for me.'

'Just fit on a pair of tusks and go as a mammoth,' suggests Makri, who's still showing signs of resentment at my plan to attend the ball. I ignore her jibe.

'Bring me my toga.'

'You have a toga?'

'Yes, from my days at the Palace. It's under the bed. And some sort of mask. You can find one in the market.'

'It won't be as good as my bodyguard costume,' says Makri. 'Where will I find you?'

'I'm going to hide in the stock pens at the harbour. There's a warehouse there waiting for some horses to be shipped in, it'll be empty for a day or two.'

Makri agrees to bring me my toga there tomorrow. I steal away along Quintessence Street, heading off down the first alley I come to. With my excellent knowledge of Twelve Sea's back roads and alleyways, I should be able to make my way to the harbour undetected by the Civil Guards. It's lucky I went to see Tanrose. Without her food inside me, I'd never make it through the night.

Chapter Eighteen

I spend a not too uncomfortable night on a pile of hay in a warehouse and remain there as the sun climbs into the sky. The warehouse has stalls and troughs, and is used as a pen for animals brought into the city by sea. Fortunately the owner is still waiting for his imported horses to arrive, so I have the place to myself. Apart from the smell of livestock, it doesn't compare too badly with the Avenging Axe for comfort. I find some bread and dried meat in an unattended office which keeps me going. A watchman looks in every few hours, which has me diving under the hay, but other than that I'm undisturbed. It's the first quiet day I've had for a long time. After nine or ten hours lounging in the hay my head is clearer and I'm feeling rested. Maybe it's not so bad being a horse. In the early evening Makri wanders into the warehouse, whistling softly. I emerge from the hay to greet her.

'Did you bring my toga?'

'Toga, sandals and a mask. And beer.'

Makri empties the contents of her bag. I'm immensely grateful for the beer. I drink it while I get the toga out. It could be cleaner but it'll do. 'They're difficult to wear, you know. You have to drape it just right. Any sudden movement and it's liable to fall off. That's why you never see Senators running around, it's too risky. What sort of mask did you bring?'

Makri has purchased a cheap mask from the market. It's a comic representation of Deputy Consul Cicerius.

'It was the only one they had.'

Makri wonders why I don't give her the pendant to return. I point out that it's already driven her mad once.

'You'd be tempted to look again.'

'You're right. It was so good being captain of the armies.'

'What have you done to your hair?' I ask, suddenly noticing that her already voluminous mane is looking even fuller than usual.

'I washed it in a lotion of pixlas herbs.'

'What?'

'They sell it at the market. It adds volume. And conditioning. I'm not turning up at Lisutaris's ball looking like a homeless tramp. It will be full of Senators' wives. I have to go now.'

'To do your make-up?'

'Possibly.'

Around the time of the Sorcerers Assemblage, Makri encountered Copro, the city's finest beautician. She was later forced to kill him after he turned out to be a rather deadly enemy, but even so, it had an effect. Previously dismissive of upper-class frippery, Makri can now be found worrying about her hair.

'How are things out there?'

'Hell,' replies Makri. 'Unicorns, centaurs, fire, death, delusions. The city's in chaos. I really wish I could afford to go to the beautician. Lisutaris has a team of them booked for the entire day. Maybe if I turn up early she'll let me share.'

Makri departs. Night is approaching and I struggle into my toga and put the mask in my bag. I try my best to hide my hair down the back of my toga. Then, hoping that I look something like a Senator who's on his way to a masked ball, I emerge on to the streets of Twelve Seas to be immediately ridiculed by some small children who wonder out loud if I'm a sorcerous apparition. I chase them off with language they're not expecting to hear from a Senator.

'That's no way to talk to children.'

Captain Rallee is looking at me with some amusement. Behind him are three Civil Guards.

'You're under arrest, Senator Thraxas.'

I'm carrying one spell. I mutter the correct arcane words and the Captain and his companions fall to the ground. The sleep spell is very effective, one of the few I can still use with authority. Unfortunately I've now run out of magic completely and won't be able to load any more into my memory till I consult my grimoire. I had been hoping to save that one spell for the masked ball in case I run into trouble there. Of course, having used a spell on a Guards Captain I'm already in big trouble. Resisting arrest by use of sorcery is a serious crime. I hurry off and wave down the first landus I see.

'The home of Lisutaris, Mistress of the Sky. At great speed.'

I squirm around a little, trying not to sit on my sword, which is concealed under my toga. Only a few months ago I saw a group of travelling actors performing a sketch at the Pleasure Gardens in which a bumbling Senator's toga fell off just as the princess walked into the room. I wouldn't bet against that happening tonight. I wonder if Lisutaris has invited any princesses. Probably. Young Princess Du-Akai is a keen socialite. Also a former client of mine, in a confidential matter. I'd best try to stay out of her way. I keep my head down all the way through town. When we join the throng of vehicles making their way into Truth is Beauty Lane, I risk a glance. All around are splendid carriages filled with people in elaborate costumes. Sitting in a hired landus with an old toga and an unimpressive mask, I already feel cheap. I still figure I can carry it off. I won't be the only one in attendance without two gurans to rub together. You don't have to look too far among Turai's upper classes to find men so far in debt they're never coming out.

I toss some money at the driver, leap out of the landus and lose myself in a crowd of giggling young ladies who're swaying up the driveway dressed as dancers. Unless they really are dancers. Assuming the air of a benevolent patriarch shepherding his flock, I stride confidently through the doors, take a glass of wine from a servant and look for the party.

Mostly the party is outside, and I'm directed by a series of servants through to the extensive grounds in the back where music is coming from every corner and a great throng of people, all elegantly costumed and masked, are walking in and out of a series of large marquees. It strikes me for the first time that it may not be easy to locate Lisutaris. I'd hoped she'd be welcoming guests at the door, but she could be the midst of the throng. Unless she's still getting dressed, which is possible. Having worked for her last year, I've had experience of the staggering amount of time she can take to get ready. I'm guessing that as a matter of pride Lisutaris will be wearing the fanciest costume on view, so I look around for anyone who looks particularly fabulous. Unfortunately there are a lot to choose from. The gardens contain all manner of costumes, from men who, like myself, are merely clad in their formal togas with the addition of a mask, to others who've spent weeks preparing the most elaborate of outfits. Pirates, soldiers, Elves, famous historical figures, snow pixies, angels, barbarians, all manner of masks and costumes. I approach a fantastic-looking figure clad in a rather graceful eagle's mask, hoping it might be Lisutaris, but am disappointed to hear her complaining to her companion about the price of merchandise in the market these days. Lisutaris would regard it as beneath her to complain of such a thing.

I wonder where Makri is. She might be upstairs sharing a beautician with Lisutaris. More to the point, sharing a thazis pipe, which means they might not appear for hours. I'm becoming uncomfortable carrying the pendant around. I keep fearing that the latent power it contains might leak out somehow and affect me. Already I've seen a wood nymph who seemed alarmingly real. I should return the pendant as swiftly as possible. There's no telling when Consul Kalius will take it into his head to confront Lisutaris and demand to see it. And if Horm the Dead really does plan to pay us a visit, I'd rather the jewel was with Lisutaris than me. Let her deal with his sorcerous malevolence. I must waste no time in hunting for Lisutaris. I need beer. The only unmasked people in the gardens are the waiters.

'I don't suppose there's any beer on offer?' I ask one of them, eyeing his tray of wine with dissatisfaction.

'I believe they have beer in the blue marquee, for the musicians,' he informs me.

Still not wasting any time in hunting for Lisutaris, I make a swift detour to the blue marquee, where couples dance to the stately music played by a chamber orchestra. It's a good steer by the waiter. No professional musicians are going to play the whole night fuelled only by vintage wine. Beer is available and I avail myself of it, raising a tankard to the band in appreciation. I watch the dancers while I wait for more beer. They're performing the slow, formal and rather intricate court dances as taught by Turai's dancing masters and performed in the best houses. I did actually learn something of the sort while working at the Palace, though it wasn't an art I was ever comfortable with. A man dressed as some sort of jester guides a woman in a nun's costume round, leading off the next part of the dance, and a great troop of pirates and barbarians follow them round the floor. From the number of dancers in the marquee and the amount of civilised revellers outside, I'd say that Lisutaris's masked ball was a success. I should find her quickly. The night being warm, I take in some more beer, just to be on the safe side, then set off, intending to try the house. Outside the marquee I meet the waiter again.

'Have you seen Lisutaris?' I ask. 'Do you know what costume she's wearing?'

'Are you unaware of the etiquette of the masked ball?'

'Which piece of etiquette would that be?'

'One must never enquire who anyone is,' he says, haughtily. 'It's the height of bad manners.'

I head for the house, rather abashed. Coming towards me is the Deputy Consul. Cicerius, though masked, is wearing his official toga, and is easily recognisable. If he catches me here wearing my cheap Cicerius mask, trouble will follow. I leap into the bushes to hide. There I find myself face to face with a large man incongruously garbed as a snow pixie.

'I'm the richest man in the world,' he says.

'Well good for you.'

His knees sag and he tumbles to the ground. I kneel over him. He's dead. Another victim of the jewel? He can't be. The jewel is safe in my bag. I take off the man's mask but it's no one I recognise. Just a Senator who always dreamed of being the richest man in the world. I feel something hard beneath my knee. It's a familiar-looking pendant. The missing pendant, in fact. I open the small bag I've strapped under my toga. It also contains the missing pendant. I now have two missing pendants. There's only meant to be one. Everyone was very clear on that. I scoop the new pendant into my bag and make for the house. As I'm nearing the back door, a unicorn trots across my path. People applaud, thinking it to be part of the entertainment.

Indoors the staff are directing guests through the hallways into the gardens, not allowing anyone to climb the stairs to the sorcerer's private apartments. I wait for a quiet moment before slipping a few gurans to a boy in a smart red tunic.

'Private business,' I say. 'Look the other way.'

He looks the other way and I hurry up the staircase. I'm familiar with this house and know that if Lisutaris has not yet made her entrance she'll be in the suite of rooms at the far end, doing her hair, or smoking thazis. Makri appears in the corridor, striding along confidently in her dark Orcish armour.

'Makri–'

She walks past, completely ignoring me.

'To hell with you,' I call after her. She must still be upset that I've gatecrashed the ball. I find Lisutaris's main salon and dive through the door.

'Lisutaris, we have big problems.'

Lisutaris is sitting in front of a mirror, with a stylist beside her doing her hair. Consul Kalius is sitting nearby on a couch. He's dressed as a pirate but has discarded his mask. Makri is standing by the window.

The Consul rises. 'What problems?'

'The musicians are running out of beer.'

The Consul laughs, and compliments me on my amusing Cicerius mask. Makri - who can't be here because she just walked down the corridor - looks surprised to see me. Lisutaris is annoyed.

'Who are you?' she demands.

I can't identify myself in front of Kalius before I've cleared things up.

'Etiquette prevents me from saying,' I reply.

'Well get the hell out of my rooms before I have my staff toss you out into the street,' says Lisutaris.

She's wearing a magnificent winged costume; the Angel of the Southern Hurricane, I believe, though with rather more cleavage shown than might be expected from an angel.

'The musicians really need beer. And Deputy Consul Cicerius is looking for the Consul on a matter of great urgency.'

Lisutaris now recognises my voice and looks alarmed. She turns to the Consul. 'Perhaps you should–'

Kalius smiles. He's looking quite jovial. Not like a man who's just denounced Lisutaris for betraying the city.

'I will sort things out,' he says, affably. 'You mustn't be disturbed while you're making ready for your grand entrance. The musicians need beer, you say? I'm sure I can rectify that. And Cicerius wishes to see me? No doubt on some affair of state. The Deputy Consul can never bring himself to fully relax on these occasions.'

He rises, bows formally to Lisutaris and departs. I remove my mask. 'The Consul's looking happy.'

'What are you doing here?' demands Lisutaris.

'He's jealous because you invited me,' says Makri. 'It's completely childish. Just like the Elvish princess in the story.'

'What story?'

'The Elvish Princess Who Was Completely Childish.'

Not for the first time I glare at Makri with loathing. 'There is no such story.'

'Yes there is. I translated it last year.'

'Is this true?' demands Lisutaris. 'You have invaded my house in a fit of pique?'

'A fit of pique!' I roar. 'Have you forgotten you hired me to retrieve the fantastically important jewel? Well I've done it.'

'But I've already done that,' protests Lisutaris. 'I retrieved the jewel myself. I have just been showing it to the Consul. Didn't you notice how cheerful he was?'

'Well this might make everybody less cheerful,' I say, and produce the two pendants from my bag.

'Obvious fakes,' says Lisutaris.

'Oh yes? There's a dead man in the bushes who doesn't agree. Take a look.'

Lisutaris takes one of the pendants and stares deeply into it. She frowns. She studies the other jewel. She places it on her bureau and opens a drawer, producing a third jewel.

'They are all real.'

'You didn't mention there were three of them,' I say.

'There aren't three of them! There's only one. But these are all the real one.'

'Well that's a mystery,' I say, sitting down on the couch. 'But it does explain why people have been being trampled by unicorns all over Turai. The place is awash with sorcerous pendants.'

'You say there's a dead man in my garden?'

'Yes. But well-hidden in the bushes. We might expect worse. Apparitions are still going on, and I know several other people who claim to have the pendant. God knows how many of these things are out there, each of them potentially lethal. If they all turn up in the same place I'm guessing we're in for a memorable party.'

There's a discreet knock on the door and a maid enters.

'Centaurs are destroying the green marquee, miss,' she says, politely.

Lisutaris looks to Makri.

'I'll deal with it,' says Makri, and puts on her helmet before hurrying off.

'You feel the need to stay?' says Lisutaris.

'There are some things we should discuss. Like how there are suddenly a lot of pendants. And what we're going to do about it.'

'I really can't be dealing with this sort of thing at my ball,' protests the sorcerer. 'It's time for my entrance.'

'Don't you realise what's about to happen out there? If centaurs are eating your marquee it means they're being produced by more of these jewels. Anyone in the gardens is quite likely to die because they find one and stare into it. Or else there will be a panic when a marquee appears to catch fire. Don't forget Horm the Dead has promised to pay you a visit. Which might mean another appearance from Glixius Dragon Killer. Also, Sarin the Merciless is still trying to sell a pendant. I'd say this ball might be remembered as the social occasion when everybody died.'

'You really know how to spoil a party, don't you?' says Lisutaris, angrily, like it's all my fault.

'Do you have any idea how the pendant might have mysteriously multiplied? Is there a spell which could do that?'

Lisutaris is still fussing with her hair in the mirror. It's the largest, most perfectly made dressing mirror I've ever seen. Buying a piece of glass like that must have been prohibitively expensive. I doubt if there's a better one at the Imperial Palace.

'It might possibly be done by a very experienced practitioner,' mutters Lisutaris. 'Though it would take an immense amount of skill. But who would do such a thing?'

I shrug. 'Look at the people who've been involved. Horm, Glixius. There's no telling what their motives might be. Horm has been keen to discredit you from the start. Maybe he thought he could take the pendant back for Prince Amrag and still make you look foolish by leaving some counterfeits behind. Maybe he cunningly planned it so they'd all end up here and destroy your guests. Good way to get rid of Turai's leaders. Whoever's behind it we have to do something. You ought to know better than me that having this many sorcerous items together is dangerous. What if the copies are unstable? Either the magic space is going to invade your gardens or there's going to be an almighty explosion.'

Last century, for reasons which were never clear, the great Simnian sorcerer Balanius the Most Powerful made a duplicate of himself. By all accounts it was a perfect copy, but when he shook hands with himself there was an explosion which flattened his city. You can still see the crater in Simnia.

Lisutaris drags herself away from the mirror. 'We don't know there are any more in the vicinity. There might be only these three. I can contain them.'

'I feel there are others.'

'How?'

'Intuition.'

Lisutaris is dubious about my intuition. She crosses to the window and gazes out at the gardens for a moment. 'You're right, unfortunately. I can sense more of them. I'm not sure how many. You may also be correct about their instability.'

Lisutaris walks over to a painting on her wall. She speaks to it and the painting shifts to one side. Behind the painting there's a safe. She mutters a rather long series of ancient words and it opens. From the safe she withdraws a bag.

'This is made of red Elvish cloth. If you put the pendants in here it should dampen the effect. Be careful not to let anyone see what you're doing. It's illegal for any private citizen, even me, to own this cloth. The King will be down on me like a bad spell if he knows I have it.'

I notice that Lisutaris seems to be talking about me doing the dirty work. 'You want me to gather up an unknown number of dangerous sorcerous pendants? I've been nervous enough carrying round one. Can't you help?'

'I have a ball to host. What will people say if I'm scurrying round with a bag rather than mingling with my guests? Is this not what I hired you for? To protect my reputation? Don't let Consul Kalius discover what you're doing. Having fake gems turn up isn't going to make me look good. Take this.'

Lisutaris hands me a copper bracelet.

'This will glow when in the vicinity of any sorcerous item.'

'It's glowing right now.'

'That's because my rooms are full of sorcerous items. It will help you to search in the gardens. If you find any more bodies, have my staff remove them discreetly.'

'I really don't like this.'

'We have no choice. I'll do my best to control any apparitions. I have to go. I'm due to lead off a dance with Prince Frisen Akan.'

'Take care he doesn't tread on your toes.'

'I expect he will.'

I step out into the corridor. I'm heading for the gardens but I hesitate. Avenaris's private rooms are on the next floor. With no one around to observe me, I hurry upstairs to check them out. Lisutaris will fume if she catches me, but what is she going to do? She needs me to do her dirty work outside. I remember I forgot to ask about the other person in Orcish armour I thought was Makri. Maybe it's nothing. No, it's something bad, I know it. Might it be Sarin? I'll deal with it later.

Avenaris's room is locked. I try a minor word of power, to no effect. I put my weight against the door and push. It gives slowly. It takes a strong door to resist my bulk. Inside I find a suite of rooms decorated in a restrained and tasteful style. Nothing too bright or harsh on the eye. I get to work.

Chapter Nineteen

The gardens are a scene of revelry. Apart from the music, dancing, costumes and fine provisions on offer, there are spectacular lighting effects and frequent appearances of otherworldly creatures. The genteel crowds, thinking these to be part of Lisutaris's sorcerous entertainment, are enchanted. Only Makri and I realise the danger. Makri tries to prevent the creatures from doing too much damage, which leads to the odd sight of a woman in Orcish armour walking round the gardens being followed by a long line of centaurs and unicorns. Centaurs, lascivious creatures at the best of times, can't help being attracted to Makri - I saw it happen in the fairy glade - and while Makri does her best to shoo them away, they continue to follow her until the magic which has produced them becomes unstable and they fade into space. As for the unicorns, I don't know why they should take to her. It's not like she's pure of heart.

'I've never seen anything like it,' says a wealthy-looking pirate to his companion as a rather harassed Makri jogs past with a long line of mythical beasts in close pursuit. 'Lisutaris has really laid on the entertainment.'

A bolt of blue lightning cracks the sky overhead.

'She's the best sorcerer in the city!' enthuses the pirate.

Meanwhile I'm looking for pendants. This is not so easy because Lisutaris's bracelet keeps lighting up any time a naiad or mermaid appears. With so many false alarms it's difficult to concentrate. When I notice two Makris at opposite ends of the gardens, one with unicorns and one without, I sprint towards the lone figure. I have a feeling that Makri's imitator has something to do with all this. The figure disappears into the bushes and I follow. As I step into the undergrowth, my bracelet lights up. There's a man in a bishop's costume bending down in the shadows to pick something up. I leap for him and wrestle the object out of his hands.

'That's mine!' says the bishop.

I shove the pendant into my bag. He lets go with some language very unsuitable for a man of the cloth.

'You'll thank me later,' I say, and hurry on. Some success at least. I find another pendant in a fountain full of mermaids and another in the hands of a Palace official who, while talking wildly about the coup he's planning, is at least not dead. I retrieve the pendant and leave him to sleep off his dreams of power. I now have three pendants. From the way a comet is currently hovering over the gardens, I'd guess there were more to be collected.

'Why did they all end up here?' I say out loud, angry and puzzled.

'I'm partly responsible,' says an elegant voice at my shoulder. It's Horm the Dead, dressed as a mythical King of the Depths, complete with trident.

'I figured you would be.'

'It wasn't my original plan,' confesses Horm. 'When I finally got my hands on the pendant I intended to leave the city. Unfortunately I then located a second pendant and realised that someone had been duplicating them. In the past day I've come across rather a lot of them.'

'So you sent them all to Lisutaris's ball?'

'It seemed like the helpful thing to do.'

Horm laughs. 'I have always wanted to see what would happen when so many unstable sorcerous elements were brought together. With luck we may all disappear in an explosion which will flatten the entire city. Look above. The stars are multiplying in the sky.'

They do seem to be. A million extra points of light. The points grow larger, resolving into a shower of comets heading our way. They start raining down on the garden, each one tiny and brightly coloured. The guests applaud wildly.

'This is splendid,' enthuses Horm. 'Everyone is about to die and they're all applauding. And you have the task of gathering pendants in a bag! Really, I've never seen anything so funny.'

There's a movement in the bushes and Makri appears. Or rather, a woman in Orcish armour. I can tell it's not Makri. My senses go into overdrive as the woman pulls a pendant from her pocket and holds it towards me.

'Not so fast, Sarin!' I cry, and strike her so she falls heavily to the ground. I grab the pendant from her hands and thrust it in my bag. 'You think you can just wave a pendant in my face, do you?' I rip off her helmet. Unfortunately it's not Sarin. It's Princess Du-Akai, the highest-ranking woman in Turai, third in line to the throne. 'Excuse me, Princess Du-Akai. There has been a misunderstanding.'

There's no way I'm talking my way out of this one. You can't strike a royal princess and get away with it. I'm heading for a prison galley.

'I was swimming with the dolphins,' mumbles the Princess, and looks confused.

Of course. She's been looking at the pendant. She doesn't realise what's happening. Thank God for that. Unless she dies. That won't be so good. Horm the Dead is laughing so much he can hardly catch his breath. Not wanting to leave the Princess close to the malevolent sorcerer, I cram her helmet back on her head, hoist her over my shoulder and march towards the house.

'Look after this woman,' I instruct a group of household servants. 'She's been drinking too much and needs to sleep it off.'

I'm now completely fed up with everything. There seems to be no end in sight to this madness. There could be forty of these pendants scattered around here for all I know. Some of the guests are now looking nervous as a new flock of centaurs stampedes through a marquee and show less willingness to dematerialise, even when Makri threatens them. Lisutaris appears to quickly banish them by sorcery but it's clear things are getting out of hand.

'It bit me!' complains a woman loudly to Lisutaris.

I need to know how many pendants there are. It's time to threaten someone. I look around for the most senior household servant I can find.

'I have to find Lisutaris's secretary right now. What costume is she wearing?'

'That would be a breach of etiquette, I'm afraid–'

I offer him a bribe. He looks uninterested. I take him by the neck and push him against the wall, ignoring the consternation this causes among his fellow servants.

'She's wearing a wood nymph's costume with yellow flowers!'

Now I've assaulted a princess and threatened Lisutaris's staff. Not forgetting the spell I worked on Captain Rallee. The courts may have to invent some new punishment to deal with my vast catalogue of crime. I start hunting the gardens for a wood nymph with yellow flowers. Makri spots me and hurries to my side.

'Have you got all the jewels yet? No? You'd better hurry, things are getting out of hand. There are centaurs everywhere and they keep trying to chew my clothes off.'

'Centaurs are like that. Any deaths?'

'Maybe one or two. You want me to keep count for our bet?'

'No, I was just wondering how things were going. But now you mention it, keep a count anyway. I'm looking for Avenaris. I figure she can tell me how many jewels there are.'

'Lisutaris will be down on you like a bad spell if you bother her secretary.'

'I already searched her rooms.'

'You did?'

'I did. I found various Barius-related items. She's been snuggling up with Professor Toarius's son. And no doubt funding his dwa habit after his father cut him off.'

I tell Makri about Princess Du-Akai. Makri is annoyed to hear that a royal princess has been masquerading as an Orcish gladiator.

'I'm insulted.'

'That's not the point. The point is I hit the Princess. If she remembers I'll be executed.'

'We could fight our way out.'

'We might have to. Now help me look for Avenaris.'

By now the masked ball has become a fantastic affair of flashing illuminations and rampaging sorcerous beasts. It's fabulous entertainment. I'd stop to enjoy it if I didn't know the city was going to explode any minute. It's difficult working our way through the crowds. Even among the garishly dressed revellers Makri's unusual costume draws attention. My funny Cicerius mask gets a few smiles too, though not from Cicerius himself when I bump into him outside the green marquee. He stares balefully at me and I can see him trying to work out where he's seen this large figure before.

'Wood nymph with yellow flowers over there,' yells Makri, and we set off in pursuit.

We catch up with Avenaris near the orchard.

'Don't be too harsh with her,' suggests Makri.

A great blast overhead signals the arrival of another shower of small meteors, which thud into the ground around us. 'No time to be nice,' I grunt. I grab Avenaris, shove her into the darkness beneath the trees and rip my mask off.

'I need some answers and I need them right now.'

Avenaris shrinks back. 'Go away,' she pleads.

I point to the lights in the sky. 'You see all this? It's getting out of control and it's going to end in disaster unless I recover every duplicate pendant. So tell me how many there are.'

The secretary starts crying. Tears pour from under her mask. I take out my sword.

'People are dying. Tell me what I want to know or I'll kill you.'

'Help me!' wails Avenaris to Makri.

Makri draws her sword. 'Sorry,' she says. 'It's time to talk.'

Avenaris slides down the trunk of a tree till she's sitting with her back to it, looking like a child. She sniffs, and takes off her mask.

'I didn't know all this was going to happen. I gave Barius the jewel. He needed money.'

'I know. For dwa. Bad choice for a boyfriend.'

'He said he would give it back. He was going to copy it and sell the copy. I didn't know he would make so many.'

'How did he make the copies?'

'I stole a spell,' sniffs Avenaris. 'From Lisutaris's private library. Barius took it to a sorcerer's apprentice he knows.'

'You realise the danger you've put everyone in?'

Avenaris looks miserable, but whether it's due to the trouble she's caused I'm not sure. She might just be sad about her boyfriend's problems.

'It was very disloyal to Lisutaris,' says Makri, disapprovingly.

Avenaris raises her head. A strange expression flickers across her face. For a moment she looks almost defiant.

'I should have been the rich one,' she says. 'My father was head of the family.'

She lowers her head and looks pathetic again.

'How many pendants did he make?'

'Fifteen. Then the spell wouldn't work any more.'

'I have nine pendants in my bag. Lisutaris has three. That's twelve. Four more to collect.'

'Three more,' says Makri, and takes one from her purse.

'You found one? And didn't stare into it?'

'I have will power.'

We hurry off, leaving Avenaris crying under the trees. Three pendants to find, which quickly becomes two as we stumble across the body of a young man who's still clutching one between his fingers. I scoop it into my bag. I hope that the red Elvish cloth will contain them as effectively as Lisutaris claims.

'Will the city really be flattened?' asks Makri.

'It's possible.'

'But I've got an examination tomorrow. I really studied hard.'

A unicorn trots out from the trees. They're pleasant animals. I never thought I'd get so sick of seeing them. It approaches Makri and starts nuzzling her face.

'I don't see why these unicorns like you so much. It's not like you're a virgin.'

'Is that an insult?' says Makri, suspiciously.

'No, just a statement of fact.'

'I'm sure that virginity has nothing to do with it,' says Makri, patting the unicorn. 'That's just a stupid thing men say. It's probably my sunny personality. Or maybe it's the Elvish blood. Is this actually a real unicorn?'

'I don't know. It doesn't show any sign of disappearing. Neither does that mermaid who's hypnotising the man in a sailor's costume. Come on, we have two pendants to find.'

My bracelet is glowing. I climb into the fountain, push the mermaid out of the way and scoop up another pendant. Only one more to go. Lisutaris, in her splendid angel costume, arrives in the company of someone who might be Prince Frisen Akan. On seeing us Lisutaris sends him gently on his way and asks about our progress.

'One more to go.'

'Are you sure only one is missing?'

'Yes.'

'Then we are finished,' proclaims the sorcerer. 'I have it. I found it with two Senators who'd taken it from a naiad. They were about to fight. Fortunately I interrupted them before their venal dreams could drive them mad or kill them.'

Lisutaris breathes a great sigh of relief. 'I'm glad that's over. Things were becoming hectic. I had to banish a troop of mountain trolls who were eating all the food, and the Consul got tangled up with an angry dryad. Unless that was just an angry citizen in a costume, it's been hard to tell.'

We withdraw under the privacy of a clump of trees. It's a hot night and sweat is running down my face beneath my mask. Makri removes her helmet to wipe her brow. Lisutaris takes the bag of pendants and rummages around inside. After a few moments she draws out a jewel.

'This is the real one.'

'How can you tell?'

'I'm Head of the Sorcerers Guild.'

'You were fooled by an imitation before.'

'I didn't have the rest to compare then. Besides, I had to show the Consul something.'

I take the pendant in my hand. It seems the same as all the others. But you have to trust Lisutaris on matters like this. She's number one chariot in all matters of sorcery. I hand it back.

'Congratulations,' comes a familiar voice. It's Horm the Dead.

Lisutaris greets him coldly. 'I don't believe I invited you.'

'I did not wish to miss such a glittering occasion. Or the chance of meeting Makri again.'

He bows to Makri, who looks uncomfortable, and may be blushing. In the shadow of the trees it's hard to tell. Horm looks at the pendant in Lisutaris's hand.

'You know, I went to some trouble to send these all to your ball. Some I retrieved by sorcery, some I bought, some I acquired from people I… removed.'

'Tough luck,' I say. 'Your plan failed.'

'My plan?'

'To cause such sorcerous instability that a disaster happened.'

'Yes,' agrees Horm. 'That would have been excellent. But that was not exactly my plan. Merely an entertaining lie. I still intend to take the pendant back to Prince Amrag. Till they were all gathered together, I couldn't be certain which was the original. Since you, Lisutaris, had already managed to retrieve one of the pendants, I felt that here would be as good a place as any to bring them all together. And now you've picked out the real one for me.'

'Your power does not equal mine, Horm the Dead.'

'It does. But we don't have to battle each other now. You will simply hand over the original pendant to me and I will not drop this handful of powder on your bag.'

'What?'

'My own preparation. It will rot the red Elvish cloth in a matter of seconds. Unprotected by the magical barrier provided by the cloth, the fifteen pendants in close proximity to each other will cause a sorcerous event of such magnitude that few of your guests will survive.' Horm turns his head towards me. 'Do not try any sudden movement. I'm quite prepared for it, and you will die. Lisutaris, the pendant.'

We seem to be stuck. It's the sort of moment a man needs to think of a quick plan. I can't come up with anything. Horm lets a little dust trickle from his fingers. The Elvish cloth starts to decay before our eyes.

'You will still have a fake jewel for fooling the Consul,' says Horm, and holds out his hand. Lisutaris has no choice. Everyone here will die. She hands over the original. Horm tucks the pendant into the folds of his costume and then, unexpectedly, he removes his mask. He moves a step closer to Makri and leans towards her, quite slowly. He kisses her lightly on her lips. Makri doesn't move at all. Horm steps back.

'You will one day visit my Kingdom,' he says, before turning on his heel and hurrying off, leaving Makri looking embarrassed.

Horm doesn't get far. A masked figure steps out from behind a tree with a short club in his hand and slugs Horm on the back of the head. Horm crumples to the ground. It's nice work. The figure reaches down to wrench the pendant from Horm's grasp.

'Good work, Demanius,' I say.

The masked figure looks over in surprise.

'I recognised the clubbing action. How did you get past his protection charm?'

'Got a spell on my club,' says Demanius. 'From the Palace.'

'Good thinking. Give the pendant to Lisutaris and we'll get rid of Horm.'

The investigator draws his mask up, revealing his features. 'Can't do that, Thraxas. I'm working for Rittius at the Palace. The pendant goes to him.'

'That's ridiculous.'

'I'm not paid to argue.' Demanius makes to leave.

'Stop him,' cries Lisutaris.

Demanius, almost at the edge of the trees, jerks backwards. For a moment I think that Lisutaris has halted him with a spell. Then, as his body spins and falls, I notice a crossbow bolt sticking from his chest. Another masked figure, tall and slender, darts from behind the tree. She grabs the pendant and leaps into the crowd, disappearing among the throng. Sarin the Merciless. I wondered where she'd got to.

Chapter Twenty

'You didn't find her?'

Makri arrives in Lisutaris's private chambers some time after the death of Demanius. She shakes her head.

'She's a slippery woman, Sarin. Probably climbed the outside wall while you were still searching the marquees.'

'I didn't see you rushing to help,' complains Makri, and sits down heavily on a gilded couch.

'I've done enough rushing around.'

Lisutaris herself is sitting dejectedly on another couch.

'You still have a lot of fakes,' says Makri.

'Old Hasius the Brilliant will spot it. I can't believe we lost the real pendant after we went to so much trouble.'

I'm sorry about Demanius. He was a good man. His body has been removed discreetly by Lisutaris's staff and now lies in a cellar, along with another two unfortunate souls who met their end as a result of the pendants. Two dead guests. Not as bad as it could have been. Lisutaris can probably explain it away as natural causes. The way some of these elderly Senators have been drinking and dancing, you'd expect a few fatalities.

I take a bottle of wine from under my toga.

'Help yourself to my supplies,' says Lisutaris.

'I earned it.'

I'm tempted to demand an explanation for my not being invited to the ball. It still rankles. I swallow it back. No need to hear Lisutaris explain in detail that I'm just not the right class of person.

'This whole thing was started off by your secretary.'

'So you say.'

'I don't just say. I know. I searched her rooms. You'd be surprised what I found. Letters to Barius. A diary full of some interesting observations about you. And a few items she's probably stolen from you over the years. Didn't you suspect her at all?'

'I told you to leave her out of this.'

'She resents you for inheriting the family fortune. It wouldn't surprise me if she blames you for her father's death.'

Lisutaris glares at me. 'Thraxas. Do you think that this is unknown to me? Do you seriously believe it has never crossed my mind that my brother's daughter may be jealous of my position? That she might have acted unwisely out of resentment at me inheriting the bulk of the family's wealth?'

'Well shouldn't you be doing something–'

The Sorceress raises her hand. 'I am doing something. I'm protecting her. I have a duty to my family. You will not mention her part in this to anyone and you will not raise the subject with me again. Count yourself fortunate that I do not punish you for searching her room.'

I shrug. If Lisutaris wants to wake up one day with a knife in her ribs, courtesy of her disgruntled niece, that's her problem. 'You hired me to get the pendant. So I did what I had to do. It's my job.'

'You failed.'

Poor Lisutaris. Downstairs her ball is a raging success and here she is, slumped on a couch smoking thazis and looking as miserable as a Niojan whore. It's a tough life as Head of the Sorcerers Guild.

'Failed? Me? Failure is an alien concept to Thraxas the investigator.' I take the real pendant out of my bag. 'Number one chariot at investigating, as is commonly said.'

Lisutaris leaps off the couch to grab the pendant. 'How did you get this?'

'I palmed it, of course, when you were showing it off. I made a switch right under your nose. It's the sort of thing I do well.'

'But why?'

'Why? You think I was going to let you keep the pendant when the gardens were full of people like Horm and Sarin? It was asking for trouble.'

'Couldn't you have told me that before I went chasing after Sarin?' says Makri.

'You ran off too quickly. You're impetuous, Makri, I've mentioned it before. Anyway, you wanted to kill her and I wasn't going to stand in your way.'

Lisutaris, no longer as miserable as a Niojan whore, congratulates me. 'I have the pendant. I have all the fakes. The one Sarin took will destabilise and disappear soon. I'm in the clear!'

'You are indeed. Unfortunately, I'm not. I'm in trouble for not answering a summons from Palace Security.'

'I can have that rescinded,' says Lisutaris.

'I put a guards captain to sleep with a spell.'

'I can probably smooth that over,' says Lisutaris.

'I hit Princess Du-Akai.'

'You're in big trouble. I could act as character witness.'

The sorcerer offers me some thazis and I accept it gratefully. As I inhale the pungent smoke I can feel my body relaxing.

'And what,' asks Lisutaris, turning to Makri, 'is the idea of kissing Horm the Dead?'

'I didn't kiss him! He kissed me.'

'I didn't see you putting up much of a struggle.'

Makri looks embarrassed again. 'He took me by surprise.'

Lisutaris doesn't look convinced. 'I was expecting you to punch him.'

'I tried that already,' says Makri. 'It didn't seem to put him off.'

Lisutaris frowns. 'I can see he's quite good looking in a pale, high-cheekboned sort of way, but really you ought to be careful. You don't want to go around getting involved with someone like Horm. You know it's rumoured he's already been dead?'

'Thraxas mentioned it,' mutters Makri, and starts inhaling deeply from the water pipe, not wanting to discuss it any further.

'Well, he's gone now,' continues Lisutaris. 'I scanned the gardens. If he comes back I recommend staying well clear of him.'

'He offered Makri a position as captain of his armies,' I tell her.

'Really?'

'Could we just stop talking about this now?' says Makri crossly.

We let the matter drop. I suppose if some insane sorcerer takes a shine to Makri it's not really her fault, though it might not happen if she could learn to dress properly. A man like Horm, living out in the wastelands, is bound to be affected when he hits the city and the first thing he runs into is Makri in her chainmail bikini.

I leave Makri and Lisutaris fuelling up with thazis before they go off to enjoy the rest of the ball. I've had enough excitement and decide to head home. I slip on my mask. In the hallway I run into Deputy Consul Cicerius.

'You are Thraxas, I believe,' he says acidly.

'I am. But about the mask, it was the only one I could find in a hurry–'

'I am not concerned with your grotesque likeness of me. I am concerned with your treatment of Princess Du-Akai.'

Here it comes. Thraxas heads for prison ship.

'She tells me she was assailed in the gardens by a unicorn and you rescued her. Is this true?'

The Princess is suffering from some very garbled memories.

'Yes, it's true. But I don't want to make too much of it. It was very dangerous but anyone would have done the same.'

'Nonetheless, it was a spirited action. Some of Lisutaris's entertainments have been far too adventurous. I'm furious that our royal princess was endangered.'

The Deputy Consul is one of the city's strongest supporters of the royal family. He's really grateful to me.

'Could have my investigator's licence back?' I ask.

'Yes,' says Cicerius. 'I will arrange it.'

'Can you have the charge of throwing away my shield dropped?'

'Unfortunately not. That must go through its due process. You were mistaken about Praetor Capatius. It was not he who initiated the charge. It was Professor Toarius. He was endeavouring to prevent you from investigating his son.'

'That figures. You know his son's a dwa addict who's heading for trouble?'

Cicerius declines to comment. As I leave he's looking on with distaste at four dancing girls who are probably Senators' daughters but aren't behaving appropriately. Or maybe they are behaving appropriately. Senators' daughters are notoriously badly-behaved.

Next afternoon I'm sitting downstairs in the Avenging Axe. Gurd is beside me at the table, laboriously writing a letter to Tanrose. He's finding it difficult.

'I've never written a letter before.'

'It'll be fine. Put in more compliments. Tell her that Thraxas is getting thin.'

'She won't believe that.'

I encourage Gurd to get on with repairing his relationship with the cook. Neither of us can carry on without her. I'm fairly satisfied with events. Most things worked out well enough. I did good service, for which Lisutaris is grateful, and the Deputy Consul is back on my side. The only bad thing is that I'm still faced with a charge of cowardice dating back seventeen years. I wonder if Professor Toarius will pursue it, now his son has been exposed. He wanted to prevent me from investigating, but now that the truth has come out about his son's behaviour anyway, perhaps he'll drop it. I sigh. Dwa addicts. They lose all responsibility. Prepared to steal five gurans from a locker, or one of the most valuable items in the city. It makes no difference to them.

I'm keeping an eye on the next table, where young Moxalan, surrounded by onlookers, is working things out on sheets of paper. Calculating how many deaths actually occurred as a result of the case of the missing pendant is a tricky business. There were fatalities all over the city, many of which could be ascribed, directly or indirectly, to the pendants.

The front door flies open and Makri strides dramatically into the room. She flings her bag on the floor, drags her tunic over her head and throws it against the wall, then starts parading round in her chainmail bikini, arms aloft, a look of triumph on her face. I've never seen her behave like this. It must be something she learned to do in the gladiator pits after slaughtering her enemies. She marches round the room, arms still in the air, grinning arrogantly, so that people start applauding even though they don't know what for. 'Makri!' she says eventually. 'Number one chariot at examinations!'

'You passed?'

'Passed? Passed doesn't do my performance justice. I set new standards. Never has a class been declaimed to in such an authoritative manner. The students were awestruck. When I finished my speech they stood up and cheered.'

Gurd grins. Dandelion, still in residence, brings Makri a beer to celebrate. I congratulate her warmly.

'Well done. I knew you'd pass.'

'It was a triumph,' she enthuses. 'Not even Professor Toarius could say a word against it. I tell you, I was great. And all this on no sleep. You know I spent the whole night dancing at Lisutaris's ball? It was the social event of the season. I walked from her house to college this morning and did my examination. I'm sailing into my final year as top student. Word got round about Barius. Now no one thinks I'm a thief.'

A good day all round. And it might get better. Moxalan is ready to make his announcement.

'With the help of my fellow adjudicators,' he announces, 'I proclaim that the final death total in the case of Thraxas and the missing pendant is sixty-three.'

There are groans from all round the room. No one seems to have picked this total. Moxalan's eye glints greedily. 'No winners at sixty-three? Then we move on to the reduced-odds winner for closest bet. Anyone with sixty-two? No? Sixty-one? Sixty?'

'Me!' yells Makri, leaping to her feet once more. 'I have sixty.' She retrieves her bag from the floor and hunts for her ticket.

'I'm not happy at this,' complains Parax the shoemaker. 'She had inside information.'

Many suspicious eyes are turned on me. I splutter in protest. 'Makri had no inside information from me. I have remained aloof from the entire contest, thinking it to be in the poorest taste. I am disgusted with you all and will now retire upstairs to forget I ever met any of you.'

I leave with dignity, and beer.

A while later Makri appears upstairs, still on a high after her examination triumph. She starts counting out her bag of money, splitting it three ways for herself, Lisutaris and me.

'Twenty to one, not bad. We lost a lot of stake money on our first bets but we've still got a good profit. This will get me started at college next year. That was a good wager, Thraxas. You picked sixty, it was well worked out.'

'I'm sharp as an Elf's ear. Incidentally, before this all started, did you tell Lisutaris that she shouldn't invite me to her ball because I didn't like that sort of thing?'

'No,' says Makri, sharply. 'Why would you think that?'

'Investigator's intuition.'

'Well your intuition is quite mistaken. It's not all you make it out to be, you know. Here, take this pile of money. It'll make you feel better.'

The End